# A SEA OF GREEN UNFOLDING

# A SEA OF GREEN UNFOLDING

THE LONG TRAILS BOOK 3

LIZZI TREMAYNE

Lizzi Tremayne / Blue Mist Publishing

Franklin Road, RD 2

Waihi, New Zealand 3682

www.lizzitremayne.com

Publisher's Note: This is a work of fiction. Names, characters, places, and incidents are a product of the author's imagination. Locales and public names are sometimes used for atmospheric purposes. Any resemblance to actual people, living or dead, or to businesses, companies, events, institutions, or locales is completely coincidental.

Formatting and artwork by Lizzi Tremayne

Interior artwork by Made by B 4 U

Cover design by Safeword! Author Services and Lizzi Tremayne

Acknowledgement for cover image to Auckland Libraries Heritage Collections Reference # 589-352 by artist Samuel Stuart

*The Long Trails* series Book 3

**A Sea of Green Unfolding/ Lizzi Tremayne** 1st Edition May 2017

Draft2Digital Paperback Edition 2019 08 29

Reloaded 2022-09-06 -V19

Print ISBN 978-0-9951157-8-1

# DEDICATED TO

… the *Māori* students of my 2014 Paeroa College maths class, born into a
culture embracing an oral history:

You didn't think you knew any *Māori* history, local or otherwise, did you?
You didn't believe me, when I said the stories your *kuia* and *koroua* told
you were real history.
You know more than you think you do.

… and to those descended from old and displaced cultures, whether they
be American Indian, Hispanic, *Moriori, Māori*, Syrian, or others too
numerous to mention:

Your forefathers lived, breathed and died in your country.
It is *your* history.
No one, but *no* one, can take that away from you.
**Be proud of your heritage.**

# CONTENTS

# LIZZI'S BOOK LIST AND SERIES ORDERS

### *The Long Trails* Series
*A Long Trail Rolling (Book One)*
*The Hills of Gold Unchanging (Book Two)*
*A Sea of Green Unfolding (Book Three)*
*The Long Trails Box Set: Historical Western Family Saga: Books 1-3*

### *Multi-Series Samplers*
*Lizzi Tremayne First Chapter Sampler*

### The *Once Upon a Vet School* Series
### *~Vet School 24/7~*
*Fifty Miles at a Breath*
*Lena Takes a Foal*
### *~Practice Time~*
*Greener Pastures Calling*

### Boxed sets with Bluestocking Belles
*Follow Your Star Home*

*Sign up for Lizzi's VIP Club to hear about new releases and specials, plus get your free sampler gift here:*
www.lizzitremayne.com/VIPSea

# PRAISE FOR LIZZI TREMAYNE

**With her debut A long Trail Rolling,** *Lizzi was:*

Winner 2016 True West Magazine
Best Western Romance
Winner 2015 RWNZ Koru Award
Finalist 2015 Best Indie Book Award
Winner 2014 RWNZ Pacific Hearts Award
Finalist 2013 RWNZ Great Beginnings

"vivid, light and fast-paced… a ripping good read. " *–Deborah Challinor,*
*#1 bestselling author and historian*

"An authentic, emotional story of one woman's fight for survival in an
unforgiving landscape." *–Leeanna Morgan, USA Today bestselling author*

"An impressive debut…a romance, a western, and an adventure story, all
rolled up into a compelling read." *–Booksellers NZ*

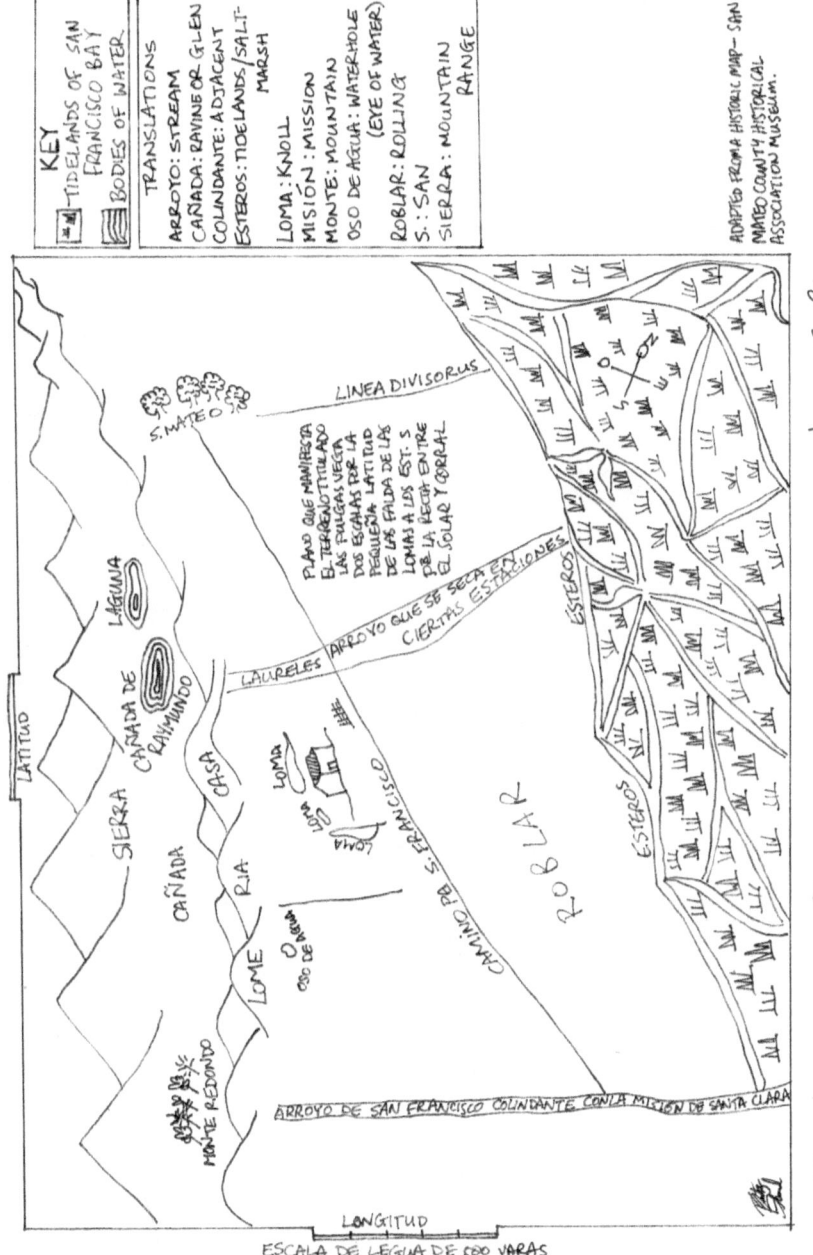

The Lands of Rancho de las Pulgas, San Mateo Co., CA

**KEY**

- Tidelands of San Francisco Bay
- Bodies of Water

**TRANSLATIONS**

ARROYO: STREAM
CAÑADA: RAVINE OR GLEN
COLINDANTE: ADJACENT
ESTEROS: TIDELANDS/SALT-
  MARSH

LOMA: KNOLL
MISIÓN: MISSION
MONTE: MOUNTAIN
OSO DE AGUA: WATERHOLE
  (EYE OF WATER)
ROBLAR: ROLLING
S.: SAN
SIERRA: MOUNTAIN
  RANGE

ADAPTED FROM A HISTORIC MAP — SAN
MATEO COUNTY HISTORICAL
ASSOCIATION MUSEUM.

LINEA DIVISORIA

S. MATEO

CAÑADA DE RAYMUNDO

LAGUNA

SIERRA

LAURELES ARROYO QUE SE SECA EN CIERTAS ESTACIONES

PLANO QUE MANIFIESTA EL TERRENO TITULADO LAS PULGAS VEGA DOS ESCALAS POR LA PEQUEÑA LATITUD DE LAS FALDA DE LAS LOMA A LOS EST. S POR LA REGION ENTRE EL OLAR Y ORBAL

CAÑADA

CASA

LOMA
LOMA
LOMA

RIA

LOME

OSO DE AGUA

CAMINO PR S. FRANCISCO

ROBLAR

ESTEROS

ESTEROS

MONTE REDONDO

ARROYO DE SAN FRANCISCO COLINDANTE CON LA MISION DE SANTA CLARA

LATITUD

LONGITUD

ESCALA DE LEGUA DE 600 VARAS

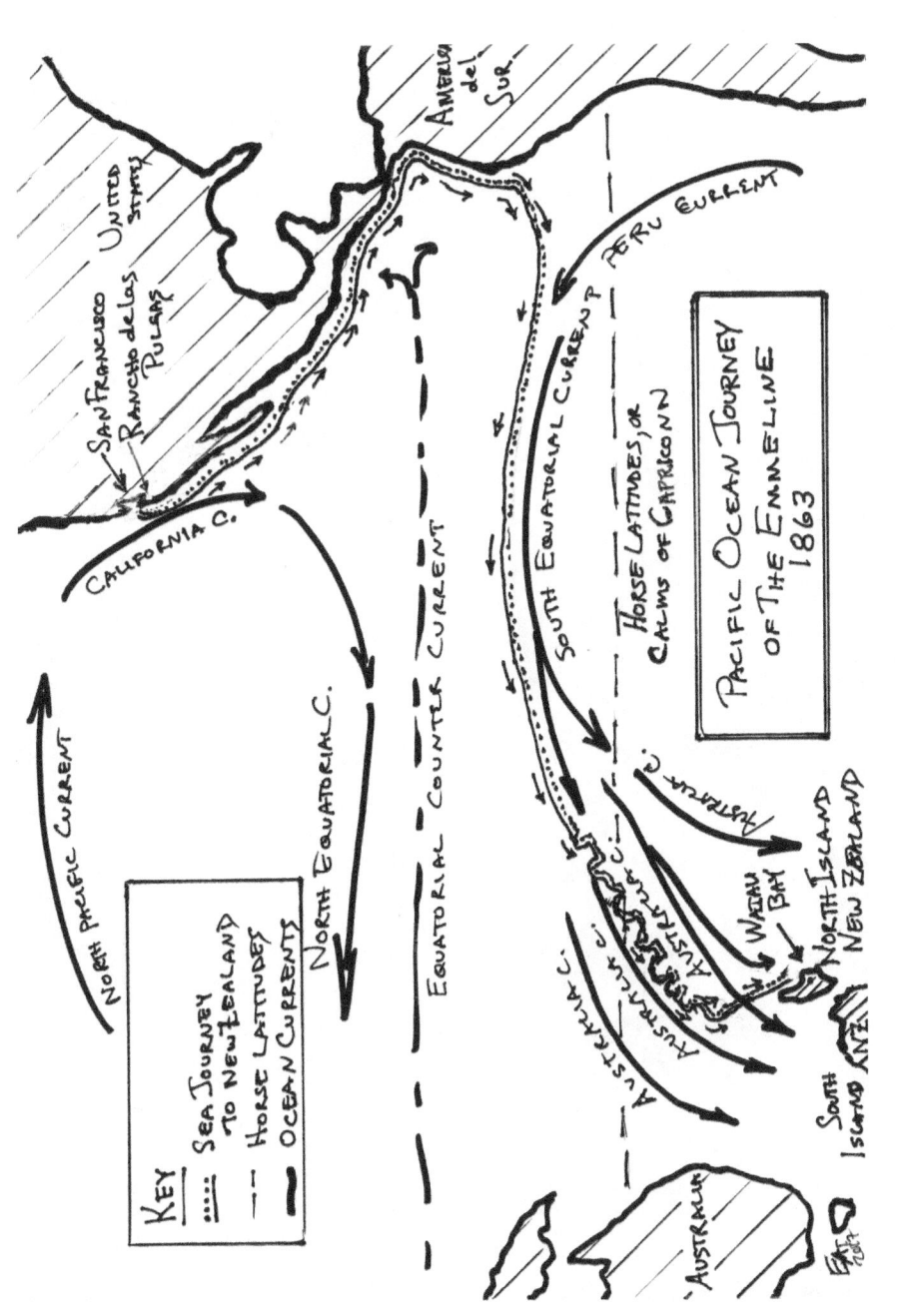

KEY
x REDOUBTS
SWAMP
GREY'S LINE

NEW ZEALAND
TOKOMARU BAY
TO
AUCKLAND
1863

JOURNEYS
ALEKS' JOURNEY
XAVIER'S JOURNEY

GREAT BARRIER ISLAND

PORT JACKSON
PORT CHARLES
COROMANDEL

RANGITOTO IS.
WAIHEKE IS.

PORT JACKSON

MAUAO OR MAUNGANUI
TAURANGA
WAIHOU RIVER
ORAKARANGI PÁ

MATATA
WHAKATU
LAKE ROTORUA

WAIAU BAY
TOKOMARU BAY
HICKS BAY
POVERTY BAY

AUCKLAND

PORT WAIKATO
WAIKATO RIVER

FERRY
TUAKAU
WHAT
WAIKATO
NGARUAWAHIA
KARAPIRO
ORAKAU
PIRONGIA
KAWHIA HARBOUR
WAROKOPA

MARIU

N

E F

Waihou Through to Pukorokoro

Frith of Thames

Coromandel Ranges

Waihou R.

Ōruarangi Pā

Hikutaia R.

Piako R.

Whitiakaurū R.

Pukorokoro
al. Miranda

KEY:
- -- A Leo's Journey
- ... Mud flats
- --- Swamp
- ▨ Free Passage
- ⌃ Mountains

EMT
2017

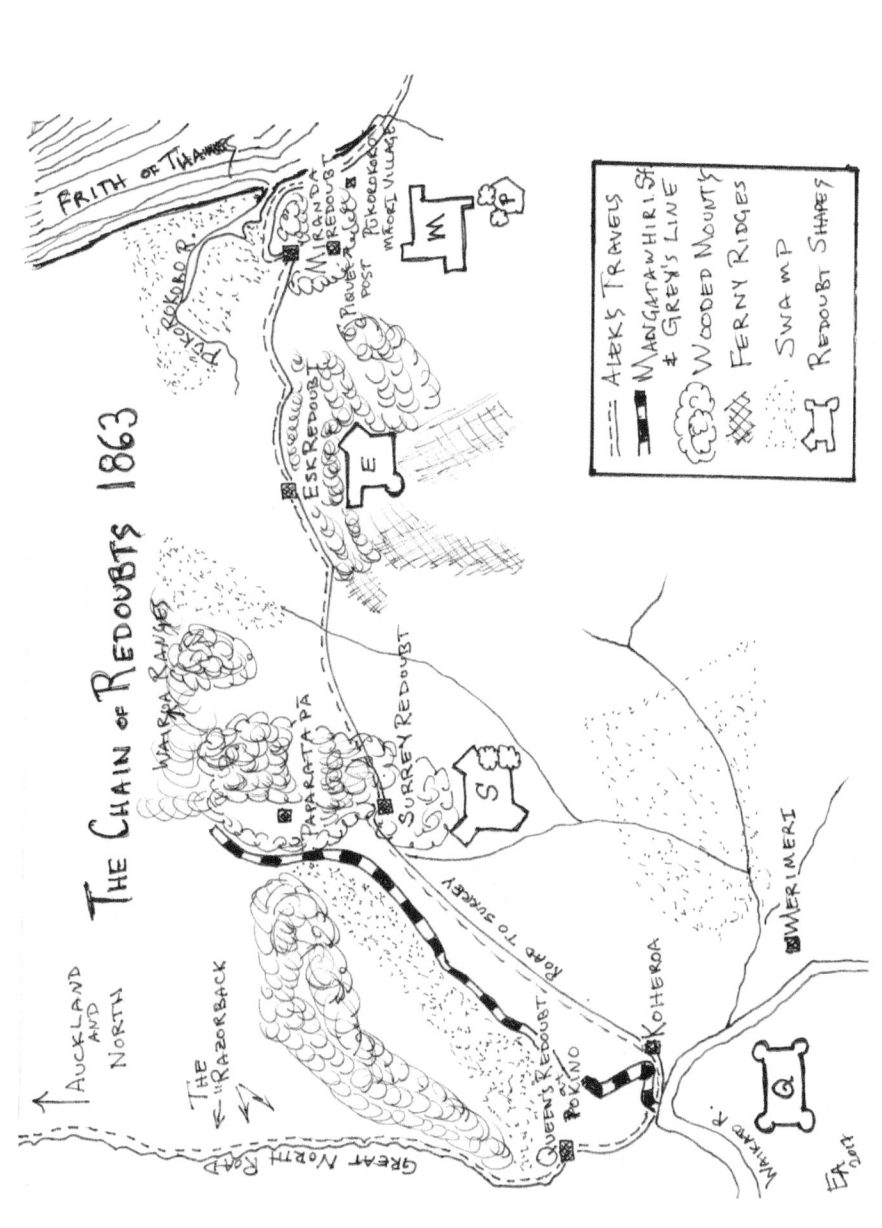

The Chain of Redoubts 1863

# Waitemata Harbour Auckland

## Then and Now

Now

1863

GRAFTON RD

SYMONDS ST

QUEEN ST

VICTORIA ST

**Reference**

1 Freemans Bay
2 Point Stanley
3 Commercial Bay
4 Point (&Fort) Britomart
5 Official Bay
6 Mechanics Bay

**Key**

Shoreline 1863

Shortland St., Previously along waterfront

Modern Waterfront

# PART I

RANCHO DE LAS PULGAS,
SAN FRANCISCO BAY

# 1

---

*March 1863, Rancho de las Pulgas, San Mateo County, California*

ALEKSANDRA ARGÜELLO's brother-in-law peeked out through the slits between his lashes and his bloodshot eyes widened at her in horror. He scrambled to his feet and bolted for the kitchen door—but she beat him to it.

"I repeat, Sancho, what did you mean when you said Xavier's and my baby wouldn't inherit the *rancho?*" she said past gritted teeth, as she stood against the plank of solid oak barring his way.

"*No se, no se,* I don't know," he stammered, and began to spin toward the window. He froze at the sharp edge of Aleksandra's sword across his throat.

Xavier Argüello chose that moment to open the door and stopped short.

"*¿Cómo?* What's going on?" Aleksandra's husband's eyes narrowed at the pair of them.

"That's what I'd like to know," Aleksandra said. Sancho turned his head and she winced, blinking at the alcohol fumes wafting from his breath.

"Sancho?" Xavier's long legs covered the distance to them in two steps.

Aleksandra tightened her grip on the sword and the miscreant inhaled sharply, but otherwise didn't move.

"*Su hermano*," she said, directing her words to Xavier, though she never looked away from Sancho, "your brother, showed up three hours ago, just after you left for morning feeding, reeking of *tequila* and looking like he'd been out drinking all night. He was mumbling something about Melissandra, our 'poor little girl', I think he said, '*pobre niña*'."

"That's right," Xavier said.

"And that Rancho de las Pulgas should be hers, but it was 'too bad she was born out of wedlock'. Then he passed out on the floor. When he finally stirred just now, I asked him to explain himself. He tried to bolt, so I'm encouraging him to stay and talk awhile." She gave Xavier the hint of a grin.

Xavier's brows shot up as he flicked his head sideways, his frown now fully on his brother. "Illegitimate, eh, *hermano*? *¿Come se dice?* What *did* you say? Out with it."

With a desperate sideways glance, Sancho ducked and spun, swinging a fist at Aleksandra as he pulled away. Xavier's punch caught him first, and Sancho's head snapped back as he dropped to the floor.

Aleksandra ducked down beside him to check his pulse, then stood up and shook her head as she sheathed her *shashka*.

"Are you even carrying your sword around the house?" Xavier asked, his dark brows lowering.

"It's only been two weeks since your daughter and I were kidnapped *from* this house," she said, fixing him with a stare. "I'm happier with it by my side." Xavier must be upset to even think of asking about it.

Xavier shifted his gaze to his brother. "I thought he'd stopped the drinking episodes," he said.

"So did I, but in the three days he's been gone, I guess he had plenty of time to get drunk."

Xavier's jaw was tight as he reached for her. He closed his eyes for a moment as he pulled her in close, and slid his fingers along her arms. "Mmmmm. You've been baking. You're covered in flour." He looked down at her with a hint of a smile, then a frown. "And you've gotten dough in your hair," he said, picking up her long blonde braid from where it hung down nearly to her knees.

Aleksandra shook her head. "It happens," she said, and glanced toward the kitchen table. "Adelita's already begun making the *tortillas* without me, while we've been playing here."

"I'm worried about Sancho. Mama is too," he murmured.

"Xavier, do you know anything about what he said?"

"He doesn't know what he's talking about," he said, and turned toward their Indian *sirvienta*.

She stared at them all, her mouth agape.

He nodded to her. "*Buenos tardes*, Adelita," he said, and reached for the water jug. He poured himself a cup and took a long drink. "We were married in Virginia City," he told her. "Sancho is drunk. *Está borracho*."

"But what if it were true?" Aleksandra looked sideways at him. "My mama and papa would turn over in their Catholic graves if it were."

Xavier stilled. The black fringe of his forelock half-hid his brown eyes, flecked with gold, as he shifted his gaze to his brother. "Sancho," he said, loudly.

Nothing.

"It's an issue easily resolved for us, really," Xavier said, as he knelt beside Sancho and shook him, "but it could be a little tricky in that Melissandra should by rights be first in line to inherit Rancho de las Pulgas. *Mi hermano* knows it well.

"Sancho," he barked again, but his younger brother never flinched. He shook his head.

"What if he knows something we don't?" Aleksandra said, shivering as a chill settled in her gut. Sancho could be telling the truth. "The Methodist pastor in Virginia City thought he could perform the ceremony in the absence of a priest, but what if…"

"*Señor* Argüello," Adelita bit her lip, and looked at them, her brow furrowed, "a letter came for you and *la señorita*," she nodded at Aleksandra. "It was from Virginia City, but I don't know who it was from. I put it on the desk of *el señorito*."

"Sancho's desk? When was that, Adelita?"

"*Sí*," she nodded. "It was many months ago, just before you returned from picking up the colts from Utah, and Molly and Sebastian from Virginia City. Before the *bebé* was born."

"I think it's time to look around the office," Xavier said. "Let us know if he moves, *por favor*, Adelita?"

They left her patting out *tortillas*, between nervous glances at Sancho, and headed for the *rancho* office.

"*Sí, sí, por supuesto*," she called after them.

They searched the desktop and shelves for an hour, but found only piles of long-overdue bills. In a bottom drawer, they found a stack of notes with scribbles scrawled upon their faces. The only decipherable figures on the notes seemed to be rather large dollar amounts.

"More bills, no doubt," Xavier said, with a shake of his head. "Guess I'll have to take over the books, too."

"We should've looked before, but…Sancho *has* been a bit displaced, with your return." Aleksandra winced.

"I wanted to leave him a little pride," Xavier lifted a brow, "but we need to keep the *rancho* solvent." He looked at the heap of chits, his lips in a hard line. "Difficult enough, without having creditors breathing down our necks. I wondered why all the storekeepers were giving me sour looks."

"We've found nothing here. Perhaps he's ready to wake up now," Aleksandra said.

This time, when Xavier shook his shoulder, Sancho struggled to a sitting position.

"Wha—? Oh, Xavier," he said, his brows narrowing at his brother for a moment, then he shrugged and rubbed his eyes.

"*Buenos días, hermano.*" Xavier sat on a stool beside him and regarded him over his coffee. "Hard night?"

"Must've been. I feel like—"

"—don't say it," Aleksandra cut in. "My Spanish is improving."

He turned to face her, an odd look upon his face.

"I was wondering," she went on, "what you meant, earlier, when you said Melissandra was born out of wedlock?"

Sancho's mouth dropped slowly open and his eyes widened, then he glanced toward the doorway. He lunged for it, but Xavier had him in a head lock before he took three steps.

"Tell us about it, *hermano*," Xavier said, his voice cold steel.

"Ah, ah…I was going to give you the letter, but I…lost it."

"You can do better than that," Xavier growled low.

"Maybe, if you let me go, I can…"

Xavier's jaw locked, along with the grip on his brother's throat.

"Where are we looking?" Xavier enunciated each word.

"The office," he whispered, eyes closed.

Xavier hustled him along before him, his arm still locked around his neck.

"You can let go, now," Sancho whined.

"If you like," Xavier said, and shoved him through the open office doorway.

After Aleksandra entered, the door slammed shut behind her, and a key scraped in the lock. Xavier pocketed it.

"Now, tell us about it," he said.

"Well, it should be here." Sancho riffled through piles on the desk, then glanced at the drawers down the side.

"Granted, we don't know exactly what we're looking for," Xavier said, "but we've already looked."

Sancho stopped, mid-shuffle, and turned, a tight smile on his face.

"Then, I don't know what you're talking about. She's lying." He looked at Aleksandra in triumph.

Xavier narrowed his eyes at them both for a moment.

She raised her brows in return. "Absolutely not," she said, and drew her *shashka* from its place at her hip. She walked with measured tread toward Sancho. Morning sunlight glinted off the polished metal of the short Cossack sword.

Her brother-in-law paled and took a step back and whipped around toward the window. He stopped short just before he got there, with a whimper.

ALEKSANDRA HELD the razor-edge of the *shashka* against Sancho's throat until he started talking.

"The letter came before you did, but I forgot—"

"The facts, please," she said, her voice as icy as the steel.

"I put it in a special drawer for you—so I wouldn't lose—" He stopped speaking and bit his lips together.

A drop of blood appeared at his throat.

"Where is it now?" She wasn't about to let him stop talking.

"Inside the bottom drawer *a la derecha*, to the right, up high, a secret shelf."

Sancho made no sound as Xavier fumbled around and pulled out a much-handled envelope from deep inside the drawer. Its flap was wrinkled where it had clearly been steamed open and resealed; by the look of it, several times.

"Is this it?" Xavier's voice brooked no argument.

Sancho glanced at him and gulped. "*Sí*," he whispered. "It is delivered. Let me go now."

Aleksandra took the letter from him and picked up a silver letter opener, shaped like a tiny sword.

Xavier unlocked the door and let Sancho escape, then locked it again and turned back to her.

She sat down with a thump on the desk chair and began to read the unfamiliar handwriting.

*Dearest Aleksandra and Xavier,*

*Jason, Billy and the rest of the family send their love and hope you are all doing well, as we are here. I am sorry to be the bearer of bad news, but when the traveling priest visited town today, he was incensed that dispensation for your marriage was given by Reverend Clay, without the Bishop's blessing. He says you are not, in truth, married, in the eyes of the Catholic Church, that you are living in sin, and that your child will be illegitimate unless you marry before its birth.*

*I hope you can find a priest to marry you at your earliest convenience, and that everything is well with the impending birth of your child. I'm glad Molly will be at your side for your birth and hope her new midwifery practice is going well. She and Seb left earlier this week with Xavier.*

*Until we meet again, all our love and regards,*

*Sarah (and Billy and Jason, by proxy)*

SHE HANDED it in silence to Xavier and leaned against his long, lean bulk. When he'd finished, he sat down on the desk before her, with a wry grin.

"Whatever do we do now?" she said.

"I guess Mama didn't miss the wedding after all?"

She shook her head. "But Xavier, this isn't funny. We've not been married all this time, over two years." It didn't bear thinking about.

"We've done our best. It will all be sorted." He was silent for a moment, then his eyes lit up. "Let's go tell Mama. She can give us a big *fiesta* and her priest can come and marry us properly, since our marriage...isn't." His attempt at a straight face failed and he grinned. "I only hope her current priest isn't the bishop of San Francisco. He's the one upset about our current marriage." He cocked an eyebrow at her, and then he frowned. "I don't know what it will take to ensure Melissandra's legitimacy, but we'll sort that out."

"Surely Mama's lawyer can fix it," Aleksandra said, but her smile was more of a wince.

ALEKSANDRA'S MOTHER-IN-LAW took the news with her usual aplomb. Only her frequent lapses into *español* gave her away.

She summoned her priest, and her *modiste*, within ten minutes of hearing their news.

"Mama, Aleksandra and I were thinking," Xavier said, and took another bite of *chiles rellenos* as the cheese dripped from his fork, "your birthday is in just a few months. What do you say we combine the wedding with your sixty-fifth birthday? Make it *la fiesta del año*?"

Maria stared at him. "But I couldn't possibly intrude on your—"

"—we insist, Mama," Aleksandra said, reaching for her hand. "Nothing would give either of us greater pleasure than to share our day with you."

"Well, if you're sure," Maria said. A frown marred her brow until she relented, with a big smile, and squeezed both of their hands.

"If you two don't need me here," Xavier said, standing up from the table, "Marcelo is waiting, so I'll be going." He kissed Aleksandra and the sleepy baby on her lap, and gave his mama a hug.

"*Gracias*, Adelita, *por la cena*," he nodded to her.

"*De nada*," she said, with a smile.

Maria looked around and took a deep breath. "Well then," she said, "we must get started. *No puedo, lo seinto,* sorry Aleksandra—English. We cannot wait upon the local mail service. *Los invitaciones de boda*—the invitations for the wedding—they must go out right away. Some must reach as far as Méjico and España, and our guests must have time to journey here." She sent a message for Miguel, the head stableman, to be ready to saddle his fastest horse to post *las cartas* from San Francisco.

Aleksandra's eyes goggled at the stack of envelopes as Maria sat her down at the table to help pen out wedding invitations—the list Maria held out to her contained four pages of names.

Her heart sank. She'd nearly turned around at the door and bolted before their first wedding when she saw the crowd of miners filling the tiny Virginia City Methodist Church.

"You can't mean to be inviting so many, can you?" Aleksandra looked up at her mother-in law, as her hands began to shake. "I'd best get Molly to take care of *nuestro bebé* for a little while."

"Ah, *señorita, lo siento,* Molly left early this morning to deliver *un bebé en* Redwood City, but I will get Consuelo to help," Adelita said, as she left to find her.

"Molly is getting to be a busy lady," Maria said, with a smile. "You will be fine, Aleks. And not everyone who is invited will be coming. The invitations we're sending to España won't even reach Europe before the wedding, but we'll send them, nonetheless," her mother-in-law said, dipping her nib again and starting on another invitation.

"I'd be happy with a small family ceremony," Aleksandra said, just above a whisper.

Maria's eyes opened wide and she nearly dropped the inkwell. "*Pero, Querida,*" she shook her head, "but darling, you are an Argüello now, or you should be, anyway." She chuckled. "We are a fine, old family. This is my gift to you and Xavier. I have missed him for many long years. I hope this can help make up for the time we have lost through misunderstanding."

"But—"

"There will be no 'buts'," Maria said. "Only the best will do for you two. Enjoy it."

Aleksandra managed a smile, and shook her head. "Very well. Just so you know, I'm not good with crowds. Fur trapping in Utah Territory with only my papa for company gave me little cause or opportunity to be social."

"You are perfect just the way you are. You are a gift from God for my Xavier," Maria said, as she kissed her grandbaby Melissandra on the forehead.

SANCHO. He remained an enigma.

After the incident about the letter from Sarah, he'd been respectful, but not really friendly. Against Xavier's better judgement, he still allowed Sancho to deal with the *rancho* accounting, especially as it seemed his brother would rather die than go out on the farm to work. Xavier didn't know what else to do with him.

"How do you know what to put in the accounting books, if you don't ever go out there?" Xavier asked him, in exasperation, one evening.

"Jose always told me what I need to know."

Xavier stopped dead. "Do you mean Jose's been doing all the farm work since I left ho—' "

Sancho's smug grin said it all, and the air left Xavier's lungs like he'd been punched.

*I left them to do all the work and now I expect to just waltz in and take it back over?*

"Right. Let's start over." Xavier pinched the bridge of his nose, elbows on the table. "How can I help on the *rancho?*"

"I'll keep doing the books and you can do the rest. It'll all be yours, anyway, *hermano.*"

Xavier shook his head. "This is a huge place. Plenty for all of us. I'd like you to show me how the books are run in case you want to leave, too," Xavier said, with a smile that wasn't returned. The back of his neck tingled as his hackles raised.

"Like I said, it'll all be yours. When you never came home, it didn't look like you'd be taking over after all, so Jose and I ran it like it were our own. Now you're back…well…things aren't the same now, are they?"

Xavier's head was close to splitting. "Sancho, won't you—"

"—I don't want to hear *su mierda,* now or ever," Sancho interrupted. He turned on his heel and stormed from the room.

LATER THAT DAY, footsteps sounded on the stairs outside his office.

Maria entered and slumped into the chair beside Xavier's desk, shaking her head. "Your brother, he has been strange for the past several years; fits of temper, drinking, staying away for days at a time, but always he comes back and asks what he can do to help me. I don't know what to do with him. He won't tell me where he goes, though he's been seen drinking at some saloons in Redwood City, and up north as well."

"I don't know what I can do to change it," Xavier said, with a sigh. "I've just asked him what I can do to help, and he says everything but the books."

"He's been doing them for the past four years or so. I have left him to it, given him some pride."

"I can do the same, Mama, but…"

"But?"

"When Aleksandra and I were looking for the fated…" he grinned, "letter, we found piles of unpaid bills. I'm concerned." He hesitated. "Isn't the *rancho* making money?"

"It is," she frowned, "so I wonder why he isn't paying the bills?"

"I'll ask him. I'm sure there's a good reason."

She squeezed his cheek between her fingers and kissed him on the other side.

"I have so missed you, my firstborn. I have missed you every day since the morning you left, but you're here now, and your lovely Aleks with you."

"Thank you for making her so welcome and planning a special wedding for her. Our last one was a bit of a rush, as she was to begin teaching school in Virginia City immediately. She's been lonely—she misses her family more than she will admit."

"How could I not make her feel at home? She is lovely, *y para ti, mi primogénito, ella es perfecta.*"

Xavier shook his head, tears in his eyes, and took her in his arms. He held her close for long minutes. How could he have ever misunderstood her so…blindly?

Maria's French *modiste* came all the way from San Francisco to measure Aleksandra for her dress.

The two older women thumbed through the book of sketches. Aleksandra was completely lost, sitting still and staring, trying to keep her jaw from dropping at the exquisite gowns displayed on the pages before her. One, though, caught her eye. She looked up as the dressmaker spoke.

"For you," *Madame* Lavigne pointed to the same design, "I have designed especially this gown in the Spanish style."

"It belongs on a princess," Aleksandra breathed.

"It is…*magnífico*," Maria said.

Aleksandra's face heated and she lowered her eyes to the ground as the *modiste* stood back and looked her up and down, as if she were assessing a horse.

"No, no, *mademoiselle*," she picked up Aleksandra's chin with a forefinger, "do not look embarrassed, you are lovely. I simply must see how it would fit on you," she admonished. "It would be a good design for your figure, with your tiny waist, and Madame says you have a wee baby?

So we will have no need for any padding of the 'boosies'?" She patted her own ample bosom, beaming.

Aleksandra offered her a wan smile. "It's a beautiful design, but I couldn't imagine myself in anything so grand," she said softly.

"I certainly could," Maria said, and it was decided.

For the better part of the next hour, Aleksandra was turned this way and that while the dressmaker wrapped her knotted string around her in every possible direction, barking dimensions to her young assistants in French. By the time the girls came to her, armed with fabrics, she'd forgotten to be embarrassed. They held swatch after beautiful swatch against her face and hair, while the *modiste* sat with Maria. The two of them commented in a combination of English, French and Spanish.

"How do you like this fabric, *Querida*?" Maria asked her, as she stroked a bolt of smoky golden silk taffeta.

"I...I..." Aleksandra gulped. She'd worn muslin and buckskin most of her life, then donned her mother's delaine for her first wedding. For teaching in Virginia City, she'd quickly cobbled together two more dresses, one of linen and another of wool. She couldn't begin to imagine what the fabric might cost, much less the making. She blinked and took a deep breath. "It is beautiful beyond my expectations, but isn't it..."

Maria shook her head. "Aleksandra, you are an Argüello now. We have a proud history and will spare nothing for the wedding of you and my firstborn. It was the same for my wedding. Xavier's father would be so..." she hesitated, then wiped a tear from her cheek and swallowed hard, "... proud. Most importantly, though, it looks magnificent on you—" she reached out and pulled some of Aleksandra's long curls over the top of the fabric and smiled "—with your beautiful hair and lovely complexion."

"Thank you, Maria. I've never even touched anything so beautiful," she said.

The *modiste* tut-tutted and flashed her a grin.

Maria turned to the other woman. "And what shall we use to accent it?"

"I had in mind, *Madame* and *Mademoiselle*, this." When she herself brought forth the roll of burgundy, gold and russet brocade, both Aleksandra and Maria blinked. "And this." She held out a cocoa silk floss fringe and a few matching spherical buttons of crocheted cord and fine silk thread.

Aleksandra could only stare.

Maria glanced at her. "*Sí, Querida?*"

*"Sí, Mama. Están tan magníficos."*

"Nothing is too magnificent for you, Aleksandra," she smiled and reached for her hand, "and your Spanish is improving daily. You have made my Xavier happy, given him back his heart and brought him home. *No*, nada *es tan magnifico, recuerda*," she said. She stood and pulled Aleksandra into her arms for a hug. "I cannot take the place of your mama, but I hope you will let me spoil you a little for your big day, as she would have."

Aleksandra couldn't hold back the tears, but it didn't seem to matter to Maria, nor to *Madame* Lavigne and her girls. Surely their brides-to-be exhibited the full range of womanly emotions. Only moments later, she nearly giggled at the thought that flashed through her mind. She daren't say it aloud.

*She couldn't get closer to the color of her buckskins if she tried.*

PLANS for the grand wedding party—the *gran banquete de boda*—moved quickly, faster than Xavier could have ever dreamed, driven by his *mama*.

They were to be married at the chapel of the Rancho de las Pulgas, the same one in which Xavier had been christened, and where Maria had married Xavier's father so many years ago.

"I'm going with Santiago to dig the pit for the bull, if anyone needs me," Sancho said, as he left the office. "Mama's gone to Redwood City to order supplies from the grocer."

"Thank you, Sancho. I appreciate your help with the wedding," Xavier said, smiling at his little brother. "I know it's been difficult."

"No problem. I know you'd do it for me," Sancho said, but his jaw tensed as he turned to go.

Xavier's heart sank. He'd hoped Sancho would come around, but it looked like it wouldn't be happening anytime soon.

Esi appeared at the door, with Melissandra in her arms. "Do you know vhere Aleks is? The *modiste, Madame* Lavigne, she has arrived and I'm oop to my ears here."

"Thanks, Esi, I'll find her," he said, and stepped out the back door into the spring sunshine. The heady scent of his mother's gardens filled the air. He smiled, thinking of Esi. She was finally coming out of her shell. She'd been a slave on the Confederate ship where Aleksandra had been held by a kidnapper. When the US Navy boarded and captured the schooner, he and Dancing Wolf, Aleksandra's childhood friend, had rescued them both. Without Esi's efforts to delay the ship, they might not have been so lucky, and after the drama was over, they had made sure Esi was freed. She was working at the *rancho* while she made her next plans.

"Aleks! Where are you?" Xavier called out, and looked around the corner of the barn, then stopped short. "The dressmak—"

His words died on his lips.

# 2

"It just won't work," Aleksandra said to Molly, her voice filled with frustration.

Xavier could only shake his head and cover his mouth so she didn't hear him laugh, as he leaned back against the wooden wall of the barn.

His bride-to-be lay sprawled in the dirt, brushing volumes of netting and shimmering silk away from her face, trying to shove them down toward her feet. She heaved a sigh and sat up, biting her lip, her forehead furrowed.

Molly gripped the end of Rogan's reins with both hands. "I don't think he likes the crinoline," she threw over her shoulder, never taking her eyes from the bucking and snorting bay. "I'll go put him away. I think he's done for today."

"Got that. Thanks Molly," Aleksandra grumbled, as she struggled to her feet, avoiding the hoops.

Xavier pushed off the wall and went toward her, exchanging a grin with Molly as she passed. "We'll geld you yet," he growled in an undertone to the wayward stallion. Rogan only shook his head, his glossy mane flying in all directions.

Aleksandra spun to face him as he spoke, a flush rising from her neck toward her face.

"Ahhh, *Querida*," Xavier shook his head, "I want to marry you, not attend your funeral." He found a handkerchief and wiped the dirt off her cheek, then touched his lips gently to hers. Wrapping both arms around her, he held her against him. "Are you hurt?"

She peered up at him from beneath lowered brows. "Only my pride."

"What were you thinking? Rogan?"

She hesitated. "I wanted it to be a surprise for you. He and Charro look so good beside each other. I wanted them to be in the ceremony."

Xavier hugged her close, only partly so she didn't see his grin. As he took a deep breath, it came to him.

*Dzień.*

"They do look nice together," he said, "but Dzień's been with you through thick and thin. Don't you think he'd like to carry you to the altar?"

She leaned back and looked him in the eyes. "You understand, don't you? You always understand me, and you always love me, no matter what."

"And you understand me. And I *do* love you. Now go get your pony and let's try this again—oh! *Madame* Lavigne is here, I almost forgot." He shook his head.

Aleksandra's eyes snapped full open. "Oh no! We need to clean the petticoats. She'll have a fit."

They began to laugh and couldn't stop. She untied the skirts and he shook the dirt from the voluminous folds of the crinoline and petticoat.

"Now get back to the house, before she comes looking for you," he said, swatting at her bottom as she dashed for the *hacienda*.

"I COULDN'T BELIEVE it when Mama said we could be ready for a big wedding in only three weeks," Xavier said, shaking his head, as he knocked the dust out of the body brush and returned to grooming Charro, "but she's done it—herded us all into making it happen."

"I told her I'd be happy with a small wedding." Aleksandra quirked her lips at him over the top of Dzień's rump, and kept brushing.

Jose, grooming his own horse in the aisle of the barn, laughed aloud.

Xavier stared at her, then found his voice again. "Mama hasn't waited all these years to have a tiny wedding. I'm sure that went over well."

"Ummm…let's just say I was overruled."

"She'll want it to be as well known as the love story *de nuestro tía abuela,* Conchita."

"Conchita?" Aleksandra said, one brow raised at Xavier. "You haven't spoken of her."

"María de la Concepción Marcela Argüello y Moraga," Jose said, "our great auntie."

Aleksandra blinked. "What a magnificent name."

"She's been invited to the wedding, of course?" Xavier turned to Aleksandra.

"*Lo siento*, I don't remember her name, but there were far too many people invited, so probably." Aleksandra's brow furrowed.

"Unfortunately, she died six years ago," Jose said, with a sigh.

Xavier spun toward his brother, his mouth open. "But, she was young, she couldn't be more than..." he bit his lip as his heart plummeted, "sixty-odd?"

Jose nodded. "She's buried at Benicia."

"But I saw her in Monterey, at the St. Catherine Academy, just after I left, soon after she'd joined their order. I wanted to see her before I left for the gold country." His eyes blurred and he brushed his sleeve across his face to clear them.

"They moved the community to Benicia the year after you left."

He clenched his hands on the brushes. He'd missed her, all the years he'd been away. Conchita had always been kind. She'd sheltered and cared for him, a heartbroken fourteen-year-old, when he needed the love of a family. Her own heart had been broken as a young woman and she'd chosen to never love a man again.

"Benicia?"

"Yes."

Xavier looked at Aleksandra and she took his hand. "We could have visited her grave, if we'd known," he said.

"Big brother, you didn't know," Jose winced, "but if you'd let us know where you were, we could have told you."

"I'm sorry, Jose," Xavier hugged his brother, "sorry for so many things. I hope I can make it up to you all."

"All is forgiven." Jose smiled. "We're just glad you're back."

Xavier turned to Aleksandra. "Father's aunt Concepcíon fell in love, as a fifteen-year-old, with a visiting Russian statesman called Nikolai Rezanov. Her father held the Presidio at Yerba Buena, the name for San

Francisco at the time. They became engaged, to the family's horror, as Rezanov was of the Russian Orthodox faith. Rezanov wrote to the Pope and the King of Spain to gain their dispensation for the marriage, then left for home, promising to return. While traveling across Siberia to gain approval from the tsar for a treaty he'd struck with Concepcíon's father, as well as for their wedding, he fell from his horse, sickened and died."

Aleksandra took a deep breath and held it for a moment, staring at him. "I'm sorry for your *tía abuela*, but I don't think we want that sort of fame, do you?"

He shook his head and grinned. "No, but Mama might."

"She might, at that." Her brow creased as she picked up a comb and started on the end of the Mustang's tail. "Yesterday, she said her priest has secured the bishop from San Francisco."

"The bishop?" He froze. "For the ceremony?"

She nodded, her eyes wide.

"The same one who declared our first marriage null and void?"

"As far as I know, there's only one bishop in San Francisco," she said, dryly.

"It should be an interesting ceremony, then." He quirked a brow at her. "It's a good thing few of the people to attend will understand Latin."

He caught Jose's grin.

"On to more exciting things," Jose said. "I was telling Aleks about my plans for Spain."

"I'm so glad we caught you in Monterrey before you took ship. We thought you'd be long gone," Aleksandra said.

"Are you sure you don't want to stay?" Xavier said. "As I told Sancho, there's plenty of *rancho* to go around."

"Maybe someday, but my heart isn't in *las Pulgas*. Mama yearned for you so, I knew you'd someday hear her call and come home. I've been awaiting your return to travel the world."

"*¿De seguro?* Are you sure? I'd love to have you here with us."

"*De seguro*," Jose said, with a smile. "I wish you both the best, but I will leave just after the wedding... and Mama's birthday celebration." He shuddered. "Can you imagine what Mama would say if I were to leave before then? It would take a stronger man than I to do such a thing."

Xavier laughed and clapped his brother over his shoulders as he passed him to get his saddle. As young boys, they'd always been close. It was Mama and Jose he'd missed every day of his self-imposed exile, for many long years. He'd miss him even more, now his brother was in his life once again.

The three swung up on their horses and rode from the stableyard. The *rancho* shone like never before. The adobe buildings gleamed with new whitewash, from the house to the stables. Even the fences lining the driveway were brushed clean of dust.

Jose went to town on an errand for Maria while Aleksandra rode with Xavier toward the flat area down the hill from *la casa grande,* where she practiced *džigitovka.* She rode out onto the *rancho* to check cattle with him whenever she could steal time away from Maria's wedding preparations and Melissandra, but today she was going to teach him more Cossack riding skills.

Today, they were to work on some basic vaults on Charro. He wanted to show them off when he mounted up after the wedding ceremony.

"Well done," she said, when he could finally flick himself onto the massive stallion as he struck off into a canter from a standstill.

"I'm sure this would have been easier to learn as a ten-year old," he said, his face heating at her praise.

"Doubtless. I've started you a bit late."

"Not your fault, but I'll do my best," he said, winking at her, as they led the horses home to cool off. "I'm glad we can steal these few moments together." He pulled her tightly against his side as they walked.

"I couldn't do it without Molly's help with Melissandra," she said, and shook her head, "and your mother is so organized. Even in the midst of all this, I'm finally getting the time to learn Mexican cookery from her and Adelita."

"Now that, I like to hear," he said, beaming. "Other than Mama and Jose, Mexican food was the thing I missed most during my exile from here."

"Everything's just perfect," Aleksandra's eyes glowed, "everyone's happy and Melissandra seems to think she has two mothers. I don't have a problem with that at all," Aleksandra said, then her brows narrowed for a moment.

"What?" he asked.

"Nothing much."

He raised a brow at her and waited.

"Sancho's still acting oddly," she said.

"How oddly?"

"Whenever he runs into me, he sets his jaw and spins the other way. Maybe I'm just being overly sensitive."

He frowned.

"But nothing's been said," she shrugged, "so it's probably my imagination."

He took a deep breath and held it. She hadn't said anything about this before. Maria hadn't, either, though once he'd heard her exchanging curt words with her youngest son in the hallway beyond his office. Nothing had otherwise been brought to Xavier's attention, so it hadn't entered his mind.

"So we'll have the bull's head, along with the rest of him, of course, *carne asada, enchiladas*—" Maria stopped, frowned, and looked at Aleksandra. "Would you like to create some of your magical *żurek* for the wedding? Then I can learn how to make it."

Aleksandra's face grew warm and she smiled down at Melissandra. Her daughter had just fallen asleep and a nipple slid from between her lips as her rosebud mouth opened.

"I'd be happy to, Mama. *Żurek* is my happy-food, for when I'm sad."

"I know you miss your family," Maria said, sitting down on the bench beside her, "but I hope you know, you're *familia* to all of us, now."

"I know. I appreciate that," a cold tear ran down Aleksandra's cheek, "but I can't help missing them sometimes."

"*Por supuesto.* Of course, you can't. Just know we love you, too." She hugged her and kissed her forehead, careful not to disturb the sleeping baby.

"Maria, *sus palillis!*" Adelita said, up to her elbows in yet another bowl of wet *masa harina*. Maria leapt back to the stove, where her frying breads had begun to smoke.

"I'll go put Melissandra into bed and be right back." Aleksandra stood carefully and lifted the sleeping infant to her shoulder.

"Good idea." Maria glanced over at the bassinet in the corner of the kitchen nearest to the stove, then smiled at Aleksandra. "There's too much hot oil and too many helpers in here today for her to get a good sleep."

A knock came upon the frame of the open front door as Aleksandra passed it on her way to their bedroom.

"Yes?" She looked up to see a small man standing in the doorway with a large suitcase in each hand.

"May I see the mistress of the house?" He smiled at her, his face wan.

"How may I help you? She's busy in the kitchen."

"I understand." He coughed, then looked up at her again. "I am a peddler. I have many wares which might be of use in preparation for the big celebration you're to have. I heard about it in town and hurried right out."

"Are you all right? You don't look well." Aleksandra frowned, as the man wobbled on his feet.

"Oh, just a bit of a cough," he said, and blinked as he tried to hold in the next spasm.

"If you hold on one minute," Aleksandra said, "I'll be right back. Come on inside and sit on this bench."

The man removed his hat and held it before him. He left his bags where they stood, stepped over the sill and moved toward the seat.

"Thank you. I would appreciate sitting—" cut off as the man launched into a coughing fit, all over Aleksandra and her daughter.

Aleksandra winced and shook her head. Melissandra slept on, undisturbed by Aleksandra's sudden leap backward.

He kept coughing as she headed up the hallway. From the first stair, she turned to see the man. He was still hacking, and blue in the face. He struggled to breathe, making strange sounds with every breath.

She trotted up the steps and placed Melissandra in her bassinet, adjusted the fly screen, kissed her, then hurried back downstairs, grabbing her medical kit from beside the door. The man might even now be collapsed upon the floor.

He was still there when she came down the stairs, but so was Maria.

"No sir, there is nothing we need," the matriarch said. "Thank you very much. We are cooking for a hundred guests here, so I'd thank you to take your contagion elsewhere, please," she said, her voice sharp.

He gave a little bow and stepped outside, then dragged his cases away behind him.

Maria closed the door with firm finality and turned toward the kitchen. Aleksandra sighed and turned to return the kit back upstairs.

The greengrocer had come from San Francisco with the last of the delicacies and the produce wagon was parked at the back door of the kitchen. Indian girls, their long black braids hanging past their waists, had been borrowed from the other local *rancho* kitchens. They'd been there for the past several days, stirring pots and patting out *tortillas* and other breads, stacks upon stacks of them. The kitchen had been humming with Spanish words and songs as they all worked together. Now these women nearly ran in a continuous stream, fetching and carrying the fresh goods as they were handed down from the oversized conveyance, drawn by two massive draft horses. Aleksandra jumped into the procession to help unload and put away.

"Oh, Aleks," Maria said, pulling her out of the line and handing her a glass of water, "there are plenty of women to unload the goods. You need to keep your fluids up to feed my granddaughter. Let's see how your *zakwas* culture is going? I know it takes many days to make it large enough for the amount of *żurek* we need for all of our guests."

"I think there'll be plenty of food, with or without the *żurek*," Aleksandra raised a brow, surveying the bustling kitchen, but she smiled and took a deep breath. *Żurek,* she could do, with her eyes closed.

They escaped the flurry into the quiet back pantry and Aleksandra could breathe again. "Too many people," she said, to Maria's questioning look.

"They will not be here for long, and we need their help."

Aleksandra smiled and nodded.

"Aleks!" Xavier called from outside the door, "Mama's dressmaker is coming up the drive."

"She's a *modiste*, Xavier, don't let her hear you call her a dressmaker. That's as bad as a tailor, to her," Maria hissed. "Heaven knows what your bride's dress will look like, else." She turned to Aleksandra. "Aleks, can you get cleaned up for your fitting? You're covered with flour."

Maria continued to rattle off instructions like she'd been born to it, which of course, Aleksandra grinned at the thought, she had been.

"Xavier, don't let me see you *near* this house for the next hour while the *modiste* performs her magic. Adelita, can you watch the pots on the stove and bring refreshments for the ladies to the drawing room?" This last as she disappeared onto the porch to greet the women in their shiny black carriage.

"Mario," Maria called out. The young man popped his head into the doorway. "Oh, there you are. Please take the ladies' bags to their rooms?" she said, and disappeared.

Xavier and Aleksandra blinked at each other.

"She gets things done," he said sheepishly, then wrapped his arms around her and kissed her until her knees wobbled.

"Xave—she'll be—" Aleksandra struggled to get the words past her lips.

"*Te quiero*," he murmured as he dragged himself away from her. "I can't wait to see you in your gown."

"You'd better go, or you might not live long enough to get to the wedding." Aleksandra looked over his shoulder. "She's coming back," she whispered. "Out, you." She swung a slap at his buttocks.

He laughed as he spun away, then held open the door for the incoming ladies and bowed properly over the *modiste's* hand, while the little Frenchwoman beamed at him.

The dress would be a success.

Fifteen minutes later, *Madame* Lavigne slipped the gown over Aleksandra's corseted and crinolined body and laced it up tightly. She could scarcely even blink when she looked in the mirror—she certainly didn't recognize the girl in the ballgown. The woman had wrought a miracle.

The neckline of the golden taffeta dress scooped deeply and barely sat on the shoulders, while the bodice dropped to a deep "V" over her abdomen in the front and back. The short sleeves were embellished with the exquisite brocade and Aleksandra's arms tingled where the silky fringe brushed them as she moved, and she shivered.

"Are you cold, Aleks?" Maria said, frowning.

"Oh no, nothing like that," she said, turning before the mirror and looking over her shoulder to see the back. Nearly forty hand-sewn eyelets graced each side of the back and she was laced to within an inch of her life. She tried to take a deep breath and gave up, then took in the cartridge-pleated skirt, spreading wide over the hoops beneath.

"The brocade strips are magnificent on that skirt, are they not?" Maria breathed.

"They look like sashes running down the sides." Aleksandra beamed, now.

"We also have the sleeves, in case it is cold on your day." The *modiste* pushed up the short sleeves to tie the long, full ones—edged with matching brocade and floss—beneath them.

The bodice lining was cool linen, but the sleeves, oh, the sleeves. They were lined with silk that whispered with the slightest movement. Aleksandra hugged her arms to herself and Maria chuckled.

The dressmaker tut-tutted. "We must not forget the pelerine."

The short cape was draped over her shoulders, its "v" hem repeating that of the bodice.

"Oh Lord, look at the buttons, Maria!" Aleksandra said.

"They are rather magnificent, aren't they?" She bent down to examine one. "We saw them before, but on the dress, well, they are something special," she said, shaking her head.

Aleksandra still couldn't believe it was really her in the mirror.

"Thank you, *Madame*, ladies, and you, Maria. It is more lovely than I could have ever imagined."

"Let's get you out of it. There is only the hem to be done, and I have that in hand," the *modiste* murmured, "and then we will finish up the last details." Her satisfied smile boded well.

Aleksandra smoothed her hands down the bodice and skirt, over brocade so rich she was almost afraid to touch it. Her cheeks grew warm, thinking of her wedding night, their second one, and of her husband's hands sliding down the smooth taffeta. She swallowed hard and schooled her features into something that wouldn't beg for questions.

ALL TOO SOON, the day before the wedding arrived, and with it, the guests. The women packed themselves six to a bedroom, while the men made their beds in the stable before donning work clothes to help dig the pit for the bull barbecue.

The hole they dug in the field nearest to *la casa grande* was huge. Big enough to fit a whole bull carcass, four feet by seven, and as deep as Xavier's shoulders when he stood on its floor.

"¡*Niños!*" Xavier called, and the little ones all came running. "We need smooth stones from the creek, the biggest ones you can carry. Then I'll let you climb down into the pit to place them."

They ran for their lives.

"They've been dying to get in there all day," Aleksandra said, with a laugh. "I'll go get a snack for them. They'll be hungry after carrying rocks for the next hour."

Xavier reached his grimy hands up to capture Aleksandra's and she leaned down for his kiss. "Thank you, *Querida*. They'll need it. After that, they'll be gathering kindling and downed oak branches from all over the *rancho*."

She waved over her shoulder and headed for the house.

The pantry was filled to bursting with Adelita and Maria's specialty dishes and vast pots of *żurek*, and the huge kitchen was packed with bull meat in preparation for the barbecue.

"Can you grind this up, please, Aleks?" Maria handed her a big marble mortar and pestle and indicated a tray full of spices on a side-table: pepper, chiles, salt, marjoram and a vast number of garlic cloves.

She ground a few handfuls of the dry herbs, then smashed the garlic cloves on a board with her fist against the side of a knife. After picking out the skins, she added the garlic to the herbs in the mortar to make a paste. Dumping the paste into a bowl, she started again, grinding and grinding, as the other women began rubbing the spicy paste onto the full beef quarters and smaller cuts of meat. They loaded them into thin muslin bags soaked in wine, then carried them outside and placed each cloth bag into a water-soaked burlap bag. Men stood by to wire the tops closed and load them into a vast tub in a wagon bed, ready to go into the pit at daybreak.

Once the meat preparation was finished, the women took a well-deserved break. Aleksandra went with Maria to stand before the porch to greet the *Californios* as they arrived. What a cacophony of color they made. The women's bright linen *camisas* were tucked under snug bodices and their colorful flounced *faldas* hung down their horses' sides. The glistening white ruffles of the men's *camisas* peeked from beneath their richly embroidered, fitted *chalecos* and short tight *chaquetas* of dark silk. They wore glossy red sashes over their velvet pantaloons or *calzones cortos,* trimmed with silver or gold braid, and their deerskin boots disappeared into their saddles' long *tapaderos,* which trailed nearly to the ground. Their outfits were completed by velvet and wool *serapes* and topped with gaudily embellished wide-brimmed *sombreros Cordobés*. She shook her head. The people were colorful enough…but the horses…oh Lord, the *horses…*

One look at the Spaniard's mounts as they danced through the gates of the hacienda, and she could see where Charro got his flowing wavy mane and tail, magnificent build and exquisite movement. These were the progeny of their Spanish ancestors—necks arched and hindquarters full. Almost all, to a horse, of regal bearing. One massive stallion daintily reached out to touch her hand, his brown eyes big and liquid, as he gazed at her. Little ears pricked, he nuzzled her, then turned aside to wait patiently as his rider dismounted, one of yet another party of fifteen or more. Many came from as far away as Santa Barbara, and one family all the way from Mexico, spending nights on other *ranchos* as they travelled north, donning their finery at the last *rancho* before this one.

She was lost in a blur of horseflesh, cooking pots and swirling colors, meeting guest after guest. She had no hope of remembering any of their names, except perhaps, those of the horses.

Xavier found her alone and pulled her into the small pantry that was becoming her favorite kitchen hideout.

"I never get to see you," he said, with a frown. "I don't get to sleep with you tonight, either," he murmured, then his eyes lit up, "but after this night, no one will keep us apart, ever again." He kissed her, his mouth exploring hers, and she his, then he nipped her neck below her ear and kissed her forehead.

With a furtive look, he peeked out the door. "The coast is clear. You go first…imagine the scandal." He grinned. "*Te quiero, mi amor*," he whispered, and pushed her gently out the door.

She bolted, not looking back, heading for their room and Melissandra.

ALEKSANDRA FROWNED over the cot at Molly.

"Poor darling, not the best time for the her to get a cold," she said, as she picked Melissandra up and cuddled her to her chest. The baby reached for her shirt as she sat down in the rocking chair and untied her blouse, then Aleksandra put her to her breast and latched her on.

Melissandra began to nurse, then jerked her head away, struggling to draw air through her blocked, snotty nose. She struggled to inhale, then began to cry, between gasps.

"Poor wee tot, give her to me. I'll wipe her nose, then she'll be able to nurse." Molly smiled at the sad-looking baby and whisked her away, returning soon with a clean-nosed little one with a slightly happier look on her dear face.

Molly, ever the midwife, expertly latched her onto Aleksandra with a triumphant grin. "Now she'll be able to drink."

Aleksandra's heart sank when Melissandra made a halfhearted attempt to suck and then let go, her tiny head lolling back against Aleksandra's chest.

"Maybe she's just scared she won't be able to breathe, or tired," Molly said, cheerfully, in her best bedside manner. "She's a bit warm, and with all the excitement, none of us is sleeping as well as we should."

"I have to admit," Aleksandra lifted a brow at her, "I could use a rest." She looked out the window. Guests were still arriving. Even with the draw of the horses, the crowds were beginning to unnerve her.

Molly followed her gaze and nodded. "I'll get you a cup of cocoa, and the two of you can have a nice little sleep. You both need it," Molly said, and smiled, but Aleksandra caught the tightening of her jaw, as she closed the door.

"Melissandra's not well?" Xavier leaned over to kiss her as she sat in the rocker with the fitfully-sleeping infant.

Aleksandra's brow furrowed. "She's probably just got a cold. She's snuffly and irritable, and she won't nurse because of it. It's going to be a long night."

"I'm sorry I can't be with you tonight," he chewed the inside of his cheek, "but Molly just told me to tell you she'd be happy to sleep in our room to help you with her."

"That would be helpful. Otherwise, I'll be a mess tomorrow." She sighed, and smiled at him. "You're a sight cleaner than you were earlier."

"The creek will be running dirty after all the diggers are finished washing themselves."

"What's left to do tonight?"

"We've just set up the kindling on top of the stones lining the pit. Jose won the draw for the honor of feeding the fire, so he'll light it in a few hours and feed it more and more seasoned oak for the next six hours. By morning, the coals will be reduced to a white-hot layer, then it's time for the meat to go in."

"Poor Jose, he has to stay up all night?"

Xavier grinned. "Not to worry. He won't be lonely. There will be plenty of people sharing the time with him—drinking, singing to their guitars and telling stories, late into the night."

"Ah, of course." Aleksandra stroked their baby's reddened face with a wet cloth and smoothed back the damp wisps of curling hair.

He reached out and touched Melissandra's forehead. It was burning hot. "Is she all right?" He swallowed hard.

"I hope so." Aleksandra bit her lip. "Other than feeding her some willow bark and thyme tisane and keeping her from getting too hot, there's little else I can do." Tears filled her eyes as she spoke.

He kneeled beside them. Careful not to disturb the fitfully-sleeping baby, he wrapped an arm around Aleksandra and kissed her lips. "I won't be out late. I'm sleeping in the barn with Charro. It's probably the only place I'll get any rest. If you need me, customs be damned, send someone for me and I'll be here. *Te quiero, Querida. Y mi poquita,*" he murmured, and touched his lips to Melissandra's forehead, then slipped from the room. "*Adiós, mi amor.*"

He slipped down the stairs, his breath tight in his chest, and found Molly.

"Yes, she's got a cold," the midwife said. "She's having a hard time drinking, because her nose is stuffy, but…she really has lost her appetite. A good sleep, and she should be feeling a little better in the morning."

She didn't sound nearly as sure as she usually did, but he'd just have to trust them to do their best. "Aleks would be happy for your help tonight, so thank you. If you need me, send someone for me."

"We'll be fine," she said with a smile. "Now shoo, off you go."

He went, but his feet were more leaden than they should have ever been on the eve of his wedding.

"A toast to your lovely bride?" Jose handed him a bottle of wine.

"You toast her. I'll drink my own, thanks," Xavier patted the water-filled wineskin at his side.

"You really don't drink at all, do you?"

"Not a drop. Too many memories of your father, my stepfather."

"A good reason to quit." Jose sobered, and raised a brow at Xavier. "What's the matter? You should be the happiest man alive, wedding Aleks tomorrow."

"Melissandra's sick."

"With what?" The merriment died in his eyes.

"Molly thinks it's just a cold. Melissandra's little forehead is burning hot and she doesn't want to eat."

"I'm sure it's just a cold. All babies have them. She's got the best of care. How many *bebés* have their own midwife? You're just lucky it's the first cold she's had."

"You're probably right," Xavier said. He took a deep breath, and gazed over the people clustered in groups around tables or sitting on logs, the scene lit by torches, flickering in the evening breeze.

"I just saw Sancho. He told me to tell you he couldn't help in the ceremony tomorrow. No explanation."

Xavier closed his eyes for a moment. He'd asked both brothers to stand with him in the church, but Sancho clearly wanted no part of it.

"So be it," Xavier said, but still, it was hard to accept.

## 3

The biggest difference between their two weddings was that in this second one, Aleksandra was led up the aisle by an aging relative of Xavier's. Otherwise, this ceremony, too, went by in a blur.

Her Xavier waited at the altar beside Jose. His glowing eyes drew her, heart in her throat and hands cold as ice, as she floated across the miles of people thronging the chapel. Her taffeta and silk whispered with every step, amidst murmurs of appreciation, as she slipped past row after row of strangers.

A tiny cough caught her attention as she passed the first pew. Molly, seated beside Maria, held Melissandra in her arms. Aleksandra gulped and began to turn aside, but then Xavier's hand was in hers and his warmth flooded through her. She dragged her attention back to Xavier and the bishop.

"I thought you couldn't be more lovely than the last time we did this," he murmured, the corners of his mouth lifting for a moment, "but I was so very, very wrong." He squeezed her fingers as the holy man droned on, his words unintelligible.

*I never was very good at Latin.*

When Xavier took her other hand and faced her, she blinked, coming out of a dream. He slipped the pocket-warm ring back onto her finger again, its stone shimmering in the light of the candles on the altar before them.

*I've missed it on my finger, these past few days.*

She smiled as his face drew near and he took her lips with his. People clapped and cheered as he led her from the church and lifted her onto Dzień. He laughed as they both scrambled to keep the crinoline and skirts where they belonged.

"Thank God Papa had the foresight to train both Dzień and me to a side-saddle," she said, under her breath, as her husband tucked the folds of her skirt under her top leg.

"Crushing this skirt makes me cringe," he said, with a shudder.

"Me too," she said, "but Mama won't care, just so we're married, and in style." She gazed into his eyes, then took as deep a breath as she could.

His face at breast height, Xavier's eyes goggled. "Don't do that, all the men can see your—"

"—I have to breathe, Xavier," she hissed, then laughed out loud. "Jealous?"

"Of course not—well, maybe."

"You've no reason." She laughed again. "See?" The men were cheering, and one came forward to clap Xavier across the shoulders.

"Quite the bride you have there, young man. Off you go, *vamos a la fiesta de boda!*"

IT WAS ONLY a short ride from the chapel back to the hacienda, after Xavier successfully vaulted onto Charro as they left the steps of the chapel, amidst applause from the assembled crowd.

"Oh, they've been busy," Aleksandra said with a smile and a wave at the farmhands and servants, who stopped what they were doing to cheer as the newlyweds rode in.

"They asked to stay behind to put the finishing touched around *la casa grande.* Look, a dance floor." He pointed at the planked area next to the musicians. "Mama brought a mariachi band, all the way from San Francisco." The players nodded to the newcomers as they tuned their guitars and harps.

Ribbons and fabric buntings hung from the huge oaks. In their shade were laid out the fruits of everyone's labor in the kitchen for the last week: *paella, empanadas, tamales, enchiladas, carne asada, palillis,* cornbread, tortillas, and other breads of every description, Spanish rice, *arroz con pollo*, and the quarters of pit-barbecued beef. Crowning the center of the biggest plank table was the massive bull's head, stuffed with fresh herbs.

Xavier slid from Charro and held his arms up for his bride to dismount into his arms, amidst clapping and shouting.

He led her to the long table covered with food, took the proffered plates and together they selected their dinner and sat down at their table to enjoy their first meal as true husband and wife.

Xavier's eyes were soft as she looked into them. "I like being married to you, Mr. Argüello."

"Again. And I love being married to you, Mrs. Argüello."

The serving platters were kept filled to overflowing by the kitchen ladies, overseen by Adelita, as their guests lined up and selected their food. Tables set up beneath the spreading oaks were at capacity with their guests. Some sat to eat, while others moved around visiting with family and friends they hadn't seen in years.

"Oh look, there's señora Martinez. She came to visit a few months ago," Aleksandra said.

"Yes, and her friend…or maybe not…señora Diaz." Xavier cleared his throat and looked sideways in the direction of a portly girl standing off to one side. She was stuffing *palillis* into her mouth, but leaving most of the powdered sugar down the front of her dress.

"Who is that?" Aleksandra nodded in the direction of the girl.

"Ah…señorita Diaz…" He winced, took a deep breath, then continued. "My stepfather made some sort of a deal with her father, just before I…left home."

Aleksandra choked on her *carne asada*, with an unladylike snort, then recovered, trying not to laugh.

"Seriously?" she whispered, then glanced at señoras Diaz and Martinez. They were engaged in a lively, if serious-looking, conversation. The former shot a glare in her direction. "Oh. I see," Aleksandra managed to control her face, "I might not be in her good books."

"Through no fault of your own. I will introduce you to them later."

"I can't wait," Aleksandra said, with a lift of her brows, then she apologized. "The poor girl, was she heartbroken?"

"I doubt it. She was in love with someone else—a stableman, I believe. Hence her father wanting her married off. It coincided with a particularly bad beating by my stepfather, and I'd had enough."

Aleksandra inhaled slowly and took his hand.

"It's all over now," she said. "It won't happen again. We have each other now."

"I believe you. *Te quiero*," he said, with a smile.

Señora Díaz looked down her nose at Aleksandra, holding hands with her new husband as they selected their food from the plank before them. She turned away to listen to her friend for a few moments, then returned her attention to the newlyweds as the bridegroom picked out a choice morsel of the succulent *carne asada* and served it to his bride at their private table beneath the lofty trees of the *hacienda*.

"Have you heard," she said, "that these two travelled all the way from Utah to here, without a *duenna*?" She wrinkled her nose.

"I heard they were married," señora Martínez said, reaching for another hot, fresh *tortilla*, and ladling the spicy *mole* sauce over it, "or thought they were." Señora Martínez tried not to roll her eyes at the woman. Who was she to insult the new daughter-by-marriage of their hostess?

"How could they possibly have thought they were?" Señora Diaz nearly dropped her plate as she spun back toward her in her excitement, then set it down on the table beside her. "Either one is or one is not!"

"A Methodist pastor performed the ceremony in Virginia City in the absence of a Catholic priest. It is acceptable to the church, but it turns out that's only the case when the bishop has given his approval."

"And he hadn't?" Señora Díaz's eyes nearly popped out of her head, and she turned to glare at the pair.

Señora Martínez pursed her lips.

"Well. Well…" Señora Díaz couldn't seem to come up with a suitable reply.

"Weren't you planning on Xavier for your daughter?" Señora Martínez looked at her sideways, her voice hushed, behind her fluttering fan.

Señora Díaz glanced at her overblown daughter and her face tightened. "My husband and Xavier's deceased stepfather had an agreement."

"And?"

"Well, it seems the lad ran away from home at fourteen, only to be seen again this year, with this…this…*blonde*." She glanced at the bride, slim and glowing in her exquisite gown of bronze-gold silk taffeta and burgundy brocade, her *mantilla* floating down her back. Like molten gold. She gritted her teeth and turned back toward her daughter.

Señora Martínez took in señora Diaz's dark-haired, *Californio* daughter, stuffing her face with yet another *palillis* and liberally dusting her wine-colored gown with the fried pastry's generous sprinkling of powdered sugar. She winced.

"Nothing wrong with my daughter," señora Diaz whispered to herself, a bit sharply.

Señora Martínez blinked and imperceptibly shook her head. "They came here from Sacramento during the flood last winter, and saw the inauguration of Leland Stanford, our Governor. Did you know, they went with him to the Capitol building, in a rowboat?"

"How do you know all this?" Señora Diaz's brows turned hawk-like.

"I met them here, earlier in the year, and they told me the story."

"Ah, so you've met them already." Señora Díaz gulped, looking sideways at her companion. "I had no idea."

At least she had the grace to look embarrassed.

"Yes, Xavier told me Aleksandra suggested to Governor Stanford that they jack up the buildings of downtown Sacramento, like they did recently in Chicago."

Señora Díaz's brows shot up.

"He also told me," señora Martínez positively smirked, "that Aleksandra rode the Pony Express, as a *boy*!"

Señora Díaz paled and allowed herself to be led to a seat beneath a tree. She sat facing away from the crowd, fanning herself for all she was worth, while señora Martinez hurried off to get her a cold drink.

THE FEASTING WENT on for hours.

"*Dios mío*, but I love *palillis*," Xavier said, selecting another of the delicately browned, fried snow-covered puffs from the platter before them. He glanced downward. Powdered sugar already coated his, thankfully white, shirt and another puff drifted downward toward his lap.

"I don't dare eat them without a plate under my chin," Aleksandra said. "I'm off to shed my sleeves and see to Melissandra." Her face was flushed and perspiration glowed at her temples.

"I'll come with you," Xavier said, as he stood and set down his plate.

They accepted congratulations as they moved through the crowd, filling a plate for Molly on their way past the still-loaded table.

Upstairs, Melissandra drank a little milk, but stopped after five or six feeble attempts at suckling. Her flushed skin remained hot and sweaty.

"I've been getting her to suck on a bit of ice wrapped in a muslin," Molly said. "Thankfully, there was ice for the wedding feast."

"There's more willow and thyme tisane steeping, but is there anything else I can do for her, Molly?" Aleksandra swallowed hard as she put her lips to the infant's forehead. She looked about to burst into tears.

Xavier pulled them close and kissed Melissandra on top of the head.

"Truthfully, I don't think so. Try feeding her again in an hour or so. I'll be here."

"Would you like to go down to the fiesta? I can stay with her," Xavier said.

"Maybe for a little while, then I'll come back," Molly said.

"I don't want to leave her," Aleksandra said firmly.

"You go on with Molly," he said, nodding at the door, "and we can trade places in an hour, OK? We'll just have a cuddle together and you go have fun."

Xavier took Melissandra from her and lay down in their bed as the door closed with a quiet click.

He gazed at her usually-lively eyes, now dull in her peaked face. None of them had slept well in the past few nights—Melissandra with her congestion, and them with their concern. He kissed her again and covered her with a light muslin wrap, then curled up around her little body. He cringed at her next coughing spell, and then they both slept.

As THE DAY drew to a close, torches were lit all around the dance floor and the musicians stood up from their dining table. Their glowing white peasant blouses and dark pants, over woven leather *huaraches,* stood out in the crowd. They took up their instruments to rowdy applause and stood, gazing with expectation, at Jose.

"Aleksandra, Maria and Xavier, would you please join me?" he said, from the middle of the dance floor.

Xavier held out one hand to his wife and the other to his mother and together they took the stage with Jose.

His brother's congratulatory speech to the newlyweds was short, flowery and bawdy. The fact they already had a baby on the ground let him use jokes he wouldn't have otherwise attempted. His birthday wishes for Maria brought everyone to their feet and tears to their eyes.

He signaled the musicians and the party began.

Xavier bowed over Aleksandra's hand and Jose over his mother's, and they led them into the first dance. The wooden floor soon overflowed onto the ground and still more people got up to dance.

Aleksandra's eyes were wide, staring around as they danced. His arms held her snugly, protecting her as they glided around the floor. She was a wonderful dancer, light and easy to lead. "I can't believe you've only danced with your brother and father," Xavier murmured into her hair, as the first dance ended.

She looked up at him and put her lips to his. "Dance with Mama now, and I'll dance with Jose?"

He nodded, kissed her again, and handed her off to his brother, then took his mother's hands.

THE DANCING DIDN'T STOP that night, or at least Xavier never heard the music end after he and Aleksandra fell into bed beside their hot and irritable *bebé*, well past the early hours of the morning.

*Huevos Rancheros* saw everyone through the exodus of the hundred-odd guests, threaded through with many congratulations on their *casamiento* and on the *cumpleaños de* Maria. After waving goodbye to the last of the stragglers, Xavier and Aleksandra retreated to the kitchen. She sank down beside him on the long bench at the kitchen table and heaved a sigh of relief as Molly handed Melissandra to her.

He looked up to see Sancho coming through the kitchen doorway. His brother glanced through them as he grabbed a mug from the cupboard and headed for the coffee pot.

"*Mierda*," Sancho growled and jerked his hand back from the steaming enamel pot. It clattered back onto the stovetop and he yanked a towel from the rack and tried again.

"Had a good night, Sancho?" Aleksandra asked.

A scowl. "Lost my ta—" he said, and clamped his mouth shut.

"I didn't see you on the dance floor, *hermano*," Xavier said.

"I was playing ca—entertaining." He flushed and sat on the nearest seat.

"I heard there was a card game going on in the study," Jose said, and Xavier raised a brow at him.

"All night," Jose added.

*All night? Cards?*

Xavier exchanged a glance with Aleksandra. So he was gambling again. Even as a boy, Sancho had been obsessed with games of chance, but Xavier didn't know he'd continued it.

But with so many old friends, stories to tell and dancing? He watched Sancho's face, returned to a pale hue, in the afternoon sunshine. Xavier's jaw tightened as Sancho merely stared into the depths of his mug.

Maria stepped into the room and Xavier smiled up at her. She'd worked hard to run the *hacienda*, and had done it well over the years, despite the abuse from her second husband. For her sixty-five years, she looked remarkable, although after the late night, the lines on her face were more evident than usual.

"Thank you, all of you, for the splendid *fiesta*. I never thought to see most of those people again in this life." Her eyes brimmed with unshed tears. "And now, you've made my life complete by coming home," she glanced at Aleksandra and Xavier, her gaze warm, "marrying, having one dear *bebé*, and hopefully soon bringing into the world another little Argüello to continue our old line." She sat down at the head of the table, just before the silver drops ran down her cheeks.

Sancho's chair scraped against the floor as he stood, not looking at any of them. He turned and walked out in silence. Xavier closed his eyes for a moment, his breath constricting in his chest, then stood to go after him.

Maria stopped him with a hand on his arm. "Leave him, Xave. He's bitter, but he'll have to get used to the idea. He's been muttering about how much he's done around the place and how you're usurping, but in reality, Jose did all the work, not him. His sense of entitlement grows stronger by the day. It is not endearing him to me. His disappearances worried me in the past, but they're becoming more frequent, and longer. I used to ask where he went, but no longer. I dread the anger he turns upon everyone in response. He is, unfortunately, his father's son—more prone to violence than love."

Everyone sat, silent.

Xavier's guts slowly unclenched as he took deep breaths and counted to ten. "Mama," he said, "I'm sorry I left you to all this. I truly thought it would be best for all if I left when I did—"

"—*hijo mío*, you did what you had to do. We've been through all this." She reached for his hand and squeezed it. "*Qué será, será.* Sancho has chosen his life path and I have, as well. I've chosen to continue to love." She gazed at the everyone in her kitchen. "All of you. And soon," her face lightened, "there will be the patter of many *piececitos en la casa.*"

Xavier gazed at Aleksandra, and they shared a long look.

"And Jose, soon you, too, will be away. I will miss you, but I know you have waited long enough."

"My heart will always be here with you, Mama, *y con todo mi familia,*" Jose said, taking Maria's hand.

# 4

---

"Up until Melissandra got sick, you've seemed generally happier than I've seen you before, Aleks," Xavier said, as they rode along together, checking the furthest fence lines for breaks.

Her brow furrowed for a moment, then she answered. "I have a family again," she smiled at him, "and life has settled out. I'm even enjoying the time I spend doing "womanly" things, things I once despised." She chuckled and shook her head, then her face fell. "I'm just worried about Melissandra. I only left her today because Molly made me go."

"All children get colds and you needed to get outside. She'll be fine."

Aleksandra was silent for long moments.

"She'll be fine," Xavier repeated. "Was she sleeping when you left her?"

"Yes, and Molly won't leave her alone while we're away," she said, idly scratching Dzień's withers. The mustang stretched out his neck and gave a little shake of delight.

"Good. Dzień's been missing you, too."

Today, though, his wife looked far from the happy newlywed. She hadn't slept much with the hacking, feverish child beside her every night. They were both terrified, but they tried to stay calm for their baby's sake, if nothing else. He swallowed hard. Melissandra didn't seem to be getting better—if anything, she was worse.

"Well, they're paying off, your cooking lessons." He found a smile from somewhere and gave her a wink to draw her thoughts away from their *bebé* for a few moments. "Your *tortillas*, and especially…" he shivered, "your *mole* sauce, will keep me around for a long time."

"Ah, just want me for my food?" Aleksandra's grin wasn't big, but it was a try.

"No, but that'll guarantee it." He laughed and ducked as she flicked the end of Dzień"s reins at him. Charro laid his ears back at the insult.

"Sorry, Charro, my fault." Aleksandra reached out toward his nose, but he ignored her.

"Now you've annoyed him," Xavier said. "Payback…"

"Promise?" Aleksandra eyed him sideways, the corners of her mouth lifting a little, before she bit her lip. Remembering Melissandra at home?

"*Sí, Querida.*" He edged Charro closer, his eyes locking with hers. The buckskin covering her thigh was warm where he touched it, and his hand slid upwards. "We just need to—"

"*Hola señor, señorita.*" A loud voice interrupted them and Aleksandra's head shot up.

Miguel choked behind his hand, nearly losing the battle to keep from smirking at his employer.

"Ah, *hola,* Miguel," Xavier said, his cheeks heating.

"*Las vacas,* ah, the cows up this end are fine, and this youngster," he gestured at the bay horse beneath him, "is coming along well."

"*Bien, gracias,*" Xavier said. "Have you checked South yet?"

The man shook his head.

"We'll go back that way, then," Xavier said.

"*Gracias,*" Miguel grinned, "I'll see you *en la cena,* eh?" His mouth quirked as he passed them, a glint in his eyes.

Aleksandra regarded Xavier from beneath her brows, silent until the man was gone from sight, then she burst out laughing.

"He tried so hard not to laugh at his boss, groping his wife in full view of God and man," she said.

"Well, that's his place."

"True, so far as that goes," she dropped her head, "but really, all of your people seem to adore you. They can't do enough for you or Mama."

"We've always done our best by them, when we could…"

"Your stepfather? He didn't approve?"

He shook his head. "We worked around him, but sometimes it backfired. Then there was hell to pay."

She reached for his hand. He looked up and the tension melted.

"We'll do our best to keep that from ever happening again, *sí?*" she said.

"*Sí.* I'm so thankful I found you, and that you kept me."

They were silent for a while, then she frowned at him. "What did Miguel say? That he'd see us at *supper?*"

"Yes?"

"Supper is three hours away," Aleksandra said, "and it's only fifteen minutes to South."

Xavier laughed.

"My old hideout is down in South fields. When Melissandra is better, I'll show it to you. Miguel's found me there often enough in my younger days. I think you'll find that little can be hidden when one is heir to the Argüello estate," he said, and leaned across from Charro to kiss her.

"Melissandra's cough—it's getting worse, not better. She's vomiting after she coughs, and losing what little milk she's taken," Aleksandra said. "I don't know what to do, how to help her." She wrung her hands in her lap and bit her lip.

Maria looked up from her plate.

"That man was not well," Aleksandra said.

"What man?" Xavier frowned.

"A peddler who came to the door before the wedding."

"No, he was not," Maria said. "I'm glad we got him away before anyone else caught it," she said, then her mouth dropped open and her face lost two shades of brown as Maria stared at her.

A chill ran up the back of Aleksandra's neck.

"What's the matter, Mama?" Xavier said.

"No, it cannot be. I sent him away." Maria turned to Aleksandra. "You were never near him, please, *dios mío, digame*, tell me you weren't near him," she said, barely audible.

Aleksandra's jaw dropped. "I was, we were…what…what…what do you think he…"

Xavier wrapped an arm around her as she struggled to get the words out.

"He coughed on Melissandra," Aleksandra whispered.

"*Dios mío*," her mother-in-law breathed, then swallowed hard. She couldn't go much whiter. "He didn't. *Por favor*, please, tell me he didn't."

"What?" Aleksandra pleaded, tears beginning to flow as her hands shook. Nothing ever upset Maria like this.

"He sounded like he had…whooping cough," her mother-in-law said.

No wonder Aleksandra had recognized the odd sound of the trader' hacking. Papa trained her in medicine. It had been thorough…but it hadn't been enough.

*"Pertussis. Whooping cough. Causes a chronic cough in adults, but death to babies," Papa's voice echoed inside her head. "Next, Diphtheria. Aleks, can you tell me the signs?"*

She hadn't recognized the sound of Pertussis in this man and she'd let him cough on her. Because of that, their baby might die. And there wasn't a thing she, or anyone, could do about it.

Aleksandra woke up and stretched with relief. The night had started out badly, but in the end they'd finally all had some sleep. Melissandra had coughed until she was blue, vomited, and then dry retched for what seemed forever. She'd had another fitful nurse, then gone to sleep.

Sleep, blessed sleep.

Xavier turned over. His fingers ran down Aleksandra's neck to her shoulder. "So, she finally got some rest?" he said.

"She's slept like a baby, or like a baby should, after I last nursed her." She reached out a hand to touch Melissandra's forehead, then let out the breath she'd been holding. "Thank God, she's cool."

"Her fever's broken?"

Aleksandra pulled herself up onto an elbow and leaned over the infant, careful not to wake her, and froze, her heart in her throat. She sat up and took Melissandra into her arms. She was limp. Her face was pale on the top side and blue on the bottom. "Xavier, get my stethoscope, please," she somehow got out.

"What is it?" He sat up beside her and gripped her shoulder.

"Get it," she shrieked.

She put her ear against the baby's chest for a few moments, then let out a sob. Aleksandra tucked Melissandra up close and held her cheek to her baby's little face. She held her breath, hoping, praying for a miracle. Praying for a breath.

Xavier placed the earpieces into Aleksandra's ears and handed her the end of the stethoscope, then wrapped his arms around them both. After long minutes of hopeless despair, she gave up. They clung to each other like they'd never let go, sobbing around the shell of their firstborn.

They cried and comforted each other as best they could. Finally, Aleksandra fell into a fitful doze, waking with a cry every few minutes and burrowing deeper into Xavier's arms, closing out the world.

They lay locked together until a knock on the door heralded breakfast, and the need to tell the family.

SILENCE REIGNED over the *rancho* for the rest of the day.

Aleksandra wouldn't let anyone near Melissandra's body until the evening came. While Xavier tended to the barest of necessities on the farm, Molly and Maria took it in turns to sit with Aleksandra, then they helped her dress the baby and lay her out. They'd just finished when Xavier returned.

"Aleksandra," Maria said, and waited. "Aleksandra," she repeated.

Aleksandra finally glanced up at her.

"Let's take her downstairs to the parlor. Melissandra needs to go downstairs," her mother-in-law said softly.

Xavier looked over her head at Maria and shook his head, then nodded toward the door.

When the door closed on everyone else, Xavier took her into his arms and sat in the big chair by the window. "Aleks?"

She finally took a breath and looked up at him, her eyes dull.

"Are you...is there anything I can do to help?"

She closed her eyes and seemed to shrink into herself again.

"I love you. I'm so sorry we lost Melissandra, but... you still have me, and we're a family."

"I can't do it. I can't keep a baby alive," she whispered. "I've tried and tried. It's no use."

"You're not a broodmare. You are my wife."

"Just." The shadow of a grin, then it was gone.

"No, you've been my wife for a long time and will continue to be so, regardless of your baby-producing state."

"But she was…so young…never had a chance to live."

"No, she didn't, but we gave her the best life we could for the time she was with us on this earth."

"But we killed her, I killed her."

"You did not."

"I let that peddler cough on her. I killed her."

"You couldn't have known. If you had, you'd not have gone near him."

"My vanity, thinking I'm such a wonderful healer, and that I could help him. I'm not."

"You always do your best. That's all you can do. Thank God she went peacefully in her sleep, if she had to go."

She whimpered and pulled him to her, then slept in his arms.

XAVIER EYED the burlap sacks of oats stacked to the ceiling of the barn.

*I wonder if it'll still work?*

It had worked when he was young and later, when he'd wanted to kill the bastard that was his father—*no, his stepfather*—he corrected himself. The man was evil itself, with the abuse he'd handed out to his mother and him.

The feed bags stared back at him. What else could he do? He'd proven himself helpless to prevent his wife's pain and he let his daughter die. What kind of a father, or husband, would do that?

He started swinging. Soon, all he knew was the numbing pain of his fists, split and bloodied. He smiled grimly and renewed his attack. The pain was beginning to dull the jagged edges of the fragments of his heart.

"Whoa, whoa, whoa," came a voice from behind him. Strong fingers gripped his shoulders. He turned to let fly at the one trying to stop his pain—the pain he wanted, needed, deserved.

"HOLD, Xavier," the voice growled, then an arm came around his neck and he was lifted off the floor.

He struggled, shouting every swear word he knew in his native tongue, then started on the English ones, kicking and swinging his arms, but the man behind him would not be denied.

"Hold, my friend, I would know what this is about."

The man's voice finally penetrated the fog. The deep timbre, the accent. He slumped. "I am done, Dancing Wolf," Xavier murmured. "You can let go, now."

The Indian took a deep breath. "Are you sure?" he said.

Xavier nodded. The arms fell away and he slowly turned to face his new, and Aleksandra's lifelong, friend.

"Come and sit," Dancing Wolf said, as he pulled a sack down, raising a brow at the red soaking its surface. "Sit here." He patted the burlap, then looked him in the eyes until Xavier sat, his whole body shaking.

Xavier put his head in his hands, then noticed the blood, sat up and shook his head.

"I've come late for your wedding, for I cannot fly," Dancing Wolf murmured, "and find you like this. What is going on here?"

Xavier gritted his teeth and closed his eyes again, then opened them and looked at the Shoshone warrior. "Melissandra died two days ago."

Dancing Wolf blinked, then his mouth dropped open and his brows lowered.

"You couldn't have come at a better time," Xavier whispered. "Maybe you can get through to Aleks. She won't eat, or sleep—just sits, her eyes glazed. I can't do a thing to help. If I touch her, she cries. If I hold her, she cries. If I leave her alone, she cries. I guess it's better than watching her stare off into space or scream in the night." He looked up at the Indian, who blurred before his eyes. "I think she *wants* to die. It's like the last time, when she tried to rescue me in Utah and fell off that Express horse. She lost the baby she was carrying... but she's worse this time, Molly says."

"What happened to Melissandra?"

"Whooping cough. A peddler at the door coughed on her and the baby. Aleks believes it's her fault she got the infection and died."

Dancing Wolf let out a breath and stood.

"You've come just when you were needed, once again." Xavier winced at the bitterness in his own voice, but he was angry at everyone except for Aleks. If the bag of oats had been the peddler, he might have had some satisfaction, but as it was—he stopped himself and took a deep breath. He reached out to the Indian and gave him his hand. Dancing Wolf pulled him to his feet and wrapped him in a bearhug, hard and tight, then released him.

"*Kwahaten*, your Aleks," Dancing Wolf said, clenching his jaw, "she has always taken things upon herself. This is another one, I see. Let's go see if we can get through to her."

Aleksandra never looked up at their knock on the open bedroom door. Dancing Wolf kneeled beside her seat before the window. The spring sunshine shone on her wan face, but no light came from her eyes.

"*Kwahaten*," he said, and she twitched. He repeated it, louder this time. She looked up, straight at him. Her eyes widened and her mouth quivered.

"No, he's not dead too, don't tell me," she whispered. "No more ghosts," she said, and began to sob.

"Would a ghost do this?" Dancing Wolf pulled her out of the chair and into his arms. He hugged her tight to his chest, then stood, with Aleksandra still clutched in his arms.

"Dancing Wolf!" she shrieked, then sobbed harder and clung to him like she'd never let go.

"*Gracias a Dios*," Xavier murmured, though his heart broke a little bit more to see her reaction to Dancing Wolf, when he'd been unable to reach her himself. He took a deep breath and looked up toward Aleksandra. Her arms were wrapped around her Indian friend, but her face was turned toward him. She opened her eyes and saw Xavier, as if for the first time.

"*Querido*," she whispered to him.

"I'm here," he said, and approached the pair.

"Xavier, what have you done to your poor hands?" she said, her voice strangled. She hugged Dancing Wolf tightly for a moment, then let go. "Come, both of you." She led them to a bench beside her seat. She sat between them and took her husband's hands in her own. She moved the joints and Xavier flinched at the third one. "You've broken it."

"It'll mend," he murmured. "Are you back, then, *Querida*?"

She nodded slowly. "Thank you, both of you," she said, looking from one to the other, before she dropped her head to gaze at Xavier's hands again.

"I am so sorry for both," Dancing Wolf nodded at them both, "of your loss, but you cannot put Melissandra death upon your shoulders and give up, *Kwahaten*. You cannot."

"But—"

"—you both grieve," he continued, looking at Xavier's bloodied fingers, "but it is time to let your husband in. He is as affected as you by Melissandra's death, but in addition, he has to worry about you. This selfishness is unacceptable."

Aleksandra's mouth dropped open, and her brows narrowed. She started to speak, but he cut in.

"Unacceptable. It is time, as I once told you, to grow up. At least you have your family to hold. You have the chance to create new life from yourselves."

Aleksandra snapped her mouth shut, and her gaze softened. "Oh, Dancing Wolf, I am so sorry."

"Not nearly as sorry as I am," he said, as he looked out the window, at nothing.

"Is any of your family… "

"Gone, all gone," he growled, and shuddered. "Now I help those that remain. They are said to be moving our people to another reservation, but who knows for certain?" He finished on a whisper.

"I am ashamed, my friend," she returned. "We have lost, but it is nothing to what you and yours have endured."

"I am away from it for a few days," the Indian said. "We can comfort each other and strengthen ourselves, for who knows what is around the corner?"

"How long can you stay?" Xavier said, glancing at him.

"I must go tomorrow."

"Can you not stay another day, for the funeral?" Aleksandra swallowed hard.

"No, *Kwahaten*. I'm sorry, but I cannot. I promised those I accompanied I would return then, and they are not well. I cannot fail them."

She bowed her head in acquiescence, then lifted Xavier's broken hand to her lips and took a deep breath.

"Let's go down to the kitchen. We need to sort your hands. Please," she looked imploringly into Xavier's eyes, "don't do this anymore. I will stay, and not disappear again. I cannot promise, but I'll do my best."

"That's all I can ask," he said.

"There must be something to eat in the kitchen," she said, as she stood and reached for both men's hands. "I'm starving. I feel like I haven't eaten for a week."

"You haven't," Xavier said, dryly.

THE FUNERAL WAS HELD on Sunday.

Even more people came to pay their respects than had attended the wedding. They flowed out the door of the chapel and lined the road leading to Rancho de las Pulgas. The funeral cortege, led by the cross-bearer and the priests with their candles, proceeded down the aisle created by the well-wishers, followed by Dzień. He drew Maria's finest carriage, carrying Melissandra's too-tiny casket, the whole assemblage draped in black crepe.

Maria and Molly supported Aleksandra as she climbed the stairs behind the casket, borne by Xavier, Jose, Sancho and Marcelo. Once they'd laid the casket upon its stand in the fore of the church, Xavier moved to Aleksandra's side and sat beside her, his arm tight around her shoulders.

She sat frozen beside him, present, but somehow not. She didn't respond to the priest's words, and Xavier had to help her to her feet when required. He appealed to Maria when he needed to leave her to carry Melissandra's body out.

The echo of dirt clods hitting the top of the casket shocked her out of the shell into which she'd ensconced herself yesterday when Dancing Wolf left. She cried out and he gripped her tightly to keep her beside him.

"…and the souls of all the faithful departed through the mercy of God rest in peace," the priest concluded; this part, finally, in English.

Aleksandra was done. She slumped against Xavier and he carried her back to Dzień, then placed her beside him on the box and drove her home to bed.

She slept for the best part of the next two days. Xavier, Maria or Molly were always beside her to spoon soup into her when she wakened.

Finally, she got up, and didn't cry again.

## 5

A leksandra didn't cry, but she retreated into her own world again as the weeks passed. She did her part around the *hacienda* by rote. Her only moments of peace were found in her husband's arms or with Dzień.

"It was good to see you at the table today, Aleks." Xavier gripped her hands.

She looked up at him and swallowed. "That man who visited, Joseph, he spoke of the redwood forests and the Pacific Ocean."

"Yes. They're just an easy day's ride away." He narrowed his brows at her, then took a breath. "Shall we go?"

She hesitated. She wanted to go, but... "Xavier, would you mind if I went on my own?"

"Alone?" He paled and froze.

"As you said, it's a short ride."

He shook his head. "Of course, but..."

She smiled for the first time since they'd discovered their baby lifeless beside them, and he stilled. "Would you really like to?"

She nodded. It seemed the rightest thing in the world—the *only* thing that seemed right in the world. "If nothing else, it would be a pilgrimage. Perhaps...perhaps it will give me some sense of purpose in my suddenly pointless existence. I need to be alone."

He bit his lip. "Will you, at least, check in with people we know?"

She smiled at that. "I will, and I hope to return all in one piece. I love you, Xavier. Please don't misunderstand me."

He was silent for long moments. "I understand. I don't want you go on your own, but if that's what it'll take for you to become whole again, then so be it." He gave her a tight little smile and hugged her close.

She slept peacefully that night for the first time in what seemed a lifetime.

ALEKSANDRA WAS TYING her bedroll over her saddlebags early the next morning, when Xavier came up behind her and pulled her back against him.

"I've something for you, *Querida*." He turned her in his arms.

She raised an eyebrow at him.

"Although I'd prefer to accompany you, I understand why you need to go alone. I have something for you to take along." He pulled a beautiful locket on a silver chain from his shirt pocket and closed her hand around it.

She looked up into his eyes, then opened her hand to gaze at the gift. The heart-shaped locket's filigree work and tiny silver pearls were delicate and obviously old, bespeaking generations of age. Aleksandra freed the clasp. It fell open to reveal on one side a tiny tintype of them on their wedding day. On the other, a wisp of what could only be their daughter's golden fairy-hair lay behind the tiny glass cover. She stared at the pendant in silence until Xavier reached for her and held her close.

"I wasn't sure how you'd take it, but I had to offer," he murmured against her hair.

She sobbed into his shirt and held him with all her strength. When she finally quieted, he tilted up her chin and kissed the tears from her eyes and cheeks. "Thank you with all my heart, Xavier, for thinking to save a little of Melissandra for me." She smiled up at her husband, his beautiful brown eyes peering at her from beneath the thick fringe of jet hair. Even after years together, he still made her want to melt into him with only a look.

"Maria wanted you to have the locket. It's been in our family for many generations. It came from our family in Spain." His eyes glowed with love.

"Please give Mama my love." She took a deep breath. "With you I leave half of my heart. I fear the other half has been lost, but perhaps I'll find it again on this trip. Thank you for trusting and loving me enough to let me go." She glanced up at him, her lips quivering.

"Well then, *mi querida*, off you go. The sooner you go, the sooner you'll return and we can begin to make our plans for this *rancho*, which seems to be ours, now Jose has gone."

"I hope so. Then we can make those plans... and maybe even," she peered at him from beneath her lashes, "work on growing our family again. We cannot replace Melissandra, but we can surely give her a brother or sister to remember her."

She sucked in a breath at a twinge in her breasts and the familiar wetness beneath her shirt. She gulped and hugged him close once more, then pulled away. She gently disentangled herself from his arms, stood on tiptoe, and gave him swift kiss.

Slinging her pemmican bag and canteen over her saddle horn, she gathered up her reins. She called out to Dzień and vaulted lightly into the saddle as he struck off at a lope. Turning around, she waved and blew another kiss before he had a chance to see the new tears that already ran cold down her cheeks.

DZIEŃ'S HOOFBEATS echoed on the hard-packed earth when they crossed over El Camino Real, the old mission trail. Aleksandra's hair streamed behind her in the wind as they raced toward the water's edge and turned south. She slowed the pony and looked behind at the San Francisco Bay, spreading far to the north. In the tidal sloughs beside her, hundreds of waterbirds pecked their long beaks into the wet sand like so many tiny sewing machines. Snowy egrets and great blue herons stood frozen, long-shadowed statues in the early dawn light. Only their heads turned to follow her.

She wiped the tears that hadn't yet dried in the breeze of their passing with the sleeve of her buckskin shirt and shook her head. She closed her eyes, her heart numb. Pushing aside the bedroll tied over her saddlebags, she slipped her fingers inside the flap and pulled out the locket. She clutched it to her heart before clasping it around her neck and letting it drop inside her neckline, between her still-enlarged breasts. Her tears rained down again as she gazed west, up into the blurry coastal ranges. A memory of her mother's voice came unbidden...

. . .

*"I WILL LIFT mine eyes unto the hills, from whence cometh my help..."*

SHE RESOLUTELY SET her jaw and turned back to face the distant sea of masts filling Redwood Creek Wharf before her, one hand gripping the pendant through her shirt and the other on the reins.

Even from this distance, she could see Redwood City's wharf, crowded with ships. The city was named for named for the creek, or maybe for the many trees cut from the coastal ranges, carted down from the hills by bullock train and loaded onto ships. As the only deepwater channel into the San Francisco Bay for many miles, Redwood Creek was perfect for the transport of timber to the ever-growing San Francisco, and beyond.

Grand houses and warehouses clustered near the road leading to the embarcadero—a far cry from its beginnings as a squatter colony of lumber trade laborers on Rancho de las Pulgas land. They'd built homes and businesses there, assuming the Argüellos would be denied their land claim, but when señor Mezes successfully defended the Rancho de las Pulgas claim, he was paid the land as part of his quarter share. The city, made wealthy by the humble redwood, became the county seat of San Mateo County. Señor Mezes sold lots to the new residents, rather than trying to evict them, and became a wealthy man. He looked to be getting even more so—as the railroad from San Francisco was expected to reach to here sometime this year. Aleksandra shuddered at the thought of the ensuing population explosion.

A hint of a smile escaped her tight lips. He'd wanted to call it Mezesville, but the name "Redwood City" had stuck and wouldn't be budged.

In the early morning sunshine, rough workers' huts near the water's edge emptied as the men trudged towards the wharves. They nodded to her as they headed for a day shifting timber, shingles, hay and wheat from laden wagons onto outward bound ships and barges.

The putrid odor of the tannery turned her stomach when she rode past. She put a hand over her mouth and nose, as if she could stop the smell.

From the alley between the blacksmith shop and the shipbuilding yard, several men turned to stare at her. One whistled low under his breath, but she hardly noticed him. The courthouse loomed on her left, the newly-begun fire station beside it, but they, too, barely signified. Her goal was Dr. Tripp's store and Mr. Parkhurst's road west into the mountains to Arroyo Honda, then on to the coast.

She'd never seen the ocean, other than a peek out through the Golden Gate on the steamer from Sacramento when they'd just come to San Francisco. Under the circumstances, visiting the Pacific seemed the right thing to do.

SHE TOOK a deep breath and patted Dzień's neck, then turned the buckskin away from the waterfront and onto the trail heading for the redwood forests towering on the distant mountains to the west.

She choked back a sob as she thought of Xavier and, too late, of Melissandra. He'd been kind, understanding her need to be alone. She shook her head to clear it, but her thoughts continued to drift. All she wanted was a family with Xavier, to have his children, and to share them with the rest of his kin. At the thought of their firstborn sleeping forever in the cold ground, a rough block of ice grated where her heart should lie.

A shout from a Punch, walking beside an oxen-drawn dray carrying a massive log, yanked her from her reverie. She aimed Dzień up the rise of a big shellmound and they scrambled out of the way as it rumbled past. Belatedly, Aleksandra remembered to tuck her long braid up under her hat—she had no desire to attract needless attention.

Shell middens still dotted the landscape of the San Francisco Bay and throughout the Rancho de las Pulgas lands, showing where the *Lamchin*, *Ssalson*, *Puichon*, and *Suchihin* tribes of the *Ohlone* Indians lived, died and buried their own. The *Lamchin*, and maybe many of the others, were long extinct. By the old mission records, probably since 1790. The other local Indians were rarely seen living free outside a *rancho* or emigrant's house these days. For thousands of years, the peaceful coastal tribes existed by hunting, fishing, and gathering the bounty of this temperate corner of the world before the arrival of the Spaniard Portolà's military expedition in the late 1700's. It took only fifty years for him and his accompanying Franciscan missionaries, led by Father Serra, to nearly obliterate the native population, culture, and way of life.

"No Indians get out alive when the white settlers and missionaries set their minds to it, Dzień." She closed her eyes and sent up a prayer, thinking of Dancing Wolf and her Shoshone family. How many of them yet lived? She forced her mind away from the thought before the tears rained down again.

The pony flicked his ears back at her as he climbed down the other side of the midden and resumed the trail.

She rode on over rolling hills and golden fields dotted with ancient spreading oaks. There were no houses out here, but huge piles of redwood bark and sawdust showed where sawmills had been, evidencing the fate of many great trees. The air became drier as the road rose up from the valley floor toward the Sierra Morena range. The landscape here was dotted with the occasional oak and scrub pine which had escaped the loggers, their leaves gray-green against the deeper verdure of the redwood forest higher on the mountains behind them. Burnt sienna-barked madrone and manzanita were rarely seen as far down as the *rancho*, but they grew prolifically up here in the slag of the logged-out forest.

Sweating even at this early hour, horse and oxen teams passed them, pulling wagons loaded with cut shingles and timber. In the distance, surrounded by oak trees, the steeply sloping roof of a massive wooden building came into view. It was just where Xavier said it would be.

*"Woodside Store"* was painted upon its huge sign, beside a smaller sign over a side door, with *"Dr. Tripp, Dentist"*, in gold lettering. Wagons rolled to and fro in the yard and men were everywhere; loading, unloading, or lounging near the steps around a spittoon. No one took notice of the boy in buckskins riding up on an Indian pony. As she dismounted, two men looked her way.

"Hey Teague, you'd never believe what I just saw," one rough-looking, musclebound man called out across the yard.

Aleksandra ducked her head, hands suddenly clammy, and held her breath. Her hand strayed to her hip, where her *shashka* sat in its sheath beneath her oversized shirt.

"What?"

"Old Prior, the beggar, standing right here, yeste'day."

Aleksandra let out her breath against her Mustang's side and willed her heart to slow. She busied herself with opening a saddlebag while she listened to the men and peeked over Dzień's back, her hat tilted low.

"Didn't think he'd show his face in town again after last time we caught up with him." The man addressed as Teague, a wiry, well-dressed blond, raised an eyebrow.

"Well, maybe ropin' 'n draggin' 'em through that slough did the old wife-whipper some good. He actually brought his poor wife in to see Dr.

Tripp about a toothache, never mind he prob'ly broke her tooth himself."
He broke off muttering and spat into the brass vessel.

"Maybe it'll keep him from being such a lunatic drunk when he starts going back to the saloons up Whisky Hill." Teague gave him a wry grin.

"Who you kiddin'?" The first man scowled. "He could sure use attendin' some of the Dell Temperance Hall meetin's. Awfully good of Mr. Greer and Dr. Tripp, puttin' up that hall."

"I hear," the blond man said, his head cocked, "we might be getting Mr. Loveland from over on the coast to lecture on 'The Evils of Intemperance'. I was told he spoke well there, last year."

"Lookin' forward to it," the muscular man said, and glanced at Aleksandra as she walked past them. His brows shot skyward and he spun to face her, nodding and tipping his hat.

Teague inhaled sharply, but recovered quickly. "Pardon us, madam, for our rough speech," he murmured, as he whipped off his hat and swept her a bow. "We failed to notice there was a lady present." He grinned briefly at her buckskin shirt and trousers, his eyes wide.

"Gentlemen," Aleksandra inclined her head and gave them her best smile before escaping up the steps and into the main storeroom. She paused just inside the door and moved aside, out of the way of two bustled ladies, chattering as they flounced out the door. They swept past her, scarcely glancing her way, then paused to bat their eyes at the men she'd just passed.

Aleksandra gazed about her at the abundant wares on display for the homemaker, rancher, and logger. Barrels of dry goods stood beside racks of fabrics, kitchenware, harness and stock feed. She sighed with pleasure and walked to the counter.

"Hello, how can I help you…madame?" The shopkeeper sniffed, glancing down at her masculine attire.

"Good morning. Would Dr. Tripp be present?" Aleksandra arched one eyebrow at him.

"And what would be your name, please?" He sighed in her general direction, his gaze straying to the countertop before him.

"Mrs. Argüello, from Rancho de las Pulgas," she said.

He jerked upright and blinked. "One moment, madame!" he said, and bit his lip as he spun on his heel. He ducked through a door into the back room faster than she'd imagined he could even move.

Aleksandra heard raised voices, then a tall, graying man strode into the store, a big smile across his face. "Mrs. Argüello, please allow me to introduce myself. I am Dr. Tripp. I apologize for my shopkeeper. While his manners are lacking, even *he* has heard of your family." He grinned and one brow shot up. "I trust he's learned his lesson. He'll be stacking boxes for the next few hours."

Aleksandra smiled at him as he bent over her hand and kissed it.

"You don't look much like my friend Maria, I would say."

She chuckled. "Maria asked me to call upon you and give you her regards."

"I would imagine you're the new wife of our long-lost Xavier, are you not?" His eyes glinted with suppressed merriment.

Aleksandra laughed for the first time in weeks. "That I am. He swept me off my feet, literally." Actually, he'd thrown her over his shoulder and dragged her back into the Pony Express Station when she'd threatened to work in a brothel if he wouldn't hire her as an Express rider, albeit as a boy.

"So where are you headed, little lady? Where's Xavier?" He peered past her, out the open door.

"He remained at the *rancho*. There is much for him to do there." She averted her gaze and stared at a bucket near his feet, then glanced up to see Dr. Tripp's brows draw together.

"Why don't you come on out back? My housekeeper's just put my dinner on the table and she always makes enough to feed a horde. My belly could do with sharing some," he said, patting his rounded stomach.

"Well, if you put it like that," Aleksandra said, "it seems I'll have to save you from yourself. Let me unsaddle my Mustang. I'll be right back."

She slid onto a bench at the table a few minutes later, her enamel spatterware plate heaped with roast venison and potatoes from a large platter. A plump woman peeked into the dining room and waved, before ducking back outside, presumably to her kitchen shed.

"Thank you for dinner!" Aleksandra called after her.

Dr. Tripp sat across from her and studied her face for a moment before he spoke. "Mrs. Argüello, please excuse my impertinence, but I've been friends with the Argüello family for many years. May I ask why are you traveling unaccompanied, and especially, without Xavier?" He frowned. "I understood you were with child some time ago, but I see no child with you." He tilted his head and gazed at her, his brow furrowed. "Is everything all right?"

It didn't take long for the hot tears to form and roll down her cheeks. The dentist reached out a hand and took hers in his firm grip.

Aleksandra swallowed hard and sniffed. "She died. Whooping cough, a few weeks ago," she whispered. "I've never been to the ocean and I thought it would be good to get away for a few days, have some time alone."

"I'm so very sorry for your loss." He sighed and shook his head. "Some things are just too unfair for words." The ticking of the cuckoo clock was the only sound for long minutes.

She gulped and shook her head to clear it.

"Are you sure you'll be safe by yourself?" His brows were nearly touching by now.

"My papa and I were trappers and best friends with a Shoshone Chief and his family. Pa trained me in the Cossack arts and I rode for the Pony Express in Utah." She looked him in the eyes, her tears cooling on her cheeks as she spoke. "I'm handy with a sword, on and off a horse, so I think so." She gave him a hint of a smile and he shook his head, his eyes sparkling.

They finished their meal in silence, then Dr. Tripp put down his fork and looked her way.

"Not a surprise you've captured Xavier's heart." He reached out and squeezed her hand, then let go. "I still can't believe he'd let you go off on your own, though, despite your abilities. You're too valuable a treasure to risk."

She ducked her head, but a warmth glowed in her heart at his words. "I've spent much of my life on my own and sometimes I need the solitude." She gave him a little smile. "I'm also quite determined," she said, and then sobered. "I need some time to come to terms with the loss of our daughter. Xavier has been wonderful and he understands my need for this time. I think the ocean might be just what my heart needs."

He didn't look convinced. "All right, but you take care, OK? It's getting a little more civilized up there in the mountains, but there are still plenty of drunken loggers and stray bandits hanging about. I'd hate to see anything happen to you."

"That makes two of us. There's been too much sorrow in my life in the past five years, more than I'd ever hoped to see in my whole life. It's got to get better." She gritted her teeth and closed her eyes. "It's just got to."

"Then I imagine it will," he said, as he rose from the table. "Let me send a letter of introduction with you, in case you should find the need. If you wish to make friends, you might take a few of these newspapers to Arroyo Honda, with my compliments."

"Thank you, Dr. Tripp, I'd appreciate that," she said, as they passed through the open doorway back into the front of the store.

She turned to thank him again as she left, his letter and newspapers in hand.

"Keep your wits about you, young lady. " He frowned. "There are plenty of mountain lions up there and the bears will be coming out of their dens—grumpy and hungry." He hesitated for a moment, then seemed to come to a decision. "Worse, I heard two of the Younger brothers are hiding out in Arroyo Honda, up at the Ray's ranch. More vicious criminals I've not heard the likes of, worse than any grizzly. They're going by the aliases of Hardin and Parsons. An acquaintance of mine recognized them and warned me. Be careful. If you find yourself in trouble, send someone to get me." He fixed her with a steely gaze.

There was no question in her mind that he wouldn't be a man to cross.

# 6

———

The eastbound stagecoach clattered to a halt before Aleksandra as she stood on the Woodside Store's veranda. The six lathered horses hitched to the coach stood, but only barely, shifting their feet and champing their bits. She nodded to the driver as she passed behind it and reached for Dzień's saddle, then watched as three men unfastened the traces and led the horses away to replace them with a fresh team.

Aleksandra gave the cinch latigo a final tug and led her pony from the crowded yard, then she swung up and headed west along Tripp's road. From the open window of the schoolhouse came the sound of children's voices reciting from a speller. She looked up at the blue sky shining through the oaks overhead and gave thanks to her parents for the love and excellent education they gave her, both at home and while out trapping on the slopes of the Rocky Mountains. She wouldn't have liked a closed-in schoolroom, but then again, was it the classroom or the way students were taught? In her time teaching in Virginia City, she'd found students learned well, even in a classroom, when she used practical examples about things of interest to them, as she herself had learned. By all accounts, it wasn't the way most schools were taught.

A whitewashed building stood just along from the schoolhouse. Mr. Teague, from Mr. Tripp's store, nodded to her as he walked up the wooden steps across the front of the hall. He turned a key in the lock and disappeared inside while she read the sign on the gateway:

. . .

*DELL TEMPERANCE HALL*
  *Presiding Officer of the Mountain Dell Division:*
  *Andrew Teague*

"No wonder he knew so much about the doings at the hall," she murmured to Dzień. The pony flicked one ear back at her and increased his pace.

Her breath caught in her throat at the sea of reddish-brown, forlorn stumps, scrap and sawdust littering the lands back from the road as she and Dzień trotted from Mr. Tripp's store towards the distant mountains. Any tree of millable size had already been cut down. As the foothills were timbered out, the mills had been moved up the canyons, as Xavier had said. She sighed at the emptiness in her heart at their loss. Only the tattered remains of the once-proud redwood forests bespoke their presence at all.

The track wound along beside one stream after another and gradually rose through the steeper foothills of the Sierra Moreno mountains. As they climbed, they passed the mills currently in work, their yards full of sweating men dragging heavy, freshly-sawn planks or stacking shingles on drying racks.

From around a bend in the track ahead came the sounds of men shouting and oxen lowing. They rounded the corner and Aleksandra slowed Dzień to a halt. The road before them crossed a swampy area. It had been built up with scrap timber and topped with narrow, twisting logs that might have been madrone and thick planks laid in parallel. Across this "bridge", a team of fourteen bulls, wooden yokes tight against their shoulders, pulled six huge logs attached end to end by great chains.

A young man ran ahead of the team with a bucket and swab, spreading a layer of thick, gray-brown slime onto the already-blackened boards.

"This could take a while," she murmured to Dzień. A touch of her leg moved Dzień off the side of the track and she dismounted to give the pony a rest while they waited.

"Good aft'noon, miss," the boy said, stopping his painting for a moment.

"Good afternoon." Aleksandra smiled at him. "What's in the bucket? Uggh!" She blinked and put her hand over her mouth as her stomach churned from the smell.

The boy grinned. "Hain't you never seen a skid row before? Oh, you'll get used t' the smell. I did, and now I'm the best grease monkey around," he said, then trotted back and greased the last few boards. He flew back to her side, his eyes alight.

"What *is* in your bucket, young man?" she asked faintly.

"It's bear grease, th' best grease ever! This bucket's a bit old, but it don't matter, it's still better'n sheep tallow, an' it makes th' logs slide better across th' row, so's it's easier on the bulls. Sometimes we use hosses," he stopped and took a deep breath, then rattled on. "They're faster, but only oxen can pull the logs out o' the trees when we've jes' cut 'em." His smile stretched from ear to ear.

"How far will they haul those logs today?"

"All goin' well, we should get t' the Redwood Embarc'dero in three 'r four hours. A'fore dark, anyways, so long as nothin' happ'ns t' the oxen."

He glanced at the oncoming team, which had nearly crossed the whole skid row.

"Are there many more skid rows between here and the summit?"

"Sure are, mostly on th' steep grades 'n sharp corners. On th' sharp corners, them'r banked tow'rd the hillside so's they don't let th' logs fall down th' hill." He nodded emphatically, eyebrows raised. He flicked a glance at the long braid that hung over Aleksandra's shoulder and studied her face briefly. His cheeks pinkened and he looked at his feet. "Well, got to be goin', ma'am," he said, as he shuffled backwards, then spun and ran back to his post.

"Thanks for telling me about the skid row!" Aleksandra called after him, then turned back to watch the leading bulls, nearly level with them now.

A big red and white right-hand bull in the leader yoke, eyeing Aleksandra and Dzień with interest, began moving toward them—and started to pull the front log off the side of the skid row.

"Haw," yelled the bull punch.

The massive Ayrshire ignored him and kept coming.

Aleksandra backed up, glancing behind her for somewhere to go on the narrow track, dragging Dzień along with her.

The bull punch whipped out his goad and poked the bull in the side of his neck. The massive beast snorted and shook his head, then jumped back toward his partner. He reluctantly returned his attention to his job, the whites of his eyes showing as he kept one eye on Aleksandra and the horse.

"Good save, thank you." Aleksandra gave the punch the ghost of a smile as he walked past her with his team.

"Sorry 'bout that, ma'am. It's his first day in the leader position. He's usually a wheeler, but thought I'd try him with my good leader to see how he went." He sighed. "Tomorrow he goes back where he can keep his mind on his work. This isn't his first time out of line today, but he's young yet. He'll be a good bull one day if I don't rush him." He laughed and tipped his cap to her, then sauntered after his leaders.

The suglar, mounted on the first log, waved at her and grinned. "The smell's a help, didn't you know ma'am?"

"How*ever* could it help?" Aleksandra was nearly gagging.

"Word around here's that the vapors from the rancid fat are so bad the logs could float on the stench alone!" He laughed as his log was dragged past her.

She couldn't help giggling.

SOON A FEW TREES still stood proudly before them, and then a few more, as the number of cut stumps declined and the forest began. Aleksandra heaved a sigh of relief. The logging road before them wound its way around the mountain, dwindling to a narrow horse trail as they entered the coolness of the virgin redwood forest.

She lay back on Dzień and looked upward. The tall, tall trees seemed to go up forever, and a soft light filtered down, glittering between millions of tiny redwood needles. She filled her lungs with moist, clean air that tasted of freshness. Sitting up, she gazed around. Even in the high alpine valleys of the Rockies, she'd never known peace and stillness like this. Beside a tinkling stream, ferns and wood sorrel grew in abundance in the soft duff layer of the open forest floor. Heeding Dr. Tripp's warning, Aleksandra checked the terrain around them before dismounting.

"What do you say we take a break here, pony?" Aleksandra rubbed his forehead.

The buckskin shook his head and lipped at her sleeve as she leaned back against him and closed her eyes.

"I knew this would be a good idea." They wandered a little way up the stream until they found a level area, then Aleksandra pulled off his bridle and loosened his cinch. She pulled a nosebag of feed and the heel of a crusty loaf from her saddlebags, collected her pemmican bag and canteen, then sat down and tucked in. Dzień munched grain from his nosebag while Aleksandra dreamily nibbled her bread. Slowly but surely, the soul of the forest helped her refill the emptiness in her heart as she lay back under the great *Sequoias'* healing canopy.

Aleksandra hadn't meant to sleep, but she awoke to Dzień's nosebag pushing at her chest, more rested and relaxed than she'd been in months. Sitting up, she stretched and looked around her, then stood and hugged the Mustang. They stood still for long minutes before Aleksandra stepped away.

She sighed as she looked down at her hair, stuck full of the little redwood cones. Memories of her Shoshone family flowed through her as she stood and picked the prickly bits of redwood from her braid and the back of her head. She shook her head. It would take some time to get them all out. Next time, she'd lie on her *serape*.

She tightened Dzień's cinch, then packed up and mounted. Her family's link with the Shoshone tribe went way back. Over a decade ago, Aleksandra's father, a trapper in the Rockies near Salt Lake City, found a young Indian boy clinging to a branch in a swollen and freezing stream. Her papa rescued him and returned the young Dancing Wolf to his father, the chief of the tribe. In time, the two young fathers became blood brothers and the families spent much time together over the succeeding years. In their tenth year, the chief gifted Aleksandra and Dancing Wolf with yearling colts on the same day. They raised and trained those colts together. Since that day, Dzień, one of those foals, had rarely left her side.

Aleksandra took a deep breath. She missed her deceased father and mother almost unbearably, but Xavier had helped appease her pain at their loss. Now she had to somehow get over Melissandra's death. Her mama, from her own sad experiences in Poland and again in America, would've told her to think of little Melissandra with love, let her go, and get on with life. She gulped.

Dzień shook his head and she returned to the present. Letting her go with love was the best, but at the same time, the hardest thing she could imagine—both for herself and her husband.

The trail rose steeply before them as they approached the summit and the game little Mustang clambered to the top as if he carried no rider or heavy pack. Aleksandra scratched his withers and he shook his head, flicking his ears at her.

They came to a clear point on the crest of the range and she sat in awed silence. The view over Utah's Salt Lake was amazing, but this—miles of rolling mountains carpeted with deep blue-green trees, framed by the distant Pacific Ocean beyond, completely took her breath away and something in her broke.

She began to cry. She slid from Dzień's back and wept into his mane. She cried for her lost baby, her mother, brothers and father. Life in the West was tenuous at best, but in exchange, people could live free. Her papa brought his family here from Poland in search of freedom and he had given it to them.

As she stared into the immensity of the panorama before her, her thoughts began to slide into better perspective. What did her own small problems really matter to the universe? What difference would they make in a month? A year? A decade? Somehow, in the vast forest, with the limitless ocean at her feet, her worries dwindled to a mere drop in the great bucket of the universe. She wanted to be at the ocean's side so badly she could taste it.

She could breathe again and smiled as she wiped her tears onto Dzień's mane and hugged him. Tucking her hair back under her hat, she took his reins and led him down the steep trail toward the ocean, and freedom.

THE TRAIL LEVELLED out after an hour of downhill trail through the redwood forest and they broke out into wide-open pastures. Aleksandra mounted up, blinking in the full sunlight of late afternoon. She turned her gaze down the hill and her jaw dropped in astonishment. It could only be the Weeks' ranch

Before her, a two-story farmhouse and a massive barn stood proudly over pristine pastures. A herd of shining cows headed for a cluster of buildings in the distance.

Two black and white dogs ran out to greet them at the house gate as Aleksandra rode up. She tied Dzień to the tie-rail and pulled her braid from beneath her hat.

A strong-looking, fair-haired woman walked out the front door, untying her apron as she approached.

"Good afternoon," she said.

"Good afternoon, I'm looking for Mr. and Mrs. Weeks."

"I'm Mrs. Weeks, how can I help you?"

Aleksandra introduced herself, adding, "my mother-in-law, Maria Argüello, and my husband, Xavier, asked me to give you their regards."

"Well, why didn't you say so?" She chortled. "It's been ages since I saw Maria, and I'd heard young Xavier had returned from the dead, with a wife, no less. Well, I can see why he brought you home, you're a pretty little thing! You just come on in and have a cool drink! I'll get one of the boys to care for your horse. Nice Indian pony, that!" She showed Aleksandra in through the front door, then stuck her head back outside and yelled. A young man appeared as if by magic and hustled to take Dzień to a trough.

"Thank you, Mrs. Weeks," Aleksandra said, as she accepted the drink, then blinked. "Lemonade! Where did you get *lemons* at this time of year?"

"We grow them in the orchard behind the house, make them into a sugary syrup, then bottle it. I don't think my men would get the hay made without it in the hot summer weather." She shot Aleksandra a quick grin.

"It's lovely, thank you so much, and your ranch is splendid. I've not seen the likes." Aleksandra stared out the window across the acres of meadows, rolling down toward the sea.

"It's a lot of work, but we love it. I've been to Rancho de las Pulgas, and it's just as beautiful." Mrs. Weeks smiled.

"Is all the cleared land I see part of your ranch, Mrs. Weeks?"

"Please, call me Cordelia. We don't stand on ceremony out here. We bought several thousand acres of government land ten years ago for a dairy and grain farm, so it's kept us busy."

And what a farm it had become. Aleksandra shook her head. "It's magnificent. You've worked hard."

Cordelia smiled. "How is Maria keeping?"

They passed the next hour talking of family. If she wondered why Aleksandra traveled this rough country alone in boys' garb, she was too polite to ask, and sent her on her way with a sugar cookie the size of her hand. The woman was clearly used to cooking for big, hungry men.

Aleksandra thanked her as she swung up onto Dzień and rode out the gateway.

The trail ran for another half hour between the Weeks' open fields of winter wheat. The track dived back into the forest and continued along a creek, crossing it at intervals. A few miles further along the softly-patterned path, they entered a clearing with a deep pit to the right of the trail. Aleksandra nudged Dzień closer for a look, but the Mustang snorted and laid back his ears, reluctant to approach it.

"Come on, Dzień," she said, and pushed him on. He acquiesced, but every muscle in his body was tensed. By the pit's size and smooth, hard-packed base, along with Dzień's response, it could be a bear pit. She gritted her teeth. Many of the *Californio* families thought it great sport to pit a grizzly against a bull and bet on the outcome. She shuddered. How could people be so cruel to animals?

Half a dozen bends of the creek later, at the junction of three creeks, a small rectangular building with a covered porch came into view. Andrew Sausman's Store looked just as Xavier had described it. Aleksandra left Dzień at the hitching rail with several horses already tied there.

She shook her head at the difference between peoples' attitudes in California and the Great Basin. In Utah, the sound of hoofbeats was cause for an urgent gathering of rifles and preparation for Indian attack at any hour. It was so restful here.

She sighed. While it was restful, it was also sad. The peaceful *Ohlones* had given up their way of life for that in the missions, whether they liked it or not. Those who chose to return home to their tribes were pursued by other mission Indians. If that proved unsuccessful, soldiers returned them to the mission fathers. Their numbers were decimated by the abhorrent living conditions, overwork by the fathers, and the effect of the white man's diseases on a population with no resistance.

She shook her head to clear it of the disquieting thoughts as she mounted the steps and entered the store. Every face in the room turned toward her when she walked into the room.

## 7

"Gentlemen," Aleksandra said, nodding to them. "Is Mr. Sausman in the house, please?"

"I'm Sausman." A tall, dark man stepped out from behind the bar.

Aleksandra introduced herself and offered him the copies of the San Mateo County Gazette with a smile. "Compliments of Dr. Tripp at Woodside."

"My thanks for those, Mrs. Argüello," he said, and handed one to a young man seated at a table.

She took the lemonade Sausman offered, with thanks, and a grin. Everyone here must make lemonade syrup. She glanced over to see the young man reading the newspaper, his eyes alight.

"You grow wheat, Red. This ought to make you happy," he said, as his finger slid down the page.

*"Half-Moon Bay Flour Mills. —Messrs. Halstead & Brother, we learn, are pushing their new mill forward with energy. When completed it will one of the largest and best out of San Francisco."*

"That's all the way up in Spanishtown, isn't it?"

"It is," said a black haired, sharply-dressed man sitting beside Red.

"Won't do me any better than taking it to Redwood City." Red shook his head and stared into his mug. "How am I supposed to get my wheat to San Gregorio with only a horse trail? Same as to Redwood."

"It'd be closer, for one. I like the sound of the new mill." Red's companion raised an eyebrow at him. "I have 400 acres in wheat and barley and I'm ready to start planting coffee to see if it'll grow. I heard they're looking to build a road from here to San Gregorio." He looked around the room. "That should solve our transport problems. When it's done, we can take our wagons straight out to the coast and north to Spanishtown. Easy as pie."

"It'll be years," the redhead said.

"It's a start, though," said the young reader, as he continued perusing the gazette. "Plenty of hearings on Land Cases. I'll bet most of the *Californios* won't get to keep their land grants. Too many squatters who want the land. All that land south of San Francisco? The hordes'll have to win in the end."

Aleksandra sighed. At least the Argüellos didn't have to worry anymore, now their grant was finally confirmed. The squatters *had* made things difficult for Mezes in the beginning, some threatening his life, but in the end, he did okay out of it. Better than OK.

As she passed on the Argüello's greetings, the well-informed, dapper farmer approached and cleared his throat.

"Mrs. Argüello," Sausman nodded to the man, "I'd like to introduce you to John Sears, a new landowner hereabouts. Mrs. Argüello is the wife of Maria Argüello's son, Xavier."

"Nice to meet you, Mrs. Argüello," Sears said. "I had the pleasure of employing your husband when he'd just left home, many years ago. He worked for me in my blacksmith shop at Searsville." Sears smiled at her. "He's a hard worker, and a good man."

"Thank you. I think so too." Aleksandra's face, and her heart, warmed.

"Where're you heading? Is Xavier here?" Sears glanced toward the closed door.

"No, I'm sorry, he had business at the *rancho*." Aleksandra took a deep breath. "Perhaps next time?"

"I'm sorry to hear that. I'd like to see him." His brow furrowed. "You're traveling alone?"

"Yes, and I've so enjoyed my trip through the redwoods." She said, in a rush. "I can't wait to see the ocean. I've been told to visit with the John family near San Gregorio."

"Have a safe trip, then, and give my best to your husband. It was good to meet you." Sears nodded and gave a little bow.

"Thank you. You too, sir," Aleksandra said, as he returned to his barstool.

"Going t' the John's sounds a good plan," Sausman said. "If yer goin' tonight, you'd best think about gettin' on. Is there anythin' ye need?"

"No, I'm all set, thanks."

"I'll make ye up some bread 'n beef from last night's supper if ye like. It's a good couple hours t' the John's place." Mr. Sausman went behind the counter, then inhaled sharply, brows furrowed, and motioned for her to come closer. "Ye sure ye wanna go out there by yerself?" he said, under his breath, when she reached him. "Them Younger Brothers 'n some of their gang 'r about, though they go by differ'nt names. They're a mean lot, 'specially if they've got a bit o' whiskey in 'em."

"Dr. Tripp said they were staying at the Ray Ranch, where is that?"

"Back a ways and up the hill, but there's no tellin' where they might wander. D'you wanna wait 'til some other folk 'r headin' out that way?"

"No, it'll be fine. I've my rifle, *shashka*, and a handful of knives," she said, patting her buckskin shirt over the sword, "plus a fast pony."

The shopkeeper blinked and looked at her from the corners of his eyes. "You'd give 'em a run fer their money. Take care out there 'n we'll see you in… how many days?"

"I should be back tomorrow or the next day, all going well."

"Well then, as your new family would say, *hasta luego!*" He saw her out the door and she rode away along the meandering San Gregorio Creek, headed for the coast.

NOT FAR DOWN THE ROAD, a mill perched beside the creek. A pack of barking dogs raced up to Aleksandra and Dzień They wriggled around the pair, teeth bared and grinning as they vied for her attention. A burly man left a saw and walked toward her. She laughed at the dogs and stroked their sleek heads.

"Good afternoon. Are you George Carter?" Aleksandra called, as he approached.

"That I am. What can I do for you?"

"I'm Mrs. Argüello, and my husband sends his regards."

"Argüello? Not Xavier?"

Aleksandra nodded.

"He's come home!" He set down the tools in his hand and sighed. "Can't tell you how happy I am to hear that. His mother was so worried. So he's your husband? Where is he?" He glanced behind her, then returned his gaze to her, his brow furrowed.

"He's back at the *rancho* and I'm going to the beach for the first time."

"I remember my first look at the sea—most awesome thing I'd ever seen." He smiled, then sobered. "You can't go out there by yourself, though. Some baddies just rode through and I don't want you near 'em."

"I'm just planning on going to the John Ranch tonight."

"You set on that?"

She nodded.

"I'll go with you, then. I'm pretty much done for the day, anyway."

"You don't have to do that," Aleksandra protested.

"Oh yes, I do," he said, through tight lips. "I know these men and you don't."

He wouldn't say any more about them, and just packed up his tools and saddled his horse. They shared Aleksandra's pemmican and Sausman's sandwiches as they rode.

Around a corner of the trail, a doe and her spotted newborn fawn came into view. They stared at the horses for a moment, then turned tail and bolted into the bushes, with a flash of their white backsides. The only sign they'd been there was the movement of the ferns as they sprang back to cover their exit.

Late afternoon sunlight drifting through the dense clusters of redwood needles caught a little waterfall as they rode past, its gurgling nearly muting the blue and black birds constantly squawking like small crows and hopping around.

"What are those birds?" Aleksandra said, with a laugh.

"They should be called 'Little Thieves', but they're Steller's Jays. They live in the redwoods. They'd steal the shirt off your back if they could carry it," he said.

Aleksandra laughed, then breathed deeply and stared up into the tops of the redwoods, enjoying the peace. After growing up in the wilderness of Utah with only her family for company, the densely-populated area around the San Francisco Bay was foreign. She loved Rancho de las Pulgas, but the sheer number of people on the *rancho* and in the towns springing up around it made her squirm.

"So how long have you lived out here?" Aleksandra spread her arms and looked up again. They hadn't seen a soul for the past half hour.

"It's been a while now. I was the first European to settle in the Arroyo Honda area."

"Is it looking crowded to you already?" She raised an eyebrow at him.

"Sure is. Sausman actually rents his store from me. It was my home until I built the mill three years ago."

Aleksandra stilled at the voices, coming from around the next bend. Carter glanced at her.

"Might want to stuff that hair up under your hat and act like a boy," he muttered, as he cocked his rifle.

"Some of your friends?" she breathed, as she released the safety on her own, then shoved her hair under her ten-gallon hat. She tucked her shirt up to free her *shashka*, then reached behind her leg to check for her knives.

NOT TEN YARDS from the road, a gutted deer hung from a tree branch next to several horses and five men seated on logs around a campfire.

A dark-haired man was tipping a whiskey jug back for a drink when he caught sight of them. He lowered the bottle and got to his feet, grinning at Aleksandra and Carter with an evil glint in his eyes.

"Well, lookee what we got here, Col—ahh—Hardin. If it ain't your friend from the mill, Carter."

"And a little friend, eh?" said a rough-looking man with a receding hairline, as he stood up. "Ever wanted to join an outlaw band, young man?"

The others laughed menacingly.

"A young relative of Mr. Weeks'." Carter raised an eyebrow at him.

The first speaker bit his lip and sat down with a scowl, then took a long draw of the whiskey.

"Enjoy your venison, lads," Carter said, with the hint of a smile, as he and Aleksandra walked on past.

The man called Hardin watched them go, brows drawn together and mouth pursed. His hand was too close to his six-shooter for Aleksandra's comfort, but he never moved.

After they turned the corner and walked for a few minutes, Carter glanced her way. "Shall we clear out of here?" he said.

"Thought you'd never ask." Aleksandra shook her braid out from under her hat and jammed the felt firmly onto her head. She whispered to Dzień and he broke into a gallop down the twisting path along the creek.

The trail broke out of the trees and they entered a wonderland of rolling grassy pastures. Aleksandra glanced behind, but no one followed. She slowed Dzień to a trot and held the pace for few more minutes before dropping to a walk.

"That was interesting." Aleksandra raised an eyebrow at Carter. "Recruiting, are they?"

"So I've heard."

"That would've been Cole Younger doing the questioning, I take it?"

He nodded.

"I see Mr. Weeks isn't their friend?" Aleksandra glanced across at Carter.

"Well, yes. They tried to recruit one of his sons recently and Mr. Weeks had a little discussion with Cole and his brother when he found them alone. He'd brought every cowhand in his employ. A considerable militia, I understand. He's got quite a spread."

"Yes, I was there yesterday. How big is their ranch?"

"They started with nearly two and a half thousand acres, might have even more by now. More'n a few men on a place that size, all loyal to him. Even an outlaw like Younger's smart enough not to cross him again."

There were fewer redwoods on this side of the Sierra Morena, and only in the sheltered gullies, but more manzanitas, madrones and pines. The alteration in trees changed the color of the gullies from green to tawny as they neared the coastline. Half an hour later, they rode down the last hill into a wide alluvial plain with the creek running through the middle of it. Aleksandra scanned the plain, every little while checking behind them for followers.

"It's all cropped," she said, staring over the growing grain covering nearly all of the flats. "I hadn't expected that."

"This is the beginning of the John's place," Carter said. "Burns John bought up the finest land out here about six years ago, 1500 acres of it, and farms wheat and other grains, hay, beef, and a big dairy as well. He and his wife Martha have done well for themselves. They work it with a man called Michael Dubbs. It's been a lot of work, but they're making a go of it, though they've had to pack all their produce to Redwood City over the horse trail."

She smiled. "They'll be pleased about the new mill up at Spanishtown."

"What mill?" Carter's brows shot up.

"The Half-Moon Bay Flour Mills. There was an article about it in the Gazette I delivered to Mr. Sausman from Dr. Tripp.

"The Johns can drive a wagon from their place to Spanishtown. That'll make the world of difference to them." He nodded and smiled. "The world of difference."

Half an hour later, they rode up before the ranch house. The men were just driving a mower and a hay rake into the yard. Smoke wisped from the kitchen shack, and a young girl lugged a heaped platter of meat into the ranch house as the men tied up the workhorses and slipped nosebags onto their heads.

"Seems we've arrived at a busy time." Aleksandra winced.

"Looks like just in time for supper!" Carter grinned as he swung his leg over his mount's head. Aleksandra dismounted and rubbed Dzień on his forehead, then told him to stand and followed Carter toward the door.

"George! So nice to see you!" A slim young woman ran down the steps and grasped both of Carter's hands. "And you've brought...?" She shifted her gaze to Aleksandra.

Mr. Carter laughed. "Martha John, this is Mrs. Argüello, Maria's new daughter-in-law. She's married to Xavier. I don't believe you would've met him, Maria's eldest?"

"No, but welcome to you both. Would you care for some supper? I'm afraid it's already on the table."

"Don't mind if I do, thank you, and I believe Mrs. Argüello—"

"Aleksandra, please," she cut in.

"Aleksandra, then, has been sent to hopefully stay with you for a day or two while she visits the ocean."

"You're welcome, Aleksandra." Martha reached for her hand and pulled her along. "Sarah!" she called out. The girl she'd seen with the platter stepped out of the house. "Sarah, please see Mrs. Argüello to the guest room while I get supper on for the men."

"Yes ma'am," Sarah said.

Mrs. John turned back to Aleksandra with a smile. "There will be water in your room. I'll see you at supper?" She raised an eyebrow at her.

"Thank you Mrs. John, I'll just care for my pony first," Aleksandra said, and returned to Dzień to untie her bedroll and saddlebags.

"I'll take care of him. You go get cleaned up." George said, as he patted the Mustang on the neck and pushed her towards the house.

IT WAS HEAVEN to strip off her dusty traveling clothes and bathe in the cool water from the lovely china pitcher and basin. She lay for a few minutes, wrapped in a drying sheet on the patchwork quilt-covered bed. Her heart was a bit empty yet, but warmed by her welcome here and by the care shown her by George Carter. She sighed as she reached above her head and fingered the tiny flowers painted on the porcelain baubles of the fine brass bedstead, thinking of her husband and new family. Melissandra's death had come as a shock. It hadn't been easy on any of them, and Xavier had taken tender care of her. She hoped he and the rest of the family were dealing well back home.

A soft knock came upon the door.

"Yes?"

"It's Sarah, Mrs. Argüello. I have your things."

"Thank you, Sarah. Please come in," Aleksandra said, as she stood and walked to the door.

Sarah placed the heavy bedroll on the floor and the saddlebags on a trunk beside the door.

"Thank you, Sarah. Now I can dress as a lady should," Aleksandra offered a wry grin to the girl, who looked to be near her own age.

"I'd be happy to help you with your buttons and hair," she offered. "I often help Ma with hers."

"That would be nice, thank you." Aleksandra smiled as she unrolled the bedroll and pulled out her fine blue delaine and two petticoats. She shook them out and pulled the petticoats, and then the dress, over her head.

"Your dress is beautiful, Mrs. Argüello. So many buttons, all the way down your back," Sarah said, as she did up the last one at the nape of Aleksandra's neck.

"Thank you, Sarah. Please call me Aleks."

"If you'd care to sit down, I can do your hair." Sarah held the back of the carved chair before the bureau, with its three angled looking glasses. She gently touched the lace about the wrist and neck of Aleksandra's gown. "My mama and I are making a special dress for me, now." The girl's eyes shone in the mirror as she began to unbraid Aleksandra's hair.

"A special dress, Sarah? And what might that be for, may I ask?"

"I'm to be married later this summer, after the harvest," she whispered, her heart in her eyes as she looked at Aleksandra in the glass. "It's so long, your hair, it goes all the way to your knees," she continued, her eyes wide, as she reached for the ivory comb on the corner what-not and began to comb it out. Aleksandra's heart warmed to her. She didn't have many friends her own age. Perhaps Sarah would become one of the first.

"Oh you are, are you? And who is the lucky man?"

"His name is John Sears. He's been courting me from Searsville for months, imagine that, but he's just moved to Arroyo Honda." She beamed. "Now we'll be able to see more of each other."

"I actually met him today," Aleksandra said. "You're a lucky girl. He's a kind man, bright and isn't afraid to speak his mind. He looks to have done well for himself, too. Even better, he speaks to a woman as an equal, unlike some men. He wanted to be introduced to me when he heard me speak of my family. He knows my husband, you see."

"He's a lot older than me, but I think that's a good thing. He'll know how to treat a girl, my mother says."

"He'll be lucky to have you for a wife." Aleksandra smiled up at Sarah. "My hair is lovely now, thank you. Shall we go down to eat before the men eat it all? And thank you for telling me about your engagement."

Supper was well underway when they slid into their seats.

"I'm sorry we didn't hold the meal for you, but the men were starving," Mrs. John said, as she placed their plates before them and sat down opposite.

"It's not a problem, Mrs. John. I'm sorry to have come at your supper hour. Thank you for having me, and at short notice. I needed to get away and Maria said you were great friends. She was sure I'd be welcomed here."

"Of course. We're happy to have you, but you must call me Martha. George says you wish to see the ocean? We can take a drive there tomorrow." She smiled at two men further down the table who glanced at her with furrowed brows, perhaps at the thought of missing a meal with the womenfolk gone.

"I'd not disturb your day like that, Martha. I'm happy to ride there on my own." She hesitated, then continued. "I actually," she gave her a crooked grin, "rode for the Pony Express…as a boy…so I'm quite used to riding alone."

"I can't wait to hear your stories tonight in the parlor!" She chuckled.

"Me either," George grumbled and scrunched up his face. "And here I was, thinking I was going to save you from the Younger Gang, when you've braved Indians on the warpath! That's a little embarrassing."

"I appreciate the thought, and the company." Aleksandra laughed. "Thank you so much for escorting me today. Xavier and Maria would appreciate it, too."

Sarah just sat quietly, hands in her lap, but her eyes shone as they met Aleksandra's. She looked like she'd just found a new hero.

## 8

---

In the morning, Aleksandra found her hostess seated in the kitchen mending a man's work shirt before a sunny window.

Martha glanced up with a smile. "Good morning, did you sleep well?"

"Like a baby," Aleksandra said, and bit her lip. She closed her eyes for a moment as the familiar darkness washed over her.

"Won't you join me?" Martha patted the seat beside her.

Aleksandra swallowed hard and willed the already-welling tears to go away. "Only if I can help you with your sewing," Aleksandra managed, and handed Martha a paper-wrapped packet as she sat down. "Maria asked me to give this to you."

Martha opened it and exclaimed with pleasure as she lovingly touched the piece of delicate French lace. "How did she know I needed just this piece for Sarah's wedding gown? Please give her my thanks, and Sarah's as well."

As together they wielded needles and thread, Aleksandra took a deep breath and quietly told Martha the reason for her trip to the coast.

"Come here," Martha said, taking Aleksandra in her arms. "I am sorry for you, my dear, but I'm glad you've come to stay with us and see our ocean. Death of our loved ones is a reality of life, especially out here. People die, in particular, our children, because they're more delicate than we adults. We love them all we can for the time they are given to us. When they go, we must let their little spirits fly free and release our hearts from the sorrow and guilt that we should have done something more to prevent their deaths. If we've done something wrong, we need to learn from that, but if not, we must let it go. Else we, and others around us, suffer needlessly. That doesn't mean we didn't love them, but that we let them go with love.

"The ocean will be wonderfully healing for you. I suggest you wear the buckskins you arrived in yesterday, roll up the legs and wade in. If you can find a private little cove, you might even bathe, if you are so inclined, but have a care of the riptide. It will pull you out to sea, so don't go beyond your waist. Many have died at these beaches in the rip."

"Thank you for that, Martha." Aleksandra sniffed, then took a deep breath. She smiled at the older woman, and they sewed in peace until Martha sent her away.

"There's a parcel of food on the table for you. I'll not expect you back until suppertime, unless you wish to return earlier." She smiled and waved her hand. "Off with you, young lady!"

Aleksandra left for the beach, Dzień keenly stepping out beneath her. Her heart still ached for her little one, but it was diminishing to a dull emptiness, rather than the sharp, aching pain that had constantly consumed her since her baby's death.

THE BLUE, blue Pacific spread out before Aleksandra, its border an endless flat line and its hue approaching black as it deepened toward the horizon. She stood beside Dzień on the sandstone cliffs high above the beach, just gazing, then followed a track that meandered toward the mouth of the San Gregorio Creek and down to the sand of the beach itself.

Aleksandra giggled with anticipation. She didn't remember seeing the open sea before. She'd only been an infant when her family took ship to America from Vienna and she'd certainly never wriggled her toes in the sand, as she was doing now. She tied Dzień's reins high up on his neck and let him go.

The Mustang snorted and hung back as Aleksandra approached the rolling waves, but he came when she called. He touched his nose to the receding wave, then curled his upper lip at its taste. The pony threw his head up and bolted when a bigger wave chased him up the beach and returned at a trot, snorting, to her side. She laughed and gave him a rub.

While not belittling the life and death of Melissandra, nor the family's sorrow, the infinity of the millions of drops of water before her lent perspective to these small events in the greater scheme of things. She'd thought the Great Basin Desert near her Utah Mountain home did the same, but the ocean spelled it out for her even more clearly in its immensity. The small things were important, but they had their own place in the world. A world which would continue, despite her private challenges. It would certainly go on and she could finally see that she could, as well.

She played the whole of the day in the water and sand, as if she were playing with her own small child—she who would never grow to a child. She cried and she laughed, she laughed and she cried. What fun she would've had with her here, if she'd only had the chance to grow older. Aleksandra bit her lip and cried some more, then offered Melissandra's memory the gift of this time together.

By the time the sun neared the horizon, Aleksandra could let her go. She wished Xavier could have been with her, but he would understand anyway, when she told him what she'd found here today.

ALEKSANDRA STAYED to watch the sun set, its glowing golden globe slowly sinking over the edge of the world. The sky was more shades of pink and purple than she could count as she turned Dzień away from the immensity that was the Pacific Ocean and they walked back the way they'd come. At the top of the trail to the wagon road, she looked back over her shoulder at the faded glory of the sunset and gave thanks for the healing she'd found today.

She smiled all the way back to the John's ranch, watching the clouds in the sky before her. They still held the remnant colors of the sunset at her back.

The front door slammed as she rode into the darkening yard and footsteps sounded on the porch.

"Aleks, we were getting worried about you. It's been dark a long time already!" Sara said.

"Thank you for your concern, but I'm used to riding in the dark and it's still a little bit light yet." Aleksandra squeezed the hand Sarah offered and smiled down at her, then released it and slid from Dzień's back.

"But Aleks, what's happened to your saddle?"

"I left it here." She grinned. "I didn't have a saddle until I'd been riding for three years and I much prefer to ride bareback when I can."

Sarah's smile and glowing eyes showed even in the dim light. "I used to ride bareback on the work horses in the fields, but since I've grown up, Mama says a lady should ride sidesaddle. It would be fun to ride astride again," she whispered. "Perhaps you could talk to Mama about letting me do it with you."

"I'll do my best, but perhaps it's not the ladylike thing to do," Aleksandra said, in an undertone.

"Do you think my husband-to-be would mind?"

"Why don't you ask him? He seems a sensible man and I'd think it a reasonable request." Aleks slipped Dzień's headstall off and let him go, after a quick hug.

"I've already put hay and water out for him." Sarah pointed out the feed.

"You're amazing. That Mr. Sears is one lucky man!"

Sarah smiled. "We saved you some food. It's on the back of the stove, so come on in."

After supper, Aleksandra and Martha talked over the washing up while Sarah helped her father melt lead for bullets.

"Thank you, Martha. This visit with you has given me the peace I sought. Melissandra's death has shown me that life is for living—and that one must go past the sorrow, learn from it, and go on. I'll always remember those I've lost, but those who loved us would prefer to see us happy in our life, not sad for their loss."

"You're becoming wise, my dear," Martha said. She hugged Aleksandra and sent her to bed.

"So TELL me of Maria and your Xavier," Martha said, after the men left for the fields in the morning.

"Maria is well, but her heart hasn't been the best for some time." Aleksandra ran her fingers through her hair. "She tries to hide it, but she's often short of breath and pale. She's happy to have been reconciled with Xavier and have him home again, which she feared would never happen. Melissandra was Maria's first grandchild and this been hard on her. The loss of our baby and my melancholy has been hard on Xavier. He's been busy on the *rancho*, but I fear he's buried much of his grief."

"They're lucky to have been given the opportunity to reconcile." Martha sighed, with slight upturn of the corners of her mouth. "And what of her other sons?"

"José is doing well. With Xavier is back, he's headed for Spain to study law at a university. Sancho is…let's say he's not been living the healthiest of lives for many years.

"Ah, well. People make their choices, it seems. You, though, seem more peaceful now." Martha smiled and took her hand.

"Yes. I so appreciate your caring words. They helped me tie things together. Now I can return and face my life with more peace and equanimity."

"Your strength has inspired my Sarah." Martha smiled. "She's always wanted to show her strength, but was constrained by her vision of 'ladies' as weak, simpering things. You have shown her a woman can be strong, yet not have it detract from her ability to be ladylike."

"I'm afraid I'm not very ladylike," Aleksandra's lips quirked, "in fact, she wanted me to ask if you'd allow her to ride astride, but I'm glad if I could help her to be strong in her lovely self. Her promised seems bright and sensible. It should be a good match."

"My husband and I believe so too. He's much older, but I don't think it's a bad thing for a young girl to have a settled man."

"Sarah's given me a letter to leave for him at Mr. Sausman's store. Do you mind?"

"No, that's fine. She's already shown it to me." She gripped both of Aleksandra's hands. "It's truly been lovely having you to stay. Please come back soon." She embraced Aleksandra warmly and gave her a peck on the cheek.

"I've enjoyed my time with you, but I'm missing my husband terribly," Aleksandra said. "Unless you need my help with anything, I'll be on my way, but only if you promise to visit us soon."

"No, thanks. You should be on the road. You have a long ride ahead," Martha said, as they walked into the guest room. "You'd best take care, those dratted Younger brothers are probably still out there."

"I'll be watching for them." Aleksandra picked up her assorted weapons and began stowing them on her person.

"Are you sure you don't want an escort?"

"Thank you. You know as well as I that you haven't the men to spare right now," Aleksandra smiled, "but thank you for the offer. Anyway," she grinned, "I'm armed like Fort Knox."

"You're a bit of a worry, aren't you?" Martha grinned and shook her head at the sight of Aleksandra, fairly bristling with knives, rifle and *shashka*.

"It helps keep me out of trouble," Aleksandra said.

"Why do I doubt that?" Martha smirked, as she picked up the bedroll and led the way outside to Dzień's pen.

"You be careful, weapons or no weapons," Sarah said when she joined them, just as Aleksandra finished saddling and tying her belongings onto Dzień.

"I'm always careful. I have to be. I have new friends to consider." She hugged the women. "Thanks again to both of you," she said, then swung up and rode away, waving over her shoulder as she left the yard.

The coolness of the redwood forest enveloped her when they rode into it a few hours later. The creek beside them bubbling happily and a warm breeze blew at her back. Aleksandra was staring into the stream, looking for fish, when Dzień's head swung up and he stopped abruptly, then started to swerve back the way they'd come. Aleksandra whipped her head around and stared.

"I don't believe we've been properly introduced," Cole Younger said, as he stepped into the middle of the trail in front of Dzień.

# 9

---

Dzień started backing up as Cole's men stepped out from behind trees to her right and left. Then more appeared just behind her.

"Yah! Let's go boy!" Aleksandra shouted. Dzień bolted, but Cole caught him. He holstered his revolver and tightened his fist on the reins as the plunging pony tried to pull away. One of his men dragged her from the saddle and she struggled against his tight hold on her arms.

"Let him go," Cole said, walking over to where his men surrounded her. "Let's see what he has to say without Carter's help," he growled.

Aleksandra flicked a glance at Dzień to measure the distance. The Mustang stared at the men, ears flat back, but not moving.

Without a doubt, they wouldn't her go alive if she didn't join them—they were too afraid of Weeks to let her go back and tell tales. An image of Xavier flashed through her mind and her guts wrenched at the thought she might not see him again, then her chin came up.

"Can't see much of you in that big hat and it ain't respectful." Cole reached out and jerked it from her head.

Her coiled silky locks tumbled down around her and the men froze.

The man holding her loosened his grip only a fraction, but it was enough.

"Hold her," Cole growled, but it was too late.

Everything seemed to move in slow motion as she jerked her arms from his grip and threw her weight forward. She whipped out her *shashka* and struck, slashing her captor's forearm as she spun away.

She crouched in the center of the circle of men. Two of them backed away, but Cole came for her and she dived at him. She managed to slice his gun hand as she ducked past him, grabbed her hat and raced for Dzień. Barking a command to him in Polish, Aleksandra vaulted into the saddle, somehow scrambling over the bedroll, as the pony struck off into a canter.

The reports of the guns behind her were deafening. Bullets whined past as they raced away. The trail ahead curved to the left. Praying they wouldn't shoot Dzień, she threw the reins at him, gripped the saddle horn with her right hand, twisted her right leg into the stirrup leather and dropped down to the side of her mount in a Cossack Hang. The shooting stopped as their target disappeared. She wondered, perhaps irrelevantly, whether they were short of horses and wanted Dzień, or if they couldn't be bothered moving a dead horse off the trail. As her beloved pony raced toward Arroyo Honda, she sent a brief prayer of thanks to her father, and even to Vladimir, for teaching her the ways of the Cossack warrior.

AFTER THEY ROUNDED the next bend, she flicked herself back into the saddle and they bolted down the trail. Aleksandra crouched low on Dzień's neck, but she didn't hear hoofbeats behind them. It was a blessing the gang's horses weren't saddled. That might give her a short respite. They clearly hadn't expected a fight, much less having to pursue their quarry.

Aleksandra was still two turns away from the sawmill when Carter's blond head showed above a stack of timber and she shouted something in his direction. His head flicked up from the board he was cutting, then Aleksandra lost sight of him. By the time she arrived at the mill, Carter had already gathered five of his men and they stood ranged across the road, rifles at the ready.

"It's Cole and his gang," Aleksandra said, glancing behind her, as Dzień slid to a halt, blowing.

"You go, girl," Carter growled. "We'll slow him down a little. Head for the Weeks' place." He cocked his rifle and spun around to face the coast road, backed by his men.

"Thank you, Mr. Carter, I owe you and your boys one." Aleksandra tipped her hat at them and galloped away, blonde hair flying out behind her. Dzień shook his head and bucked, then stuffed his head down and flew up the trail.

"Cole and his boys might be giving George Carter a bit of trouble. You might want to lend a hand," she shouted to the men lounging in the doorway of Sausman's store, as Dzień stopped just short of the porch steps.

"What's het up Cole?" Sausman's brows narrowed.

"Me, and he's bleeding," she said. "He'll be mad as a hornet, so please take care! Oh yes," she threw over her shoulder, then turned back, "letter from young Sarah for Mr. Sears." She pulled it out of her shirt front and handed it to Sausman.

"I'll see he gets it," he shouted after her. "You head for the summit and don't look back."

They shot off, the miles evaporating beneath Dzień's hooves as he sprinted along the creek trail and burst into the open fields of the Weeks property. She had no way of knowing whether any or all of the Younger Gang had made it past the gauntlet of Carter's and Sausman's men, so better safe than sorry. She raced up to the porch as Mr. and Mrs. Weeks came out the front door. She apprised them of the situation. Mr. Weeks headed for the kitchen to rouse his men, who'd just washed up for dinner. Cordelia ran inside to pack food for the men to eat as they rode. Rifle and paper wrapped packet of dinner in hand, each man was soon mounted and heading back along the way she'd just come, at speed.

Aleksandra looked down from the saddle as Cordelia thrust a packet of food into her hands as well. Aleksandra thanked her and swung Dzień's head around for the last leg of the winding trail toward the crest of the Sierra Morena.

When they finally reached the skyline, Aleksandra reined in and slid from the saddle, hugging her tired pony. She scanned as far as she could see back down the road they'd just traveled, but there was no visible movement. She poured some water from her canteen into her hat and Dzień drank thirstily. She gave him a few handfuls of feed while she rubbed his forehead and ate the dinner Cordelia had provided. The pony sighed at the same time as she did, then she patted his neck and they turned back down the trail, Aleksandra trotting beside Dzień over the dappled redwood duff on their way to Dr. Tripp's store.

She looked back wistfully as she left the shade of the redwood forest and entered the logging-slag covered foothills. Over the next few hours, they passed several unladen oxen teams heading up the hill for more timber. In no time at all, they were at the steps of the Woodside Store. Dr. Tripp turned aside from his conversation and stared at her pony's curly, sweat-laden coat and then at her own disheveled locks.

"You look like the devil's been after you, girl," Dr. Tripp raised his eyebrows as Aleksandra slid to the ground before the steps.

"It was a bit like that," she said, looking at the blood on her sleeve.

"You're bleeding," he growled. "What's happened?"

"Not my blood. Cole Younger's."

"You cannot be serious," he said, under his breath. "Come on into the barn and we'll untack in there."

He helped her unsaddle the Mustang and rub him down while she told her story in private.

"Lucky my hair fell down. If not for that, I'd be likely head down in a ditch, somewhere no one would ever find me," she said, with a twist of her lips.

"You've made a powerful enemy, Aleksandra. He's not likely to forget someone who's cut him." His brows nearly touched, his mouth a firm line, but then he gave it up and grinned for a moment. "Not sure anyone's ever done that. Most of the people he associates with use guns, not little short swords."

"A *shashka*'s got its strong points," she said, as she turned to finish Dzień off with a flourish. She stroked him as he munched hay contentedly in a box stall—in the furthest, darkest corner of the barn, where Dr. Tripp had hidden him away.

Tripp wasn't taking any chances of the outlaw finding her before she made it home. He'd already sent his right hand man to find Xavier and inform him his wife was going nowhere until he arrived to escort her home safely—and then only with a few of Tripp's men.

"Really," Aleksandra protested, "I can get home, in half the time."

"Over my dead body." Tripp raised an eyebrow at her. His housekeeper was in her element and fussed over her. She fed her roasted chicken, gravy and biscuits, and then thrust before her what had to be a quarter of a loganberry pie, crusty and dripping with juice.

"I give, I give…" Aleksandra smiled her thanks at the beaming woman and downed the whole piece. "If I keep eating like this, Xavier will be finding himself a new wife," she groaned, as she leaned back in her chair.

"What's this about finding myself a new wife?" Xavier strode into Tripp's back room and clasped Dr. Tripp's hand as he walked past him. "My thanks, Doc. Good to see you again," he said shortly, before he sat on the bench beside Aleksandra and pulled her onto his lap. He held her tight, her head tucked into the crook of his neck in silence. Finally, he sat up and sighed, looking her in the eyes. "Just what kind of trouble did you find this time?"

"Mmmm... well...Cole Younger—"

He blinked. "Not Younger." He shook his head and buried his face in her hair. "How do you do it?"

"I didn't just go looking for trouble," she said, frowning at him.

"I know. It just finds you." He shook his head and smiled at her. "You have to be the luckiest girl alive, with the scrapes you've weaseled out of, *Querida*."

"Sorry Xave," Dr. Tripp grinned at him, "but I couldn't let her leave here by herself. I did it once, against my better judgement, and decided I wouldn't do it again after seeing what she means by 'being careful'."

"And for that, I thank you. She's pretty special to me." He kissed the top of her head and hugged her close again.

"You were quick," Aleksandra said, "between Dr. Tripp's man and you, for a twenty-mile round trip."

"Well," Xavier squirmed, "sorry Doc, but your man ought to be along sometime soon. I couldn't wait and didn't want him to push his horse."

"So how's Charro looking about now?" Aleksandra looked sideways at him.

"He's fit. A little gallop won't hurt him. You galloped your Express ponies over the same distance and worse terrain." Xavier stood up and stretched. "I can't say the same for my fitness. Charro's in better shape after his run than I am."

She couldn't argue with him about the Express ponies, and Charro was an exquisite example of a Spanish horse. He was probably just getting warmed up.

"Xave!" Dr. Tripp's housekeeper shrieked, as she came in the door from the kitchen shed, hugged him and ran back out, only to return with another huge slab of her pie. "You won't go without some of my pie! You never could do without it when you were a boy!"

"No, ma'am, and I can't resist it now, either," he grinned up at her as she slid the pie, drenched with cream, before him.

$$\leadsto$$

XAVIER REACHED across the space between their horses for Aleksandra's hand as they rode home from Dr. Tripp's. "I'm so glad you're here with me and coming home," he smiled down at her.

"Me too," she said, meeting his gaze. "Oh Xave, the redwoods are beautiful."

"I knew you'd love them. If I'd known the Younger brothers were up there, I'd never have let you go alone."

"I needed to go, you know that." She looked down at their entwined fingers.

"Yes, but..." He sighed. "I know you need your freedom, but I can't bear the thought of losing you. I've nearly lost you too many times already."

"I've always returned, haven't I?"

"Yes, but it's that first time you don't that I'm scared of."

"OK. Truce?"

"Truce." He smiled, then his brow furrowed. "We've got a little problem at home. Sancho's missing."

"Oh no. I hope he's OK." He'd been agreeable to Xavier, almost obsequiously so, but many times Aleksandra had caught him sending sly glances toward his elder brother when Xavier's back was turned. Sancho was still routinely rude to her when he chanced to catch her alone, so she avoided him unless she was with Xavier or Maria.

"I've never been through here before," she said, staring across the oak-studded rolling grasslands as they traveled cross-country. "Only deer and cattle trails. No people. I like it."

"We're near the boundaries of the *rancho*," he said.

"Where are we going?".

"You'll see in a moment."

The trail followed the bottoms of a deep canyon winding its way east, between high hills that blocked out the sun.

"We're on our place now," he said.

"Really? Already? Oh yes, I recognize it now."

Half an hour later, they exited the big canyon and Redwood City appeared in the distance. Soon the *hacienda* came into view.

"Few people would know that way, besides, much of it's our property. We'll have to spend some more time riding about the *rancho*, now that you can ride again." He took her fingers again and kissed her palm, his gaze smoldered as he looked into her eyes.

"Is that a promise?" she murmured.

"Try me," he whispered, as they rode toward the stableyard.

# 10

Maria's brows lowered as someone pounded on the door during their breakfast, a bit of poached egg halfway to her mouth. "Whoever could that be at this hour, and unannounced?"

"I have no idea." Xavier stood and headed toward the front door.

"So what have you planned for today, Aleksandra?" Maria cut a piece of bacon and added it to her egg, while she remained turned away from the raised voices in the front hallway.

"I'd planned to look at the new foals to see which need handling the most, there's—"

A crash from the front door cut Aleksandra's answer short and she swung around at the sound. She and Maria raced each other to the door and froze in horror at the sight of a tall man lying flat on the floor before the door. Xavier stood over him, swearing in Spanish and rubbing his fist. Two other men stood quietly just outside the door.

"Xavier, what is the meaning of this?" his tiny mother thundered.

"Whoever he is, said he's now the owner of Rancho de las Pulgas, and that my no-good scum of a brother lost it to him gambling." Xavier glared at the still form on the ground.

"How did he end up on the floor?" Aleksandra said, with a frown.

"He came at me when I told him to get out and then ran into my fist as he tried to punch me."

"Begging your pardon, Mrs. Argüello, but that is truly exactly what happened." A grey-haired man took a hesitant step toward the door and stopped, his eyes wide, looking at Xavier.

"Mr. Fraser, what is the meaning of all this?" Maria's voice was clipped.

"I'm afraid I'm still trying to get to the bottom of it myself." Fraser's brow furrowed as he took a deep breath and stepped past Xavier toward Maria. "This man appeared on my front doorstep this morning, waving the deed to Rancho de las Pulgas, shouting about how he'd won it in a bet from Sancho."

"Oh well, if that's all it is," Maria sighed and smiled at her lawyer, "of course, you can make it right. Do you have any idea where Sancho might be?"

Fraser didn't return her smile. He stood frozen and said nothing.

Aleksandra shot a look at Xavier, who came to her side. Together they approached Maria and Mr. Fraser.

"Mr. Fraser," Xavier said slowly, "is this man correct?"

"He does hold the deed for the property."

"He must be mistaken." Maria shook her head and smiled again. "The deed couldn't be signed over by anyone but me."

Fraser was staring at his feet. He slowly lifted his eyes to hers. "Mrs. Argüello, I'm afraid that isn't true. Do you remember, before you left for Carson City a few years ago, how worried you were about your heart? You'd hoped to find Xavier and make him your heir, but in case you didn't find him, you signed a power of attorney... giving Sancho full rights to make binding decisions regarding this property until such time as the power of attorney could be transferred to Xavier, if you did indeed find him? I'm afraid we have both neglected to change the documents after Xavier's return home."

Maria's paled and Aleksandra grabbed her shaking hand. She clutched at her chest and gasped for breath like a fish out of water, then slumped toward the floor.

Xavier kneeled and picked her up gently, his visage nearly as white as hers. "Aleksandra, ride for Doctor Furniss in Redwood City. His house is at Broadway and Main, just near the docks," he said over his shoulder, as he strode down the hall. He took the stairs two at a time, pausing for a moment halfway up. "Take Charro, Dzień will still be tired."

Aleksandra shot out the door and into the barn, then slipped a bridle over the ears of the gray Spanish stallion. Not taking the time to saddle him, she swung up and they hurtled down the road she'd followed on her way to the coast, only a few short days before.

His mane whipped back into her eyes and tears streamed as the miles flew by. They galloped up the main street, quiet at this early hour, and Charro slid to a halt at Aleksandra's request. She pounded on the door below the gold leafed sign, "Dr. Furniss, Surgeon", then chewed her nails as she stood waiting.

A maid in a mob cap answered the door. "Good morning, I'm sorry, the doctor is at his breakfast," she said, with a smile.

"Oh please, miss, I'm sorry to bother him at this hour, but could you please tell him Mrs. Argüello has collapsed. She has a bad heart. Can he please come to Rancho de las Pulgas?"

"I'm coming." Dr. Furniss was already pulling his coat from the hook behind the door. "Hello Aleksandra. James is putting my chestnut to the gig. You fly on home. I'd ride your gray if I could, but I'd be safer in the gig." He smiled and squeezed her hand. "I'll be there as fast as my horse can trot."

Aleksandra burst into tears and wobbled, her knees turned to jelly.

"Mabel!" he shouted over his shoulder into the house, "can you get Aleksandra some strong tea with honey? She's had a shock. I must be off!"

"I'm f-f-fine," she mumbled.

"Poor dear," he said to Aleksandra. "It's always like this. You did well getting the message to me. You just take a moment to let your nerves settle. A nice cup of tea will do you the world of good." He guided her to a seat in the front hallway and she sank into it, with a sob of gratitude.

The doctor patted her shoulder and hurried away as a horse clip-clopped sharply up to the porch. He exited with a slam of the door, bells in the entryway jangling in protest. His carriage springs squeaked as he climbed in, then the sound of hooves at a strong trot echoed in the lane, diminishing as he headed for de las Pulgas.

"Aleksandra, would you like to sit there or come through to the kitchen? Oh my, aren't we looking a bit peaky this morning?" Mrs. Furniss clucked over her while she set a piece of buttered toast and a cup of dark brown liquid before her.

"Thank you, Mrs. Furniss. It's Maria. She's had a terrible shock and collapsed. I think she's had a heart attack. Some man just arrived and claimed to have won Rancho de las Pulgas in a bet from Xavier's brother. Maria's lawyer was there too. I think it might be for real." She stared up into the horrified eyes of the doctor's wife. "Not only is Maria unconscious, we might have lost the *rancho*, too."

"Oh," Mrs. Furniss sat down with a plunk on her seat, her eyes wide, her mouth an "o". She gathered herself together and put on her best doctor's-wife face. "I'm sure it will all be fine," she said, as she made an effort to school her face into some semblance of a grimace-like smile.

"Thank you for the tea, madam, but I must be back at the *rancho* to help out." Aleksandra stood and clasped Mrs. Furniss' hands in hers for a moment, then spun to go. She glanced back at her hostess as she let herself out the door. Mrs. Furniss looked to be in worse shape than she was, sitting frozen, staring at the unlit table lamp with a bemused look upon her face.

THE CLUSTER of visitor's horses still stood outside the front door of the *hacienda* when Aleksandra returned. Miguel, the head stableman, hurried to her and reached for Charro's reins.

"I'll cool him out, you go see to Xavier." He smiled at her, but his brow was furrowed as he led the gray away toward the barn.

She quietly opened the door to the front hallway to find Fraser scribbling furiously on a piece of paper. The big man still measured his full length on the floor. He might have been taking a nap, other than the blood running from his nostrils. Another man sat beside the lawyer.

She resisted the rather inappropriate urge to laugh. Xavier's tutoring in hand-to-hand combat back in Utah by Vladimir Chabardine had certainly come in handy this morning.

Dismayed by Xavier's total lack of aptitude for fighting, the Russian had made it his life's ambition to teach the *Californio* to defend himself, and more. She couldn't hold back a little smile. Vladimir hadn't entered their life as a friend, but he'd become one in the ensuing weeks.

She nodded to Fraser and brushed past him on her way to Maria's room. She peeked in the open door to see the doctor leaning over her mother-in-law, his stethoscope against her chest.

"Thank you for getting Dr. Furniss, Aleks." Xavier tried to smile, but his brow wouldn't smooth out and his mouth remained tense. He sat beside his mother and gripped her hand as she stared into space.

"How is she?" Aleksandra dropped to her knees beside the bed and leaned against Xavier's knees.

"She's been in and out of consciousness, but she's very weak."

"It's her heart?" It was a statement, rather than a question.

"Yes." He looked down at Maria. "She's been lucid, though. She wants to revoke the power of attorney and update her will. Fraser's writing it up now. It might be too late for the *rancho*, but she wants to do it anyway, before Sancho can do any more damage."

"Have you found your brother, or discovered any more details?"

"The man on the floor's name is Skinner. The other man, not the one on the floor," the corners of his lips turned up a touch, "was apparently present at the saloon when the final bet was made, when my idiot *hermano* placed the deed for this *rancho* on the table." Xavier's voice shook. "It seems he was into the house for many, many thousands of dollars and made a bet with which he was sure to win it all back…but he lost it, and with it, our heritage." Xavier sighed as he ran his fingers through his hair and slumped forward, his forehead in his hands.

"Oh, Xavier." Aleksandra wrapped her arms about him and rocked him gently.

"Not only that, but he was caught cheating, so he's now in jail."

"At least we won't have to go far to find him." Aleksandra's words were clipped, her lips tight.

"I don't dare go." Xavier closed his eyes. "I'm afraid of what I might do to him for causing this shock *a mi madre*, not to mention losing Rancho de las Pulgas."

"Where's he now?"

"In San Francisco."

"That's a long ride from here for a few hours of gambling." She shook her head. "No wonder he was gone for days at a time."

"He's in the Presidio jail."

"The Presidio?" She stared at him. "Why the Presidio? It's military."

"One of the men accusing him of cheating was high up in the U.S. Army. Unfortunate choice on my blasted brother's part."

"Xavier," Fraser said, from his elbow, "I have the revocation letter and your mama's will. Would you care to read it while Mrs. Argüello is still asleep?"

Xavier took the document and perused it as a tear leaked from one eye. Aleksandra gripped his other hand.

Maria groaned and blinked, then turned her head to look at Xavier and Aleksandra. She was deathly pale.

"How are you feeling, Maria?" the doctor said, his voice velvet.

She motioned to the glass of water on her bedside table. She took a sip when he held it to her lips. "Xavier," she whispered, "the law will take care of him for his cheating and the Lord will take his due for the abuse of his family and heritage."

"But Mama, for this, what he has done to you...I cannot forgive him."

"I was unwell before. This is just a hiccup. Unfortunately, one from which I may not recover, but it is the will of God that I should have a heart with this weakness." She'd regained some color, but her skin was still mostly tinged blue.

"Madam," Fraser said, "I have prepared the papers as you requested and only require you go sign them. They are here." Xavier placed it before her, atop a book. He took the dip pen from the lawyer and helped his mother to hold it in her quivering hand.

"Yes, thank you, Fraser," she whispered. "I wanted this done. It is my fault you have lost your heritage, Xavier. If I had not—"

"—Mama, it's not your fault, even if you signed that power of attorney. I relinquished my claim to the *rancho* when I left, many years ago. It isn't nearly as important to me as you are."

"And you to me, *mi querido*." Her heart was in her eyes as she gazed upon her firstborn. "I am eternally thankful for the opportunity to know the son I believed lost and the daughter I'd never before had." She looked at Aleksandra, the corners of her mouth upturned, then took a deep breath and waited a moment before speaking again. "It is worth every hardship. I know both of you are feeling crowded by the masses of people so close to us, so when I have breathed my last—"

"—don't speak like that, Mama, you'll get better." Xavier's voice was forceful.

She gazed at him, a faraway look in her eyes, and smiled.

"Xavier, do not lie to me. We both know I am living on borrowed time." She looked up at the crumpled face of her doctor, then back to her son. Her skin became more and more blue as her voice weakened. "Thank you, Fraser. That is all. Please be sure to have all of these witnesses sign that revocation," she said, dismissing the lawyer.

"I will let you rest, madam. Fare well." He gripped her hands and exited the room.

"Xave, remember," his mother said, "the deed is for the land alone. Everything else is yours. You and Aleks will have more than enough to make a good start somewhere and still invest the rest wisely." Her voice dropped to a dry whisper. "Perhaps you will find a place with fewer people clamoring on your boundaries, where you can live in peace."

Xavier held the glass to her lips again and took a deep breath. Tears were seeping from the corners of both eyes now.

Aleksandra gave her a brave smile and held one of her hands tightly. Maria, and everything else, were blurry beyond recognition.

"My Aleksandra, you have been a joy to me in the short time we have had together. Perhaps this is for the best. I know you have chafed at the crowds, even on our *rancho*.

Aleks couldn't help but send her a watery grin.

"Didn't you two receive a letter from a man in New Zealand, that von Tempsky?" Maria whispered. "Maybe that is to be your new home."

"But Mama, we won't leave you," Xavier said. "I've only just gotten you back." His voice threatened to break, and he let out a sob.

"I'll never leave you, Xave. I'll always be in your heart, but we both know this is goodbye. I'd scarcely dreamed to see you again, yet I was gifted with many months of your love. You've grown into a man of whom your father would have been proud. Bury your hatchet with your wayward brother and let him know I love him, despite his shortcomings. He's always lived in your shadow, though you were far from us." Her voice was like dry crepe and they leaned in close to hear her words. "To your brother Jose in Spain, please also give my love. I wish I could see him again, but it is not to be."

She gazed at them all, the smile of an angel on her lips, and closed her eyes. "It no longer hurts," she breathed.

"THE POST, *SEÑOR*," Miguel said, with a knock on the office door frame.

Xavier turned in his seat, the ghost of a smile on his face for his stableman, and thanked him.

Miguel looked like he might say something, bit his lips together, then shook his head and turned to go.

"Miguel, did you have…" Xavier started.

"No," he murmured, "just that we're all so sad for the loss of Mrs. Argüello. We don't know how we'll go on without her." The tough old man's eyes leaked as Xavier got up and gave him a tight hug. Miguel had always been there—Xavier couldn't remember a time he hadn't been part of the Argüello household. Xavier thanked him and sent him to the kitchen. Doubtless, Adelita's morning baking would help, if only a little.

He wiped the tears from his own eyes and closed them, willing the hole in his chest to stop aching so. It would be a long time before that happened. He took a deep breath, sat up, and turned to the pile of post on the desk before him. Anything not to think of the mother he loved, lying in state in the parlor so long before her time, like her granddaughter before her. He'd missed years of her love in his self-imposed exile. He shook his head and swallowed hard.

"Addressee not found, return to sender," was scrawled across the front of the first letter. It was from Sancho to a Mr. Ryan, at a San Francisco address. It had been returned, unopened. He frowned.

Xavier leaned back in his chair, his jaw tight. He didn't know if Sancho knew about their mama's death yet. He needed to see him to make sure; ideally, before the funeral. He didn't trust himself to visit just yet. Perhaps he could forward this letter on…

He stilled at the odd feeling coming over him, the one that told him he needed to open it.

Taking his father's letter opener, a tiny, finely-wrought silver sword, he slowly slit the top of the envelope and pulled out the single sheet of folded paper.

*Dear Mr. Ryan,*

*I hope this finds you before you take ship.*

*As per your request, I have just delivered Mrs. Argüello (somewhat the worse for the chloroform), the baby, and the pony into your waiting hands.*

*You should have had no problems leaving undetected, as I have just told Xavier she ran off with that Indian friend of hers. He's currently sulking over being a cuckold. I'm proud to have had the opportunity to help him escape this wench; I hope you find some distasteful and permanent position for her —far, far away. She has caused nothing but trouble for my family.*

*Your welcome promise to pay off my unlucky debt with you, as well as to send $500.00 more, is appreciated.*

*Please pay the sum to my account at the Bank of—*

Xavier sat, frozen in place. He could read no further.

The letter dropped from his hand to the floor, forgotten, as his world spun.

*Sancho? Aleksandra's and Melissandra's kidnapper?*

He slumped forward, his head cradled in his arms on the desk before him and his guts clenched. He didn't move for what seemed an eternity.

There was nothing for them here anymore, not even a brother to support in jail. At least he would no longer feel guilty about leaving him behind.

Sancho would be incarcerated for a long, long time.

ALEKSANDRA, understandably, did not take it well.

"But Xavier, finally…a family…and they do *this?*" She cried softly into his shirt.

"I know," he said, rocking her gently. "I've been trying to figure out how to tell you. I know he was never kind to you, but this…this…*es inconfesable*…unspeakable."

"We have no reason to stay," she said, her voice lifeless.

"Is there somewhere you'd like to go?"

"I don't want to return to Utah. It's no longer the same as the place I grew up in. It is death, pain for my Indian family, nothing…"

"I've been thinking…as Mama said, about the letters from von Tempsky."

She looked up, a light beginning to flicker in her eyes, and a question. "Von Tempsky said the natives in New Zealand and the settlers work together, unlike the way the 'Americans' are abusing and slaughtering the Indians here," Aleksandra said. "The problem is too big here, and too few people care—well, they care, but they care only for their land."

"I want to get away from the fools trying to turn this into a Southern state." He brushed the hair back from his face with a quick movement. "This whole country is in an uproar. If the Confederates and the Knights of the Golden Circle win out here, California will go to the South, and…" he shuddered, "slavery will become an everyday part of life, even more than it is now," he finished on a whisper, then gulped and began again. "I cannot abide it."

"Maybe, just maybe, it's the place for us to make a new start, away from all this death."

"We have all the money we could want from Mama," he said, "and from the sale of the stock…and she wanted us to go. There's nothing here for me anymore. My family and Rancho de las Pulgas are gone. We can write to Jose to let him know where we are, if you'd like to go."

"We also have the two gold pieces an old prospector left for my brother and me, so many years ago. They would go a long way to paying for a ship to get us and our stock to New Zealand," Aleksandra said.

"It seems as good a place as any, and a sight better than most," he said, and pulled her more tightly into his arms.

# 11

S ancho sat slumped in a chair in the Presidio prison visitor's room.

"So, why'd you do it?" Xavier said, as he entered the room. His brother picked up his head and stared at him with bleary eyes.

"Do what?" Sancho said, and looked away, but not before he pressed his lips together.

Xavier tossed the envelope, addressed to Mr. Ryan, onto the wooden table before him.

Sancho glanced toward it and flinched. Neither man spoke for long minutes.

"Well?" Xavier said, finally.

Sancho took a deep breath, opened his mouth to speak, then shut it again. "I don't have to tell you anything."

"No, you don't, but I'd really like to know what makes you tick. I've always loved you, and wanted the best for you, but it's not the same for you, is it?"

Sancho shook his head, then seemed to come to a decision. He sat up and fixed Xavier with a glare. "You weren't meant to return."

Xavier blinked.

"I thought you'd go away for good, after all I did."

"*¿Cómo?*" Xavier frowned at him. "What?"

He clamped his mouth shut, then finally spoke. "I guess Mama'll be mad at me anyway, so I might as well tell you," Sancho said.

Xavier bit his tongue. He wouldn't say a word, for now.

"You were always Mama's favorite. I knew that, even though I was the baby. I wanted you gone, oh, for as long as I can remember. Papa would beat you, then Mama would try to take your beatings for you. I couldn't stand it, so I did something about it." Sancho straightened up and looking coldly at Xavier. "I couldn't have been more than eight or nine when I started."

"Started?"

"Trying to make you go. If you went, I knew I could have anything I wanted. Papa said so. I know he tried to kill you. I saw it."

Xavier could only stare.

"Anyway, I started getting you into more and more trouble. I told on you when you did anything wrong, so he'd beat you again."

"Wrong? What did I do wrong?" Xavier's mouth dropped open as his brother went on.

"Whatever you did wrong, and things you didn't. I may not have been Mama's favorite, but I was smart. Smarter than you. I risked getting Mama beaten more, but it was the only way to make it work."

"I'm intrigued," Xavier said, the blood beginning to turn to ice in his veins .

"But that's not all." His little brother's eyes glinted in an unnatural way and Xavier shivered. "I used to creep up beside your pillow when you were asleep and whisper things to you. It seemed to work, because you got more and more nervous and distant. I knew I was winning."

"What things?" Xavier said, keeping his voice level.

"Like... that Mama didn't love you, that no one could ever love you, that you needed to go, and never come back."

Xavier had no words, but his brother's ones gut-punched him and he could only sit, frozen, as flashes of his life raced through his head. He'd taken it all on, believed the hateful thoughts and left home. Still those lies ruled him, years later—until Aleksandra had shaken him to his boots and made him start to believe... to believe none of it was true. His brother's voice continued, as if through a fog.

"And you went. I was glad. I lived as I wished and encouraged Jose to go. He was devoted to you—he wouldn't go until he was sure you had your *rancho*. Silly of him. I was going to have to get rid of him, too."

"And then I returned," prompted Xavier. He gritted his teeth and pulled back a little from the man across from him. The glimpses inside this man's mind were frightening.

"And brought that troublemaker with you," he snapped. "She saw through me from the first, even if you didn't. I'll give her that, she's smart, but not as smart as me. That's why I was all too happy to hand her and the baby over. The baby…" he hesitated and frowned, then went on, "I felt a little bad for, it had our own blood, after all, but a deal's a deal."

"So you wanted her gone, and then?" Xavier managed, from between gritted teeth. He gripped his hands together in his lap to keep climbing over the table and ripping out his brother's throat.

"And then you'd go away and never return. I could run the *rancho* on my own, because Jose would know you didn't want it. I could do whatever I wanted, as Papa promised me." The fanatical stare was even stronger now.

Xavier shook his head. "And Rancho de las Pulgas? What about that?" Xavier pushed.

"What about it?" Sancho said, his brows lowering as he bit his lip.

"You've gambled it away. We just found out."

"No loss, I'd saved enough money to take care of Mama and Isabel—" he broke off and flushed red, "Mama and me," he corrected, and seemed to draw into himself.

"Isabel?"

Sancho didn't respond.

"Who is she?" Xavier said, his fingers drumming on the table.

Sancho, his eyes full of hate, finally spoke. "Isabella. The only person other than Mama and Papa who ever loved me. She wanted to marry me, have my children to carry on our name, but you wrecked it."

Xavier blinked. "And how would I have done that?" Xavier lifted a brow at him, his face otherwise still.

"You came back. When I told her, she dropped me and went back to her husband."

"Was that when you still held power of attorney and she thought Rancho de las Pulgas would be yours?"

Sancho flinched. "I still hold it," he snarled.

"I beg to differ."

Sancho peered out the corners of his eyes from beneath his fringe of lank, dirty hair. "You didn't deserve to have it," he said. "That's why I put it up as a bet."

"So you'd kick your own mama off her *rancho*? Did you stop to think what that might do to her?"

Sancho didn't respond, just stared at his dirty fingernails, lips pursed.

"That money that you've 'saved' belonged to Mama." Xavier stood and leaned over the table, close to his brother's face. Tears ran cold down his heated cheeks as he spoke. "There was precious little of that left, with what you've filched for these past four years; I've seen the books."

"Mama won't need it, I have plenty."

"Well, you won't have to spend it on Mama." Xavier sat down in his chair with a thump and the chair legs screeched across the tile floor.

Sancho looked at Xavier's face and his sneer turned to confusion. "But it would give me pleasure," he said, as if speaking to a small child. "Unlike you, who left her, I love her. I just wanted to get her free of your influence, then she'd come back to me again…and love me like she did, before you returned."

"Mama made me promise to let you know she loves you, and for us to bury our hatchets."

"Never will that happen. She'll have to go on hoping." He gave a short bark of laughter and derision, looking at Xavier's tears. "Still soft, aren't you? Anyway, is she coming to get me out soon or are you taking me home?"

"It'll be a cold day in Hell before I take you anywhere." Xavier enunciated each word.

Sancho rolled his eyes. "Well then, when's Mama coming?"

"She's not."

He turned his head to face Xavier. "She will. She loves me. No matter how bad I am." He sat up straight and tried to smile. "No, really, when's she coming? I have to get out of here. I haven't had a drink in days."

"You killed her." Flatly.

He looked sideways at Xavier. "What?"

"You heard me. Your gambling buddy, the man you lost Rancho de las Pulgas to? The *rancho's* new owner? He came calling the other day. Mama heard what you'd done with her heritage and her home. She had a heart attack on the spot. She died an hour later."

Sancho melted, like a candle in the heat of the summer sun. "You're lying," he whispered, after long moments, then staggered to his feet. "Not Mama, not her." He shook his head, his eyes wild. "That wasn't in the plan." He stood up straight and looked at Xavier with haunted eyes. "You bastard, you're lying," he screamed, and launched himself at Xavier.

The guards outside thrust open the door, rifles at the ready, but there was no need.

Sancho lay on the ground before Xavier, knocked out with one punch.

One punch, but it held a lifetime of frustration, self loathing and fear.

"Take him back to his cell, please. I've heard enough from him to last me forever," Xavier said.

His hands shook as he walked out the front doors of the jail and through the Presidio to Charro. He wrapped his arms around the great horse's neck and let his tears flow. The ones he hadn't cried since he was a child, not understanding why so much hatred had been directed his way —for no reason, and to no purpose.

He finally picked up his head and stared out over the cliffs of the Golden Gate to the Pacific beyond. Boundless sea. Freedom?

At least now, he had some answers.

Late, but never too late.

## 12
_____

The funeral of Maria Argüello would be the talk of the county for years, but Xavier couldn't wait to get rid of the houseful of well-wishers, still talking and sharing stories, so he and Aleksandra could grieve for the woman who had given her life for him.

His tears had flowed for hours over the past week. They still returned when he least expected it—looking at her what-not in the corner with its tiny Spanish figurines, her sewing basket, her handwoven shawl, his horse. He shook his head. Even when he was only a young boy, his mother had already instilled in him her unique way with horses.

"I cannot bear another moment of this," he whispered into Aleksandra's hair when he caught her in the kitchen. He pulled her into the pantry and closed the door.

"It will soon be over." She pulled his head down and kissed him deeply. "Maria was well-loved. Her friends want to be sure you know how much they care about both you and her," she said against his lips.

"I just want to be away." He kissed her on the forehead and held her hard against him.

"Away, we will be, and soon." She bit her lip. "Thankfully, Skinner is a gentleman, despite his drunken visit that first morning. He apologized profusely the other day when he was here. He said he won't be drinking for awhile, if ever, after he was kissed by your fist—more than I can say for your brother, I'm afraid, but we can do little for him now."

"Skinner didn't have to offer us the use of the *rancho* for six months. I sure appreciate that," Xavier said, with the hint of a smile, "especially after his welcome in the hallway."

"I'm grateful to Mama for encouraging us to go to New Zealand," she said. "It was like being thrown a rope in a rough sea. She was right. All the people around Rancho de las Pulgas overwhelm me."

"We can create a place of peace for our family in New Zealand. It's meant to be vast."

"All I ask is a chance to start anew in a peaceful country, away from all this death and destruction."

They were silent for a moment.

"Have you found out when the barque is to sail?" she asked. Her lovely blue eyes shone with such trust, he felt inadequate to the task of creating this new life, but he'd give it everything he had, with all his heart.

"Captain Rach said we sail in late August. We have plenty of time."

"August will come sooner than we think." She pulled his hips to hers and leaned back, their eyes locked together.

"Mama and Melissandra," Xavier gulped, squeezing her tightly again, "they'll forever be in our hearts, but we're ready to move on to a place we can call home."

She nodded. "But for now, let's go give Mama's guests the sendoff she would have done." Aleksandra smiled through her tears and hugged him close one more time before they emerged to face the crowd.

"A FINE LOT of horses and cattle you have here, Xavier." Josh Skinner scanned the herd of cows before him. "I'd be pleased to buy any animals you wish to sell. You just name your price."

"Now that I've been to your ranch and seen how you keep your stock," Xavier sighed, "I'm relieved to know you're buying them. I'm also pleased they'll stay on the *rancho* they've always known, especially the horses."

"I don't imagine that gray Spanish horse would be for sale?" Skinner raised an eyebrow over laughing eyes. "Just kidding. I know what he means to you. I'd sure like some of his get, though. Those horses you brought back from Utah on your last trip would suit me just fine."

"Charro over Doc Faust's Thoroughbred mares gave us some stunning foals," Xavier nodded, "but they won't come cheap."

"I've seen the sale list you made up and I'm prepared to pay." He took a deep breath, hesitated for a moment, then went on. "Xavier, you're taking this whole ordeal like the man your father was. He would have been proud of you."

"You knew my father?" Xavier glanced up as tears filled his eyes. He shook his head. This was happening all too often for his liking.

"Yes, I was just a bit younger than you are now when I worked for him on this very *rancho*, before I left for the gold fields."

Skinner blurred before his eyes. "Sorry," Xavier said, as he wiped his eyes.

"No need, no need. You've both had a rough time of it lately. You're not half as sorry as I am." Josh put an arm over his shoulder and they walked toward the broodmare pasture. "Your Papa was a good man, and fair. I've tried to follow his example in my life, but I will forever regret my part in your mother's death." He shook his head and closed his eyes.

"Her heart was not good, you know that." Xavier said, and looked away.

"I also realize I'm taking your birthright, but as you've told me, this place is too crowded for you and that lovely little woman of yours. You both need some time away, and an adventuresome life for awhile yet. There was too much unhappiness for you here with your abominable stepfather and the loss of your firstborn, as well as your mother. We won't even discuss your youngest brother. Money will be no object. I'll do right by you with the stock from this place and any farm implements and equipment you care to let go my way. I can help you invest it, so you always have a springboard and money to educate the many young ones you're sure to have." He dropped his arm from Xavier's shoulders.

Xavier turned to face him and clasped his hand. The older man clapped him on the shoulder as they turned and walked into the horse barn to view the rest of the stock.

A feminine shriek came from the front of the house. They exchanged a glance and bolted toward the house.

Xavier ran around the corner of the barn in time to see Aleksandra leap into a familiar wagon beside two mounted riders and throw her arms around…Tatiana!

"It looks like you have company, so I'll just leave you to it and return tomorrow?" Skinner shook his hand and turned to go.

"Thank you for coming by, sir. We'll speak tomorrow," Xavier said, as the new owner of de las Pulgas turned toward his horse in the barn, and he hurried on to meet their guests.

⌒

"Nikolai, how you've grown!" Aleksandra said, hopping off the cart to greet Tatiana and Vladimir's son. The young man slid from his horse and picked her up in a bear hug.

Xavier reached the mob as Vladimir dismounted. He reached for his hand.

"Xavier, what's this I hear in town about you two leaving for New Zealand?"

Xavier frowned, then he hugged his friend and clapped him across the back. "Quite a few changes around here, but I suspect it'll all be for the best." Xavier tried to smile as he made his way to the wagon and helped Tatiana down. The dogcart, which actually belonged to Aleksandra and her papa, was drawn by two chestnuts and loaded to within an inch of its life, piled high with belongings. Vladimir must have adapted it with a singletree, so two horses could pull it instead of one.

"You took that over the Sierras?" Aleksandra's mouth dropped open.

"The southern road around Lake Bigler through Placerville is much easier than the northern route you took." Tatiana smiled.

"What have you brought? The whole cabin?"

"You'd be surprised," the Russian woman said, and raised a brow at Xavier.

"Miguel, please meet our old friends: Tatiana, Vladimir and their son Nikolai. Would you please see their horses are put up?" Aleksandra asked.

"I'll help, Aleks," Nikolai said. "You just take Mama and Papa in with you."

Aleks and Tatiana shared a glance and a smile. The boy was indeed growing up.

"Come on in," Aleksandra said, as she led them onto the porch and into the house.

"What possessed you to leave this beautiful *rancho* and go to New Zealand, of all places?" Vladimir said, his brow furrowed.

Xavier gripped Aleksandra's hand tightly and told them. "And so," Xavier said, when he'd finished the story and taken the last sip of his *mocha Mexicano*, "we take ship soon. I can't say how glad I am you showed up before we left."

"We sure are, too," Nikolai piped in. He'd slipped into the room a few minutes before and heard the last of the story.

"I wish I could still offer you a place on Rancho de las Pulgas," Xavier said, "but it's no longer ours. I could speak with the new owner, if you wish. He's a good man and was a friend of my real father."

"Our thanks, but it is not necessary," Vladimir said. "We are going north to a settlement on the coast. It was a Russian Fort until twenty years ago, but some of the settlers chose to stay when the fort was sold."

"It sounds lovely, it's right on the sea. Some friends I met on my trip here from Russia live there now." Tatiana gave them a wistful smile. "It'll be like a little bit of home, albeit warmer and with more freedom."

"I wish we had time to see it before we leave, but we leave soon."

"Don't remind me," Xavier said, wincing. "I have far too much to do before we leave."

"We're just glad we caught you," Tatiana said, and hugged Aleksandra to her side, seated beside her on the wooden bench in the comfortable old farmhouse kitchen. "We will only stay a few days to help you if we can, and then we'll be on our way north."

"I'm just so glad we were able to see you before we left," Aleksandra said again, and gave Tatiana another hug.

"Xavier," Aleksandra called, "Mr. Fraser is here."

"I'll be right there," he said, shaking the water from his hands at the pump beside the porch. Aleksandra handed him a towel and he grabbed her hand and pulled her toward him for a kiss. "Nearly there, *Querida*. We're nearly done."

"Can't be soon enough for me," she said, shaking her head.

"Are you still happy with our decision about our *sirvientes*?"

"More sure than sure can be." She reached up and kissed him again, then preceded him through the front door.

The lawyer sat at the kitchen table, his papers already spread out around him. He stood at their entrance and shook Xavier's hand. "Mr. Argüello, thank you for coming in during the middle of the day, especially during this busy time of year," he said.

"I'm glad you could make it out here," Xavier said. "You have the stock sale contracts for Mr. Skinner drawn up?"

"I do, ready for you to sign," he said, peering at him over his glasses.

Xavier slid onto the bench opposite and took the sheaf of papers. He was one page through it when the lawyer sat up straight and looked at Xavier and Aleksandra, a frown on his face.

"I don't seem to see, however, a list of the indentured and apprenticed Indian servants. Mr. Skinner was asking about them yesterday. He wondered how much you wanted for their contracts. Are they to remain on Rancho de las Pulgas or do you intend to sell their papers elsewhere?"

Xavier and Aleksandra looked at each other in silence.

Mr. Fraser's eyebrows shot up.

"You have itemized them, haven't you?"

Xavier shook his head.

"But those indentures are worth a lot of money. Surely you've considered that?" Fraser said, as if speaking to small children. "You've lost enough money out of this farce of a land transaction, thanks to your sainted brother. The sale of the indentures and those of the apprentices would go a long way to helping you both get a new start. You can't mean to just leave them for nothing on the *rancho* for Skinner?"

"Actually, that wasn't our intent, sir," Xavier said.

The lawyer's brow furrowed and he looked at him sideways. "What *is* it, then? Because I cannot see any other choice."

"Aleksandra and I have discussed this at length," said Xavier, "and given our abhorrence of slavery, which is what these forced indentures and apprenticeships truly are, we see another choice entirely."

Fraser's jaw dropped and he could only stare.

"We require you to draw up letters for each servant. Here's the list," Xavier took the list from Aleksandra and handed it to him, "detailing that their indentures and apprenticeships have been fulfilled in their entirety with no exchange of money by any parties."

"But..." Mr. Fraser had no words for a moment, then he found them, in earnest, "but those contracts are worth a small fortune, and the government doesn't believe the natives can govern themselves, which is why they support—"

"—Mr. Fraser," Aleksandra cut in, "do you wish to draw up the papers or shall we find another solicitor?"

The man went white as a sheet and stared at the long list of men, women and children before him.

"These *people*, I prefer to think of them as *people*, Mr. Fraser," Xavier enunciated every word, "are essentially slaves. While some were born on this *rancho*, most were kidnapped from their families and forced to become slaves for decades."

"But Xavier," the lawyer tried again, "you must realiz—"

"—Mr. Fraser, this is the end of the discussion. Do you wish to draw up the papers or shall we find someone else?"

He closed his eyes and took a deep breath, his hands shaking. "Yes, Mr. Argüello," he whispered.

"She looks a strong ship." Aleksandra said to Captain Rach, as he prepared to lower the ramp for them to enter the hold. "It'll be a long trip for the stock, but it's for the best."

He pulled the lever releasing the winch and the ramp slowly moved downwards, ropes creaking as they unwound. "We can carry feed and water to accommodate the eight horses and dozen beasts for the time of the trip and then some. Yours will be the only stock on board," he said, as he watched the ropes.

Aleksandra inspected the tie stalls in the hold, stamping on the floorboards to assure herself of their condition. "Brilliant, sir. There's plenty of room for our stock. They'll do fine down here," she said, as they climbed back up the ramp to the deck. "We chose the *Emmeline* specifically because of her ramp setup—so the horses can be walked on the deck for exercise—and because you came so highly recommended."

"Thank you," Rach said. "Your husband was most particular about the horse quarters and access. He said it would matter to you."

She smiled. "The horses and stock will certainly be happier with ramps than with harnesses," she said. "It will be easier for everyone."

"I'm looking forward to having you and Mr. Argüello on board for the trip," he said. "You'll be the only immigrant family. This trip is mostly cargo to supply the colonies."

"Do you know when we're to leave San Francisco?"

"I'll send a barge to the Redwood City docks to pick up your stock and goods in three weeks, on the Monday." He ran his fingers through his hair, biting his lip. "I might be able to get the *Emmeline* into the deep water channel at Redwood Creek, but I suspect she might not come out in one piece, so we'll have to load everything twice, sorry." He took a deep breath and shook his head. "We'll transfer everything from the barge to the *Emmeline* back here in San Francisco."

"We wouldn't expect you to take that sort of a chance." Aleksandra said. "The stock will be waiting in the corrals near the Redwood City docks. You'll send word if you're delayed?"

"Of course, Mrs. Argüello," he said, as he took her hand to assist her across the gangplank. "Oh, one last thing," he turned to her and spoke across the ramp. "I'm an abstentionist, and the crew will be allowed no alcohol of any sort, whether as ale, porter, spirits or otherwise, including laudanum. I would appreciate it if you do not supply them with any. I will not put this restriction upon you and Xavier, but I require your word that you will not provide it to any of the men."

"Xavier doesn't drink alcohol and neither do I," she said, "so we'll have no problem with that, and won't be bringing any on board."

"That is as it should be. Thank you," he said, with a smile.

"Until then, Captain Rach." She nodded to him and walked along the dock in search of her wagon.

"Clumsy oaf!" An unnervingly familiar voice came from the other side of a wagon as she walked past. "Take better care of her case, damn you! If I wasn't in a hurry, I'd string you up and use you for target practice," the man menaced.

*Cole Younger*. It had to be. There was no one meaner than he, it was reckoned. She pulled the brim of her bonnet further forward over her face and slipped her braid underneath the shawl covering her plain cotton gown. She kept her head down and walked faster. She tripped over an uneven cobble in the road beside the wharf and began to fall forward, her feet tangling in her petticoats. Her heart was in her throat when someone grabbed her roughly by the arm.

## 13

"Oh, missy, let me help you." The voice chilled her to the bone. "Up you get!"

Aleksandra's heart plummeted at the sight of his boots and buckskins. It was indeed Cole Younger. She daren't look up.

"Cole, where've ya gone? My new hatbox is in the mud! Oh there ya are. Who's that yer talkin' to?" a woman's shrill voice demanded.

"Thank you, my mother is waiting," Aleksandra whispered in a tiny voice, picked up her skirts and scurried off, not looking back. She ducked into the next side street and ran as fast as her legs would carry her until she reached the milliners shop. She needed to visit it today, anyway. Better yet, it was one place a man like Cole would never be found.

Aleksandra took a breath to compose herself before she entered the open door.

"Oh, and you should have seen the money he had in his pouch!" the blonde shop girl, ringlets peeking coyly from beneath her bonnet, said to a woman standing before a counter full of gloves. "And he said she could have whatever hat she wanted, but I suppose that's because he's practically bought her from a Pacific Avenue saloon owner, down on the Barbary Coast." She jumped and spun around when she realized a customer stood waiting near the door.

Aleksandra smiled at her.

"Good afternoon, madam. How may I help you?" the blonde smiled, an overly large smile that didn't quite reach her eyes.

"Good afternoon, I'd like to look at your hardiest hats, both for myself and my husband. We're emigrating to New Zealand."

She showed her the range and Aleksandra selected two felt work hats for Xavier, several work sunbonnets, two straw hats for gardening and a beautiful headpiece that made her feel like a real lady—all felt, feathers and veil. She finished her order with a fine silk top hat, charcoal, to accent Xavier's dark coloring.

"Good choices." The shop girl nodded. Her smile was genuine now, and somehow calculating. "The shop owner will be back soon, but I can measure you now." She whipped out a knotted string and took several measurements of Aleksandra's head, marking them down in a book. "Do you have the measurements for your husband's hats?"

"No, I'm sorry, I don't, but he has purchased here before, Xavier Argüello?"

The girl gulped. "Um, Mrs. Argüello," she managed, "from Rancho de las Pulgas? Ahem. Yes, we'll have the whole family's measurements. One moment please." She scurried back with a black book and checked Xavier's measurements. "Yes, all here, and Xavier's measurements are current, thank you."

"Yes, he came in a month ago to be measured. When shall I call to pick them up?"

"They should all be ready in four weeks."

Aleksandra blinked and took a deep breath. "I'm afraid we need them before that. Our ship leaves three weeks from today."

She considered for a moment. "They'll be ready. Can you call to pick them up here?"

"Yes, but we'll be quite busy," she said, counting out the necessary coin. "Perhaps you could deliver them to Captain Rach of the *Emmeline*? We sail with him."

"Thank you. They will be there," the attendant said, as she glanced down at the counter and turned away, a secretive little smile on her face.

ALEKSANDRA TOOK another street back to the wharf and looked carefully up and down the docks to ensure Cole was gone. Her wagon, already filled with goods she'd picked up earlier in the day, stood where she'd left it and the big bay cart horse slept between his shafts. She slipped the feedbag from his nose, untied him and climbed up onto the box. With another surreptitious look around, she turned him and they headed for home at a good trot, slowing to a walk once they were out of town.

She kept an eye out for the outlaw and his cronies all the way home. She shivered at the thought of how close she'd come to real danger.

Xavier was grooming a young colt in the barn, singing to him in Spanish. The colt's near ear was tipped back, his eyes half closed. He jumped when Aleksandra came around the corner, but quieted quickly and nosed towards her as she neared him.

"Good trip?" Xavier smiled at her.

Together they'd begun to smile again. Life was beginning to hold hope once more and they anticipated their trip with excitement as the sailing date neared.

"It was good until the end. The ship is most satisfactory. I like the captain and the tie stalls are big enough for the horses." She took a deep breath. "Had a scare, though."

Xavier lifted an eyebrow, his head cocked, and waited.

"Cole Younger."

"In San Francisco?" Xavier growled low.

"Yes." She bit her lip, then told him of the encounter. "I should've taken someone with me, but it's such a busy time of year. I didn't want to take anyone off the place just for a drive to San Francisco."

He put his brush down and they moved away from the tied colt. His arms held her snugly, his body firm and hard against hers. "We're not leaving a moment too soon." He shook his head and looked her in the eyes. "He's a bad one. Every day, I'm more glad we're leaving. We have no reason to stay and every reason to go."

"I'd like to have a home, but a bit of an adventure sounds good right now, as long as it's far away from Younger." She hugged him tight, inhaling his scent along with the beloved smell of horse and let it calm her soul. "Have you chosen which stock we're to take?" Aleksandra looked up at him and leaned back against the stable wall.

"Of course, we'll take Charro, Dzień and Rogan, plus we'll need two of the heavier workhorse geldings and our five best broodmares. That makes ten, instead of the original eight we discussed, but we'll need them. For cattle, six cows, two with bull calves, and one bull. With the two stallions and five mares, it'll be a noisy trip, but they're as fine a lot of stock as will be found in New Zealand and probably better than most.

Their get will pay for us to set ourselves up many times over, all going to plan."

She glanced at the open stable door and returned her gaze to his face, then her fingers slowly found the buttons of his shirt and began to unbutton them, one by one, her gaze holding his.

His eyes smoldered, the golden flecks in the brown brightening as his eyes blackened with desire. He pulled her to him and crushed her mouth beneath his as they slid down the wall to the soft, thick straw beneath their feet.

SKINNER'LL BE poor for most of his life, with the prices he paid for the stock and the farm implements, much less the household goods," Xavier said, and chuckled.

"Feeling guilty for taking the *rancho* and helping Mama from this world? He did get the place for a song." Aleksandra's lips twisted into a wry grin. "His fortune from the gold fields is legendary, and I understand he's quite the businessman. I wouldn't worry too much about him. Plus, he doesn't have to purchase the *sirvientes* contracts, though he'll spend plenty for their wages."

"True. You've picked all you want from the house?"

"Already sorted and in trunks, ready to go on the barge next week. The farm and horse gear?"

"I'm keeping what we're taking in one stall, but we need to use most of it until we go." He lifted her fingers to his lips and kissed them. "We'll be away before you know it."

"The shoemaker delivered the boots and shoes yesterday." Aleksandra stroked the hair back from his forehead with her free hand.

"I know." His brows drew together. "I just paid his bill. What were they made from, gold?"

Aleksandra laughed. "Enough boots and shoes to last us for five years are bound to cost a bit, sorry. Our priest sent me the list that they give to the missionary ladies. You'd be astonished." She shook her head.

"Like what?" His brow furrowed.

"Aprons, petticoats, skirts, dresses, stockings, hats, shoes, trousers, shirts, jackets, bed sheets—enough of everything to last for three to five years. Do you have any idea what that pile would look like?"

Xavier's brows lowered now and he bit his lip.

"Don't worry, I can sew what we need. We're bringing plenty of calico, linen and wool, but the shoes we buy. You picked up the extra wheels, harnesses and leather oil? I hear it rains a lot."

He nodded. "The mud on the roads is legendary," he sighed, "but I hear there's always grass for the stock to eat, so one balances the other, I suppose."

"A bit different from Utah." She grinned. "An inch of rain there causes flash floods."

"We might need to grow webbed feet," he said, with a smile.

THE STOCK LOWED in their pens alongside the Redwood Creek Wharf and the horses moved impatiently, tugging on their leadropes. The Argüello's big wagon stood nearby, its tarp covering the plow and the other farm implements. The gig was packed tightly with Aleksandra's and Xavier's most important personal goods, ready to accompany them to their new country.

"What's under the tarp in the wagon?" Aleksandra asked.

"Some timber I thought we'd need," Xavier said, and looked away. "Do you have everything you need?

"Timber? You can't be serious. Doesn't New Zealand have trees?" Aleksandra stared at him.

"It's special wood," he said. "Are the horses ready?"

"Yes. This trip isn't going to be much fun for the horses or the stock." Aleksandra scrunched up her face.

"At least we can walk the horses around the decks. It's the cows and bulls I'm sorry for. They'll have to stay below," Xavier said.

"I brought all the bottles of lemon syrup I made this year, thanks to Mrs. Weeks' recipe, enough to last all year for the whole *hacienda*." She grinned. "We shouldn't get scurvy, anyway. For the first time, we'll be able to drink as much of it as we want."

When the barge docked beside them, all hands from the *rancho* jumped to it. The animals were soon loaded and the gig and wagon were stowed. They'd left just enough room on the box of each vehicle to drive it away when they got to the other side of the Pacific.

"Looks like that's it, only our trunks for the journey left to load," Xavier said, reaching out to shake Skinner's hand. "I thank you for making this as painless as possible, Josh."

"And we sure appreciate your willingness to employ the free *sirvientes* who've lived on the *rancho* most of their lives." Aleksandra smiled, as Skinner bowed over hers.

"Least I can do, under the circumstances. Thank you both for the stock and your good wishes. I'll do my best by your people." Skinner looked down at his feet for a moment. "Again, Xavier, your father would've been proud to see the man you've become. I wish you two the best in your new life. Stay well and Godspeed."

"Thank you, and goodbye, Mr. Skinner," Aleksandra said, as he turned to go.

Aleksandra and Xavier stopped and looked at the crowd of their old *sirvientes*—more family than servants—from the *rancho*.

"How do you say goodbye to your family?" Xavier said to the assembled people. "We love you and hope everything goes well for you in your lives, and…" Xavier and Aleksandra both melted down. They all hugged and cried until the captain of the barge yelled to say it was time to leave.

"I'll see you in New Zealand! Remember to write to tell me where I can find you," Molly shouted, as the ropes were thrown off and the barge slipped into the stream and away, bound for San Francisco.

They held each other beside the rail, saying goodbye to places they might never see again on the short trip north. Xavier pointed out landmarks and told stories. Before they knew it, Alcatraz Island showed on their right and then they were docking beside the *Emmeline* on one of the San Francisco wharfs.

The men of the barque knew their jobs and soon the horses, stock, and conveyances were stored below deck.

"I can't believe how easy that was, with the internal ramps," Aleksandra said.

"Me either," Xavier said. "I've never seen a ship loaded so fast."

Captain Rach appeared at Aleksandra's elbow. "Mrs. Argüello, my men are ready to carry your trunks on board," he said. "Let me show you to your cabin and you can tell them where you wish them stowed."

Aleksandra followed him through a labyrinth to their stateroom.

"The milliners brought a box for you yesterday," Captain Rach said, as he unlocked the door and gave her the key. "They said you were expecting it." He pointed out a large carton sitting on the bed.

Aleksandra thanked him as he left the cabin. She took just a moment to open the box and see how the hats had turned out. Unfortunately, her lovely headdress was not included. She mentally calculated the time until their departure.

"All ready to go?" Xavier said, when she found him down below.

"The milliners left something out of our order," she shouted, over the sound of the lowing cows he was settling into the hold. "I'll return in five minutes."

"We sail as soon as the trunks are loaded," he called after her and spun around to avoid a frightened cow, about to crush him against the railing.

"I can make it if I leave right now" she said, and bolted for the gangplank, dodging the men carrying their last trunk.

Aleksandra ran as fast as her feet would carry her and soon gained the shop. She took a breath to still her pounding heart before she reached for the door handle.

"Your lady's hat will be ready in just a moment, sir," the shop girl said, as Aleksandra stepped into the shop. It was the same girl who'd taken her order. "Excuse me," Aleksandra said, "but the felt hat with the veil doesn't appear to be in the box delivered to the ship."

"I'll look for it after I finish with my other customer." She looked away from Aleksandra.

"I'm sorry, but our sailing is imminent, and I have to be on board for the change in the tide. Would you please look now?"

She heaved a great sigh and looked under the bench before her. "Here it is, don't know how I missed it. My mistake," she said, as she slapped it down on the bench. Nothing about her demeanor said apology. Nothing at all.

"Thank you." Aleksandra raised her eyebrow at the girl and turned from the counter, heading for the door, then her breath caught and she froze.

To the side of the door on a chaise lounge sat a man with a bandaged right hand. Cole Younger's "lady" was draped over him, her hands inside his shirt, but his eyes were on Aleksandra as she headed for the exit. His brows were drawn together, his lips tight, but in a flash, recognition dawned and his expression changed. And not for the better.

She fled for the ship, her heart in her mouth.

# 14

Xavier waited on the dock with a grin across his face, as Aleksandra ran toward him.

"You're quick, *Querida*, but you know I'd wait for you forever," he said, reaching for her.

"No, we've got to go," she gasped, clinging to him as she bent double to get her breath. "Younger, Cole Younger. He recognized me. He's coming, I think." She took his hand and pulled him to the gangplank.

"Captain!" Xavier shouted, "we've got to leave. Long story, but it involves one of the Younger brothers."

"Leaving as we speak." The captain was as good as his word. He whistled to the tugboat captain and his sailors hustled to pull in the gangplank. The ropes attached to the screw-propelled tug tightened and they slowly pulled away from the dock. A minute later, the stream of the outgoing tide surged beneath them and the towboat threw off their ropes as the clipper picked up speed. From the dock came shouting and the sound of pistol fire.

"Get down!" shouted Captain Rach, as a ball punched a hole in a sail.

Behind the ship's solid bulwark, Aleksandra lay against her husband and closed her eyes, shaking her head.

"Guess you'll be doing some sewing." Xavier grinned down at her. "Can't leave you alone for a minute, can I?"

"This one wasn't of my making, *Querido*." She shot him a look. "I guess I didn't really need the hat, on second thought," she said, then laughed. "Look, I still have it! I don't even remember carrying it. I just ran. Truth be told, I probably just didn't want the snooty shop girl to keep it."

A few more pistol balls struck the hardwood side of the clipper, but even those stopped as they drew further away. They got to their feet to look over the rail at San Francisco, slipping into the distance. She tried not to think about Sancho in his barred home as the Presidio reared up, high on the cliffs to their left. The fort's adobe walls shone white in the sun as they picked up speed, slipping out the narrow mouth of the San Francisco Bay and into the open sea, heading for a new life.

"Eh, missy," the scarred seaman looked at her sideways, his eyebrows raised, as he moved toward her in the narrow passageway, "ain't seen you on board befo'," he said.

"We just boarded today." Aleksandra backed out of his way and glanced over her shoulder for the safest way out.

"Bound to see mo' of each other. It'll be a long trip." He looked her up and down, with a glint in his eye.

"Yes, it will be a long trip. My husband and I will no doubt be seeing more of you." Her heart thudded in her chest as she spun and ran back the way she'd come, his low laughter following her until she turned the corner and shot into the door of their compact, tightly-filled cabin with its narrow bed.

Xavier lay back on the bed, his eyes closed. As she quietly shut the door behind her and slid the bolt home, his eyes opened, one brow raised.

"Locking the door so soon, *mi querida*?" he grinned, his eyes slowly perusing her.

"There's a man, one of the crew," she took a deep breath and sat on the bed beside him. "He stood in the passageway before me and was looking me over and saying how we're bound to see "mo' of each other" on this long trip," she shuddered.

"It'll be OK. I'll make sure the Captain tells his crew that you're taken, and that I'm on board." He pulled her down and kissed her thoroughly, then rolled over and looked down at her. "Are you all right? Your heart's pounding in your chest," he said, his brows nearly touching. "Did he touch you?"

"No."

"Does he think you're traveling alone?"

"No, I told him my husband was with me, and all he did was laugh, as I bolted."

"I'm sure it'll be fine. I'll speak with the captain as soon as I see him, OK? Let's go below and check on the horses."

She sighed and followed him out the door, glancing furtively in both directions as they left the stateroom.

"They're surprisingly relaxed for their first day at sea," Aleksandra nodded at the horses, munching their supper.

"The cows act like they've been eating hay in these stanchions all their lives." Xavier said.

"The bulls, however," said Captain Rach, who had walked up behind them, "are less than impressed."

The great hairy beasts tugged at their ropes, ignoring the feed before them.

"They'll get over it," Xavier said. "Everything going to plan, captain?"

"Yes, other than an unusually rapid exit from the dock at San Francisco," he raised an eyebrow at Aleksandra, his lips turned up at the ends, "all's well."

"Captain, I was wondering if we might have a private word with you?" Xavier said.

"Come on up to my cabin, we can speak there." The gray-haired man nodded his head toward the stairs.

Xavier turned to face Captain Rach as he locked the door of his stateroom behind them. "I don't mean to cause trouble this early in the trip, but Aleksandra took a fright from one of your seamen today."

"Which man, Mrs. Argüello?" His brows drew together.

"Please, call me Aleksandra," she said. "I'm sorry, but I don't know his name. He has a long scar down one side of his face." She told him about the encounter.

The captain's face darkened as she spoke.

Aleksandra cringed. This mightn't have been a good idea.

"I think I know of whom you speak. He's a friend or relative of my first mate. In the past, the mate was always a discerning character, but I believe his judgment might be a bit flawed in this acquaintance." His brows nearly touched now, his mouth set in a grim line.

"I'm sure it won't be a problem, but would you mind speaking with the man? Just to let him know we're on to him?" Xavier said.

"I'll speak with both him and my mate. Can't have you worried to walk about my ship." He smiled at Aleksandra and shook Xavier's hand. "Be sure I'll have that word with them tonight."

"Thank you, sir. I hope I'm imagining it," she said.

"It's no problem at all." He tried to smile, but his furrowed brow quite marred the effect.

FIRST MATE BROADHURST flicked his eyes sideways to the man standing beside him at the rail. "So, have you met the emigrants yet, Symes?"

"I've met the female, just now. She'll be a treat."

Broadhurst frowned. "She has a husband. He doesn't look to be one to take lightly to that."

Symes eyes narrowed until Broadhurst stepped back a pace. "Do we have a deal, or don't we? You'll be a rich man by the end of this, if you hold your end up."

"You know we do. I wouldn't have even taken this mate's position, otherwise. Could've stayed in San Francisco." Broadhurst looked away, his voice dwindling.

"And done what, pray tell?"

Broadhurst swung his eyes back to Symes. "There are still plenty of women looking for work. You must have an endless source of jobs for them."

The man's eyes glittered in his head. "That I do, that I do, but this will be more fun. And pay off big in the end."

Broadhurst's heart twinged a little. He'd never seen any of those women again, after he'd introduced them to Symes. He didn't really want to know where they'd gone to work. The little sideline, he squirmed, the only sideline... truthfully, the only *work* he'd done in the year since he'd met Symes, was supplying him with women seeking employment. Pretty women. He swallowed hard. He never got a regular job or worked on board ships anymore, until now. His wife had begun to nag at him, though the income was sufficient to pay for their rooms and food for the children. Just. But that was enough.

The mate looked around. They were still alone. "Symes, where did you find work for those women?"

"Never you mind about that." He said, his voice sharp. "You never worried about it before, did you?"

Broadhurst gritted his teeth, thinking of opium dens and cramped trips in the holds of ships to faraway ports.

"It's none of your concern, or maybe it is now," Symes said, from the corner of his mouth.

The mate took a deep breath and changed the subject. "I'll miss our little nightly sojourns on the Barbary Coast, and," he frowned, "the laudanum. Pity Rach won't even allow opium tincture because it contains alcohol."

Symes grinned. "You don't need the stuff."

"Good thing we won't, there isn't any on board."

"It was a good year while it lasted." Symes' mouth quirked.

"You and your little brown bottles," Broadhurst grinned. "Where did you get it? You seemed to have an inexhaustible supply."

"Bit of a British-American link. Old friends of my family. The Opium Cartel. They've got plenty to spare, with importing so much of it to supply the war effort," he smirked, "on both sides."

The mate blinked at that and sighed. "Guess they have to sell where they can make the money. I still wish I could have a tipple like the one you offered every evening," Broadhurst said, with a smile. His hands shook a little, as he tightened his grip on the gunwale and watched Fort Point disappear into the distance as they headed south along the coast from the Golden Gate.

THE SHORELINE STAYED within sight as the ship sailed on the California Current, its trade winds blowing them south at a good clip.

"Captain Rach, if New Zealand is so far south and west of us, why do we stick to the California coast?" Aleksandra said.

Rach looked toward the shore through his telescope and then turned the great wheel to change the barque's course. "With the winds and current in our favor, we can make New Zealand much faster than we ever could by forcing our way across the Pacific against other currents, tacking to make the barque go where we desire." He handed the telescope to Aleksandra

She looked through the long glass at the dense green vegetation of the shore. "What are those clusters of white near the shore?"

"Rocks. Mountain ranges just under the surface of the water. Maim a ship, if it doesn't sink it outright. We stay far away from them," he said, with a smile.

"Oh," Aleksandra took a deep breath and quickly handed the scope back to him. "How long do we follow this coastline?"

"While we go past California, then Mexico."

She frowned and glanced at the white water.

"I promise we'll stay away from the rocks, but the current is fastest near the shore. It'll get you to your new home faster."

"OK." Aleksandra shook her head at him. Unconvinced, she stared toward the frothy water, its underwater peaks lying in wait to grab the barque's hull.

"Just past the equator, we'll head straight west from South America on the South Equatorial Current. Its trade winds will carry us nearly all the way to New Zealand."

As children in a Polish *schlacta* household, Aleksandra's parents had received exceptional educations, ranging from classics, to languages, to warfare tactics. "My parents educated me well, but living in the middle of America, ocean currents weren't a top priority, I guess," she said, with a rueful grin.

He smiled at her. "The South Equatorial Current runs parallel to the equator, then curves south along the east coast of Australia to become the East Australian Current. Part of that runs toward New Zealand. If you'd like, after supper, you and Xavier may join me in my cabin and I'll show you a map of the currents."

"Thanks. That would make it more clear." She frowned again. "Where does it go after it runs into New Zealand?"

"Well, most of it runs east over the top of New Zealand, then south and down its East Coast."

"I'll wait and see your map tonight," she said, with a smile.

AT SUPPER THE FIRST NIGHT, Broadhurst grinned at Symes. "Nothing to this. I feel fine."

"That's good. Me, too. As I said, you'll do fine without the laudanum." His friend returned the look.

By morning, he was shaking and felt not at all good. The day was filled with jobs Rach wanted done immediately. By suppertime, his stomach churned and his face heated. He couldn't have eaten if he'd tried.

"What's the matter, Broadhurst?" Rach frowned. "Are you coming down with something?"

"Certainly not," he snapped, then pulled himself together. "I hope not, sir. Perhaps I'd best go lie down. I think I'll skip supper."

"Good idea. I'll see you in the morning," he said, and glanced back down at his charts. "Let me know if you need me to send the surgeon to you."

"Thank you, sir," he said, closing the door of the cabin behind him.

"How are you doing? Nice cabin you have here," Broadhurst said, when he found Symes in his cabin.

"A touch unsettled in the stomach, but you're not looking so good, my man."

"I'm not. I wish I had some laudanum. It always makes me feel better."

"Ah. You 'll feel better tomorrow. Why don't you go lie down?" he said, indicating his bunk.

Broadhurst swallowed. Surely he jested. They were good friends, but to lie in another man's bed?

"Go on, you look like you need a rest."

He closed his eyes, but all he could think of was the little bottle Symes usually carried in his coat pocket. His guts started to churn like they were full of serpents and he cried out before he thought.

"What's the matter, Broadhurst?" Symes said, from the table.

"I've got food poisoning or something."

"Hmmm. Maybe it's the lack of the laudanum. I thought you could do without it, you've only been sipping it for a year or so."

"Maybe not," Broadhurst said, with a groan. "And with bloody Rach being an abstentionist, looks like I won't be getting any."

"That's too bad, you just try to rest."

He turned back to the wall. He was soon doubled over with the cramping. Sweat dripped from his brow and cheeks. He struggled to his feet and staggered toward the chamber pot on the floor.

"You'll have to use the head," Symes said, his voice firm.

"But I don't think I can make it there," Broadhurst said, swallowing hard.

"Of course, you can," he said, and steered him out the door.

Somehow he made it there, emptied his guts from both ends and stumbled back to Symes' room. He should be heading for his own stateroom, but... he needed Symes. At least he'd understand, even if he wasn't sick from the lack of laudanum.

"Ah, see? I said you'd make it, didn't I?"

"Barely." Broadhurst bit his cheek to keep from swearing at the calm, collected man.

"Now you go and lie down again."

It seemed the thing to do.

He must have slept, because when he awoke, he was drenched in perspiration and he needed to vomit again, or have diarrhea, or both. He wasn't sure.

Symes came to his side. "Have you had enough?"

Broadhurst just closed his eyes and nodded. "Dying might be preferable right now, and it's getting worse."

"It's not even begun to get bad, my friend."

He flicked a glance up at him. "What?"

"You'll truly be wanting to die in the next few days."

Broadhurst could only stare.

"But I have a solution."

He narrowed his eyes at Symes. "What?" he said, as his bowels cramped again and he hunched into a tight ball. He heard Symes' voice as if from afar.

"I have a little bottle."

Broadhurst wrenched his head back to stare at him. "Seriously? Can I have some? Please?" he said.

"Well, now, my friend. That depends."

"Upon what?"

"Well, we're such good friends and all... and I'd like to make it... a bit more."

Broadhurst frowned. Certainly he couldn't mean...

Symes nodded. "How bad do you want that laudanum?"

His jaw dropped as it became clear.

Symes reached a hand to touch him on his cheek, then drew his fingers slowly down to the soft skin inside the open neck of his shirt.

Broadhurst shuddered, but wouldn't let himself draw away.

"There, now. That wasn't so bad, was it?"

"N-no," Broadhurst whispered, as the pains took him again.

The seaman drew his signature little brown bottle from inside his coat pocket and removed the cap.

The mate's teeth clattered on the spoon and he sucked greedily, afraid to spill a drop. One spoonful and he closed his eyes to wait. "How long will it take?" he groaned, as he tucked himself around his pitching belly.

"Give it a few minutes, then I'll teach you a few things you'll never forget," the seaman said, his voice soft, as he stroked Broadhurst's back and flanks.

SOMEWHERE OFF THE coast of Mexico, Aleksandra turned around and saw the seaman, Symes, she'd learned his name was, coiling a rope on the deck, but looking at her. She turned away, but not quickly enough to miss his raised eyebrows and his sharp gray eyes raking her from head to foot and back. Shuddering, her heart clenched in her chest, she spun back to face the captain, her hands clammy.

"What's the matter, girl?" Captain Rach glanced past her to where she'd been looking. Symes stared at her, but he was beyond reproach. He continued his work, never missing a beat. He looked the captain in the eye, one brow raised, his mouth in a sardonic grin.

"Good afternoon, cap'n. Passing the time of day with the ladies, I see?" He nodded in Aleksandra's direction, his gaze on her chest, then turned on his heel and disappeared.

Aleksandra closed her eyes and sank back against the wall behind her.

"He's gone," the captain said, giving her shoulder a little shake when she didn't move.

"It's unreasonable, I know, but he frightens me." She let out a long breath.

"I'll be keeping an eye out for you, but I'm wondering about my first mate too. He's gone a little strange on me. I don't normally encourage weaponry among my passengers, but do you have any way of protecting yourself?"

She glanced around, then pulled a short sword from a sheath beneath her shawl, and gave him a glimpse of two small daggers she was wearing.

"And yes, I can use them," she said, with a smile.

"I do believe you could."

"My papa taught me. He was Cossack-trained and made sure my brother and I could acquit ourselves well in any situation."

"I'll remember to watch my step. You might be good at my back in a difficult situation. Let's hope we don't have any on this trip." He pursed his lips and turned back to the wheel.

DESPITE LIVING in tie stalls below deck, the horses fared well on the ship.

Xavier joined her on the deck when she walked horses, two at a time, around the deck.

"They're calming down nicely, no more skittishness," Aleksandra said to him.

"It's good to see them settling into a good routine, after only a few weeks on board," he said.

"Symes is keeping his distance from me, but he still looks me up and down with a great leer on his face," she said, with a shudder.

Xavier was silent for a moment.

Aleksandra glanced at him. "What?"

"You're not...encouraging him, by any chance, are you?" Xavier ventured, his brow furrowed.

Aleksandra stopped like she'd been shot and stared at him.

"Well, he hasn't stopped, despite being told, under no uncertain terms, to leave a married woman alone," Xavier said, his jaw tight.

She spun on her heel, her lips gripped together, deigning to answer such a ridiculous question, and stalked off. The surprised horses scurried to keep up, ears back and tails swishing.

By bedtime, she'd still said not a word to him. She went to bed as soon as supper was finished, turned toward the wall.

Xavier lay down in the narrow bed beside her. "Aleksandra," he said.

She lay stiff, head turned away from him.

"Aleks."

"What do you want?"

"Have you? Encouraged him?"

She turned over and sat up beside him. "How could you even imagine such a thing? I want to be as far away from him as possible," she enunciated slowly and clearly, each word like a knife.

"I just can't understand why the men are saying he wants you for his own."

"He *what*?"

"That's what the men are saying. That he plans to leave this ship with you on his arm." Xavier looked away, and took a deep breath. "If you want him—"

She swung as hard as she could and the flat of her hand struck his cheek a loud slap. "I have never, *ever* given you reason to doubt me, my love for you, nor my commitment to our marriage," she snarled, her chest heaving, "and I have no plans to ever do so. I realize you have difficulty trusting anyone, but if you plan to continue to doubt me, seek a life with someone else."

He sat frozen, eyes wide, his hand over his reddening cheek.

She lay back down and turned away as Xavier got up from the bed.

A chair scraped next to the little table, tucked tightly into the tiny stateroom between the wall and their bed.

After an eternity, Xavier returned to their bed.

"I'm sorry, Aleksandra," he said into her hair, as he pulled her backwards against his front, his tall body curled around hers in an embrace. "You know I struggle, even now. For God's sake, I'm still jealous of Dancing Wolf, if you can believe that. I don't understand how you could ever love me. It takes ridiculously little for the demons in my head to convince me of things I want to believe cannot be true."

"I have done nothing to cause you pain," she whispered.

"I know," he groaned, "please help me believe it, and get rid of the voices threatening to engulf me tonight."

"Come here," she said, her heart aching, and she turned over to face him.

He captured her mouth with his, arms folding tightly about her, and they were lost in their embrace.

"I'm getting cabin fever," Aleksandra shook her head, "and we're not even halfway there yet."

"Why? You can go anywhere on the ship," Xavier looked sideways at her. "Other than leading the horses around on deck, you've just been staying in the hold with the animals or in our cabin. You can't still be worried about Symes," he said, his brows narrowed.

She looked at him, one eyebrow lifted.

"What could he do to you?"

"I don't know. He just scares me."

"Look, Aleks, the captain has already warned him off. I'll do the same as well, if you wish."

"No, just leave him. I'll stay out of his way."

"You've got your *shashka* and knives?"

"Never leave my side," she said, patting the voluminous folds of her skirt.

"Let's go for a walk on the deck," Xavier said. "I'm told we should soon be seeing marlin. Have you ever seen one?"

"I've heard of them," she said, "but they don't frequent the waterways I used to fish."

"You lived in a desert," he said, shaking his head.

"Some seamen were talking of catching one, the other day.".

"I'd hate to catch one, but they'd feed the ship for a week."

"What's so special about them?"

"An old seamen told me they travel thousands of miles. They're deep blue on top, with a silvery belly, and have a spear on their nose. They can weigh several tons."

"They sound like they work too hard to kill them," she frowned, "but then I think most animals are too special to kill—I do it anyway, to eat."

"They're pretty hard to pull in. They fight for a long time."

"Maybe we won't catch any."

"I love the way you care for animals." Xavier smiled.

"You're just the same," she said, and hugged him. "Can we fish, anyway?"

"Yes. Shall we try for our supper?"

"I'd love it." She smiled up at him and he leaned down to kiss her.

"I'll go see Captain Rach about some fishing gear while you have a seat in the sun. You've grown pale," he said, as he led her to a seat on a sail storage box and turned away to seek the captain.

ROD IN HAND and wind blowing through her curling blonde tresses, she had to be the most beautiful thing he'd ever seen. She'd obviously tried to contain the blonde tresses in the long braid that fell far past the exquisite derriere which was, unfortunately, hidden beneath her skirts. He scowled and rubbed the long scar on his face, cursing its presence. He couldn't wait much longer to see what other treasures lay in wait for him.

He hadn't seen the likes of her since he'd left England. The debutantes and their fathers had tired of his somewhat different tastes in sexual preferences, so he'd left, in rather a hurry. Now he was at leisure to seek and sample available wares…and to pass them on to his wealthy clients in the Near East when he tired of them. At least three of the sultans he regularly supplied would bid strongly for the pleasure of adding her to their harems after, he grinned, he taught her a thing or two. His lordly parents had paid him off to leave the country, but that was nearly gone, and he needed to supplement his income.

It was lucky she had the care of the horses. He watched her daily, as she strode over the decks as freely as a man. He would soon change that. She wouldn't be able to walk much at all, for quite some time. That is, if he ever untied her from his bed, much less let her out of his cabin. He couldn't wait to get out of the disgusting seaman's disguise he'd affected on this trip, but getting caught was not part of his plans. He fully intended to enjoy his life to the fullest, but that required the utmost in discretion and control over those who would seek to curtail his pleasures.

He sniffed, thinking of the dark one, husband to the golden angel. A minor affliction, soon remedied. He smiled, fingering the sword at his side.

# 15

The weeks passed as they sailed past the endless green jungle of the South American coast. The horses sniffed the breeze and walked eagerly, trying to trot when they were led up the ramp to the deck, sometimes whinnying towards the mountains on the horizon.

The day after they'd turned west away from the coast along the South Equatorial Current, Dzień looked about, turning his head from side to side, ears pricked, when he reached the deck. He became skittish and Aleksandra had difficulty holding the usually-calm animal.

"I don't think he likes not being able to see land," Aleksandra said. "We're heading for our new life, pony," Aleksandra said, looking up at the sails. They were rounded, fluffy as clouds, filled with the trade winds that drove the ship onward

They fished every day and supplied the boat with ample fresh fish and shark. Aleksandra collected several of the barbed shark teeth to keep.

"If you keep catching so many fish, I'll have to pay you for supplying the galley," Captain Rach said. His first mate, Broadhurst, looked their way, his eyes sunken in dark sockets. He glared, his mouth in a firm line, before turning his face away from them.

"Mr. Broadhurst, don't you like fish?" Aleksandra asked, to draw him into the conversation.

"Excuse me, Mrs. Argüello?" he turned to her, his lip lifted in a sneer.

"I asked if you liked fish." Aleksandra smiled at him.

The mate narrowed his brows at her, then placed a shaking hand onto the rail and gripped it tightly. "Never touch the stuff," he said, releasing the rail and turning unsteadily away from them.

Aleksandra, Xavier and the captain stared after him as he walked away toward the bows, where Symes sat on a coil of rope. Broadhurst stood beside the seaman. The mate's lips moved, his hands clasping the nearby balustrade, but his face looked out to sea.

Aleksandra lowered the corner of the sail she was mending onto the deck, jammed the needle with some force into the canvas, and turned her back on the pair in the bows of the ship. She faced the captain and Xavier. "Can either of you explain that one?" she said.

The captain took a deep breath and looked at Xavier and Aleksandra. "They're cooking something up between them, no doubt about it, and the mate's none too well. Wish I knew what was going on."

"Has he always been like this?" Xavier's brow was creased.

"He sailed with me for a decade until three years ago, when he said he wanted a life away from the sea. He was a good fellow, certainly more hale and hearty than he is now, with his hollow eyes. I thought he'd fallen upon hard times. He used to have a wife and child, but he's said naught of them since he sought me out a month ago in San Francisco and asked me to restore him to his old position."

"Does he take laudanum?" Xavier's brows lowered. "I know many take it as a tonic, but it seems to dissipate those who take it often."

"I don't know, but it could explain some of his behavior," Rach said, with a shake of his head.

"Some time ago, you mentioned Symes seemed to hold sway over him. Perhaps he can't do without it, and Symes holds the supply." Aleksandra lifted a brow at the men, then picked up the stiff fabric again.

"He shouldn't have any supply at all, on my ship, and they both know it," Rach growled.

Aleksandra raised a brow at him and took a deep breath. She turned her attention back to the sail before her. "Captain, I've sewn more than my share of harness, but the holes were punched," she said, with a frown, "unlike your canvas. One of your men gave me this seaming palm," she held it up for him to see, and it flopped around her hand, "but it's a little big for me."

Xavier and Rach chuckled.

"That sailor's palm is twice the size of *your* palm," Xavier said.

"Between the palm and the canvas, I'm finding this hard work," she said.

"That's why we use a fid," Rach said, and pulled a long, pointed piece of bone from his belt. She grinned and took the tool from him.

"This helps," she said, as she twisted it into a small hole. In short order, it was expanded to the right size.

"You don't have to do this, you know," Rach said. "You have enough to do, both of you, just taking care of the stock."

"It wouldn't do to let me get bored," Aleksandra said.

"I promise you, captain, you wouldn't want to see it, it's not pretty," Xavier agreed, with a smile.

"Mr. Broadhurst," Symes muttered across the galley table, at the far end from where the captain sat with the angel and her dark consort, "be so good as to pass the salt."

"Symes, I am nearly out of the last bottle you gave me."

"Pass the salt, if you please, my good man." He raised a brow at the captain's second in command.

The first mate's hand shook as he lifted the bowl of salt. It fell to the table with a crash, the tiny willow spoon and pieces of the cut glass bowl scattered among the salt crystals on the table. All eyes turned toward him.

"A little accident," Symes said, almost gaily. He swept the lot onto a plate and placed it beside his bowl of chowder.

"I'm getting a little clumsy." Broadhurst's voice shook as much as his hands.

"You must be more careful," Symes said, in a low voice. "Someone might start to think you aren't capable of your duties." He lifted his brow at him and shook his head. "Now where were we? Did you say you needed another bottle?"

"Yes." Broadhurst gulped.

"Hmmm… but you just got one last week."

"It's nearly gone. It's all I can think of when I lie down to sleep." His voice raised as he spoke. "I cannot sleep—"

"Shut up, you idiot," Symes growled. "You know what you need to do to get more, don't you?" He smiled darkly at the blond man, who blushed pink and looked at the table. "Come, come, it's not that bad! Cheer up. Tonight you'll have another bottle. Just remember your promise. I'll take a little in payment from you tonight, but I will have her, and with your help." He laughed out loud at the first mate, who stared into his untouched bowl.

ᕀ

THE SALT BOWL shattered with a loud crash, spilling its contents before Broadhurst and Symes.

Broadhurst shook, his face red and sweaty, despite the coolness of galley. He reached out toward the salt, but Symes thrust his hand away and spoke sharply to him. The first mate stared into his supper, while the seaman growled at him in low tones. Broadhurst's head sank lower and lower.

"I shudder to think of what hold that man has over Broadhurst. He's reduced to a blubbering child." Aleksandra frowned, her hand twisting the napkin in her lap.

"I think your idea of laudanum is correct." Captain Rach nodded. "I'll seek some time alone with him tonight and see what all this is about. Alcohol is not allowed on this ship, in any form."

"I've had enough to eat, Xavier." Aleksandra shuddered, her bowl barely touched. She couldn't draw enough air in her lungs and needed to get onto the deck and into the light.

"I've done as well, so good afternoon, captain." Xavier nodded and pushed back his chair, then held out a hand to Aleksandra. She didn't look back toward Symes as she stood and walked before Xavier from the room.

"I'll see you both on deck soon, all being well," Rach said, his brows drawn nearly to touching.

ᕀ

ALEKSANDRA LEANED back against the wall behind her and closed her eyes. When she opened them, Symes stood at the rail close by and pulled a hand reel from his jacket pocket. She tried to prevent the shudder that ran through her. She hadn't come up on deck to spend time with him. She sat, rigid, as her eyes sought Xavier.

"So you like to fish, eh?" he said, and turned back to the rail.

She looked away, without answering. A few moments later, he was spinning a baited hook, then let it fly.

Gulls screeched and one dived down to catch his bait before it hit the water.

"Bloody gull," he growled, and jerked the line. "I'll teach it a thing or two."

Aleksandra watched in horror as he pulled the gull, flapping frantically for its life, toward him, wrapping the line back onto its reel as it came.

She jumped to her feet. "I'll help get it—" She froze as he grabbed it by the neck and turned to her, his face a mask. He dropped the reel and it clattered to the deck. Still looking at her, Symes closed his hand over one wing and ripped it from the bird's body.

She gasped, her hand going to her *shashka*, as he repeated the motion on the other wing of the screeching seagull. He ripped the hook out of its gullet and tossed what was left of the bird over the rail, never taking his eyes off her face.

He picked up his reel.

"Don't cross me," he said, and turned on his heel.

She didn't wait to see if he'd leave. She fled.

"You just have a little more and lie back for a few moments until it takes effect." Symes smiled at the shaking, sweating man on the bed in his cabin, a cabin a seaman should never have been allocated.

It was one of his conditions of passage. He'd required it of Broadhurst, and he of the captain, before Symes would agree to the trip. It helped that Symes knew of Broadhurst's inclination to boys and how much the first mate wanted to keep that information from the captain, his parents and his wife.

Blackmail was a wonderful thing.

Especially when one could make a man depend upon him with just a few little bottles of liquid.

He'd heard that the young women of New Zealand were a prize, dark as the men of Arabia, who prized them, but different, as the golden angel on board was different. They would all capture him excellent prices.

For now, this young man, dissipated from his former self almost beyond recognition, would have to do...at least until the dark *Californio*, who watched his angel like a hawk, as well as the captain, should conveniently disappear. The boundless sea was another wonderful thing.

Symes laughed as he walked to the bed and began stroking the now-quiet man. He hummed a lullaby as the blond man smiled softly and lifted a now-steady hand toward his lips.

"How did your meeting with Mr. Broadhurst go the other night?" Xavier raised an eyebrow at the captain as he fell into step beside them.

"It was interesting," the captain shook his head, "to say the least."

Aleksandra moved closer to Xavier, his arm held in her vise of a grip.

"I couldn't find him for three hours after supper, but when I did, I asked him about his family. He would hardly look at me, much less answer." The captain's gaze was out to sea, then he turned back to them. "His eyes were tearing and his pupils were tiny dots in the lantern light. His hands were steady enough, as they used to be, although they were all scratched up. More than that, though, his behavior was odd."

"How odd?" Xavier's brow knitted together.

"He seemed," the captain thought for a moment, "excited, then while we were talking he became drowsy, and then he woke up again."

"He's had more laudanum," Aleksandra whispered.

"Broadhurst kept saying what a great man Symes was." Captain Rach took a deep breath and held it, his mouth and nose wrinkled up. "It was almost as if he idolized him." He let out his air slowly, between pursed lips.

If it wasn't such a foul situation, Aleksandra would have laughed at the horror on the captain's face, but as it was, she just gulped and looked away.

"Should someone be keeping an eye on Mr. Broadhurst, for his own safety?" Xavier's brows lowered, as he tilted his head toward the captain.

"Most likely, especially as he's my first mate. I wonder about Symes, though. I fear he's not what he wishes to appear and I wonder when he's going to reveal his true self."

"He already has," Aleksandra murmured, with a furtive look about them, and told the captain about Symes and the gull.

The captain closed his eyes. "Something will have to be done about him."

"He's evil," Aleksandra said, her hands clenched at her sides as she peered around them in the darkness, looking for anyone who might be close enough to eavesdrop. "He frightened me before by just looking, but now…he's more sinister than even I could have imagined. I'm sure he's hiding something. At the very least, he's probably supplying laudanum to Mr. Broadhurst."

"But why would he do that?" Xavier's brow wrinkled.

"So he can control him, I'd guess," Aleksandra muttered.

"But why?"

"That's what's giving me more gray hair." The captain frowned. "I'd like to know what someone, clearly born a gentleman, is doing living a seaman's life, making a seaman's wage."

"What makes you think that?" The *Californio's* brows narrowed.

"His actions and speech when he thinks no one is around and the way he continues to pursue Aleksandra, despite my warnings and your presence." He glanced at Xavier, then at Aleksandra.

"Has he touched you, Aleks?" Xavier growled, looking around them now, too.

Aleksandra took a deep breath and scowled at Xavier. "No, as I've told you again and again, Xavier." She turned to the captain now. "Xavier tells me," she said, through gritted teeth, "the men have heard Symes boast that I'll be leaving with him."

"I, too, have heard this." The captain rubbed his forehead with the back of his hand. "I'm not sure what to do, besides having him watched. I have four men already doing that, in shifts." He looked down at the deck. "Unless he steps clearly out of line, I can't lock him up."

"By then, it might be too late," Xavier said. "Much too late."

"I'm sweltering in this wool dress, but all the calico ones are packed in a trunk down in the hold." Aleksandra put aside the sail she was mending and fanned herself. "I'm not sure how I missed learning how hot it was near the equator. I must not have been listening when Mama tried to teach me geography."

"Was that when you were chained to a table in the cabin?" Xavier smiled and kissed her forehead.

"Yes," Aleksandra said, with a wry grin. "Not like the mathematics or history lessons Papa taught me while we cleared traps along the Weber River. I remember all of those."

"Come along, then. I'll help you find that trunk so you can cool off." He reached out his hand and pulled her up from the coil of rope upon which she sat in the fo'c's'le.

Symes stood off to her left and followed her with his eyes as they walked past, his false smile playing upon his lips. She avoided him wherever possible, but tried not to let him know how much he unnerved her. She set her mouth, took hold of Xavier's arm and moved with him toward the entrance to the hold.

It took awhile to find the chest among the cargo and the rest of their belongings, but finally Xavier found it and placed it before her. Rogan reached out from his tie stall and lipped at the leather.

"Thank you," Aleksandra said, and stood on her tiptoes to kiss Xavier on the lips. Behind him, a blanket covering their goods slipped and the corner of a deep golden piece of furniture peeked out.

"Any time, *Querida*," he said, and reached out to wipe the sweat from her brow.

"Xavier," she frowned, "what's that?"

"What?" He turned around to see what had caught her eye and smiled.

"It isn't…" she said, her heart leaping as she reached out and flicked the cover away to reveal her mother's oaken secretary. "You brought it." She fell silent, then threw her arms around his neck. "You're the most wonderful husband in the world," she mumbled, against his neck.

"You happy now? It was truly "special wood." Your mama's precious secretary. I wanted you to have something of your family with you in New Zealand."

"But how did you get it to California?"

"You'll have to write Tatiana and Vladimir to thank them for that. They brought it out in the dogcart. Now find some more appropriate clothing for these climes. I'd prefer you in a whole lot less," he leered, "but we've got more than enough trouble on this ship, as it is."

She swatted at Xavier's buttocks and he grabbed her before she could connect.

"I'm getting faster," he said, his eyes shining in the dimness. "You'd better watch out, or it'll be me bending you over my knee, wife." He paddled her bottom lightly.

Aleksandra drew in a quick breath, her mouth in a silent "o." A pulsing began in her nether regions and her face grow hot as he watched her, a slow smile dawning on his face.

"Hold that thought, *Querida*. We've not the privacy down here to try that." He pulled her to him and kissed her, his mouth firm against hers. His tongue slipped into her mouth as he drew her close against his hard body, and his even harder erection, behind his light trousers.

It had been far and away too long since they'd made love. First, it was too soon after the birth, then the shock over Melissandra's death kept anything but the most basic of emotions at bay.

Had they feared to try again?

They held each other in their arms readily enough, spooning together as they slept on the narrow bed in their cabin, but neither had broached the subject of lovemaking.

Until now.

It seemed the time had come.

"I'll be waiting in our cabin upon your return. I fear if I stay below here with you, you'll not find that dress and I may wreck the one you're wearing as well." He grinned down at her.

Against her chest, Xavier's heart pounded beneath his shirt. His chocolate eyes were pure black with desire and she inhaled sharply as his hand grazed the surface of her bodice, her nipples tightening against the confining fabric. She moaned, her knees melting, when his strong fingers returned to pinch each of them lightly in turn. Aleksandra's world spun, her abdomen clenching at the feel of wetness between her legs. She leaned backwards in Xavier's arm as his lips trailed down the front of her neck.

A hot breath at her nape made her jump. Rogan playfully nipped at her hair and she took a deep breath and chuckled shakily.

"Thanks, Rogan. We didn't really need any help just now." She turned and lifted a quivering hand to stroke his soft muzzle while she clung to Xavier with the other one.

"I'll see you soon. *Very* soon, I hope," her husband said, twitching at his now-tight trousers, and took his leave. "I'll be waiting. Do not dally, *Querida, por favor.*"

Aleksandra gave a last pat to the stallion behind her and spun to open the latches on the trunk. It was a big chest, and full, but she finally found the three cotton dresses and petticoats. In the bottom layer, of course. She replaced the rest and closed the lid. She'd done up one of the latches when the sound of steps echoed in the hold.

"So you like it rough, do you?" A deep voice slowly drawled behind her, with an English accent. "I saw you with the dark one, the one you call husband. I'm sure you'll prefer me. I can make you—"

Aleksandra waited for just a moment to ascertain where Symes stood before she moved, her hand positioned over her *shashka*.

# 16

A thundering crash sounded beside her and Aleksandra dropped to her knees, covering her head.

"Arrrggghh," Symes shouted, staggering back and holding the side of his head. "I'll see you gelded!" he shouted at Rogan.

"No, you won't," Aleksandra stood before him, her *shashka* at the ready, aimed for his groin. "If any trouble befalls him, I'll seek you out, you misbegotten pig of a man," she spat.

"You bitch, I'll have you, if it's the last thing I ever do. You can count on it," he growled, blood dripping from beneath his fingers as he held the side of his head.

She watched in silence as he stumbled up the slope to the deck. She finally let out the breath she didn't know she'd been holding. Only when he was gone, his footsteps heading towards the fo'c'sle, did she begin to shake. She turned and wrapped her arms around the neck of the big bay. He nibbled at her derriere, just because he could get away with it, this once.

Watching closely about herself, she climbed to the lower deck, then headed straight for their cabin. No one met her in the passageway, and no alarm had been raised about the devil horse which had attacked Seaman Symes. She doubted they'd hear about it.

She slipped through the door of their cabin and turned the lock, then let out her breath, her forehead against the door.

Xavier came up behind her and kissed the top of her head. He slid his hand up her spine and stopped dead.

"What is this? Whose blood is this?" His voice chilled her to the core and she shivered.

"Symes paid me a visit while I got the dresses—"

"Symes?" He reached for the door handle, but Aleksandra grabbed his hand with both of hers.

"Good thing you placed the trunk where you did. Rogan attacked him from his stall. Symes is bleeding from the side of his head—where are you going?"

"He's not bleeding nearly as much as he needs to be, yet." Xavier let go of the door handle and pulled her to him, holding her tightly for a moment, then swung away to grab his sword belt, with Aleksandra's father's *shashka*.

"He'll kill you. No, Xavier, please don't go. Who knows what he has planned. He didn't touch me, just threatened me that he would have me, whatever that means. He's just bluffing. Really, he's a coward, only suitable for you to wipe your boots with. He only attacks women and sick, weak men."

Xavier closed his eyes, and the pulse pounded at his throat.

"Please?" Aleksandra begged. "I couldn't bear to be left alone if something happened to you, especially if he were still alive. Where would I go?"

"Aleksandra, be still. I'll speak with the captain. This man needs to be stopped. If he tries anything again, I'll kill him, have no doubt about that. A man must protect those he loves. You'll have to have some faith in the man who trained your papa and me, even if you have no faith in me.

"I do, but the risk is there, and who knows how many men he has at his disposal? I'm going with you."

The captain was less than impressed, but he was still uncertain as to what he could do about the man.

They bedding down the horses and stock for the night and retrieved Aleksandra's summer gowns from their heap on the floor of the hold, then returned to their cabin and lay down on the bed.

"All I want to do is hold you, Aleksandra," Xavier murmured into her hair.

"You've become so precious to me," she whispered.

"And you to me. Times like this remind me how precarious our life and our love, really is, now that I've found someone to truly love and believe in." Xavier held her close until both of their hearts stopped racing.

At supper, the first mate's friend was nowhere to be seen.

"I've restricted Symes to the fo'c'sle for the duration of the trip," Captain Rach said. "Broadhurst can take him meals, if he wants him to eat at all. The only alternative I've given him was to spend the rest of the trip in chains."

Broadhurst glared from his position at the other end of the table, but short of being put into chains himself, he had little choice.

There was an uneasy silence about the decks for the next few days when Aleksandra and Xavier walked the horses on their daily rounds. They stayed behind the foremast, but Symes' dark looks still followed Aleksandra as he mended sails or knotted ropes. The captain must have assigned him plenty of work—he was nearly always occupied whenever he came into view.

A week later, as she walked the last horse of the day behind Xavier and his horse, she glanced at Symes. He flicked out a knife, as if to carve on a piece of bone. His eyes held hers as he slowly placed the knife on the deck beside him and wrapped his hand around the long white object. He began to stroke it, his fingers in a ring around it, back and forth. He panted a few times, then laughed, long and low. Aleksandra dragged her eyes away, and looked toward Xavier, who was speaking with another sailor.

"Probably a good thing," she said to Dzień, as she glanced back to see Symes' gaze still focused upon her, "he missed the exchange. I'd sure like to keep Xavier alive."

The pony just shook his head and walked on.

The captain walked up to her, brows lowered, his mouth in a firm line.

"Xavier didn't see that," Aleksandra tried to smile, her legs wobbly, "but I should have known you miss nothing on this ship."

"I saw it. The man must be insane, to continue to flaunt my authority and the temper of your husband," he said, from between tight lips.

"He just threatens, as I told Xavier," she looked at the deck, "and only women and weak men."

"So far," the captain scowled, "so far."

"HE MUST HAVE FINALLY GIVEN UP," Aleksandra said, one particularly steamy evening as she measured out oats for the horses' supper. Sweat dripped from beneath her hair, down the open neckline of her cotton work dress, then in between her breasts. She blew cooling air toward her forehead, and curling wisps of escaped hair danced about her face.

"And a good thing for him," Xavier said, hanging the water bucket away on its hook.

"This weather's enough to make a saint swear." She sighed. "I'm sure it was hotter in the Utah Desert, but it was never as stifling as it is here."

"It's the humidity. Makes it so much worse—I think it makes us all a bit mad."

"I'd love to feel your hands all over me—like we…started to a few weeks ago, before—"

"—best not to think on that night, eh, *Querida?*"

"What I was going to say was, how I'd love to feel your hands on me, but it's just too hot for even that" she said, with a smile.

"It is, at that, but I'd be game to give it a try." He laughed. "It's nearly supper time. How about you get our meals and take them to our room, while I finish up here. We could have a little wash and then…see how we go?"

Aleksandra took a sharp breath, quivering, and looked up at him from beneath her lashes. Her cheeks heated and her core gripped tightly. She backed away, watching him all the while, then turned and walked swiftly up the ramp without looking back. She sped down the passageway toward the galley, nearly dancing, a smile stretched wide across her face.

"What's the hurry, love?" Symes whispered into her ear.

Her breath caught in her throat as he grabbed her and ducked into an open doorway.

"Were you so eager to join me in my love nest that you had to run here?" He smiled as he clamped one hand over her mouth and held her tightly against him with the other. He swiftly replaced his hand with his mouth and his tongue forced its way between her gritted teeth as she gagged.

Aleksandra bit down hard and he moved back half a step, his fingers flying to his mouth, then drew his other hand to strike her. Aleksandra stepped back and reached for her hip, but she came up short against a cabinet and knocked her head. While the room spun about her, he grabbed her again, holding her close.

"There is an easy way for you and a hard way. I'd like to show you the easy way, but you're not giving me much chance for that, my darling," he growled.

He gripped her right arm tightly, and her left was trapped behind her, so she couldn't get at her *shashka*. If she could reach the knife in her boot, she could surprise him. Symes hadn't expected a fight, and certainly not an armed one, so a false faint might let her reach it. It went against all her instincts to do so, but she couldn't think of anything else to do, so she closed her eyes and let herself go limp in his arms.

"That's the good girl," he chuckled. "Come to daddy, my little one." He let go of her arms and supported her with one arm. "Open up, dearest," he murmured, as something cool and smooth slid between her lips and a bitter taste stung her tongue.

Her eyes flew open the instant she tasted it, and her knife was in her hand, even as he slid the bottle under her tongue and tipped it up.

She slashed at his chest, but only succeeded in scoring the skin over his ribs before he grabbed her wrist and twisted it. The knife flew from her hand and clattered somewhere against metal. He threw his weight on her body, one hand holding her hands above her head, and the other gripping her throat. She couldn't breathe, but soon she felt nothing, in a blessed blackness that blotted out even the sight of his sweaty, red, contorted face above her.

SYMES LEFT HER, stripped and spread, on the bed in the Broadhurst's room where he'd drugged her, then hunkered down behind the door to wait.

*Nice bed, Broadhurst's, much better than the one in the cabin allotted to me.*

He nearly spit at the injustice.

He'd given the girl enough to knock her out for awhile, so he was in no hurry. By the time the rest of them figured out their first mate was drugged to the eyeballs in Seaman Symes' cabin and thought to look in Broadhurst's, he'd have had his first of many "experiences" with his new plaything on the bed. Her idiot husband wouldn't expect to find him still with her, so he'd just jump him when he entered the cabin and the girl would belong to him. The captain should be easy to convince, with his promise of a portion of the profit from the girl's impending sale.

He couldn't help laughing. If only his misguided, noble family could see him now. Soon he'd be making money hand over fist, living the high life he always had, while they drowned in their moldering old manor house, running out of the rest of the family's money…helping their tenants, of all things. *Noblesse oblige* be damned. His father had tried, but what was the use? He just couldn't have cared less, then or now. He'd never worked an honest day in his life… and he never planned to.

Even with these titillating images to entertain him, crouching like a thief behind the door bored him within minutes. His attention span was short at the best of times.

"Doubtless, your loving, but stupid, husband will take quite some time to find us," he said softly, to the still form on the bed. "Perhaps we should begin enjoying our time together now." He untied the laces of his trousers and climbed onto the bed to kneel beside her.

"So lovely," he breathed, as he smoothed his hands from the inside of her thigh up over her taut belly, just the faintest of stretch marks…

"Stretch marks?" His head shot up and he looked closer. Surely, they were. He frowned. That would change things. "No matter for now," he muttered beneath his breath, with a scowl.

His hands slid up to her breast, taking his time. He pursed his lips at his work-roughened hands in disgust. A gentleman should never have stooped to the work he'd been doing, but it would be worth it. Her sale alone would restore his fortune. The peers who now snubbed him would be throwing their daughters at him by this time next year.

He smiled as his other hand slid up toward her crotch.

## 17

"The mate's not been in to pick up Symes' supper," the galley cook frowned, "and he's always here early."

The captain looked at him, his own brows lowering.

"When did you last see him?"

"Breakfast time, it was. Bright and early, as usual."

"Thank you for that." Rach turned on his heel and strode toward Symes' cabin. Before him, Xavier stalked up the ramp from the hold, his mouth set in a grim line.

"Have you seen Aleksandra? I sent her to get our supper from the galley and she's not returned."

Rach filled him in as they quickly checked the fo'c'sle, then raced to Symes' cabin. Rach unlocked the door and they slowly entered the darkened room, weapons drawn. The only occupant was a nearly comatose... *Broadhurst?* He lay naked on the bunk, atop a rumpled woolen blanket.

"Where's Symes?" the captain thundered, blinking at the strong smell of sex in the room.

His mate turned toward him with the small, soft face of a bewildered child and Rach spun around in disgust. He motioned Xavier out and padlocked the door behind them.

"Broadhurst's cabin?" Xavier skipped into a full run toward it. "Makes sense, she was on her way to the galley. All he needed to do was grab her," he growled.

They made it to the door of the mate's cabin in seconds. Rach had no desire to bother unlocking the door this time.

"Be my guest," Rach murmured with a grim smile, nodding at the door.

Xavier threw his shoulder against it. It gave with a splintering of timber and the two men rushed into the cabin, swords at the ready.

The seaman kneeled on the bed beside the still form of Aleksandra, one hand near the triangle of curly hair at the juncture of her legs. He spun to face them and froze, staring, as they stepped through the remains of the cabin doorway.

Xavier never even stopped. His *shashka* was already in one hand and he drew his bowie knife from its sheath as he raced across the few steps to the pair on the bed.

Symes looked surprised, but he wasn't stupid enough not to be prepared. He reached down beside his hip to pick up a gleaming marlinspike and Xavier stopped in his tracks, an arm's reach away.

"Looking for someone?" The greasy seaman waved the weapon, its point sharpened to a needle tip, toward Xavier. "Should I give this to you, or to her?" He pointed it at her breast, smiling. "That way, even if I don't get her, neither will you." His manic smile stretched from ear to ear.

"Leave the girl alone, Symes, and move away from the bed." Rach said, in his most authoritative captain's tone.

The seaman went on like he hadn't heard him, a wild look in his distant eyes. The drool running from the corner of his mouth bespoke his condition.

"Actually, I'd hate to mar her." He smiled tenderly at the girl beneath him, the grin grotesque on his embittered face. "I'm going to have such fun with her after I kill you both. Did you know, we're going to take over the ship, Broadhurst and I. Between us, we've accumulated quite a large proportion of the crew. They'll be ours, like that," he snapped his fingers, "and we'll collect up many more of these lovelies, but none as fine as her." He reached down and gripped her breast again, his long fingers sliding to the areola and pinching the nipple between them. He smiled again.

"Get your hands off my wife," Xavier said, enunciating every word, but he froze as the tip of the marlinspike grazed Aleksandra's breast over her heart. Blood welled from the scratch as he ran the point slowly toward the nipple.

"She's spirited now, I'll give her that, but that will be the first to go, and then, oh, the things I'll teach her. She'll be more skilled than the finest woman in any of the harems to which she'll eventually be sold when I tire of her," he muttered, almost to himself.

He lifted the marlinspike towards Xavier. His eyes seemed to focus upon him for a moment. The ends of his mouth turned up a bit, contrasting with the unholy light from his vacant eyes. He turned his gaze again to his comatose captive and laughed.

In that second, Xavier struck. He slashed at the seaman's throat with the *shashka*, but Symes ducked, lost his balance and fell backwards from the bed, the marlinspike still clutched in his hand. He flailed as he fell backwards, and his left shoulder glanced off the corner of a tea chest. He twisted and threw his right arm out to save himself, swearing as his elbow struck the floor, but his words turned into a scream, and then silence.

Rach and Xavier stepped cautiously around the end of the bed, swords and knife at the ready, but there was no need. Symes had done their work for them.

The blunt end of the sharp metal spike protruded from his eye socket, half of its length embedded in the fated man's brain.

Satisfied that Symes would fight no more, Xavier turned slowly to look at his wife on the bed, white and still as death. Terrified of what he might find, he went to her and touched her face while the captain pulled a blanket from the cupboard and covered her naked body. Xavier's hand slid to her throat. Her pulse was slow, but steady. He collapsed over her, letting out a great sob, and finally took a deep breath.

"*Gracias a Dios por la bendición y su vida...*" he muttered, on and on, a prayer of thanksgiving, as he picked her up and wrapped her in the blanket, rocking her while the captain searched the room.

"Found it," Rach said, sniffing the contents of a small glass vial. "And isn't this Aleks' knife? Looks like she tried to fight." He handed the dagger to Xavier and snapped shut the lid attached to the glass vial.

"What is it?"

"Laudanum." He showed the bottle to Xavier. "May I?"

Xavier's brows knitted together, but he pulled his head away from his wife's face.

The captain opened Aleksandra's mouth, lowered his face to hers, and sniffed.

"Yes, I can smell it on her breath."

"How much danger is she in? We don't know how much he gave her." Xavier gritted his teeth and tried to still his shaking hands.

"We only have Broadhurst to go by."

"If, indeed, he was given the same."

"He was more conscious than her, but we can check to see how awake he is now."

Rach led the way to Xavier and Aleksandra's cabin, opened the door and turned down the bed for Xavier, then retreated. Xavier laid her down as if she were crystal, carefully wiping the drops of blood from her breast before tucking her into bed.

A knock sounded. In the doorway stood Captain Rach with his cabin boy.

"How is she?"

"Much the same. I'm keeping her warm."

"Broadhurst is still locked in Symes' cabin, but he's beginning to make some noise. I thought you might like to come and help ask my mate a few questions," he said, with a ghost of a grin.

"I'd like to go with you, but I don't want to let her out of my sight. Come in, please."

"I completely understand," Rach said, as they stepped into the room. "I don't know how much sway Symes and Broadhurst had, or have, over the rest of my men, but I've gathered my best ones to guard this door. I'd trust James with my life," he said, nodding at the capable-looking young man beside him. "We can leave him before, or behind, the locked door to watch for Aleksandra's awakening."

"In that case," Xavier gave the captain a grim smile, turning to check Aleksandra once more. "Take my chair, James." He nodded at a seat near the door.

"I'll guard her with my life," the young man said, patting his revolver.

"Loaded?"

"Yessir," he said.

"Know how to shoot it?"

"Yessir," he barked.

"Good. Call me if she wakes, please." Xavier couldn't help smiling at the keen lad, then he spun on his heel and followed the Rach from the room.

"Xavier, I think you should see this," the captain said, when they were out of earshot of the cabin. "Come over here for a moment."

He handed Xavier a piece of parchment, folded and creased.

Xavier read it, then frowned. "But whose passport is this? No one on this ship goes by that name, do they?"

"It was in Symes' bunk. I saw it when we went looking for him. It's his permission to leave England and go to Arabia. If it's Symes', his real name is James Morrison Fitzwilliam III, and he's a peer of the realm. Things could get messy."

"I wonder how many others know of this?" Xavier said, his stomach turning to ice.

"Hopefully not Broadhurst, anyway," Rach said. "We can vouch for each other, you needn't worry. Anyway, let's go. The surgeon's waiting."

The ship's doctor, a tall, ruddy-complected man, stood near the hatch leading toward Symes' cabin, awaiting their arrival.

"We're lucky to have a man of his experience on this barque," the captain said in an undertone, as they neared him. "He was a proper surgeon's mate in the British Navy. You don't find men like that in San Francisco every day."

The man's eyes were warm and friendly, not at all like the doctors he'd met in California and elsewhere in America. Xavier nodded to him as they were introduced.

"I've no idea what we'll find. He could be asleep, or armed and dangerous," Rach murmured, as they approached the door.

He took a deep breath and unlocked the door, then let it swing open. The men stood back to the sides of the entryway and waited in silence.

Broadhurst still lay on the bed, but he'd covered part of his nakedness with the blanket. He lifted his head, then dropped it again, groaning. "Shut the bleedin' door, Symes, if you please," he muttered. "Come to bed with me and keep me warm. It's so cold. And bring another bottle, if you please?" His voice assumed a wheedling tone at the last.

The men looked at each other, then turned their eyes back to the pale-faced first mate.

Xavier blinked. "Well, that was a twist I hadn't considered."

"Symes and Broadhurst, lovers?" Rach shook his head.

Broadhurst sat up and stared at the men in the doorway. He started to slide from the bed, then looked down at himself and froze.

"First Mate Broadhurst, what in Hell do you think you're doing in Symes' bed?"

"I was just wondering that myself, Captain," he said, shakily. "I remember suddenly feeling ill while delivering Symes' supper, and I only now woke up." He swung his head from side to side, then staggered toward a pile of clothing, presumably his own.

"And was it necessary to unclothe yourself to deliver his supper?" Rach raised an eyebrow at him.

"I don't know how it happened, sir." Broadhurst mumbled, to his toes.

"And the bottle beside you on the bed, what was it?"

"Bottle?" He spun toward the bed, nearly falling in his haste. He scrabbled in the bedclothes, searching.

"Would this be the one?" The doctor had already retrieved it. He held it up and raised an eyebrow at Broadhurst.

"Give that to me." He lunged at the doctor, who backed up, holding it to his chest. Xavier and the captain stepped into Broadhurst's path and grabbed him, holding him fast while he struggled and mewled like a kitten.

"You've had enough from that bottle to last you a lifetime. It's laudanum, isn't it, Mr. Broadhurst?" The doctor watched his face intently.

"I don't know what you're talking about," he hissed.

"I think you do, and we are going to talk about it. Where have you been getting it?"

"I don't know what you're talking about. I'm the first mate of this ship, and I'll have you in chains for insubordination." He gasped for breath.

"I think not, Broadhurst." The captain shook his head. "You were expecting Symes to come back and get into bed with you. Is he supplying you with laudanum?"

"I cannot believe you'd think that of me, captain." His voice lowered, and he gulped.

"So where do you think Symes might be now?"

"I don't know. Why should I?"

"I thought he might have told you his plans."

"His plans?" He shuffled his feet, his face going paler, if that were possible.

"Those involving Mrs. Argüello, perhaps?" Rach moved his face close to Broadhurst's.

"I told him it'd never work," Broadhurst said. "Where is he, he said he'd return soon, with—" he stopped dead, as he noticed it was Xavier who held one of his arms, then struggled to get away.

"Your associate is dead. He killed himself with his own marlinspike," Captain Rach stated flatly.

"No, no, no!" His voice rose on a wail, and his struggles began anew.

"Lock him in the brig, for now. We can't have him running about the decks like this." Rach took a deep breath.

The men half-dragged the screaming first mate to the small, barred cabin, bearing only a wooden slat bed and a tiny table attached to the wall beside the door.

"If he's been accustomed to taking laudanum, we'll soon know it," the doctor said. Captain Rach turned the key in the door and they left, while Broadhurst howled on the other side.

"GOOD MORNING, *MI QUERIDA*," Xavier said, as entered and closed the door of their cabin the next morning. "I thought I'd let you sleep. You must have had some crazy dreams last night, the way you were talking."

Aleksandra sat up in bed and smiled at him, dragging the sheet up over her naked breasts.

"How are you feeling?" He sat on the bed beside her, pulled her into his arms and kissed her gently.

"I'm well, surprisingly well. Like I've slept for a week." She grinned up at him and kissed him again, harder this time. "I never did thank you for saving me from that lunatic."

"Any time, wife." His voice caught in his throat and he gulped. "I'd have never forgiven myself if he'd taken you and done the things he said he would."

She closed her eyes and gripped him tightly, her hands fisted in his shirt. "How's our first mate?"

"He's in pretty bad shape."

"Not a huge surprise," Aleksandra said, one eyebrow raised. "He'll have had his last dose about the same time I was drugged, I'd guess."

"Eighteen to twenty hours ago." He shook his head. "He's so loud, I'm amazed we can't hear him all the way back here."

"Papa once helped an old soldier who used to take laudanum and he told me some stories." Aleksandra shuddered. "By my reckoning, he'll be wishing he were dead before long."

"He may already be there," Xavier said, taking a deep breath. "It's hard to watch. I couldn't imagine being in his place."

"Has he started cramping and vomiting yet?"

"Yes. His skin looks like a tomato, his pupils are so big his eyes look black and his hands, no, his whole body's shaking. He's exhausted, but he can't sleep, and he keeps calling out for Symes to help him, bring him his little bottles. His nose is running and he's sweating like a pig. The stink coming from the cabin…it's…it smells like a sewer."

"Can the doctor do anything to help him? My papa gave the old soldier tiny doses of the drug until he was better, but it took weeks."

"He considered it, but there isn't much more laudanum in the doctor's stash. It seems the surgeon was allowed to hold some for medical care, but Symes must have stolen the ship's supply. The captain wants to keep it in reserve in case it's needed for emergencies, so Broadhurst'll have to sweat it out."

"That's tough for him," she said, gritting her teeth.

"He's pretty upset about Symes, too." Xavier closed his eyes and was silent for a moment.

"Well, come here and hold me tight. I, for one, will never voluntarily take that drug." She shivered. "The dreams were frightening. I was half-conscious as he stripped me. I honestly don't know what happened next," she said, and blushed. Her voice dropped to a whisper. "I have no idea if, or how, he touched me."

"He wouldn't have had time to do more than just touch you by the time we found you. I think he was about to start exploring, thinking we'd take longer than we did."

She buried her face in his shirt front.

"It's a good thing he didn't," Xavier said. "I think he was poxed."

She stared up at him, her eyes wide, and he kissed her lips.

"I'll never let anything happen to you." He stroked the soft skin beneath her chin with his forefinger and lightly kissed the tears from the corners of her eyes.

"So you say…but we go to New Zealand," she gave him a little smile, "and it's wilder than either of us can even imagine. Wilder than the Pony Express Trail through Utah, Nevada and the rest of America combined. I appreciate the sentiment, but I fear we'll both have to take good care of each other, and ourselves, if we're to survive. Especially," she said, "if we're to find von Tempsky, our mercenary journalist."

ANOTHER WEEK PASSED and the horizon rolled on, straight as an arrow, broken only by fluffy clouds, and the occasional cloud-capped verdure of a small island in the distance.

"Broadhurst looked pitifully thin," Aleksandra said, with a frown, "before he was locked up. Is he any better, or is that his usual condition? More, is that him or the laudanum?"

"I understand he was a strapping big fellow when he worked for the captain before. That was one of the reasons Rach took him on again. He thought he'd fallen upon hard times and wanted to help him. He must have started taking laudanum some time ago. He seems less crazy this week, though. His howls have diminished to moans and whines."

"That's got to mean something," she said.

"What hasn't altered, however, is his judgment that I'm to blame for the death of Symes."

"Symes?" She looked up, her eyes wide and mouth fallen open. "But he killed himself with his own marlinspike, the same one he scratched me with." She glanced down at her just-healed breast, then stared at him with incredulity.

"Be that as it may, his twisted mind has placed me as Symes' murderer and he wants me locked up immediately, put in chains, and turned over to the authorities when we get to New Zealand."

"The captain wouldn't allow that, would he?"

"Rach won't hear a bar of it, but Broadhurst rants on," Xavier took a deep breath and looked into Aleksandra's eyes, "constantly."

"They cannot possibly hold it against you."

"He seems to think they can, but he's currently the one locked up." Xavier raised a brow at her. "The doctor is in charge of him now. He gave him a tiny dose to keep him from vomiting his empty stomach out so he's quiet again, but Lord only knows how long that will last."

"Does Broadhurst hold any sway on this ship?"

"Not sure, but Symes said he and Broadhurst had gleaned their own crew from the seamen here to mutiny, so who knows? It may have been the talk of a madman, but Rach's keeping Broadhurst under lock and key. It shouldn't be long, anyway. The captain's expecting the North Island of New Zealand any day n —"

"STORM AFT!" the watch shrieked, from his position high in the sails.

Xavier grabbed her hand and they ran up onto the deck. They could only stare at the tempest clustered on the horizon—big black clouds, growing larger and even blacker as they approached.

"The watch saw a darkness behind him and went up to investigate," a sailor told them.

"Good thing we've been keepin' an eye out for land, else we might not've seen this comin'," another said, with a grimace. "They're runnin' on the Trade Winds... and they're goin' a lot faster than we are."

"HANDS ALOFT!" came the captain's call. Men swung out over the bulwarks and dived for the main shrouds, then sprinted up the ratlines, racing the squall for the yardarms.

Xavier held tightly to Aleksandra. They tried to stay out of the way as the squall pursued the little barque like a pack of hounds after a rabbit.

It was only a matter of minutes before the storm hit them with a scream like the opening of the gates of Hell and the world of those on the ship went dark.

# 18

The tempest hit with a vengeance. Everything not bolted or cleated down flew and the main deck was in chaos. During the pitifully few moments between the sighting of the storm and its arrival, the captain shouted orders to the men. They sprinted from the ratlines to the fighting top and thence to the yardarms, trying to keep their balance as they stood beside each other on the foot ropes. Against the wind, they held themselves to the yards with one hand and pulled in the great sails with the other.

"One hand for the ship, one for yourself," Aleksandra whispered.

"Pardon?" Xavier's brows narrowed, his knuckles white on the door frame, trying to stay upright as the ship pitched and rolled.

"Something an 'Old Salt' told me, back in Utah."

"*Dios mío,*" Xavier murmured, gripping Aleksandra with his free arm. He nodded his head upward at a man dangling from the yards, swinging to and fro. Only seconds later, he was pitched into the water, screaming, as the ship bounced in the wild seas.

"What happened to him?" Aleksandra strained to spot him in the churning waves.

"Instead of climbing across the foot ropes to move along the yardarm, he pulled himself up onto the yard and tried to run along it. We fell into a trough and he was flicked off," he said, and said a prayer for the sailor in Spanish.

"Why do they risk themselves, just to save some sail?" Aleksandra wailed.

"It's more than the sails. They're trying to reef them to save the masts," Xavier said.

Aleksandra shivered and held tighter to Xavier.

The remaining crew still on deck tried to pivot the yards around so they were all in the wind, but the storm swirled inconsistently and their efforts to set the sails parallel to the blasts were in vain.

"I always thought the *Emmeline* was a substantial ship, but now... now she's like a cork tossing in this big sea," Aleksandra said.

Waves washed over the deck with startling regularity as the ship listed far enough sideways to dip what sails remained unfurled into the foaming maelstrom.

"This is no ordinary storm." Aleksandra's chest tightened and it was hard to draw a breath.

"No. I didn't think Captain Rach could ever look terrified." The great man was ashen-faced, his forehead wrinkled almost beyond recognition.

"He's trying to sound cheerful for his crew, but there's little chance of that," she muttered.

"All hands, lash yourselves to your post. Don't want to lose anybody else!" Rach shouted, trying to make himself heard above the screeching of the wind in the wires and the frantic flapping of loose sails. He raced fore and aft, dashing from handhold to handhold as he tried to coordinate the ship's survival against terrible odds.

"He needs his first mate." Xavier said. "Hold tight, I'll be right back." He followed the captain, grabbing at anchor points as he moved across the heaving deck.

Their shouted conversation was brief. Xavier headed fore and shortly returned with the mate, who saluted the captain. With a dark look at Xavier, Broadhurst headed forward and began shouting orders. The captain nodded his thanks to Xavier, then return aft to help the crew.

"Captain said to see to our stock as best we can," Xavier puffed. He grabbed Aleksandra's hand and pulled her with him down the ramps below the deck.

"It's a lot quieter down here." Aleksandra drew a breath and slowly released it as they entered the hold.

"Yeah, well, we're two decks away from the screaming wires, so that should help," he returned.

"Good thing this isn't a passenger ship. She managed a wry grin.

"Instead of people crying and screaming, the animals are just focused on keeping their feet."

"And doing an admirable job of it." He stroked Charro's face with one hand and Rogan with the other, while Dzień's rubbed his head hard against Aleksandra.

"He does this when he's nervous. Used to knock me over when he was little." She tried to smile and wrapped her arms around her old friend. "Of course, I was a lot smaller then, too." She gave him a last scratch and moved down the line to check the others. The broodmares were worried. Their muzzles were tensed and the wrinkles around their eyes were deep furrows, but they were stable, their forefeet in a wide stance. The stoic cows and bulls stood strongly on their four legs, heads lowered, but they still lowed softly.

"There's less motion down here, which would make sense," Xavier said. "The creaking of the ship's timbers is louder, though."

"Luckily they don't understand the danger we've put them in." Aleksandra's jaw clenched and her lips pursed. She grabbed a pitchfork and began to feed them their supper. Xavier joined her and soon all were munching as contentedly as could be expected.

"Are you OK?" Xavier murmured into her hair when they finally finished and leaned together against the wall of Dzień's stall.

"Work always helps." She leaned back against him, inhaling his scent. She wanted to brand it forever into her mind. Who knew might happen in the next few hours?

He slid an arm around Aleksandra and they walked unsteadily toward the hay, piled in a corner near the horse stalls.

"Is there anything we can do to help up top?" She looked toward the ramp.

"Nope. Captain said for us to stay below so we won't get bumped around so much."

Something about the way he said it made her turn and look at him closely.

Xavier's jaw was tight, but he wore a wide grin.

"What?" Aleksandra looked at him from the corners of her eyes, trying to keep her feet as another wave crashed against the hull.

"Rach said," Xavier twisted his lips, then hesitated and bit them together, his brow furrowing, "that if his loving wife were here, and if he weren't needed up top, that he'd make the most of the situation and make love with her just one more time…because it could well be their last."

"That makes me want to cry, the poor man," she said, and swallowed hard.

"He also told me I was lucky to be given this chance, and that the rest of the hands are needed on deck... so there was little likelihood of interruption."

Aleksandra looked up at him and her vision blurred for a moment, then tears ran cold down her heated cheeks. "I hadn't realized it was quite as bad as that, but I think my mama would think it sound advice," she smiled faintly, "and Papa definitely would. It'll keep us out from under the sailors' feet, anyway." Xavier's dark eyes glowed in the semi-darkness and she held him tightly.

Xavier placed her hand on the last tie stall "Hold to this, I'll be right back." He smiled and pulled away from her arms. He soon returned, picked her up and carried her to the top of the soft pile of hay that smelled of California summertime, now covered with the thick wool blanket he'd retrieved from a trunk. The horses glanced their way, but returned to their own meal. The sound of their chewing nearly drowning out the creaking of the timbers as the waves smacked the hull, but not the more ominous cracking noises coming from somewhere near the main mast—just fore of their tryst site.

"Would that I had forever to love you, Aleksandra." He lay over her, kissing her lips, her face, her throat, as his hands slid down her bodice and past.

Aleksandra gasped at his hands on her body, first soft and gentle, then hard. Hands nearly crackling with electricity through the thin calico of her gown as they ran down her full length.

"I don't plan to let you go that easily, Xave." She smiled and slid her fingers through his thick hair, pulling his lips down to hers, letting the waves rock as they rolled in each others arms; the immensity of their lovemaking, their cries and sounds soon drowning out the storm that raged all around.

WHEN ALEKSANDRA and Xavier finally made their way back up top, the storm was worse. The deck was tipped to a crazy angle and loose pieces of mostly-furled sails flapped in the gale. They made for the galley, clinging to the walls of the passageway as the ship tossed first one way, then the other. The few hardy souls ensconced there huddled in the moving shadows from a hurricane lamp as it swung wildly from its hook. Clutching the table with one hand and hardtack with the other, they nodded at the pair as they entered and sat beside them.

"Are the rest of the men in their bunks?" Xavier reached a hand to take their biscuits from the cook, with a nod of thanks.

"Yep, trying fer some sleep while they can. Sorry lad, missus," the cook nodded to Aleksandra, "but it's too rough to feed ye," he muttered, as he turned and walked back to his chair by the cold stove.

"We're not terribly hungry, anyway." Aleksandra smiled at him and was rewarded with a brief lift of the corners of his mouth as he sat down with a sigh.

"Captain in his cabin?" Xavier raised an eyebrow at the cook.

"Said he was going there—you'd best have a care for the mate, son."

"What's up with him? He seemed normal, if angry, when I went to get him this afternoon." Xavier looked sideways at him.

"He's got it out for ye. Ranting as how ye killed his 'friend' Symes." The cook's mouth pursed, his brows nearly touching. "No good can come o' it. He wants ye locked up in chains, though Cap'n's told him to pull his haid in and leave ye 'lone."

"So I've heard." Xavier gritted his teeth.

"Just ye take care. He's got some friends on board, few though they be."

"Thank you for that. I'll keep my wits about me and stick close to the captain." Xavier smiled. "Thanks for the biscuit, we'll be off now. Best wishes for the night."

Aleksandra nodded to the rest of the sailors and smiled at the grizzled old salt, giving his shoulder a squeeze as she walked past on the way to the captain's cabin.

"I'm worried about Mr. Broadhurst's threats." Aleksandra clung to his hand as they groped their way along the dark passageway.

"We'll just have to take care."

"You've your *shashka*?" she murmured.

"Always."

"Good."

At the sound of shouting from the other side of the *Rach's* cabin door, Xavier raised his eyebrows and looked down at Aleksandra. He knocked loudly and the ranting ceased.

"Xavier, just the man I wanted to see," Captain Rach said. "Come on in."

Aleksandra slipped in behind Xavier and glanced around the room. Broadhurst stood up from his seat on the far side of the room as they entered, eyes narrowed at Xavier. His reddened face glistened in the flickering lamplight.

"My mate thinks you killed Mr. Symes. I've told him what I saw. Could you please enlighten him as to what you saw on that night?"

Xavier detailed the scene, omitting Aleksandra's nudity. Broadhurst's jaw remained clenched, but he held his peace while Xavier spoke.

"I know he killed him," the mate nearly shouted. "He knew Symes wanted his wife. Of course, he killed him." By now, the mate's tremors had taken hold of his whole body. "You have no right to keep me locked up. He's the one who should be in chains." Broadhurst's voice raised shrilly as he pointed his finger at Xavier.

"He's done nothing wrong," the captain growled. "What do you think Symes' part in this was? He had the lass stripped and spreadeagled on the bed. He was going to rape her. He cut her with the same marlinspike he stabbed through his own eye."

"She must have enticed him." He looked at Aleksandra like she was anathema.

"She was drugged to the gills with opium just like you were." Xavier spat out, his hand straying to the hilt of his *shashka*.

"And you were naked in Symes' bed when we entered the cabin," said Rach, "asking for him to keep you warm and for his bottle. Of laudanum, I imagine?"

"I admit, he'd been giving me a little. It was for medicinal use." The mate looked down at his feet.

"He's been using you. He provided you the laudanum so he could control you." Rach shook his head. "I want to give you a chance, but I need to know I can trust you; sober, of sound mind, and without the help of opium. How long have you been taking it and why?"

Broadhurst stared at the floor for long minutes before answering.

"Symes met me about a year ago. I was out of work and trying to feed a family. He told me it would fix it, and it did."

"It fixed his control over you, likely little else. What did he require of you? How did you feed the family with his help?"

"I only had to help him find women who wanted work. He found work for them."

"He sold them on as white slaves to wealthy men in the Near East,"

Rach said, enunciating every word. "And I think you know that," he added.

"He wouldn't do that." Broadhurst looked away. "Besides, this isn't about him, it's about his murderer." His eyes shot daggers at Xavier.

"You're about to find yourself locked up again, Broadhurst," the captain said, steel in his voice. "Not another word of this and you'll stay a free man. If I ever learn any different or hear of you using laudanum again, you're out."

"I don't need it. I'm just... disturbed... because he killed my friend." He returned his gaze to Xavier.

"Get out, Broadhurst. Your cabin's been changed and your old one is now unavailable to you." The captain's eyes glittered. "There's no more laudanum for you, so you'd best buck up. Stay away from these two and out of the hold. If I hear you or any of your henchmen have been near them or creating trouble, you'll answer to me. Got that?"

"Clear as crystal," the first mate spat out. With one more baleful look in Xavier's direction, he exited, with a slam of the door.

"I'm NOT sure exactly where this storm's blown us." Captain Rach rubbed his forearm across his sweating brow as he held to the pitching hatchway. "My compass says we're heading in the right direction, but I'm not sure how far off course the storm drove us before I was able to take readings when it first hit.

"I don't suppose we'll know until the storm's over, either." Xavier took a deep breath and looked at Aleksandra.

"Captain, we wanted to tell you, there's an awful lot of creaking around the midship mast." Aleksandra frowned.

The captain seemed to be struggling with something. He broke into a grin, and then a chuckle. "Where you two were 'spending time'?"

Aleksandra's face heated. She sighed, and then laughed. "Well, yes, Captain, but the sounds—they seem to be coming from the mast itself. Little cracking sounds."

His eyebrows lowered and his mouth became a grim line. "You'd best show me, please."

"Of course," she said, as the three rose.

"I'll place guards outside your door tonight. Broadhurst's not coming to grips with the truth," Captain Rach murmured, before they headed down the passageway and below.

In the hold, the captain examined the main mast and its attachments. "It's beginning to crack," he said slowly, his jaw clenched tight. "It shouldn't, it's New Zealand *Kauri*. It's rare they would ever break—they're flexible and strong." He took a deep breath.

"But this isn't your usual squall, is it?" Aleksandra swallowed noisily.

"No, madam, it isn't," Rach said, as the hold shuddered. A loud crack sounded like a thunderclap. The ship heeled sideways, as the stock scrambled on the tilted floor.

"We'd better check that out. I'll get Broadhurst to go out on deck and inspect it with me."

"Can you take a rope with you and some sort of a harness?" Aleksandra looked at him, frowning.

"I'll try," the captain said.

"Can I help you on deck?" Xavier raised an eyebrow at him.

"You'd be more use here, keeping an eye on Aleksandra and your stock. If the worst happens, perhaps we're close enough to shore to save yourselves and some of your stock. You might make ready a small kit to take with you. Can you swim?" He looked at both of them in turn.

"Sure can, but I'd really like to go with—"

"—you stay safe, you two. I've got a bad feeling about this, but I've got to see what's happened to my ship," he called over his shoulder as he disappeared up the ramp.

"I do too," she said.

Aleksandra and Xavier waited up for the captain to return to his cabin.

"We should be able to see him when he comes back," Aleksandra said, as she propped their door slightly ajar.

No noise except for the sound of the storm came from the direction of the deck. After an hour, they started to look for him. In the galley, only a few exhausted sailors still slouched, half asleep, on the benches. There was no sign of the captain in his cabin, either.

Thankfully, the storm seemed to be abating. They stood in the hatchway to topside and surveyed the disastrous scene of the storm-lashed deck.

From the corner of her eye, Aleksandra caught a movement aft and pointed it out to Xavier. In the driving rain, she couldn't quite make it out, but when she heard a bitten-off scream, they both bolted for the back of the barque, *shashkas* at the ready.

Aleksandra spun when she saw the trap, as five men closed in behind them. A lantern was uncovered before them, and in its light, three more men appeared. Broadhurst, at their head, laughed.

"Seems the captain had a mishap," Broadhurst shouted above the storm. "Unfortunate. He fell overboard while checking his broken mast." The former first mate looked toward the mast, lying on its side, half in the water, still connected to the ship and the other masts. "I couldn't save him. A big wave took him away." He sniffed.

*Rach? Drowned?*

Aleksandra's heart froze in her chest. The waters closed over her head as surely as if she were already underwater, as their current position became clear.

"I'm the captain now, so you'd best look sharp, boys, and tie this murderer up. He'll answer to the authorities when we get to New Zealand, wherever the godforsaken place might actually be." He laughed, a harsh bark that chilled her to the marrow. She gripped Xavier's shirt as the men headed their way and hid the *shashka* in her skirts.

"Better yet, put him in chains. He can go in the brig and see how pleasant it was for me, locked away all that time."

Two burly men grabbed Xavier and wrenched his arms behind his back, pushing Aleksandra out of the way. Broadhurst spat in Xavier's face as they dragged him away, and below.

Xavier's *shashka* bumped against her foot and she grabbed it just before it clattered to the deck. She tried still her heart, racing at the thought of the sound it would have made. He'd somehow managed to drop it beside her. He was right; it would be of more use to her than to him.

She ducked down and concealed it before her next move. "Captain." She bit her cheek to keep from shrieking at him and took a deep breath while he turned toward her. "Xavier had no part in the death of your Mr. Symes. What will it take for you to understand this?"

"Well, if it isn't the little temptress." He strode to her and grabbed her wrist. "Do we have to lock you up too?"

"And just where would I go if you didn't?" She looked him full in the face, her voice belying her quaking heart at the thumping sounds of her husband being dragged across the deck.

"That's true." He laughed. "You're not going anywhere. None of us are going anywhere, for that matter, except where the ocean might take us."

She raised an eyebrow at him.

"We've lost a mast, sweetheart, and the other two are damaged as well." He dropped her wrist and spun away from her, hands clasped behind his back, then turned toward her again. "We are Devil-knows-where, somewhere between the equator, Australia and Antarctica, by my reckoning. We may all die out here, but be certain that if we find a port, your husband will hang for the murder of my lover."

"What about your wife, and your children?" she spat. "What about the man, your captain, who gave you a chance to earn a good living for that family?"

"Don't go on about what you don't know," he growled, as he swung for her, but she ducked. She desired to draw her *shashka* and show him just how helpless a woman really was, but two more of his men stood to the side, awaiting his orders. She could do little if all three of them went for her. After these two were done with her, the attention of the rest of the men would surely kill her. She couldn't help Xavier if she were dead, so she'd hold her temper and keep her wits about her, find a way to free her husband, and get them both safely away.

Somehow.

## 19

For the past weeks, the ship had drifted wherever the ocean would take them. The men had cut the shattered main mast from its partners and attempted to make a few good sails from the shredded bits of once-glorious canvas.

Whatever Broadhurst was or wasn't, he let Aleksandra bring food to her husband, though she wasn't allowed to talk with him.

"I'm fine, *mi querida*," Xavier whispered to her when she handed him his food and water through the slot in the door. "*Ten cuidado*, you look after yourself, OK?"

She bribed the man on the door to give him blankets, candles, and a striker, so at least Xavier wouldn't freeze. She gazed at her husband with longing and slipped away.

Aleksandra had plenty to occupy her, although her thoughts strayed to Xavier constantly through the days and even more so at night. Her waking hours were spent caring for the stock, no small job on her own, and watching the horizon for any sign of land. Walking the horses on deck was hazardous now, with the damaged woodwork and bits of torn sail still flapping in the wind, but it had to be done.

Aleksandra returned from walking two broodmares to find Rogan waving his right fore in the air. He alternated between holding it up and barely touching the tip of his toe to the floor.

"Oh, what have you done now, boy?" She slid her hand down the back of his leg and felt for the pulses on the either side of his fetlock, then compared them to those on the other foreleg. She felt the structures from hoof to elbow. He blew out his breath and relaxed as she lifted his foot and supported it. He never flinched when she flexed and extended all of his joints.

"Well, at least you're not foundering," she said, "and nothing up high seems painful. Those digital pulses in your right front, though," she said, "say you've got an abscess in there. Let me get my knife."

Returning with her shoeing apron, hoof knife and pitchfork, she quickly cleaned out his stall so she wouldn't make things any worse, then picked up his foot and held it between her knees. With her knife, she gently pared a thin layer from the entire sole, looking for black fissures.

Even with the walks on deck, living in the same three-by-six-foot tie stall for months on end was bound to cause their hooves to soften and become smelly with thrush. Although she cleaned the hooves of every horse daily and brushed them with seawater, Aleksandra was still surprised it had taken this long for one of them to develop a hoof abscess.

As she carefully pared each tiny black crack in the sole, one of them at the inside heel didn't end in healthy sole, as the others had. His damp-softened hooves were compressible with the pressure of only her fingers. She squeezed her way around the hoof, staying away from the area with the deep fissure until last. When she finally put pressure across that heel, he jumped and tried to jerk the foot away.

"That's it, boy, now I can help you. Good lad." She followed the black lines with her knife, making as small a hole as possible, until Rogan reared and nearly ripped his hoof out of her hands, then dropped again to stand on the floor. She let him have his hoof and he tentatively touched it to the boards, then let it lightly rest there for a few moments, then picked it up again.

"It's okay darlin', I think we've got it," she said, as he lifted the foot and gave it to her when she touched his fetlock. Sure enough, a thick, silvery-black liquid oozed from the heel. She opened it up a little more, then left him to see if she could talk the cook out of a hot brick. A poker wouldn't do for this.

With a bucket on a rope, she collected fresh seawater from alongside the ship and took it with her into the galley. The cook took pity on her and slipped a hot brick into the bucket. It steamed and hissed until the water had taken all the heat from it, then she carried it back to Rogan.

She dumped some of the nearly-boiling water and a handful of her precious Epsom salt into another bucket.

She put a bucket of feed before him and lifted the foot. "Here, Rogan, put your foot in here," she cajoled, as she placed the tip of his hoof into the hot water. He jerked it out, nearly tipping the lot, but she eventually got him to leave his foot in the bucket. Once it was in there, he sighed again and leaned his full weight on it.

She sat on another upturned bucket, one of her legs on either side of the soak-bucket, and leaned her head on his forearm. She was so tired, she could hardly stay awake. Caring for all these animals on her own was an immeasurable amount of work, but it had to be done. She relaxed over the steaming tub, periodically adding more of the hot water from the brick bucket. They both relaxed and she even slept a little. Rogan must've not had much sleep with his sore foot overnight. It looked like she'd get plenty of soak-relax time over the next few days while the horse's hoof healed.

Aleksandra finally pulled his foot out of the water and covered his sole with a sugar and seawater hoof poultice. She wrapped the lot with a clean piece of canvas and bandaged it into place. The canvas filched from the torn sail pile came in handy; she'd have otherwise run out of muslin as the days went by.

Her time was packed full of caring for Rogan, feeding stock, cleaning stalls, and the occasional visit to the deck to fish. Several of the new captain's cronies made advances toward her in the first few weeks but each backed off at the sight of her *shashka*, glinting in the dim light of the hold. One wasn't so bright. It took the bright spurt of blood from his arm to teach him she wasn't to be toyed with. Word soon got around and the others left her alone.

A few men, no friends of Broadhurst, muttered about the murder of their captain and offered to help with the stock. Two of them also surreptitiously offered to assist with their escape, should the opportunity arise. She thanked them profusely and kept her head down.

The seamen separated themselves into two camps. The first mob was made up of Broadhurst's men. They were few in number, but this lot seethed with opportunists, bullies and braggarts. The other group comprised Rach's stalwarts. These men remained loyal to him even after his death, and seemed to have transferred their allegiance to Aleksandra and Xavier.

Jacob was a young man, one of the latter. He'd been at sea for most of his life, sailing to New Zealand first as a young cabin boy, and later as a seaman. He'd made the trip several times each year with Captain Rach. A man more devoted to the old captain and less admiring of Broadhurst probably didn't exist on the ship.

"Broadhurst, even before Cap'n Rach disappeared, ee's bin promisin' those men 'at would follow 'im a big share o' the goods we're carryin'. 'At's why 'ees got the followin' 'ee do," Jacob said. "Ee's not makin' 'imself many other friends now, though, what wit' refusin' t' give Rach a fun'ral service, or t'sailor what fell from the yardarm."

Aleksandra frowned and shook her head. "The poor men. We'll just have to pray for them ourselves." She hesitated for a moment, then went on. "I wondered how he'd gathered so many to support him.

Jacob grumbled something under his breath.

Every time she thought about how little she could do to save her husband, her heart sank further. She'd always fought her way out of situations before or found one she trusted to help, but here there was no such possibility.

*Just a crazy man with the keys to Xavier's life.*

"Broadhurst has sworn to have Xavier tried for Symes' murder in Auckland or wherever we land, but I'm not so sure he won't just kill him in one of his mad fits. His mate Symes was most likely poxed and he isn't looking quite right himself," Aleksandra said to Jacob, as they groomed Charro together.

The big gray spent most of his day looking toward the ramp, his eyelids and muzzle wrinkled. This was the longest the stallion had ever gone without Xavier since he was a foal. Aleksandra felt for him and tried to make up for it with extra attention.

" 'Ees nowt right in the heid," Jacob agreed.

"And if he does get him before a magistrate, who would he listen to, a wife or a first mate of a ship?" She gritted her teeth.

Jacob opened his mouth to speak, then shut it again.

"I don't know what to do, Jacob. We don't really know how many men are faithful to Rach, do we?"

Jacob shook his head, with a frown.

Aleksandra's stomach churned, as it had for the past few mornings, and she barely made it to the bucket outside the stall.

Jacob looked sideways at her. "Are ye—"

"—I don't know, but if I am, I'd sure like it to have a daddy. I have no more family anywhere, and no chance of ever having one."

Aleksandra's voice rose on a wail as her world started to crumble, once again.

"Then we bes' be savin' y'man," Jacob cut in firmly. "I'm sure I kin tell if'n we see New Zealand, madam," he said. "If'n I see it, I'll be comin' to get y'right away. I cain't swim, but if'n y'can…"

"I can, but what do you have in mind?"

" 'At's a bonny wee pony ye got there," he went on, grinning from ear to ear. "Can 'ee jump?"

"Jumps and flies like the wind." Aleksandra narrowed her eyes at Jacob. "Why?"

"If'n we get near land, could y'jump 'im over the gunnel? And inta the sea? Yer a braw young thing, with yer wee sword, an' horses'r good at swimmin', 'specially if'n otherwise'n they'll drown." He winked at her. "An' then, y'could get help."

"You'd help me?" Aleksandra's heart lifted for the first time since Xavier was taken, and then it fell again.

New Zealand was a wide, wild country. Would she be able to find help? Would she be more help to Xavier here or out in unknown territory? If she stayed and Broadhurst killed Xavier, what would happen to her, and to Dzień, Charro, the rest? Her thoughts spun but she had to make a decision, and soon.

"O'course I'd help. And m'friends. 'First-Mate-Captain' is'n a friend o' mine," Jacob said. " 'Ees tried 'is touchy-feely bit on me, more'n once, when 'ee was a bit full o'the bottle." He shook his head. "Me little dirk an' 'im," he waved a deadly-looking dagger he produced from beneath his shirt, "they'da like t' get close some'n day." He gave a short laugh and rubbed Dzień's nose before he slunk back into the shadows from whence he'd materialized.

THE SHIP CONTINUED TO DRIFT, the jury-rigged sails on her remaining masts flopping uselessly in what random puffs of wind came their way.

"We must have been driven into the calms." The sailor on watch turned his head to spit over the side.

Aleksandra frowned at him.

"Out of the trade winds, into the calms of Capricorn."

"I never learned about those," Aleksandra said. Even to her ears, she sounded grumpy.

"They call 'em the doldrums, where a ship can wait without wind, without sail, for weeks on end until she runs out of food and water—then people go mad." He grimaced and crashed to the deck, clutching his neck in horror.

Aleksandra rushed to his side.

"Gotcha," the seaman said, as he leapt to his feet.

"You had me there." Aleksandra shuddered. "It's getting to be less and less of a laughing matter."

"You've got to laugh a little, especially in the calms," he smiled, "otherwise, you'll indeed go mad."

"I'll try to remember that when I have something to smile about." She raised an eyebrow at him and turned on her heel.

"Mrs. Arguello, take a look, out there," he pointed off the port bow.

She returned to his side and looked. A big dark-gray body slid from the water, arced up and dived, then a split tail smacked the water with a great splash.

"Is it a whale?" she breathed.

"It is, a humped back. We must be getting close to New Zealand."

It rose from the water again, closer this time, and turned a bit, so its big, liquid eye showed. She fancied it winked at her before it glided back into the water and disappeared.

"It's so graceful, and so very, very big," Aleksandra said.

"I always think of them like sleek horses," the seaman said. "Like after they come out of the sea, all dripping wet and glistening. I was on a whaler for awhile, but couldn't stand killing the beasts, and them so old."

She shuddered. She was a hunter, but they made her think of horses, too, and she wanted to reach out and hold them safe in her arms, not stick them with harpoons.

"HANDS ALOFT!" a sailor screeched from above. Men's feet pounded on the deck as they ran for the ratlines. Aleksandra spun to see what threatened.

Another harbinger of terror darkened the sky behind them on the starboard side. Aleksandra glanced around but no one was paying any attention to her, so she ducked below to check on Xavier.

"Good afternoon, sir. Might I have a wee word with my husband, please?"

"Cap'n's orders are no one speaks with 'im."

"Come, sir," Aleksandra smiled sweetly at him. "I clearly cannot get him out, so what would it matter? It appears there's a storm coming and I might not get to say goodbye otherwise. Could you let your wife go to her death without saying goodbye?"

He twitched his mustache and shifted his weight from foot to foot, then glanced longingly toward the stairway to the deck.

"I can watch him. You can go see what they're yelling about."

He looked at her sideways, then sighed. "You can talk with him, but no funny business, OK?"

"Wouldn't dream of it," Aleksandra said, in her softest voice, and the man bolted for the hatch.

"Sweet as pie when you want to be, aren't you, *Querida?*" Xavier shook his head and grinned at her through the slit in the door.

Aleksandra pulled up her skirts and slid one of the two sword scabbards from the ties strapping them to her thigh.

"Here," she said, shoving her papa's *shashka* through the slit.

"You always were my favorite girl," he said, and blew her a kiss. "What's happening up on deck?"

"Another storm's approaching." She bit her lip.

"It shouldn't be so bad." He cocked a brow at her. "We've little more mast to lose."

"We've been stuck in the calms for the past week," she grinned faintly, "in the 'horse latitudes'. I'd hoped it would be a good omen, being horses, but it hasn't worked." She tried to smile at him. "Let's hope we get knocked out of them before we run out of food and water."

"Not much chance of that," Xavier said. Our stock will feed the crew for quite some time."

"Let's not think on that." She gritted her teeth. "I wanted you to have the *shashka* in case you get the opportunity to use it, especially if we go down."

"I've loosened the bed timbers. They're heavy enough to use as a battering ram, if need be." The door moved a little as Xavier leaned his forehead against it, and his eyes came closer. "*Te quiero, Querida, siempre,* forever. Just thought I'd let you know."

"And I, you, *Querido,*" she said, as the gaoler clomped back down the passageway above and his feet appeared on the top stair. "I must be away," she said. "I'll go back to the stock now. I have a young friend, Jacob, who's been helping me. You can trust him."

Xavier gave her a half-smile.

"I'll try to get help, if I can get off the ship."

"No, Aleksandr—" he hissed.

"—yer time's up," the guard cut in.

"Get what sleep you can. *Te quiero*," she whispered. "This storm looks much like the last one."

"*Te quiero, que le vaya bien*," he called after her.

The new storm shook the barque as if Neptune had unleashed all his furies at once. Aleksandra checked on the decks every so often. Once the sails were furled again, the men went below to wait it out. She crept back to the brig at first light.

"Good morning, sir," she said to the gaoler. He got up from his chair and glanced past her, up the stairs into passageway. She slipped him a nip of whisky and he walked toward the stairs.

"I'll just be a moment, miss. Off to use the head," he said. He nodded his thanks to her, smiled at the small bottle, then held it to his lips as he left the room.

Xavier reached his fingers through the door and Aleksandra kissed them. Her heart wrenched as she stared through the narrow gap at her husband.

"It was much like last time," she said. "The men raced up the ratlines to furl what sails remain, but no one tried to run across the yards."

"That's good. There are few enough seamen on the trip as it is. Does anyone have any idea where we are?"

"No, but the men hope we'll be driven nearer to New Zealand, or at least out of the calms, so we can make some headway."

"A storm for a storm." He grinned wryly.

"Without it, we don't look to be going much of anywhere."

FOR TWO MORE NIGHTS, the little boat tossed on the waves.

Jacob had taken to helping her with the stock any time he could slip away. It couldn't be much better—the cows tolerated him and the horses adored him.

"How do the beams of the hull hold out when the barque smacks into the bottom of a trough?" Aleksandra shook her head.

"That's why'n y'truly have t' have'n the best boat builders," the boy said smugly. "Now, this barque, she'um made 'n Liverpool, that's'n in England, and she's made with the finest timbers," he said loudly, then added in an undertone, "Miss Aleks, I b'lieve we be gettin' pulled along by a current now, the wind be slackenin', but hear the li'l waves against the side?"

Aleksandra held her breath and listened. Sure enough, little wavelets slapped against the side. Not crashing, just slipping past the hull.

"Have y'got y'li'l bag packed?"

Aleks nodded in the faint light. She had to go. There was no other choice. Broadhurst seemed more unbalanced by the day.

"Here'n some oilcloth t'wrap yer kit in," he whispered, "an' put this in it too." He dropped to his knees before her and handed her a stack of hardtack, a flask of water, some raisins and a good-sized chunk of salt pork to boot. "Cooks'n told me to giv'n this to ye. We'll be takin' care to feed y'man while y're gone." He dropped a kitbag with shoulder straps beside the pile on the ground. "There'n be 'n oilsk'n coat in t' bott'm o' the bag. It be likin' to rain here." He grinned. "More'n y've *ever* seen."

Aleks smiled her thanks and gripped his hands, then let go. On impulse, she gave him a peck on the cheek and a tight hug.

He colored so pink she could see it in the near-darkness. He stood, then leaned down to Aleksandra once more.

"If'n y'send help, know 'at the men faithful'n to the old Cap'n Rach'll be waitin' to help free Rach's friend and y'rs. Godspeed." He touched his forelock and slid away.

Aleksandra stashed her packed bag, her bow and arrows tied together inside it, under Dzień's manger and covered it well with straw. Her bedroll sat beside it. She'd taken to sleeping in Dzień's stall. It was safer with her horses near than alone in her cabin surrounded by a ship full of strange men.

Aleksandra was grooming the already-gleaming Rogan when Captain Broadhurst came calling that evening.

"We haven't seen much of you on deck lately." He stepped up to lean on the tie stall pillar, then retreated when the bay bared his teeth and lunged at him.

"There's much to be done down here, especially for one person." She bit her cheek, hard, to stop herself from laughing at his ignominious retreat.

"That's a dangerous horse." His brows narrowed at Rogan.

"He's a stallion. It's to be expected." She forced a smile. "He was my father's, and he doesn't trust people easily. I've handled him since he was a foal."

She glanced beneath the horse's neck at Broadhurst while she worked. His hands didn't appear to be shaking anymore and his eyes looked normal.

"Maybe you shouldn't be taking care of the horses. I might get someone else to do it and you can stay up top and entertain my friends." He lifted an eyebrow at her. "I'd make it worth your while." He smirked.

Her hand strayed to her waist and he laughed.

"So it is true, what the men say. You really did pull a sword on them." His head tilted to one side. "Interesting," he said, as he slowly turned on his heel and walked away. "You'll bear watching. Be sure I will be."

# 20

The winds decreased and Aleksandra resumed her daily exercising of the horses, much of it running beside them at a trot. She and Dzień needed to be fit if they were to escape and find help.

She found an old pair of Xavier's trousers in the rag-bag, cut them off just below the knee, and placed them inside the top of Jacob's kitbag. When the time came for their exit, she'd wear them next to her skin beneath a skirt. She'd pull off the heavy skirt at the last minute—just before she mounted and set him at the five-foot solid bulwark for their jump into the sea. Skirts would be the death of her in the sea.

She knew Dzień would be able to swim in if they could see land. The horse didn't seem to mind water, and they'd swum many rivers in the past. He'd be only too pleased to set out for *terra firma* once he scented it. Her heart squeezed tight in her chest and a tear squeezed from the corner of one eye. It was a big jump for the little Mustang, but she had to get help before that madman killed her husband.

*Xavier.* She wanted to see him one last time. She filled a small bottle with whisky and tucked it into her belt, then put an apron over the top.

"Good evening, Xavier," she said loudly, as the gaoler left, then dropped her voice to a whisper. "Jacob says there is a group of men faithful to the old captain who will do their part when help comes."

Xavier smiled and reached for her hand.

"YES, THE HORSES ARE FINE," she nearly shouted.

"I'll be ready for whatever opportunity avails itself," Xavier said, beneath his breath. "I'm exercising within an inch of my life and practicing with the *shashka*."

"Stay strong, *mi querido*, AND THE COWS TOO. THE BULLS HAVE BEEN A BIT RESTLESS, BUT I THINK ONE OF THE COWS IS IN SEASON," she barked.

"Von Tempsky should be at Coromandel, however you can get there, God willing. Please stay safe, *Querida*."

"YOU WANT ME TO TRY TO BREED THE COW? DOWN THERE? THERE'S PRECIOUS LITTLE ROOM, HUSBAND," she said, in her loudest voice. "I'll do my best. *Te quiero*," she whispered, as she turned to go. "OKAY, OKAY, I'LL BREED THE SILLY COW. I SURE WISH YOU WEREN'T LOCKED UP IN HERE, THEN YOU COULD DO IT. IT'S NO JOB FOR A WOMAN!" She turned to gaze back at him, only his beautiful brown eyes showing through the slit in the door of the brig.

*This can't be the last time I'll see him. It just can't.*

As she walked back topside, a man lounging just outside the entrance to the hold nodded, a smirk on his tattooed face. The corners of her mouth turned up as she ducked her head and passed him quickly.

Whenever Aleksandra walked Dzień on deck she tended to see the same four men every day. They were often employed in different jobs, but they always kept one eye on her as she walked and ran around the deck. They usually had a nod and a smile for her. Perhaps they were part of the group Jacob mentioned. Tonight, though, other men watched. These were the Broadhurst's gang. As she passed these sailors, they gave her painted-on smiles that never neared their eyes. She airily waved the end of a lead rope to them and walked on, two horses at a time.

"You gettin' them horses ready for a race?" one of her usual watchers called out.

"I'm bettin' on the big bay," another said, with a grunt.

"I've got m' money on the gray Spanish horse," a third said.

"Me, I'll take all your money with the little Indian pony," Broadhurst said. "I've seen those Mustangs before. They're tough."

Aleksandra looked at him, eyebrows raised. "Yes, he is a lovely pony, isn't he?" She gave Dzień a pat.

"Did any of you see him go on board? No?" The captain shook his head. "He never even looked at the ramp, just followed Mrs. Argüello here like he'd done it every day of his life." He looked at her out of the corners of his eyes.

"I've trained him since he was a foal. Pa was a trapper and we had to have horses who did whatever we asked, or we wouldn't have survived."

Broadhurst just looked at her as she passed. He opened his mouth to speak, but instead, he mouthed, so silently even she didn't hear the words: "I'll be watching you."

WHENEVER SHE WASN'T HANDLING the horses or bringing food to Xavier, Aleksandra took to sitting on deck in hope of being the first to sight land. The days became monotonous, but at least the ship was drifting *somewhere*.

"I'm thinkin' we be in the Aucklan' Current," Jacob confided that evening, over the supper they shared in the hold. "This time o'year it run to the east o'New Zealan', down past Poverty Bay and heads fer th'South Islan'."

"So you think we're headed for New Zealand, then? The captain doesn't know where we—"

"—this 'cap'n' ain'a real cap'n," Jacob interrupted, "and don't know sh—"

"—I understand," Aleksandra cut in, flashing him a grin. Dzień shuffled his feet. Even the little rustling of straw sounded loud to her ears.

"Jus' so we understan' each oth'r." He smirked.

"So how would I find Coromandel Town from that coast?" Aleksandra muttered into her salt pork.

"*Coro?* I don' be likin' yer chances, Mrs. Argüello."

"Jacob, you can call me Aleks, remember?"

"Aleks, then. Some awful big mount'ns a'tween that'n East Coast n' Coro Town. Y'll need'n t' find a mission house'n ask 'em fer help. They c'n prob'ly find y'a native guide," he whispered, blowing crumbs of hardtack with his words. "There be lots'a boats comin' up'n down th'coast, all a time."

"Jacob, we owe you more than you can ever know. If we get out of this alive, please come find us, wherever we are. We're seeking a man called von Tempsky. He's from Poland, where my family comes from. Xavier met him in California, and he's a bit bigger than life, so I'm sure you can find him, and through him, us. When you tire of the sea, you'll always have a place with us."

The boy's eyes shone wetly in the dimness, and he ran a sleeve across his eyes. "Thank'ee, Mrs... Aleks." He gulped. "Ain't no one never said nuthin' like 'at a'fore. My thanks. I'd best be goin' now. I'm thinkin' yer land'll be 'ere soon. I seen alb'trosses las' night, an' it smells like land. T'morro', mebbe?"

"Thank you, Jacob, from the bottom of my heart. Now go." She gave him a little push. He turned and dashed up the ramp, his light footfalls barely audible over the munching of many beasts.

Louder feet, heavier ones, and irregular, came down the ramp and she looked up, heart in her throat.

"And what was all that about?" Broadhurst strode in, the collar of Jacob's shirt in his clenched fist. "Why did the boy run out of here and why were you two talking together so quietly?"

Aleksandra looked down at the ground as her guts churned and her face heated. How could they get out of this? "Well, sir," she put her hands over her face, "I do believe I embarrassed the lad, being frank with him about a woman's needs..." She rubbed her eyes and whimpered a little. "With my man not available, why, I just wanted a little closeness, but... but the boy's as good as his word and I'm a married woman... a bad, bad married woman. Please, please don't tell my husband I've been unfaithful in my heart," she got out, between sobs.

"That true, Jacob?" Broadhurst growled.

"Well, yessir. 'Tis," he said, in a small voice.

Aleksandra peeked between her fingers. The boy was biting his cheeks, his lips quivering.

"ALEKS." She awoke to Jacob's voice beside her ear and his touch light upon her shoulder.

She bumped into Dzień's muzzle as she sat up in the darkness and reached out to the boy. The Mustang whickered softly at the diminutive seaman, then nuzzled the back of Aleksandra's neck, his whiskers tickling her fully awake.

"Good save yest'day, wi' the cap'n'. He just'n 'bout found ye out," he whispered. She could swear he grinned in the pitch-darkness. "I smell'n land fer sure. It's jus' aft'r midnight, but I smell it and I hear some o' them li'l owls them have, them'r callin' 'em moreporks."

"What do you want me to do?"

"First light, if'n it's safe, I'll knock on th' deck above ye four times. Ye come out 'n ride fer yer life. I'll have m' men ready so's ye don' get shot while yer swimmin', but there won' be much'n time. If'n it gets t' be no safe, I'll bang three times. Ye'll have to do summat else, mebbe use th' two horses'n like we talked 'bout."

"OK. I'll be ready," she said, her stomach already knotting.

"I'll be tellin' yer man how ye went," he whispered, and they clasped hands before he melted into the night.

Sleep came hard, but she got some, in fits and starts, as the ship rocked through the night.

"It must be near to dawn," Aleksandra murmured to Dzień as he nuzzled her hair and shifted his weight to his other hind leg.

She sat with her skirt loosely tied over her short trousers, arms clasped around her knees. Aleksandra's knapsack remained hidden and Dzień's bridle stowed with it. No sound had yet come from the boards above.

At the sound of footsteps, Aleksandra looked between the planks lining Dzień's stall and she frowned. This wasn't their plan.

"Over here," she whispered.

"Expecting someone, were you?" Broadhurst sauntered into view.

"Only wishful thinking," Aleksandra said, and pulled her blanket up under her chin to better cover her fully-dressed frame. Her heart pounded so loudly she was sure he'd hear it from six feet away.

"Better get used to the idea your husband won't be coming back to you. He'll be hanged for what he did to Symes. Remember that," he said. His footsteps retreated toward the ramp.

"Thank you for the visit," she said, sarcasm dripping from her voice.

"Just a reminder. I'm watching you," he said, not bothering to stop.

How she wanted to bury her throwing knife between his shoulder blades.

Four knocks came through the ceiling boards and the captain's footsteps stopped.

"What's that?" he growled, his shoes squeaking as he spun around.

"It's still dark, you've woken me up from a sound sleep, you hear noises, and you ask *me* what they are?" Her voice raised as she railed at him, making sure it reached maximum volume by the end. "Good *night*, Captain Broadhurst," she shrieked at him, her hands clenched at her sides.

He took a deep breath, then resumed his walk topside.

Two minutes later, three knocks sounded and repeated.

Aleksandra assembled all just beside the door and went for a walk to see the lay of the land. She walked the long way to the privy. It gave her a view all around the ship as she walked, slowly and a bit unsteadily, as if still groggy from sleep. She turned a corner to see the captain headed back toward the galley and Rach's old cabin, then a door clicked closed. Ducking into a narrow space from which she couldn't be observed, she strained her eyes to starboard. *There.* Rising from the straight line of the sea.

Jagged lines of mountains, glorious mountains, broke the horizon. She bit her tongue to keep from crying out as she quietly opened, then slammed the privy door shut and slipped back the way she'd come. No one else was out walking at this hour. As she entered the hold, four faint knocks sounded on the wood above.

Aleksandra smiled. Jacob was on the job.

Dzień took the bit she proffered, then her fingers flew as she slipped the crownpiece over his head, buckled the throatlatch, and flicked the split reins around his neck. Slinging the knapsack onto her back, she strapped it on tightly. One tug on the string of the waistband of her skirt and it slid to her feet. She stepped out of it and shivered, goosebumps raising against the thin men's trousers.

Leading her pony from his tie stall, she swung up and they dashed away, up the ramp from the hold to the 'tween decks. She turned the corner toward the top deck and Dzień slid to a halt as a shadow rose up before them, hands held high.

"Stop," Broadhurst barked.

The captain dropped his hands and walked toward them, shaking his head. "Stupid, stupid. That's the oldest trick in the book." He grinned as he reached for Dzień's reins.

# PART II

---

# WAIAU BAY, NEW ZEALAND

## 21

November 1863, Waiau Bay, East Coast New Zealand

ALEKSANDRA'S FATHER hadn't spent years training her and her mount in the Cossack ways for nothing. She drew her shashka as Dzień rose on his hind legs in a levade, tucking his forelegs up to protect his rider and free her to swipe at Broadhurst. He dodged, but not before he received a slice across the inside of his right forearm for his efforts.

The captain's fingers jerked backwards and he screamed.

Desperately hoping Broadhurst shot his pistol right-handed, she called out to Dzień and he swerved around the man crouching before them, holding his arm and screaming.

Dzień galloped the rest of the way up to the deck. She turned her head to sight the five-foot-high bulwark, topped by the even higher gunwale, and lined the Mustang up to give him the longest possible run. Reaching behind her, she shoved her *shashka* into the pack then loosed the reins and called to Dzień as she aimed him for the solid wall. Her heart sang as he raced toward it like he'd been shot from a cannon. The Mustang gave a great grunt as his forelegs left the ground and he shoved with his hindquarters. Then his hind hooves, softened by the long trip in the damp hold, slipped.

Heart in her mouth, Aleksandra held her breath and kept her eyes up, her legs clamped firmly on his sides. She'd never jumped this high, much less bareback. Dzień swung his hind legs sideways to miss the rail and his hind hooves clipped the top of the gunwale, but then they were over, and falling, falling until they hit the dark water.

Breath jarred out of her, she sank, and sank…far beneath the surface.

*How could I have ever thought water would be soft to land in?*

She held her breath forever as bubbles ran upwards past her face, tingling like a bath of icy champagne bubbles across her skin. Pain shot through her ears as they continued to drop like stones, deeper and deeper. In a momentary panic, she wondered if they could explode.

The water was so shockingly cold she nearly inhaled it, but the rock of a horse under her seat reassured her and she pulled herself together.

Aleksandra reached for the tendrils of mane that brushed her fingers and hung on for dear life as he surged upward, his strong legs kicking out behind him. It was all she could do to cling to his mane like a limpet and pray Jacob and Rach's friends could keep Broadhurst's men from shooting them out of the water.

They broke the surface with a roar. She wasn't sure if the sound was from her own tortured ears or from guns on the boat behind them, but all she could do was lay low on Dzień's neck, praying for a miracle.

*Just one miracle for today, please.*

Either Dzień knew where land lay or he just wanted to get away from the boat which had imprisoned him for months. Either way, he struck out for the distant ridges against the sky, tail streaming behind him. He struggled to keep his head above water with her on his back, so she knotted the reins behind his ears, slid down his back and off his rump, then let his long tail slide through her fingers. She tied a knot near the end of the long hairs and held the tail above it, letting herself float behind him.

She glanced back to the ship, its outline just showing in the pre-dawn light. There might have been some movement on board, but no flashes of pistol fire. She could only hope Broadhurst was completely incapacitated and would be dealt with appropriately until she returned with help.

However long that might be.

Captain Rach, bless his dead soul, had provided for an extra month of feed and water for the stock. Likely he'd done the same for the passengers and crew. She could only hope so, as the dark-edged, ragged mountains loomed larger in the growing light.

THE PONY's hooves pounded up the ramp toward him and Jacob ducked out of the way so he didn't spook the little horse. Dzień made so much noise that Jacob never heard Broadhurst running down the slope behind him until the captain passed him in his hiding place, and raced on down the ramp toward Aleksandra. His heart was in his throat as Broadhurst yelled and the hoofbeats stopped.

*Aleks was done for.*

He bolted after Broadhurst as fast as he could run. The captain's shout became a scream of anger and pain, then Dzień's hooves clattered up the gangway again, skidded around the corner and came on, up the next ramp, toward him. He could have cheered. Aleksandra's sword glittered red in the faint light through the portholes and he saluted her as she passed.

Jacob half-wanted and half-couldn't bear to watch them jump the solid bulwark, but the choice was out of his hands now. Broadhurst was still screaming and hadn't come up the ramp. He *had* to stop him from coming back up on deck.

Jacob clung to the shadows as he ran, then peeked around the corner into the dark depths of the hull. As his eyes adjusted to the darkness, he saw Broadhurst huddled on the floor of the ramp leading from the hold, and a stream of blood ran down the ramp below him. The captain clutched his arm and howled, still with his back to Jacob. The boy glanced both ways and behind him, but no one was there to see.

He never hesitated, though he shivered at the thought of punishments meted out to mutineers. He reversed his dagger, and with four quick steps, was onto him. One clunk over the head and the screaming stopped as Broadhurst slumped to the floor.

Feet pounded behind him and Jacob dived into the depths of Rogan's stall. The stallion shifted his feet and wuffled beneath his breath, then stood still, as Jacob waited.

Two men entered the hold and looked from side to side until they saw Broadhurst on the floor. Jacob breathed again. It was Rogers and Smithy, two of Rach's men. They were some of those who'd helped him prepare the way for Aleksandra's escape.

"Jake?"

"I'm here, Rogers."

"Did you drop him?"

"It were all m'little dirk's idea," Jacob said from the shadows, as he climbed out from between the bay's legs, flourishing his knife.

"And a good one it was," Smithy said, "but Broadhurst's men are on their way down, so clear out, boy, they've got pistols."

"So," Jacob raised a brow at them, "do I."

"Good lad. Now disappear," he said. "We don't know how many men Broadhurst has in the crew, so we won't take over just yet." He lifted one of Broadhurst's eyelids and peered into his eye.

"Someone get the surgeon," Rogers shouted, as the sound of running feet came from the ramp above them, then two more men appeared.

"Where's Broadhurst?" one of them growled, looking from side to side in the gloom.

"He's down here. He's hurt. We need the surgeon," Rogers repeated. "He's bleeding pretty bad. He must've fallen and hit his head. Help me get him up on deck, where there's some light."

"Aye," said the other newcomer. He gulped, eyeing the blood trail beside his captain, and slipped away.

Together, the men picked him up and climbed the ramp.

With a rub on the nose of the stallion, Jacob followed at a safe distance.

By the time Jacob reached the deck, the surgeon was already kneeling beside the fallen man with his bag. Jacob settled himself on deck where he couldn't be seen.

*There had to be some advantages to being small.*

The surgeon briefly checked the already-swelling egg on Broadhurst's head then turned his cut arm this way and that. He peered closely, digging around in the wound with a piece of shiny metal from his bag. He hemmed and hawed for a few more moments, then glanced up in time to see one of Broadhurst's flunkies, a big braw lad, slither to the floor beside his captain's head.

"It's always the big ones that pass out," the doctor said, and grinned. "They can't handle the blood and meat." He doused the wound with spirits and bandaged the arm, his lips in a tight line.

"Not much to stitch together, eh?" Rogers said.

"The tendons have retracted, so not much to do there," said the surgeon. "He's lost a lot of blood already... I suppose I could stitch it together, but it's probably not worth it."

"What do you mean?" Broadhurst's first mate's brows lowered, his tattoos bulging as he tensed.

"Wound that size? And him diminished from years of laudanum? He'll probably never be able to heal the wound." The surgeon shook his head. "Probably just best to wrap it up and keep him full of laudanum until the bottle—our last one—is empty."

Rogers raised a brow at the surgeon.

"But—" the mate began.

The ship lurched, her timbers creaking.

"ROCKS, ROCKS!" shouted the lookout. The men looked at each other, then at their unconscious captain.

"He won't be giving any orders soon." Rogers raised a brow at the man before him.

"Drop anchor, whoever can get there first!" yelled the mate, and ran toward it. The chain rattled shortly, then stopped short in the too-shallow depths.

In the fracas, Jacob moved from his hiding place and headed to tell Xavier. Another of Broadhurst's men stepped into his path, brows narrowed, lips tight.

"You stay away from the Spaniard," he menaced. "I'm watching you. Unless you want to be locked up with him, keep your distance until the captain wakes up."

"Yessir," Jacob dropped his eyes, "just on m'way to m'berth," he said, and ducked away from the fist the sailor swung in his direction. He met up with two of Rach's men on the other side of the ship.

"She made it. Aleks made it to shore," one of the men whispered as he sidled up to Jacob and passed a telescope behind his body. He glanced over his shoulder toward Broadhurst's men and moved to block their view of the boy looked through the glass.

"She's climbin' up Dzień's leg."

"Good. She was flat out in the sand, before," the sailor said,

"Well lordy, lordy," Jacob said, and sat down hard on a pile of shredded sails, his legs turned to jelly. "She done it." He turned his face up to thank his friends, then he frowned. They were all blurry, or maybe it was his eyes. He blinked a few times. He never cried.

"It weren't anything," one of the sailors said. "Thank Christ she had that sword. She may have just delivered us from yon madman."

"I jus hope," Jacob went on, "she be livin' long 'nuff to *find* help," he murmured. "They're at war out there."

"And thank Christ," said the sailor with the telescope, "they missed those rocks."

"THANK YOU, THANK YOU, THANK YOU," Aleksandra said to anyone who would listen, as a wake spread out behind Dzień. "You splendid pony, what would I do without you?" she murmured.

A wavelet smacked across her face and she spluttered, then swallowed a mouthful of the briny liquid. Her lips and hands were rubbery and half-numb, but she still felt the rough tail hairs slide against her palms as her grip on Dzień's tail begin to fail. Holding her breath, she wove cold fists through his tail above the knot and locked her arms so she wouldn't lose hold of the Mustang, then began kicking to help him along.

After a while, the waves came from behind them. The surges that lifted and dropped them became waves that increased in size and soon crashed all around them. Aleksandra tumbled and spun, salt water filling her nose, eyes and sinuses. Which way was up? Down? She clung to Dzień, her lifeline, as he towed her through the water. His tail jerked on her arms once, then again, and again. They were in shallow water, and Dzień's feet pounded the wet sand.

Aleksandra tried to let go of his tail before he dragged her, but her arms wouldn't mind. She called out to the pony, but all she could manage was a squeak and a barrage of coughing. She finally extricated herself and slumped on the smooth, hard sand.

"Dzień." She whispered his name.

He returned to her and nosed at her shoulder as she lay in a heap. Wavelets nudged her legs when she tried to turn toward the Mustang to rub his face, but she couldn't move, couldn't lift herself from the sand… then she remembered her knapsack and shook her head, with a ghost of a rueful grin.

"Thank you, again, my darling pony," she murmured, as he pushed at her with his nose. Aleksandra pulled her knees beneath her, then struggled to a sitting position. She sat for a few moments, then climbed up his forearm to stand on wobbly legs, her arms wrapped around his neck. Water soaked his coat and dripped off his mane and tail, and her own braid. Aleksandra took a big, stinging breath, then moved to the front of him and put her forehead against his.

"I know you hate water in your ears," she said, "but it couldn't be helped. Without it, Xavier might not be getting off that boat or surviving the exit."

She inhaled deeply and looked around into the first rays of sun shining across the sea. In its path, the barque lay silhouetted—mainsail gone, the other two masts forlorn in their nakedness. There was movement on deck, but it was too far away to make out what was happening, so she turned back to peruse the shore. In the rapidly growing light, the beautiful white sand beach arced away in a long bay. A short distance away, a wide river mouth opened onto the beach, flowing from a big valley in a nearly vertical wall of steep mountains. The beautiful sea of green beginning at the shoreline seemed to go on forever, as far as the eye could see.

"Well, boy, how about some fresh water?" Aleksandra managed a smile and took another deep breath. "I don't know where we are, but if Jacob's right this is the East Coast of New Zealand, our new home."

Dzień flicked his soggy ears, shook the rest of the sea water from his coat, and together they headed for the river.

There was so much green, green upon green, it dazzled the eyes, with no sign of habitation. The massive trees were unlike any she'd seen before. Some were like the ferns in the redwoods of California, except they weren't bushes, but big trees. Fern trees. She shook her head in amazement. Something moved in the bushes to her left and her hand slid to her hip, but her *shashka* was gone.

Her heart pounded against her ribs before she remembered it was in her pack. She reached back and felt its outline through the canvas, then broke out into a cold sweat and glanced skyward.

*Thank you again.*

Aleksandra slowly let out her breath.

A small stream crossed the beach ahead and she followed it toward the trees. Parting the branches, she peered into the darkness.

"Oh," she breathed.

From over the sea, the sun's early rays slipped inside the edge of the forest and caught a tiny, perfect, waterfall. It flowed from a stand of ferns high up a wall of rock. The water glittered as it tumbled from stone to stone until it reached the stream at her feet.

She'd never seen anything so beautiful.

Scooping up a handful of the water, she took a drink, then offered some to the old gods of the place, whoever they were. She bowed, then with one last backward glance, turned to go.

Never one to waste an opportunity, Dzień was already browsing on the trees and bushes lining the beach.

"Let's go find that river," she said, and continued on until they came to the wide river. Untying the waist strap, she slid out of her knapsack. Dzień drank while she stripped off her wet clothes, shivering in the early morning air. Aleksandra followed him in, gasping at the temperature, then ducked all the way under and came up giggling. She slid under again and rubbed her hair until it was cleaner than it had been for their months at sea. She couldn't remember being so happy to smell fresh water and have clean hair and skin.

"Everyone on board would be jealous. Fresh water—not salt, nor from a three-month old barrel." She grinned at the pony, then squeezed the water from her hair and shook it out.

Opening the pack, she pulled out her wet *shashka*, rinsed it in fresh water and wiped it dry, then extracted the oilskin-wrapped bundle. Her packed clothes were dry, as were her knives and bow.

After her sodden garments, the soft warmth of her buckskins and sequestered weapons were familiar and welcome. Dzień nearly inhaled the handfuls of corn she scooped into her hat for him, then she repacked her bag and slung it on.

"OK, pony," she said, rubbing his neck as they walked up the trail beside the river, "we're looking for a needle in the haystack here. Somehow we need to find Gustavus von Tempsky."

Something niggled at the back of her mind as she rambled on to the horse, but her brain wasn't clear enough to grasp it.

"I think we're in the right country, but I have no idea where we are, nor if there are any people here, nor how to find the—"

Aleksandra's heart froze and she stopped dead.

*The trail beside the river. With footprints.*

In an uninhabited wilderness…

It wasn't uninhabited, either.

Before her on the trail was a pair of bare feet. Big ones.

Slowly, blood pounding in her head, she lifted her eyes to meet those of what could only be a native of this land.

She gulped.

His dark face and body were covered by swirling tattoos—and little else. The massively muscled, taut warrior, for he could only be a warrior, held in his hand a heavy club, carved from a glossy green stone... *and he wasn't smiling.*

## 22

*Come on, Aleks, you didn't spend your life among the Shoshone to be frightened by a native.*

She mentally shook herself and did what she would have done if she'd unexpectedly faced an Indian of a tribe whose language she didn't know. She nodded and gave a short bow, then greeted him in Shoshone and then in English. Then she stood again, and looked him in the eyes. Despite the grimness of his fierce scowl and lowered brows, a glint of merriment lurked in his eyes. The corners of his mouth twitched, before his visage returned to that of a fierce warrior whose lands have been invaded.

"Well met, horse-woman. Why do you dress as a man and how did you come ashore from that ship?"

Aleksandra stared at him. He spoke English! She snapped her mouth shut and took another deep breath.

He raised an eyebrow as he waited.

"I'm Aleksandra and I've come from San Francisco."

"San Francisco." His smile grew wide. "I have been there. It is a place of wonders. I am Tama. You wouldn't be able to pronounce the rest of my name, but I am of the Turanganui-a-Kiwa people."

"You've been to San Francisco?" Aleksandra could only stare. Was she dreaming? She closed her eyes and pinched her arm, but when she opened them, he still stood there. She slowly shook her head.

"I've been there on a whaler. Many of the men in my *hapū* harpoon for the whalers or steer their boats."

"Oh." She blinked. "We are in New Zealand, then?" she said.

"You don't know? Yes, at Waipiro Bay." His brows narrowed and he looked at her from the corners of his eyes.

"We were heading for Auckland, but were caught by two storms. The midship mast broke in the first storm and the calms held us afterward. The next squall put us back into some current, but we had no idea which, nor where we were bound."

"The storms were big. They have damaged many of our *whares*."

"*Whares?*"

"Houses. Again, how did you get to the shore?"

"I jumped my pony over the rail and into the sea. We swam in."

"Over the gunwale?" He blinked. "The small horse has a big jump. The swim, I can see," he said, with a grin. She tried not to cringe as he reached out and lifted her braid, sodden, from where it lay on the water-stained buckskin.

"So why do you dress like a boy, which you clearly are not, and why did you make this pony leap into the sea and swim ashore?" Dzień shoved his head against him and he glanced down. He grimaced as he vigorously returned the rub on Dzień's wet forehead. "And what was the pistol shot I heard?"

"A shot? Wasn't me. Might have been *at* me, but it wasn't me." Her rifle was still wrapped up with her bow in the long kitbag. It was a wonder she hadn't cracked her head on the weapons when Dzień leapt into the water.

She took a deep breath and narrowed her eyes, considering how much to tell this man. She looked up at him, considering, for a moment. She had little to lose and Xavier needed help. There really was no choice.

"It's a long story," she stared him full in the eyes, "however, the end result is that the first mate, who probably killed the captain, has taken over the ship and is holding my husband captive. I seek a friend of ours. He is in Coromandel."

His brows shot up and he shook his head. "Do you have any idea how far away that is?"

"No," she winced, "and I'm not sure I want to know, but I'll ask anyway." She looked up at him from beneath her lashes.

"Overland, many weeks. If you can find a boat to take you and…this beast, probably less than a week." He looked at her sharply. "That is, if anyone can be convinced to guide you there. We must see the tribal elders for their permission. Some are less than pleased with the Queen's government. They are not so happy as they once were to help settlers."

Aleksandra took a big breath, then let it out. "Would you please take me to them, then? I must get help for my man."

He looked at her closely and nodded, then turned away and walked on up the path beside the river.

The trail ran nearly straight up the side of a mountain from the beach. Sunlight filtered through tall trees so densely packed together it was hard to say where one finished and another started. The big tree ferns made finely dappled patterns on the ground and across Tama's back.

Innumerable birds flew through the canopy or flitted about them.

"What are these little ones, the ones that squeak and follow us?"

"*Pīwakawaka*. Fantail," he said. "They're my favorites." He made little squeaky kissing noises and the birds flitted closer, nearly landing on his hand.

Aleksandra grinned at their antics, then practiced the sound. Soon they were approaching her too, nearly brushing her with their wings. Some other little birds made warbly sounds as they passed.

"*Tauhou*," Tama said. "Waxeyes."

A quarter of an hour later, Tama dropped back level with Aleksandra as the trail widened. "Do you not fear going before the tribal leaders?" He looked at her sideways, brows wrinkled. "Any other *Pākehā*, especially a woman, would run a thousand miles, screaming, before entering a *Māori* village, much less meeting with the leaders."

"I can't say I wasn't frightened to see you before me on the beach, but my father was blood-brother to the leader of a Shoshone Indian tribe. He loved me like a daughter. Chiefs hold no terror for me—they're people too." She looked up at him with a smile on her face, but bit her lip at his shocked expression.

It seemed his tribe's leaders were to be feared.

As they continued beside the river, higher and higher into the mountains, the track remained wide enough for them to walk abreast.

"Do you go out on whalers now?"

"No. Many of them have gone, either elsewhere to hunt whales or to take up other trades here. There is plenty to sell."

Aleksandra looked around her. She saw nothing but dense 'bush', as her new companion called it—no farms or other signs of dwellings. "What do you sell?" she said, pushing a stray curl away from her face.

"Our women make fine *kete*—bags, and baskets and such, from *kōrari*, flax, and we sell much flax fiber overseas to Australia and the rest of the world. We also grow crops for selling to the settlers—potatoes, *kumara*, gourds and wheat."

"How do you get them to Auckland?

"*Pākehā* traders used to buy them and pick them up, but our *hapū* has ships now, and sells our produce without their help." His lips formed a grim smile.

"Pardon?" She cocked her head and looked at him.

"Our tribes used to be gullible barterers, but thanks to Reverend Grace from the Church Missionary Society, we now get what our goods are worth. He taught us about business. Traders and others who weren't happy with the *Māori* producers' new knowledge drove the Reverend out, but the knowledge he offered remains. Now, with our own ships, we're able to get full value in Auckland."

"Too bad the American Indians don't have your Reverend Grace's help." She shook her head. "Life for them is getting worse by the day."

"So why do you wear men's clothing?" He was back on track.

"I grew up trapping in the mountains and it was the only sensible way to dress. Sometimes I wear skirts, but not when I plan to ride for days on end."

"And you can you do this, this sort of riding?"

"Yes," she hesitated, then went on. "I rode for the Pony Express in Utah."

"Pony Express? Even I have heard of this. And this 'pony' of yours?"

"Dzień? He's been on the trail, but not as an Express horse. Where is your village, by the way?" Aleksandra asked, between breaths, as she panted up a particularly steep hill. Their tribe must be extremely fit, if they had to walk up this slope all the time.

"Near where I found you, but our leaders are at the Te Puia Hot Springs for a day of planning and contemplation. I believed you had a certain urgency to be away, so we have come now.

The fronds of a tree fern brushed against her as they rounded a corner and turned off the river path to enter a clearing. A group of men sat before them in a ground-level, steaming pool of water.

As one, they turned. One jumped out, naked but for his tattoos, and brandished a long wooden weapon.

Tama barked something in his own language and the man put down his stick as Aleksandra looked away. A big splash sounded from the direction of the pool, then only silence.

"Shall I wait until they're finished?" Aleksandra whispered. Her cheeks were probably steaming as much as the pool.

"They'd be in there all day, but for your coming here." He grinned at her. "Go, sit," he nodded at a big rock a short distance away. "I'll drag the necessary men from the water."

He soon returned, and Aleksandra looked up at him. "What is the government doing that bothers your people?"

"The *Pākehā* want more land, the best land, of course, and authority over the native people of this land, the *Māori*. We, for some strange reason, do not agree." His eyes were steely.

Her heart jerked. She let out the breath she'd been holding.

"What is it?" His brows narrowed at her.

"I grew up among the *Shoshone*, as I said. This pony was their gift to me." She rubbed Dzień's neck as she spoke. "I am well familiar with this taking of land and life." She was silent for long moments. "It's not something I wish to see again. Ever."

"You're about to see more of it. As a *Pākehā*, I'm afraid you'll be in danger, the way things are brewing, especially where you're headed."

Aleksandra gulped and her eyes began to well up. How could governments continue to harm native peoples? "What's a *Pākehā*?" she managed.

"Many translations, not all complimentary, but let's just say your Indians would call him a White Man."

"We thought to come to New Zealand to find gold, and peace." She swallowed hard and looked down at her hands, wringing the fringe of her buckskins. "We were told the natives and the settlers got along well. How could I have believed such a thing, when I knew it could never be?" Tears fell to her hands and shirt, staining the buckskin dark.

Like blood.

*Running doesn't help. It's here, just as bad as back home.*

The dark man rose and left her.

Dzień lifted his head from the undergrowth a short time later and fluttered his nostrils at Tama, whose head appeared through the ferns.

"They're ready." He nodded his head back towards the pool.

The assembled elders stood beside the pool, fully dressed. Behind the men, a great cloud of steam billowed as several women pulled a large basket from a smaller pool and hefted it onto the ground beside it. They looked her way and whispered among themselves.

Tama motioned toward Aleksandra and spoke at length in *Māori*. The men were silent, their tattooed faces stern, then they muttered together. She stood facing the men in silence and watched the women from the corners of her eyes as they emptied the contents of the baskets onto smooth boards. The scents wafting from the steaming packets was beyond recognition, and heavenly.

Finally, one of the men spoke to Tama and he translated. "Our *rangatira*, our chief, doubts the mission station at Tokomaru Bay has the military might to free your husband and remove your belongings from the barque, but he suggests you go to the mission there. Our leaders have given me permission to guide you there and put you on a whaling boat or trading ship for the Coromandel. They won't mix themself in the disagreement between two *Pākehā*, but they're willing to help you get your own assistance."

The men nodded at her and spoke in their own language.

"They have invited us to share their meal."

She let out a long breath. She'd thought they'd never ask. "I accept, with gratitude. Please thank them for me. I would like to give them this," she said, reaching into her bag for the raisins.

They joined the men around the food and she handed the small pouch of fruit to their leader. He frowned at it and looked at her.

"Tell him they are raisins, dried grapes," she said to Tama.

He told them, and explained, with hand gestures.

Several of the men nodded and smiled as they were shared around.

"A few of the men have had grapes, and I have had raisins in my travels. They thanked you," Tama said. "And now we have," he scooped unfamiliar foods into her carved wooden bowl, "*kumara, Māori* potatoes, pork and *puha*."

She looked at the brilliantly colored foods, the unfamiliar tubers, and blinked. "That water is hot enough to cook pork?" She glanced at the men who'd just been soaking in one of the pools.

"Wait until you taste it." He laughed. "The temperatures of the pools differ. The men were in no danger of cooking."

Even if she *had* been able to eat decent meals for the past three months, it still would have been fantastic. The scent of the delicious, perfectly-cooked pork permeated everything else: the soft, fragrant, sweet *kumara*—sweet potato, the slightly bitter green *puha*, and *taewa*—the moist, little purple-brown potatoes.

"My thanks." She nodded at the women, standing by the side, and bowed to them. "It is all delicious."

They smiled and turned back to weaving and braiding long, flat strips of some green plant material.

"What are they weaving?" Aleksandra asked, with a glance at the flying hands of the women.

"They are plaiting flax. From it, they make baskets, ropes, and with more preparation, linen. As I said before, we sell much flax fiber overseas."

"We don't have flax where I come from."

"It grows in profusion here in the wet areas and near the coast."

"That would account," Aleksandra said, with a grin, "for the reason we don't have it in Utah. It's mostly desert."

He laughed. "Coming from here, it's hard to imagine a desert, but come, the men wish to speak with us some more."

WHEN THEY LEFT the hot springs an hour later, after a last wave of thanks to the leaders, Tama held out his hand for the knapsack, but Aleksandra refused.

"I can manage it," she said, and walked on ahead of him.

Fifteen minutes of straight uphill trail later, Aleksandra began to slow and her breath came faster.

"Aleks, why don't you ride the horse, then I can go at my regular speed?" he said, with the hint of a smile.

"Isn't this fast already?" Aleksandra stared at him. Sweat dripped from her brow and her legs burned. She took advantage of their stop to take a few deep breaths and a sip from her canteen.

He raised an eyebrow at her.

"I didn't realize," she bit her lip, "how unfit I've become on board the ship, despite walking the horses on deck every day."

She dropped her pack and handed it to Tama while she mounted. Once up, she held her hands out for the knapsack but Tama quirked his lips.

"I'll carry it," he said, swung it onto his back, then trotted off at an impossible pace. Aleksandra blinked, her mouth open, but Dzień began dancing on the spot.

"OK, you boys. Go." She chuckled, and slipped the reins. The Mustang shook his head as he shot forward. He followed at a trot, once he'd caught up to the flying *Māori*.

"How far is it to this Tokomaru Bay?" Aleksandra called out, over Dzień's head.

"It's nearly ten miles," he said, over his shoulder. "A little over an hour."

"And you intend to keep up this pace for the whole trip?" She raised a brow at him, then stared at the rough, steep trail ahead.

He glanced at her over his shoulder, merriment glinting in his eyes and flashed her a bright smile.

Aleksandra closed her eyes for a moment, then laughed out loud. She wanted to see him try.

The forest was even denser up here along a ridge, as they headed south. The tallest trees reached far up into the sky, and beneath that were innumerable smaller ones, along with many more of the tree-ferns. "What are the big tree-ferns called, Tama?"

"They're *ponga*," he said. "I've not see them elsewhere in the world."

"They're lovely." She gazed up at them as they passed. "The little curling bits inside, the leaves before they've completely unfurled…they're like a seashell that's been cut in half."

"That is the idea of *koru*. *Koru* symbolizes "change" or "growth". The *ponga* frond still unfurling. Endless possibilities."

"A poet and a warrior, eh Tama?"

He tossed a grin back at her. "Yes, they all laugh at me, except for the women." He raised an eyebrow at her. "They like it."

His answers, though still complete, became shorter as the hour progressed. "So this husband of yours, what did he do to get locked up?" He glanced back at her.

She told him the story.

"Well, I can see what the man was on about. If I had the chance to have you, I would," he chuckled, "but I suspect there's more to you than meets the eye. You don't give me the impression of being an easy woman to keep. Take, for instance, that sword tucked inside your pants."

She frowned. It was completely hidden from sight. "What sword?"

"It is my job to know if someone is armed," he said. "If you know how to look, you see much. It is hidden, but its shape is visible, even through the leather."

She frowned. The man was too observant, by far.

"What is it called, by the way, the leather you wear?"

"It's buckskin." She was glad to be able to answer a simple question and forget about how poorly she'd hidden her *shashka*.

"How is it made? And from what?"

"It's made from the skin of a deer—"

"—deer?"

"They're a wild grazing animal, about the size of a young horse. To make it into buckskin, the skin is worked and worked to make it soft, supple."

"I'd like one like that," he said, puffing, as he dropped back beside her. "May I?" He raised an eyebrow, as he reached towards her to touch the leather.

"Of course."

"Nice," he said, after he'd rubbed the flexible, but tough, leather between his fingers.

"I promise you'll have one for taking me to Tokomaru Bay. How would I get it to you?"

His eyes lit up and he took an extra breath.

"You can send it to the Reverend and Mrs. Blakett at Tokomaru Bay Mission House. We're going there first," he said.

"Well, if I don't return myself, I'll be sure to send it there. You've made my quest much simpler. Actually, you've made it *possible* and I thank you. Do you wish more payment for taking me today? I'm happy to pay."

"No, that shirt will be payment in plenty. Just one thing, though," he stopped for a moment to get his breath at the crest of a hill and pointed out into the distance at the curving bay before them. "Tokomaru Bay".

"One thing?" Aleksandra raised an eyebrow at him.

"One thing, yes. If you are ever at a loss for a husband, or if you are in trouble and I could be of assistance, please call upon me." He looked her straight in the eye. "Women of your bravery are prized among our people and I would be proud to call you my own."

## 23

Aleksandra could only stare at the handsome man gazing at her with such intensity. She dumbly nodded her assent until she could speak again. "It's just a bit to take in," she said, with a wry grin, "to go from terror of a half-naked native to a marriage proposal within a day." She lifted her chin and smiled. "Thank you, Tama. Your offer, coming from a man so clearly respected by his elders and so well-spoken and courteous, is a compliment indeed. I am, however, well and truly married and hope to stay that way forever."

He swept her a bow which wouldn't have been out of place before royalty and started off at a trot.

"Your English is impeccable. It's much better than mine," she shouted after him as they trotted down the hill toward Tokomaru Bay. "Where did you learn it?"

"I took lessons with the previous Reverend and his wife at the Mission House in Tokomaru Bay for many years. When I was old enough, I worked on a whaler out of St. Patrick's cove, at the other end of the bay. My English was correct, but halting. Then I whaled with a man for four years who'd been an English governor in a manor house before he'd emigrated to New Zealand. I learned much from him about life in other places, as well as proper English. He had school books from which I taught myself. He coached me, filling in the gaps left by the books."

"You've done well for yourself." She smiled.

"Thank you. I've never regretted the time spent learning. It's been helpful in our negotiations with the Queen's government. I'm afraid, however," his voice lowered, "they're not going well."

They followed a trail by a large stream, then slid down a steep bit onto some cliffs. Glimpses of blue water showed between the trees.

"That's part of Tokomaru Bay. We're on its northern edge." He continued down the cliff. The coast was rocky on this end, its water looking dark and deep, but as they followed the trail above the waterline, a pristine white beach appeared at the edge of the bay, arcing away from them for miles, its dense, green bush growing right down to the water's edge.

"Oh, it's beautiful," Aleksandra breathed. Other than Waipiro Bay, which she'd been too exhausted and cold to fully take in, the only other beach she'd seen was at San Gregorio. That had been a much smaller beach, with steep sandstone cliffs and plenty of seaweed and kelp covering much of the beach. This beach's glittering white sand ran for miles. It was simply and only the most lovely place she could ever remember seeing.

Tama stopped and pointed out landmarks. "There's the Tokomaru Bay Mission House. See the fields behind it? On the other side of that promontory at the end of the beach is St. Patrick's Cove, the site of the first whaling station around here.

"What a paradise." She shook her head, then had a thought. "Did you come all this way for your schooling?"

"Do you think it might have been worth it?" He cocked a bow at her.

"I'd just never considered running twenty miles a day to get to school, but then I was educated at home, so I guess I was one of the lucky ones."

"It was worth it. Between that education and my travels around the world on a whaler, I've been blessed to see so much."

Aleksandra slid down from Dzień's back and slipped off her knee-high moccasins to dig her toes into the sand, warm from the afternoon sun. They walked down the long, white beach that seemed to go on forever, or at least until it reached the promontory rising from the far end. As they crossed one of the little streams that emptied out into the sea, Dzień pulled Aleksandra towards the bush.

"He knows the water will be fresher up in the trees." Aleksandra laughed.

"He probably smells the good, green grass growing somewhere up there, too." Tama gave the pony a scratch as he walked past him.

"The birds sound so different from those in Utah and California." Aleksandra cocked her head to listen to one.

"That one's a Bell Bird, *korimako*."

"And what's that one?" she turned to stare into the bush, as if she might see the bird, but nothing moved.

"That's a *tūī*. Come over here. There are several." He walked to the top of the beach at the edge of the bush and pointed to a tree. "They're blue and black, with tufts of white feathers beneath their throats."

"Oooh! I see it! It's lovely! Oh, there are many of them." She grinned, but then she thought about Xavier, waiting for her in his brig. She sobered and turned to face Tama.

"I've seen as many as thirty in one *Kowhai* tree, squabbling, scolding and hopping from branch to branch," he continued.

"I'm sorry, Tame, I'd love to stay and look all day," Aleksandra sighed, "but I really must get to a boat. I'm worried for my husband. Who knows what that madman may do with him." She couldn't help but smile, however, when four more of the squabbling birds arrived at the tree. They dove into the middle of the group of three who were already there, bouncing from limb to limb and hanging upside down from the branches.

"They look like a bunch of boys playing in a tree." She bit back a grin, then turned again toward the sea and stood in silence.

"I'm sorry, Aleksandra. As much as I'd like to show you around, we'd better get on if you're to get a boat to Auckland." He looked at the ground, then took a deep breath and slowly turned to walk on up the beach.

ANOTHER RIVER CROSSED their path and emptied into the sea in the distance before them.

"What river is that, Tama?"

"That's the Mangahauini, and that," Tama turned to the right and pointed to a cluster of man-made structures near it, "is the mission station."

"Those are the first buildings I've seen since I arrived," she said.

"They are *whares*," he said.

"They look a bit like the thatched homes of the Shoshone Indians where I come from."

"They're thatched with *raupo*. They don't last as long as a wooden house but they're easy to rebuild when they burn down from a cooking fire, as they often do," he said, with a twisted grin.

They walked onto the grass verge from the beach toward the station buildings and two dogs ran toward them, hackles raised and teeth bared.

Tama gave a low whistle, and the dogs stopped short. Their tails began to wag, going faster and faster as they bounded up and danced around him until he petted each of them in turn, speaking to them in *Māori*. They settled down and led the way to the front door of the biggest *whare* on the station. A woman's shout came from a small wooden building, separated by ten feet from the main *whare*.

"*Kia ora*," called Tama, as they walked toward the small shed.

"That's hello?" Aleksandra raised a brow at him.

"Yes. The missionary's wife is in the cookhouse," Tama nodded at the outbuilding. "The cooking fires used to be within the *whare*, but the whole house burnt down not once, but twice, from cooking fires so they made a cookhouse from less-burnable planks—far away from the *whare*. Now, even if the cookhouse burns down, it might not take the whole *whare* with it."

"That sounds a lot like my Tama?" A slim woman in a black woolen dress exited the little shack. She pushed stray grey hairs, escaped from her bun, out of her eyes with the back of her floury forearms.

"It is, Mrs. Blakett. I've brought with me a foundling, Mrs. Aleks—" he turned to Aleksandra, "I'm sorry, but I don't know your surname." He looked at her, his eyes wide.

"Argüello, Aleksandra Argüello," she said, "Pleased to meet you, Mrs. Blakett."

"Welcome to the mission station. I've just finished out here. Would you like a cup of tea?" She briefly looked Aleksandra up and down. "You two look like you've had a rough day."

"That's one way of putting it, Mrs. Blakett," Tama raised an eyebrow at her and shook his head. "When I found Mrs. Argüello, she had just jumped her horse off the deck of a ship and escaped up onto the sands of Waipiro Bay, then she survived a meeting with the elders of my tribe, and then followed me here. Yes, quite a day."

The missionary's wife gazed at Aleksandra's bare feet, buckskin trousers and shirt, her lips tight and one brow raised.

"I'm sorry, I don't drink tea, but water would be appreciated." Aleksandra raised her own eyebrow at the woman's appraisal. "I was wondering if you might be able to help me, please. My husband is being held in chains on a damaged barque for a murder he didn't commit. I need to find a man, a friend of my husband's, who resides in Coromandel. Do you know of any boats which would be leaving here soon and could deliver my pony and me to Coromandel? I need to get to our friend so he can help rescue my husband."

"I'm afraid my own husband is away working with natives in the interior, but I will find out when the next boats are due."

"Thank you, I'd appreciate that. Tama offered to escort me all the way to Coromandel, but I'm sure he has other things to attend to.

"You're traveling alone?" She wrinkled her lip.

Aleksandra looked about her and returned her gaze to the woman. "It appears so," she said, then frowned. "I needed to get off the ship to reach our friend. In truth, I was lucky to escape at all. The first mate who took over the ship after the captain 'disappeared' is fond of laudanum and wants my husband dead. I believe he was responsible for killing the captain when they were alone together on deck in a storm, but I have no proof. Thus, I'm afraid propriety is secondary to necessity for me, madam." She looked directly at the woman, who bit her lip and turned away.

"Well," Mrs. Blakett sighed, "I don't suppose we could put you on a whaleboat, all alone as you are. The men are much too rough and the stench, well, you'd never get rid of it. There are flax and produce boats putting into here most days."

"Those would be more appropriate." Tama nodded. "Would you be able to keep Mrs. Argüello here until she is able to leave?"

She looked again at the trousers Aleksandra wore. "Well, we've not much room, but—"

"I'm happy to sleep outside, Mrs. Blakett and I have my own bedding, so I needn't bother you." She brushed wisps of hair back from her eyes. "I even have a skirt with me, so I can be slightly respectable."

Mrs. Blakett glanced at her, then looked down at the ground.

"I'm sorry if my buckskin trousers offend you, but they have been practical and provided me safe passage through many rough patches in my life," Aleksandra said softly.

There was a long silence while the other woman looked away out to sea, then she turned back to Aleksandra with a big sigh.

"It is I who should apologize, Mrs. Argüello." The woman took a deep breath and looked straight at her, then gulped. "It was unchristian of me to judge you in your time of hardship and I am mortified. May we start over, please?"

Tama had been shifting his feet and holding his breath. He looked like he wanted to be anywhere other than here, but now he stepped closer.

"I, for one, would love a cup of tea, Mrs. Blakett," he said, clapping his hands together. "I've missed it. Did I tell you, Aleks, that Mrs. Blakett is the very best schoolmistress? She has taught all of my nieces and nephews. Unfortunately, she came after I had already left the mission school."

Aleksandra sighed and smiled. "On second thought, a cup of tea sounds good after all. Thank you, Mrs. Blakett."

The other woman disappeared into the cook house and returned with a pot of hot water.

"Tama, would you please get some *mānuka* for me? I have some tea, but we can have *ti* tree in it, as well."

"When will tea be?" Tama said.

"We could have tea any time, but the rewena will be out in half an hour."

He smiled. "We will be back by then." He turned to Aleksandra. "Would you like to collect it with me?"

"What is *mānuka*, and what is *ti* tree?" Aleksandra asked, as they walked toward a stand of nearby bush.

"They are two names for the same plant. You can make tea from it, or you can mix it with black tea to change its flavor. They're all over New Zealand—*mānukas*, as well as *kānuka*." He gripped the rough, flaking bark of a branch. "They're good on wounds and many settlers use it to prevent scurvy."

"Handy plant," Aleksandra said, fingering the prickly leaves.

"The wood gives food that is cooked over it a unique flavor."

"May I gather some to carry with me?" Aleksandra sniffed the strong scent as she crushed a few leaves between her fingers.

"You could," he chuckled, "but you'll truly find it everywhere."

"Mrs. Blakett doesn't like women wearing trousers, does she?" Aleksandra ventured.

"Not at all, but you did just the right thing." Tama smiled down at her. "She can be a bit narrow-minded, but when confronted with facts, she usually sees the light."

"I didn't want to ask anything of her back there. I just wanted to leave, but I'm guess I'm growing up." She gave him a sheepish grin. "A short time ago, I'd have just left."

"Most of the *Pākehā* in this part of the country are either whalers or missionaries," he grinned. "Two groups more diametrically opposed, I cannot imagine."

She smiled faintly. "Where I grew up, for the most part, I had the freedom to dress and act as I wished. When I went to town I wore dresses, but the rest of the time I dressed like this or as the Shoshone women did, and rode freely through the wilds." She looked down at her feet. "I love the freedom and have difficulty conforming to society's image of women."

"Many men wouldn't mind but unfortunately, the women here don't appreciate it. It could make your life difficult, but you'll figure it out."

"Thanks. It might take a while, but I'll get there." She looked up, to see his eyes glow with warmth. It helped.

Aleksandra left Dzień happily munching grass, tied to a tree beside her pack, while she and Tama walked further down the beach. The wind was behind them, so the scent didn't hit her until they neared the southern end of the beach.

"Oh my God," she said, closing her eyes and plugging her nose. "What is that stench? Let me guess, it's a whaler, isn't it?"

"It is."

"Where?" She looked all around her, but no ships met her gaze in the bay beside them. She turned to Tama and frowned.

"St. Patrick's Bay, around the other side of Mawhai Point. Just ahead."

"I recognized the smell from a whaler that put into port at San Francisco once." She wrinkled her nose.

"It's a smell you never really get used to, even after being on a whaler for years." He gave her a wry grin.

"How close do we have to be to see the ship?"

"Not very close. We can climb up to the *pā* site up on Mawhai Point, that little promontory at the end of the beach."

They hopped and ran over the narrow spit of land connecting the point to the mainland.

"Good thing the tide's going out," Tama said, looking at the water line, just below where they now walked.

"We might be out here for a while otherwise? Unless we want to swim for it?" She glanced his way.

They climbed up the steep bank to a level area covered in grass. Circling the *pā* was a long barricade of poles. The poles were sharpened on their top ends and stood upright, but facing outward, just above a deep ditch.

"It looks like a fortress."

"It is, it's a '*pā*', a *Māori* fortress."

"I wouldn't want to have to scale that wall, especially with that ditch there. It would be pretty defensible in a siege. I'd imagine only starvation would get them out. Is there water on that point?"

"Yes, starvation, and no, no water. And there," he turned and faced south, "is your whaling station."

She stood staring at the inlet, a nearly clover-shaped, deep harbor containing two, three-masted sailing ships and numerous small whaling boats. It was the dead whales winched onto the shore that froze her heart.

Tears ran cold down her cheeks, her knuckles white, as she gripped her buckskins at the sight of the massive, once-graceful creatures lying on the shore, their flesh being stripped off by groups of men. Others cut long strips of the white blubber into thin sheets, while still others carried the sheets to big pots and dumped them in. The fires beneath the huge, three-legged pots smoked as fat dripped down their pot-bellied sides.

"It's an amazing way of life." Tama's enthusiastic voice came to her through a fog as her vision blurred. "There's nothing as thrilling as being out in the sea in a little boat with only a harpoon in your hand, knowing you can bring down something that massive. Those big cauldrons are the try pots, in which they boil down bible sheets, those thin sheets of blubber. That one they're cutting up is a Right Whale. It has baleen plates in its mouth, instead of teeth. Women use them in their dresses."

Aleksandra said nothing, unable to look away, thinking of the beautiful creatures, so much like horses to her, being destroyed for lamp oil, machine grease and whalebone stays. She sat down hard and hugged her knees to her chest.

"Aleksandra?"

She couldn't answer past the lump in her throat and the swirling darkness that threatened to engulf her.

## 24

"Aleksandra?" he repeated. She hardly heard him. When he touched her shoulder, she flinched.

He dropped to his knees beside her and peered into her face. "Are you all right?" he asked.

"How could you?" she whispered. "Those noble creatures—stripped and boiled." She gasped for air.

"Aleks, I know it's hard, but…you're a hunter. How are they different from anything else you would capture and eat?"

She shuddered, but had nothing to say to that. "It seems so foreign and violent," she said to the ground, "but when you say it like that, I guess it's not really any different."

"It may seem violent and to you, no doubt it is foreign, but you must remember," he sat down on the ground before her and tilted her chin up with a finger, "we come from a society of warriors. Warriors who ate, and some who still eat, their vanquished and their slaves. On long marches, after these slaves have carried goods for us over mountain ranges, they then become food themselves. When we came to New Zealand, there were only birds and whatever came with us on our canoes. We needed meat to live.

"This has happened for many, many generations. It would be surprising to you because it's not done that way where you come from, but it is our way.

"As to the animals and fish we kill to eat, we are grateful to them and to their *whanau*. We give thanks to them for our sustenance. Nothing is wasted and nothing taken for granted. We thank our gods, as well as our Christian god, for the gifts we have been given when we are fed, clothed and housed. Can you understand that, Aleks?"

She sat in silence for long minutes, her eyes closed, then she looked up at him and nodded.

"That is good. It will make your life here easier." He sighed and stood, reaching down for her hands. He pulled her up and they walked back down the cliffs.

She didn't look back at St. Patrick's Bay.

"MRS. ARGÜELLO, one of the natives said a boat is expected to sail in here tomorrow morning to pick up flax for shipment to Auckland." Mrs. Blakett said, holding aside the blanket hung over the doorway to admit Aleksandra and Tama.

"Thank you, I'm glad to hear that." Aleksandra said.

"The *rewena* is ready, so would you care to take tea now?"

"Yes, please," said Tama, eyeing the cast iron oven on the sideboard. "Aleks?"

"Please, and thank you," Aleksandra smiled. "May I help you?"

"It's all done," Mrs. Blakett said, "but you can set out the plates if you wish, while I collect the children from our housegirl. The crockery and cutlery are over there." She pointed at the sideboard.

The missionary's wife returned with her two small girls. They smiled and curtsied prettily to Aleksandra and Tama, then took their seats at table. Aleksandra finished setting out plates, cups and silverware while Mrs. Blakett carried the oven to the table, now open to reveal a steaming loaf of delicately browned bread.

"It's *Rewena* Bread," Tama said, "made in an *umu*. My favorite," he said, with a gulp. "We make it from potatoes, flour, sugar and water."

"No yeast?" Aleksandra asked.

"No. It uses a potato bug, like the sourdough starter you told me about, earlier."

Mrs. Blakett nodded and tipped the bread out onto a board on the hand-hewn table.

"That smells heavenly," Aleksandra said, inhaling deeply.

"Did you see any boats by the shore, Tama?" Mrs. Blakett asked.

"Not yet," he said, not looking up, his attention on the slices of smoking bread as they curled away from the woman's knife.

"It's a good thing there are flax boats coming and going. I don't think I'd do so well on a whaler." Aleksandra shuddered and looked up to find Tama watching her closely. She thanked the woman as she accepted a slice of bread.

"I would fear for the lives of the men on board." Tama's lips twitched.

Aleksandra lowered her brows at him, then let the ghost of a smile escape. "How long will your Reverend husband be away?" Aleksandra passed a piece of bread to Tama, who seemed about to melt with desire for his first piece. She shook her head and grinned at him while Mrs. Blackett began to say grace.

"I'm not exactly sure but probably about a month or so," Mrs. Blakett said, when she'd finished. She tried to smile, but swallowed noisily instead.

"That long? My, this is good, thank you, Mrs. Blackett."

"He's usually gone from here. You're welcome." She nodded. "When he's away doing missionary work, I try to keep track of the children and those in our mission."

"No small feat in itself," Tama said, raising an eyebrow at her, his piece already wolfed down.

"No, but I knew I'd be on my own much of the time when I answered the advertisement for a missionary wife in New Zealand," she said, and handed Tama another piece.

"Is that how you got here?" Aleksandra said, and took another delicious bite.

"Yes," she said. "My father is a Reverend. It was always assumed my sisters and I would go abroad as missionary wives."

Aleksandra took a deep breath, then clamped her mouth shut. It just wasn't worth it.

The clanging of a ship's bell echoed across the water.

"Excuse me," Aleksandra said, jumping up from the table.

Tama was right behind her as she slipped out beneath the doorway blanket to look across the bay.

The sails of a small barque showed white against the deep blue of the bay. Its freeboard sat clear of the water and several men were climbing down the ship's ladder into a rowboat. They rowed to shore while Aleksandra and Tama walked toward the water's edge.

"You stay here and I'll speak with the captain," Tama said and turned away.

"But I—"

Tama turned. His look stopped her in her tracks. She bit her tongue on her retort. This man was doing his best to help her. She needed to have some patience.

He spoke with a giant of a man in the back of the boat, then they clasped hands. Tama motioned to Aleksandra to come down to the water and introduced her to Captain Strange.

Tama greeted the other men in the boat, who eyed Aleksandra with interest. One short comment from Tama and they immediately turned their heads the other way.

"What did you tell them?" Aleksandra said in an undertone, as they men jumped out of the boat and pulled it onto the sand.

"The only thing that would keep them from making advances to you on the trip," Tama said, and looked away.

Aleksandra cocked an eyebrow at him and waited until his gaze returned to her face. "And what, exactly, was that?"

"I told them you were my woman and that they needn't be found to have been vying for your favors," he said, in a matter-of-fact tone.

"You had no right to tell them that. I'm a married woman." Her cheeks heated again.

"Would you prefer their advances during the next four days on this ship, all alone with them? I assure you, it will be safer for you this way."

Aleksandra was silent, then nodded. "Thank you, Tama," she said softly. "I hadn't thought about that."

"You're welcome. Just you remember my offer." He smiled at her.

Aleksandra was silent, then she was struck by a thought.

"Tama, why do these men listen to you? Better question, perhaps, what influence do you have over them that one word from you has them practically bowing?"

"It could be that I've educated myself, or that I have traveled extensively, or it could," he grinned, "have something to do with the fact that my father is the *rangatira* of the Uawa *hapū*?"

Her mouth opened but no sound came out. She took a deep breath. "No wonder the tribal leaders let you speak at their retreat." She shook her head.

Mrs. Blakett approached them, her youngest daughter on her hip. "It looks like you'll be heading out this evening," she said, "rather than tomorrow. The men usually load whatever goods have been delivered to here and leave for the north while there is still light."

"Then I'd best gather my belongings and my horse. I thank you for your hospitality," Aleksandra said, and walked back toward the *whare* with the missionary's wife.

"I hope you enjoy your time in New Zealand," she said.

"Thank you. Right now, I just need to get my husband freed."

"You do that. I'll be praying for you both."

"I'm sending a buckskin shirt to Tama after I make it for him," Aleksandra shoved her clothes down tightly and secured the top of her knapsack, "as payment for assisting me. He indicated I should send it here. Is that all right?"

"Of course. We see him regularly. He seems to like running down the hill and back up again. An interesting person. A woman could do worse than to link up with a man of his nature." She smiled. "Have a safe journey. I look forward to hearing word of your success in freeing your husband."

"Thank you, again."

"Godspeed," she said, as she turned back to her reed hut, with only her small children for company for weeks and weeks on end.

Tama waited for her at the waterline. The men had already rolled the lighter on logs from the grassy verge, across the sand, and down to the water.

"I've never seen boats moved that way, but I guess it's necessary where there aren't any docks," Aleksandra said.

"You'll see it throughout most of the country," he said.

The boat was packed to the gunwales and three more baskets of fresh produce sat beside Tama in the sand. The oarsmen took up their oars and began to row it out through the waves to the waiting ship.

"Full load?" Aleksandra's stomach churned as her boat disappeared. She looked up at him, then at the little boat crashing through the surf.

"Yes. They'll take this one and the crew will take you and the last of the potatoes out in the longboat." He smiled at her. "You know, you really are a remarkable woman."

She turned to him, with a frown.

*What was he going to say now?*

"You aren't afraid of anything." He shook his head. "After all you've done today, now you're setting off with a boatload of strange men. It's impressive," he said slowly, then took a deep breath and looked at her.

"The captain will be coming back with the lighter. I'll tell him your true story, but I wanted the crew to know you were irrevocably taken. A trading ship captain they might deny, but not the son of a powerful *rangatira*."

"Tama, thank you again for all you've done for me," she said, and meant it with all her heart. "Because of you, my husband has at least a chance of getting off that ship alive."

"I'm glad to have been of assistance. If the opportunity arises to help free him from the barque ourselves, I will see it done. Most of our warriors are away right now, but we'll see who returns first. Otherwise, I will be looking out for this von Tempsky or his representatives. We will assist if we can. Remember what I have told you."

"I promise," she said, smiling up at him.

"Do you know what a *hongi* is?"

She considered for a moment, then shook her head.

He put his face down to hers and placed his forehead against hers, nose to nose, and placed his hand on her shoulder and hers on his. Energy flowed between them and her heart ached for…she knew not what. When they drew away, she could only look at him in silence.

"It is a gesture of respect, esteem, and connection to all that was and all that will be." He took her hand and kissed it. "I will treasure the time I have been blessed to spend with you, my Aleksandra. Godspeed, and I hope to see you again in this life," he said, beneath his breath, as the lighter scraped the sand. He released her hand to grab the prow and pull the boat a little way up the beach. The captain jumped out and helped the men move it up the beach a little way. Tama introduced her to Captain Strange, then lifted Aleksandra and her pack in his strong arms as easily as if she were a small child and carried her over the shallow water. He handed Dzień's rein to one of the captain's men waiting in the longboat and handed Aleksandra in to the other crewman. Tama smiled at her, then walked briefly down the beach with the captain.

When they returned, the captain nodded to Aleksandra and took Dzień's reins from his man and handed them to her.

The pony's lips were drawn tight, his ears halfway back. She spoke to him and rubbed his forehead. Dzień stood up to the middle of his barrel in water, already wearing the harness with which he would be hoisted onto the ship.

"Welcome, madame. We should have you to Coromandel Town in

about four days, all going well." He turned to his crew and gave the order to row slowly out through the small waves at the river mouth.

Tama smiled at her as he pushed the boat from the shore, then patted Dzień on the rump as the pony stepped off the sandbar and began to swim. He blew a kiss to Aleksandra as the men rowed their craft out to the waiting ship.

Men waited on board with a hoist cable for the swimming pony. Dzień snorted as he swam beside the barque, his ears flat back now. The cable was hooked on to the big ring atop the bellyband of his harness, and its chest and rump straps kept him from falling out either end. He glared at everyone as he was lifted free of the water on the great crane and placed gently, dripping wet, onto the deck of the ship. The men had already made a small pen for him with bales of wheat straw, so he could stay on the topside deck. He soon relaxed in his makeshift corral, yanking hay from a barrel and drinking from a bucket of fresh water. He gazed at the men bustling around him and at the distant shoreline while he rested with one hind leg cocked. Aleksandra tied him firmly to the mast at the edge of the pen. "He's jumped once from the deck of a ship and I'm not about to let him free to try it again without me."

The captain blinked.

"I'll tell you the story later," Aleksandra said, one brow raised, then turned to wave goodbye to Tama, still waiting on the shore.

"I UNDERSTAND your husband is being held captive by what sounds to be a madman. That's a messy business," the captain said, two hours later, as they ate their cold meal of roast pork and *kumara*, seated away from the rest of the crew on the beach where the Waiapu River joined the sea. They could get the ship in closer here than they could at Tokomaru Bay, so the crewmen had spent the past hour picking up the goods delivered to the beach by the local *Māori* and transferring them to the ship, taking on fresh water at the same time.

"Yes, he is," Aleksandra said. "It was that damaged barque we passed in Waiau Bay, without the mainmast."

The captain's brows shot up. "You swam that horse in from there?"

She nodded. "And met Tama there, on the beach."

"So why didn't he and his men go out and deal to the crazy man?"

"The local *hapū* didn't want to get in the middle of a *Pākehā* dispute, which I can understand. We are friends with Gustavus von Tempsky, and I need to find him—"

"Von Tempsky?" The captain's head shot up.

"Yeeees," Aleksandra cocked her head at him. "Is there a problem with him?"

"No, I mean yes," the captain shook his head. "No, there isn't a problem with him, but yes, it could be a problem for you, because he's no longer in Coromandel, from what I've heard."

"Oh." Aleksandra's heart plummeted. "I thought it sounded far too easy." She took a deep breath. "Do you have any idea where he is?"

"He was in Coromandel Town. He went there to mine for gold but ended up writing for the local newspaper."

"That sound like Gustavus." Aleksandra started to smile, and then she frowned. "So he's writing again, but he's left Coromandel? What about his wife and children? I understood that they were to join him there."

"Well," the captain's brow furrowed, "it seems he met up with someone from the military and was asked to become a war correspondent, so he left Coromandel to accompany the Colonial Army to suppress the uprisings near Drury and in the Wairoas.

"Oh no. That sounds even more like him,"

"I've even heard tell," the captain continued, relentlessly, "he had extensive military training in Prussia."

"It's definitely the same man." She rolled her eyes. "He was also a mercenary in South America."

"And," the captain winced, "I hear he's to be leading his own battalion of Forest Rangers, a new crack force that's just been formed."

Aleksandra looked down at the ground and bit her lip, lost for words. How would she ever find him in time? She could only hope the foolhardy Prussian Pole didn't get himself killed before she found him. The muscles at the back of her neck froze up as she gritted her teeth to keep from growling her frustration and fear. The driftwood on the beach wobbled as her world darkened.

"Mrs. Argüello, Mrs. Argüello," someone shook her shoulder, but she couldn't be bothered attending. "Someone bring me some water."

The voice came from far away, then diminished into silence.

WHEN SHE AWAKENED, it was full dark. She lay on a soft bed in a darkened room. How had she gotten here? The last she remembered, she was sitting on the beach with the captain. She frowned.

She sat up, hitting her head on a lantern swinging from a hook above the bed. She was on a ship, then. It all came flooding back. Xavier. Von Tempsky, who wasn't where he was meant to be. She must have passed out and been returned to the ship…she hoped.

She swung her legs over the side of the bed. Everything worked, so she lifted the lantern handle from its hook and found her way to the deck. The captain stood at the wheel of his schooner in near-darkness.

"Back with the land of the living, are you?" Captain Strange sounded relieved. "You went white as a sheet and slumped to the sand. Thought I'd killed you." He took a deep breath. "Are you all right?"

"I'm fine, thank you. Sorry to have been a bother."

"Not at all. I was just afraid you had a condition that needed more than a bed and some sleep could fix. It's tough to get a good surgeon out here." He waved an arm out to the sea, glittering like a thousand diamonds in the light of the full moon.

"I've had precious little sleep for the last few days," Aleksandra gave him a little grin, then grimaced, "but I suspect hearing I might not find von Tempsky, dead or alive, was a bit too much."

"I've been thinking of the best way to find him. We're going up the Waihou River first, all the way to Ōpita, then I can take you to Miranda. You can ride up to the Miranda Redoubt and follow the chain of new redoubts until you get to Queen's. Someone there will know where he is."

"That sounds good," she said, with no idea what he meant.

"But," he was silent for a moment, "it's not without risks. The *Māori* are gathering in the Wairoa Ranges and they're not happy. In fact, things there are downright dangerous."

"I'm used to that." She raised an eyebrow at him. "Ever heard of the Pony Express?"

"In America? St. Louis, Missouri to San Francisco in ten days flat?" His eyes lit up. "Hasn't everybody?"

"Well, I rode for them for a few months."

His brows shot up and he twisted his mouth to the side. "They don't take girls," he said.

"You'd be surprised how many people were fooled when most of my hair was up under a ten-gallon hat and I dressed like I am today…a bit of a boy swagger, and voila, instant boy."

"Not very boy-looking there." He looked down at her chest, then looked away.

"A leather wrap can fix even that," she said. "Trust me. I know about dodging arrows and tomahawks. I've done my share. And seen my share of massacres, both by Indians and by the white settlers' army."

"So you're not scared to go on alone?" He looked at her with wide eyes.

"If I can save my husband, it'll be worth it." She took a deep breath. "Besides," she gave him a cheeky grin as she turned away to check on Dzień, "they don't have bows and arrows."

"Yeah, but they have muskets, and I happen to know which are deadlier.

## 25

"Mrs. Argüello, we won't stop until we reach Maketu pā," the captain said. "We've already collected all the flax we can hold, but we'll get the *kai moana*, sea food, from Maketu."

She smiled. "That's fine with me. The fewer stops, the sooner I'll get to von Tempsky," she said, and bit her lip. "Please call me Aleksandra. We'll be on this ship together for awhile and I don't stand much on ceremony."

"And I'm James," he said evenly.

The coastline, rough and rocky in some places and boasting smooth white sand in others, invariably gave way to deep gray-green bush, spreading on to infinity.

The captain pointed out many *pā* on the headlands and named the bays for her, but other than a few people waving at them from the cliffs, they saw no sign of houses or *whares* as they sailed along the shores.

She spent hours grooming Dzień and repairing clothing for the captain and his men. Once she finished those, she searched the piles of sails for those in need of patching.

"You'd best stop that or we might not let you go," one of the men joked.

"I'm not used to being idle and I have no books to read," she said.

James appeared soon afterward with a handful of well-thumbed volumes.

She caught up on sleep and read, then spent time learning how to sail the ship whenever the captain was so inclined. Anything to keep from thinking of crazy Broadhurst and her man, back there on the foundered barque.

⌁

XAVIER BLINKED IN THE DARKNESS. His heart lurched every time the ship's hull cracked against the rocks, which it was doing with increasing frequency.

For three days he'd only seen one of Broadhurst's tight-lipped henchmen. He'd punched Xavier when he'd asked after Aleksandra. There was no sign of either her or Jacob.

*Were they still alive? Had she made her escape?*

He gripped his hair and shuddered with the fear of what he might find when he finally got out of this hell-hole.

Footsteps, coming closer.

A bolt scraped and the door to his prison opened.

"We bin boarded, an' this 'ere *Māori*, 'ee asked fer ye." It was Jacob, his eyes wide. The boy looked back over his shoulder at the tower of a man filling the doorway.

The native was nearly naked, but for his short trousers and tattoos. His skin, the shade of mahogany, covered chiseled features that might have been cut from sandstone—and looked just as hard—while his long, black hair was tied back behind the nape of his neck.

"Are you Xavier Argüello?" the apparition asked.

Xavier looked at him sideways and blinked at his unexpected British accent. He nodded.

"Aleks said I'd find you here. I am Tama."

Now he had his attention. "Aleks?" Xavier struggled against his fetters.

"I put her on a trading boat heading up the coast to find your friend in Coromandel. I'm not sure how she's going to get that far, but…she seemed determined."

"You don't know the half of it." Xavier shook his head slowly. He flicked a glance out the doorway past the man, and his eyes lit on Jacob. "Come back in, man."

"I tried to t'come an' tell ye Aleks got 'way, but Broadhurst's men wouldn' let me," the boy said, his voice strained, as he rushed to Xavier's side.

"Where's Broadhurst?" he asked. His stomach clenched as the ship shuddered again, its timbers creaking and scraping on the rocks. A scent wafting in the door nearly knocked him flat. With it came a memory. Whales. Xavier's eyes watered. "That stench…"

The native's eyes softened. "Your rescuing ship is a whaler."

Xavier remembered the smell like it was yesterday. The great, greasy ship in San Francisco, its odor preceding it. But today, it meant freedom and finding Aleksandra. Xavier took a deep breath. "So be it. Thank you."

Jacob turned a key in one of his wrist irons and Xavier sighed as it clanked open.

"Gather what you need, we're leaving," Tama said.

"Thank you, Jacob," Xavier said, and reached out to put a hand on his shoulder as the young sailor continued to the other wrist, and then down to the leg irons, releasing him. He glanced up at Tama and hesitated. "I have stock on board and all of our belongings."

"Someone will look after them. Is there anyone you trust here?"

"This one," Xavier said, and smiled at Jacob, as he rubbed his chafed, sored wrists. The legs would have to wait until he sat down. He was too stiff to bend over.

"I'd be happy to do ee fer you, sir, and fer yer wife."

"Good lad. Thank you." He stretched up tall, the first time he'd been able to in since he'd been put in chains, wincing at the pain. At a thought, he inhaled sharply. "Broadhurst? Is he still here?" Xavier said.

Tama shook his head.

"Did you see his mate, a heavily tattooed seaman with almost white hair?"

Tama frowned. "I don't recall one."

"Pardon, sir, but them both disappeared las' night," Jacob said, gritting his teeth.

"Good riddance. I'll be glad to see the last of them," Xavier said.

"I ain' sure an how 'ee got Broadhurst inta th' boat—he were near ravin' with fever."

"Fever?" Xavier frowned at the boy.

"He were cut," Jacob said.

Xavier's mouth dropped open. "Was it Aleks?"

"Yep," the boy said. "Her an' that li'l sword o' hers."

"A deadly creature, your wife. Lovely, but deadly," Tama said, the corner of his lips twitching. "Broadhurst and his man shouldn't get far.

There's nothing but bush for miles. The mission might take them in—if they find it."

"Never mind," Xavier said. "You know how to care for the stock, Jacob?"

"O' course, sir. Ah've been helping yer missus while 'ee was locked up."

"We go, then." Tama turned to leave. "I assume," he threw over his shoulder, "you wish to find Aleks and this von Tempsky?"

"Aleks first, and then von Tempsky. He might be able to help get us out of this mess."

Not one of the crew knew what was to happen with the boat, with both of its captains having now disappeared. The crew wished to remain onboard until the ship was hauled wherever it was to go, and presumably, be paid their wages after the cargo was sold.

Xavier saluted them as he stood at the rail of the whaler.

Mr. Thompson, the whaler's captain, ordered his men to release the ropes holding the boats together and they drew away from the ragged remains of the once-proud ship, careful to avoid the rocks roughly caressing the *Emmeline's* hull.

"I'll return soon, Charro, for you and the rest," Xavier said, beneath his breath.

"Pardon?" Tama said.

"The horses. They're below," Xavier said. "I'd like to take them, but I'm not sure even my stallion would tolerate the scent of this floating slaughterhouse," he said, his jaw tight. "I never thanked you for helping Aleks and coming to rescue me."

Tama grinned and shook his head at the side of the ship behind them. "That woman of yours is something. Did you hear how she got that pony off the ship?"

Xavier's guts churned and he blinked. "*She took Dzień?*"

"You really believe she'd have gone without him? Think again."

Xavier slapped his mouth shut. "How?" he asked, fearing the answer.

"She jumped him over that bulwark." The *Māori* nodded back at it.

Xavier swung around to stare at it, then down at the water below it. He flicked his gaze back to Tama, closed his eyes and tried to breathe.

Five feet of solid hardwood, followed by the drop to the water.

*What if they'd landed on the rocks?*

It didn't bear considering.

"I'm glad I didn't know before," Xavier whispered. "So why else is she so amazing?" he somehow said, past the boulder in his throat.

"She kept up with me, plus she apparently dodges bullets while swimming. I eventually had to put her on that pony to keep her from killing herself, but then, I'd imagine you're used to that sort of thing?" He cocked a brow at him.

Xavier took a deep breath and gave him the merest hint of a grin as his knees wobbled. "*Bullets...*" He shut his eyes tight for a moment, then shook his head. "She's dodged arrows before, but never bullets, so far as I know."

"She should be in Coromandel soon, all going well." Tama clapped him on the shoulder. "The trading ship should have taken her around the top of the Coromandel, straight to the town itself."

Xavier let out the breath he didn't know he'd been holding. "Thank you again, Tama. You don't know what a relief it is, knowing she's safe, for once. It's a rare pleasure."

A RIVER FLOWED LAZILY out into the ocean at Maketu pā, or would have, if the tide weren't taking it back upstream.

"And here you'll find the finest, freshest and fattest fish and shellfish you've ever seen," the mate said to Aleksandra, as she climbed down the ladder behind the captain. "Enjoy your time ashore."

The captain held up a hand to steady her as she stepped into the lighter sent for them from shore.

"These *Māori* came to New Zealand on the *Te Arawa waka*. This was their final landing place when they arrived here from Hawaiki, and what a place it is," he said, as he greeted the men in the boat and introduced Aleksandra.

Aleksandra's mouth gaped at the lined-up baskets of seafood on the shore. "I'd never imagined there were so many sorts of *kai moana* in existence," she said, trying out her new words for seafood. Her heart twinged as she thought of Xavier. He'd so love to be here to see. She returned her attention to the fish, sea urchins—*kina*, mussels, abalone —*paua*, crayfish, and eels displayed on the beach in the shade of a *pohutakawa* tree, its gray-green branches nearly covered with bright red, spiky flowers.

James selected buckets full of each type of seafood, and they were tipped into wet sacks on the floor of the lighter. He haggled over the prices with the men and handed over the agreed goods, then they jumped back into the longboat. With a wave to the men on shore, the captain signaled to his men and they pulled at the oars and set off through the waves.

It was a beautiful day. The sun shone on the long white beach running along the shore. The sea smelled fresh and the salt spray splashed from an oar tingled on Aleksandra's face.

"What *is* that sound?" Aleksandra asked, shaking her head a little, as the high-pitched echo reverberated in her ears.

"Cicadas," James said. "Little insects in the bush. Rings in your head, doesn't it?"

She nodded.

Once out at the ship, the crew threw down ropes to tie to the top of the bags. They hauled them onto the deck and stored them under sails in a big basin. Aleksandra made it her job to ensure they stayed wet for the rest of her trip.

The mussels and *kina* they ate for supper that night were quite different from what she was used to, but she could sure get used to it.

XAVIER STOOD at the rail waving as Tama and his men rowed their lighter back to shore.

The captain came to his side and saluted the men in the smaller boat.

"Thank you, sir, for taking me on," Xavier said, as the whaler pulled away.

"My men were hoping for more of a scrap than we found on your ship. So the crazy mate was gone, eh? They'll find him," he said, with a grin. "Anyway, we only have a few stops to make on our way to Auckland, but we can drop you at Coromandel on our way past."

"You're not going after any whales this trip?"

The captain nodded at the barrels stacked two high, strapped to both masts. "The hold's overflowing. We've had to store the extra casks of rendered blubber up here, so no—no more hunting on this trip."

Xavier let out the breath he'd been holding.

"What's your interest in Coromandel, if I may ask?"

Xavier told him and the captain frowned. "I don't think you'll find von Tempsky in Coromandel. Last I heard, he was south of Auckland, leading colonial troops—into the bush."

Xavier stared, then he recovered. "This von Tempsky is a newspaperman," he said, as a niggle started up in his guts.

"Oh, this one went to be a war correspondent, but they discovered he had bush-fighting experience from South America. They're fighting the *Māori* for the land south of Auckland and the whole Waikato."

Xavier gripped the rail till his knuckles turned white.

*Fighting? Did Aleks know? Was she in Coromandel seeking a man who wasn't there?*

"Are you OK, lad?" the captain said, his brow narrowed. "We'll find her. She's bound to be waiting for you on the docks," he said, with a grin. "She'll be waitin', you'll see."

"Thanks for that," Xavier said, as he flicked the hair back from his eyes with one hand and rubbed his eyes.

"There's an empty hammock just below. Why don't you get some sleep? You look like you could use it."

"Best idea I've heard all day," he said, and went below.

THE TRADING SHIP began to lurch and roll. Aleksandra looked up from her book to find the bush-covered shore they'd been following for days had disappeared. She glanced up at James.

"We've just gone around Cape Colville, the top of the Coromandel," he said, and pointed north, "and that's Great Barrier Island. We're now heading straight ahead into the Hauraki Gulf."

Aleksandra forgot everything at the view that met her eyes. The waters of the gulf, silver-blue, stretched westward nearly to infinity, where a thin, black mountainous border of land edged them, but the sky, the *sky*...it took her breath away. The sun had lowered behind clouds that swirled blues, black and grays—almost to purple. She could stare at it for hours as it shifted and swirled.

James' voice brought her back. "There are many little islands, some little more than rocks, all along this coast."

"Does anyone live on them?" she said, her eyes still on the scene before her.

"On some of them, yes. Others are places the *Māori* go to fish and collect shellfish."

"I just might like Coromandel, after all." She smiled.

He pointed out several *pā* on the cliffs as they passed. "Your Coromandel town is just ahead, between those islands. We'll be there soon and we can check to see if anyone's seen von Tempsky," he said.

XAVIER STOOD beside the rail with his telescope, looking at the cliffs and the bush beyond.

"That's a *Māori pā* up there, on that rocky headland," said the captain. "You can see the palisades and parapets?"

Xavier nodded, never taking his eyes from the glass. "Have they been built since the settlers arrived?"

"They're much older than that. Long before the *Pākehā* came. They were always a warring society and needed them to protect their own from invading tribes.

Intrigued by the names of the places they passed through the day: Opotiki, Whakatane, Matata, Maketu, Xavier stayed near the quarterdeck, where the captain or his helmsman stood to steer the ship. He grinned. He must be driving them crazy by now. "I appreciate your willingness to answer my questions," Xavier said.

"Love this place," said the helmsman. Been whaling here for years. We're going to stop at Matata, then at Katikati, at Te Kura a Maia pā."

"What are we stopping there for?"

"*Kai moana*, what the *Māori* call seafood. We'll be there soon, but our landing will depend upon the tides," the captain said.

"What's that tall, round flat-topped mountain there, just on the shore? There seems to be..." Xavier lifted his telescope to his eye, "a *pā* up there."

"That's Mauao. The *Pākehā* call it Maunganui."

"It's so tall."

"It's an old volcano, like many of the hills you'll find near Auckland. There's so much old lava up around Auckland, they make their roads out of ground up scoria."

Xavier watched the mountain as they passed it and entered a big open harbor.

"Tauranga Harbour," the captain nodded, and pointed at a town on the edge of the harbor itself, "and Tauranga Town, with Matakana Island just past it."

"That's a big island. I can't see the end of it."

"It's thirteen miles long, but narrow. To get to Te Kura a Maia pā, we'll sail past the island on the sea side and anchor at the bay on the far end of Matakana, just inside the inlet to the Tauranga Harbour.

"The harbor goes all the way around the island?"

"Yes, and the water from the whole harbor has to enter and leave with the tides through narrow inlets at either end. Consequently, the inlet is swift—we can't sail against it, so we need to go in while it's going in and leave just after it turns. The channel itself has many shifting sand bars—fine in the shallow-drafted *waka* used by the *Māori*, but treacherous for a ship this size. We have to time it just right unless we want to spend another tide cycle there," Thompson said. "At least."

Xavier kept looking and talking. Anything to keep from falling into the trap of thinking too hard about Aleksandra, somewhere out there and—knowing her—more than likely in trouble.

## 26

T he trading ship's dawn stop at Coromandel, though fruitless, hadn't taken much time. Gustavus von Tempsky was truly gone. The Coromandel colonial forces recruiter said he was likely be somewhere between Auckland and the Waikato. He suggested Aleksandra make her way to Queen's Redoubt at Pokino and work her way north from there.

"Just make sure you're well-escorted, madame. We're at war."

"Yes, thank you," she'd said, and rolled her eyes as she left the office.

They sailed on south along the coast and Aleksandra saw a huge river mouth on the left before them.

"We're in the Frith of Thames, now," James said. "It's the big bay between here and Pūkorokoro. It goes all the way up toward Auckland."

A short time later, Aleksandra watched the frith's shoreline slip away as they entered the river mouth and left it behind.

"Behold, the River Thames, or so Captain Cook called it," the captain said. "The *Māori* call it the Waihou. Looks like we've just made the beginning of the flood tide," he said, peering down at the water, "so our trip up should work out just fine."

Aleksandra looked down to see the frith's wavelets ripple upstream. "It's huge," she said, her brow raised. It had to be over a hundred and fifty yards wide, lined with mangroves.

"The whole area between here and Pūkorokoro, where the Miranda Redoubt is being built, is swamp. It's passable with the right guide," James shook his head, "but otherwise, you'd likely never get out, once you got in there."

"But it looks like forest." Aleksandra frowned, staring to the southwest. "Those trees, I've never seen trees so tall, other than the redwoods of California."

"It's a forest of *kahikatea*, white pine." James returned his gaze to the fore, brow lowered, searching the depths. "They grow in the swamps."

"Do they use them for masts?"

"They do. They're straight and tall enough. The *kauri* that grow higher up in the mountains have been found to be stronger, so some boat builders prefer them, but many a good ship has had *kahikatea* masts," he murmured, his eyes still scanning the river and the mud of the low-tide shore. He inhaled and flashed her a smile. "You should come through here in the autumn. The birds come to feed on the *kahikatea's* red berries and their chatter is deafening. The *Māori* climb up to collect them, too, to eat. They call them *koroī*."

"They grow awfully close together for such large trees," Aleksandra said.

"Their roots intertwine with the roots of those beside them." He glanced back down at the water. "It keeps them from falling over in the wet ground."

Aleksandra nodded slowly as she stood looking east. The clouds above the crest of a high mountain range glowed pink.

"Might get a touch of rain today," he remarked, gazing at the clouds. "That's the Coromandel Range. Until the foothills get steep, it's mostly swamp, but the *Māori* farm the open, cleared areas along the streams and rivers that flow down to meet the Waihou."

"I'd like to see their farms sometime."

"Mmm..." the captain mused, as he checked the trim of the sails. "We have enough time to get to Ōpita before the tide turns, with the three stops we need to make. Easy as pie, but I don't think we'll have time to show you any of their plantings." James corrected the wheel, then frowned as he rocked the big wheel back and forth.

"What is it?" Aleksandra raised an eyebrow.

"There's more play than I'd like in the rudder. Did you feel it, a few minutes back, over the bar into the river? It was a little shallow," he scowled, "and we struck it."

Aleksandra's breath froze in her chest. "Will it be OK?"

He perused the sails again while he held the wheel fast. "It'll have to be, won't it, missy?" James said lightly, but his lips were drawn into a tight line.

Aleksandra took a deep breath and forced a smile. "How far upriver are we going today?"

"It's about 27 land miles, all told. It should take us the full six hours of flood tide to get to Ōpita, at the junction of this river with the Ōhinemuri. If all goes well and we get back to Ōruarangi a few hours after the tide turns, we should be OK."

"Ōruarangi?"

"It's a big *pā* at the place where the tide ends. We need to catch the ebb tide there for our return trip to the frith, for the depth. After that, I'll sail you and your pony to Pūkorokoro."

"They wouldn't have a dock there?" Aleksandra winced.

"That they wouldn't," the captain grinned, "but you won't have to jump over the rail again. We'll winch your pony off, as he came on, and he can swim in, or at least stagger through a mile of mud to get to the shore."

Aleksandra shuddered. "Even that would be good. Soft as water seems, it was a bit hard, coming down from that height," she said, with a chuckle.

An island appeared in the middle of the stream. She pointed at it, and turned a questioning brow to James.

"Tuitahi Island. Many *Māori* fish from that island and gather *pipis* and ducks. There's Ōruarangi pā, our first stop," he said, pointing to the left. "They usually have freshwater as well as seagoing fish. Oh yes, and sharks."

"Sharks?"

"Yes, but they're usually too well-fed here to bother people."

"Oh, that's good." She smiled.

The palisaded walls of the *pā* rose before them as they approached. A score of *Māori* women walked toward the shore carrying baskets of produce.

The captain shouted to the sailors in the fore of the ship and the anchor chain rattled its way into the depths. Another bark from the captain and it was made fast, the deck jerking with the sudden stop.

The women loaded their goods into a large canoe sitting in the mud and pushed the boat out into the stream, while the men rowed it out towards the ship. Aleksandra tried to look closely at the canoe without appearing to be staring. It seemed to be carved from a whole log.

James shouted out to the man at the helm in *Māori* and he laughed.

"You've come at a good time, eh?" The man rubbed at the side of his tattooed face. "We have had a good catch of flounder and mullet these past few days."

"Excellent. We'll take all you have of those. What do you have from your gardens today?"

"Potatoes, pumpkin, and the last of the corn."

"I'll have the lot, thanks." He grinned down at the tall man, whose thick raven hair was tied back from his sharply featured face with a feathered thong.

"And what have you to trade today?" the *Māori* asked, with a big smile.

"Powder." The captain raised an eyebrow at the men in the boat and they all nodded in agreement.

"Come ashore with us and bring your powder. We will discuss this."

James nodded over his shoulder to one of his men, who carried a small gunpowder keg and a bag, into which he placed the keg. The master slid down the ladder into the boat and received the bag, lowered on a gaff. Two sailors accompanied him, looking like pirates with cutlasses in their waistbands.

Aleksandra sat on an upturned barrel on deck and watched the exchange, while the big *Māori* and the captain wrangled good-naturedly over the price. Both men smiled in the end and the *Pākehā* returned to the canoe and rowed back out to the barque.

As James topped the ladder, he gave a shout that Aleksandra couldn't decipher, but someone must have, because the great anchor chain was weighed. It rose, dripping, from the depths and the ship was underway, the commander back at the wheel.

Another mile and a half saw them approaching a village on the west side of the Waihou, silhouetted against the forest.

"That's Kairere, of the swamp," James said.

"The land where their *whares* sit looks dry." Aleksandra raised an eyebrow at him and turned again to look at the raupo-roofed a-frames sitting among the clumps of flax and sedge.

"Strangely, some of the driest and best-drained ground in this area is near the river itself. Unfortunately, that means when the river is in flood simultaneously with a high tide, their villages are swamped."

"The forest can't be more than a mile away." Aleksandra gazed out at the dense thickets of towering *kahikatea* trees.

"Not too far along here, it'll be right up against the river, then you can see it up close."

As they neared the village, a woman dropped the basket she was carrying and the woman beside her began to beat her with a stick. The first woman merely ducked her head under her arms and made no sound.

Aleksandra muttered beneath her breath, knuckles white on the railing. The aggressor eventually stopped and the woman unfolded her arms and picked up her basket without looking up. She stood, with hesitation, then trudged on toward a boat at the riverbank.

James came up beside her. "Is anything amiss?"

"One woman was beating another, and she made no sound."

"*Pononga*. She's a slave."

"Is slavery common here?" Aleksandra took a deep breath, consciously released her hands from the rail and half-turned to face the captain.

"Very. The gardens here are mostly grown by slave labor. Slaves are taken in raids on other villages."

"It's just not right," Aleksandra growled.

"It's the way it is, and has been, for as long as they've been in New Zealand, maybe longer. Many hundreds of years. These are the lucky ones. They're not yet someone's supper." He raised a brow at her and looked out at the boat as it was being launched.

She sighed and gulped. "Is there much gardening in this river valley?" she managed.

"More than you'd guess," he said. "Last count, between the Kauaeranga Valley and the banks of the Waihou, there were over 500 acres of maize, 1600 of potatoes and 300 of *kumara*."

She stared at him, and he laughed.

"Here at Kairere, it's so wet that most things won't grow. Looks like they have for us today..." he stretched his neck out to peer into the baskets in the boat, "*taro* and *hue*—gourd, and gooseberries. I do love gooseberries." He grinned, and clapped her over the shoulder.

"But—" she began.

"—buck up, girl," he said in a low voice. "You can't save everyone."

"We went to California, partly to escape the pro-South, pro-slavery sentiment, but it had spread even to the West Coast. We thought we could get away from it here," she whispered, as he turned back toward the approaching boat.

Even before she and Xavier left for the California from Utah, Aleksandra's feelings on slavery ran deep, inherited from her father, who'd fled the feudal system of Poland. Slavery didn't exist there by name, but serfs were little more than slaves to the *schlacta*, and later, to their Austro-Hapsburg "protectors" in partitioned Poland.

The woman who had beaten the slave, a swirling dark *moko* tattooed on her chin, was in the boat below. Aleksandra gritted her teeth, her stomach roiling.

Her shrill voice rose from the rowboat and Aleksandra turned away to the other side of the boat. She couldn't trust herself not to say anything to the *mokoed* woman.

The captain made his selections and paid the trade price, then they were away again. He called to Aleksandra to show her what he'd purchased.

Aleksandra forced herself to relax and turned toward where James stood at the wheel, the baskets at his feet. Besides the *taro* and *hue*, there were eels, a few *kākā* birds, and a basket full of *tūī*. Aleksandra gulped at the little white tufts of the *tūīs*, protruding from beneath their necks as they lay in rows on a woven tray, gross caricatures of the once-lively and beautiful birds. Aleksandra turned away and looked at the last item, a huge bundle of *raupo*, probably destined for a roof.

"Everything they have to trade can be grown or gathered in the swamp. Luckily," he flashed her a grin, "they know their gooseberries will keep me coming back to their village whenever I'm in the area."

"MIGHT BE a good idea for you to stay with the men in the boat, Xavier," the captain said, as their longboat approached the shore at Matata. "This *hapū* is made up of what the *Pākehās* call 'friendly natives', but things are a bit unsettled right now."

Xavier nodded and pulled harder on his oar to straighten the boat. "What are those crops? They look like wheat."

"They are."

"I didn't think it was warm enough here for that."

"Sure is," he said, and greeted the man who'd come into the water to pull their boat onto the smooth sand of the sheltered harbor. "I'll just be a few minutes. I need a few more crew members and I'd like to see if their *rangatira* can recommend anyone."

A few men wandered along the beach and stopped near their boat. They looked out over the bay, one man gesturing wildly to his neighbor.

"I don't know why we couldn't all just get along with the *Pākehā*, then we could continue to become prosperous, our children could eat, and we could all have a better life," he said, in a loud voice. He pulled off his *raupo* hat, and stood, crunching its brim.

"And then we'd all have to give up our land," muttered the taller man beside him.

"No we wouldn't," the first said, leaving off his hat to stroke his <u>moko</u>.

"You *know*," his friend growled, "that if we want to build flour mills, we need the government grants. They will only give them if we agree to sell some of our land to the government and other *Pākehās*."

"It isn't written into the contracts," the first man said, his voice terse.

"Have you yet seen a case where it didn't happen?"

The shorter man hung his head. "No," he said softly.

"Have you sold any land?"

"Yes," he said, squirming.

"*All* of your extra land?"

"Yes." His voice was almost imperceptible, mumbled into his shirtfront.

"It's the best way for the government to lock us into one place, living the *Pākehā* way, on our small bit of land around our mills," the taller man said, with a shake of his head. "They know we'll behave and not revolt, so we can keep what little land we have to survive on, attached to our mills."

"Where do you hear this stuff?" his companion snapped, from beneath the brim of the crushed hat he'd replaced on his head.

"It's worse than that, actually. The government wants our land, man, and the best of it," he said forcefully, and looked off into the distance at the bush-clad mountains to the west. "For more serious reasons than even that. I heard two officers speaking on the docks a few days ago in Auckland. The land in the Waikato was already offered to the troops they brought here from Australia to fight us. If that won't motivate the *Pākehā* to fight well, I don't know what will."

## 27

Less than half an hour later, the trading ship dropped anchor off Te Puriri, its stream flowing gently into the river beside Puriri Village.

"There was a mission station here until about fifteen years ago, but it was moved to the Kauaeranga Valley," James said, to Aleksandra.

"Good morning, Captain!" shouted a tall, slender *Māori* woman on the shore as she stepped into an already-laden boat.

"Good morning, Rawinia," he called back, his eyes alight. Several men rowed the boat out to their ship.

Rawinia's enthusiasm was infectious. Aleksandra laughed and leaned over the edge of the railing as the woman danced about in the boat, ignoring the scowls and muttering of the rowers.

"What do you have for me today, then?" he called to her as they drew alongside, and the men reached for the ropes hanging from the side of the ship.

"We have *parareka*, potatoes, flax, mullet and eel!" she said, as she climbed one of the ropes like a monkey.

"And they're the best I'll ever find, eh?" he said, as he took her hands and pulled her over the rail.

"Of course!" Rawinia's eyebrows shot up, and she grinned.

"But what about *kumara*?"

"Mmmm…well, we haven't any today, sorry. Maybe next trip?" She looked at him with big eyes.

"Well, if that's a promise, I'll be back."

"Oh, but just see the quality of what we do have!"

"I'm only kidding. You know that, Rawinia." James' smile and voice were soft. "I'll always return."

She looked down at her hands and didn't say a word.

"And maybe someday, I'll stay for good."

She glanced up at him from the corners of her eyes, a smile playing about her lips. "I'd like that," she whispered.

"We'll see how I go with trading this year, then perhaps I'll speak with your *pāpara*."

The girl's hands shook as she completed the trade, then with a wistful glance over her shoulder at him, she disappeared over the side and dropped into the boat.

As the boat slid upriver, they waved to each other until the village disappeared from sight.

Aleksandra held tightly to the mast beside her, trying to swallow the lump in her throat and turn the thoughts of Xavier away before they engulfed her mind again. "What's a *parareka*?" Aleksandra raised an eyebrow at James. He jumped at the sound of her voice.

"Sorry?" He focused his eyes on her with difficulty, as if returning from somewhere else, worlds away.

"I asked you what a *parareka* was." She smiled at him.

"Oh. Fern root," he said, and rubbed his forearm across his forehead.

"She's lovely, your Rawinia." Aleksandra glanced at him from the corners of her eyes.

The tough trader blushed from his forehead to his shirt collar, loosely tied with a leather thong. "Yes, well, she's the chief's daughter. She shouldn't really be coming out on the boat, but...as you see..." he swallowed noisily, "she seems to like me. Her father is encouraging both of us, or she wouldn't be out here."

"Why would he encourage it?"

"It works well for a village when a trader marries into the chief's family. The trader guarantees their village will have its produce sold and the chief offers protection to the trader."

"It's seemed peaceful, what I've seen of it."

"What your seeing on the surface may seem so, but you'll find the country is...in a different phase," James said. "One completely at odds with what's gone before. Previously, the *Māori* warred between themselves, capturing goods, land and slaves, especially after they were provided with muskets in trade for their goods by whalers and traders. The *Pākehā* are now the focus for their grievances and they begin to work together...to an end that can only be bad for everyone who desires peace between the races." He nodded to her with a grim smile. "All because the *Pākehā* settlers are greedy for land at any cost, and only the best of it, at that," he murmured, as he returned to his wheel.

Aleksandra leaned against a crate in the shelter provided by its neighbors, as the flax and *raupo* of the swamp slid slowly by, the big trees standing guard in the distance to the west. Her heart ached at the thought of Xavier. How long would he be safe from Broadhurst? She'd be at Pūkorokoro by tonight, all going well, and hopefully find von Tempsky the next day...if he were still there. She closed her eyes and took deep breaths.

"Aleks," James said, from the back of the ship.

She sat up and looked back at him.

"Turn around." He pointed.

Aleksandra turned and inhaled sharply, then walked back to where James stood at the wheel. They sailed past a stream that entered the river from the left, then the barque slid beneath the overhanging branches of the big trees crowding the eastern, and soon the western, banks of the Waihou.

The cacophony of sound escalated as the river wound deeper into the *kahikatea* forest.

"The birds sound like none I've heard before," Aleksandra said, as she closed her eyes to focus on the music. "I was in native bush on the East Coast, but perhaps I was too worried about Xavier to notice the sounds."

"Perhaps," James said.

"What are those?" Aleksandra laughed and pointed to some big birds that looked like overgrown pigeons, impossibly hanging halfway upside down on bent-over tree limbs. "Those branches are far too small for them."

"Those are *kererū*, wood pigeons." He laughed. "They're my favorites. They're inquisitive and entertaining, but not terribly bright. *Māori* place *waka kererū*, traps with many nooses above a *waka*-shaped trough of water in the trees. When the birds go for a drink, they hang themselves."

She shuddered. "Is that another island?" she asked, turning to look upriver.

"Yes, Koputa. Te Kare pā is on its southern tip."

"In the middle of the river?" Aleksandra blinked.

"Yes. We'll stop there on our way out for more fish."

"How far up is the river tidal?"

"It stops at our next stop, Ōruarangi, where the Hikutaia River joins this one. Hikutaia means 'end of the tide'."

She nodded.

"We should reach Ōpita and be back to the frith by mid-afternoon," James glanced upriver for a moment, "then we should make Pūkorokoro before dark, all going well."

"That suits me just fine." Aleksandra breathed a sigh of relief. "The sooner the better. It seems I'll have to do some searching to find von Tempsky."

"Once we get to Pūkorokoro, you'll see the Miranda Redoubt on top of the cliffs above the bay."

"Is there a trail or road?"

"If you can call it that." He grinned. "It links Pūkorokoro with the other redoubts across the island."

The captain glanced upriver at the sound of a shout and the roar of answering voices, but all they could see was the end of Koputa Island and a large stream entering the river on the eastern bank.

They looked at each other, eyebrows raised. Aleksandra's hand went to her *shashka*, beneath her buckskin shirt.

"Ōruarangi," James announced quietly, as the palisaded sides of a massive *pā* glided into view. Men and women milled about the stronghold and James stared hard at the crowd, his brows narrowed.

Aleksandra forced her fingers to relax and dropped her hand to her side, but her heart continued to pound.

"I wonder if it's safe to land?" he said softly.

"There's a boat." Aleksandra nodded at the man rowing out. His skin was as dark as a native, but he had blonde hair.

"So there is. It's Albert Nicholas."

Aleksandra raised an eyebrow at him.

"What's he doing alone, with almost no produce?" James mused, almost to himself.

Aleksandra threw a rope down and Nicholas made it fast to the prow. The man bounded up the rope ladder and over the rail, then clasped hands with James.

"Mrs. Argüello, I'd like you to meet Albert Nicholas, a resident trader here."

"Pleasure to meet you, Mrs. Argüello." He bowed over her hand for the briefest moment, and glanced at her long, blonde braid with a fleeting smile.

"And you," she murmured, before withdrawing her hand and stepping back.

"Where is everyone?" James glanced back over his shoulder toward the *pā*, from which the noise seemed to emanate.

"At the Kakaramea pā, there." Albert pointed.

Aleksandra stared at not one, but four big *pā* along the convoluted stream's edge as it made its way up the valley.

"What's keeping them, Nicholas?" James glanced back at the trader.

"Some warriors from the Waikato arrived earlier today. They're rousing everyone about fighting the *Pākehā* in the war over there." He looked down at his feet and sighed deeply. "They're recruiting. It's about to get messier than it already is."

"Are you safe staying here?" Aleksandra asked, then she glanced at a movement on the bank. A young *Māori* looked their way, his face inscrutable. The hair raised on her arms as he stared at her. She forced herself to smile. He never moved; just continued to look at her. She returned her gaze to Albert with some effort.

"For now," the trader answered. "My wife, Ngaire, is the eldest daughter of the chief, so that should keep me protected for a while, but it seems we're moving out to the *pā* on Koputa sooner than we'd planned." His lips drew tight and he bit his lip.

"Can we do anything to help?" James asked.

"No," he said, looking down at his skiff, bobbing below. "I've brought you some potatoes and flax, but the *kumara* are in the *pā* with the crowd. I thought it unwise to disturb them." He winced.

"Smart, but that's too bad. No one else has any *kumara* today."

"Why don't you stop on the way back? Perhaps the news'll have worn off by then and I'll have some waiting."

"We'll do that. Your *kumara's* second to none," James grinned, "other than Rawinia's, of course, and it seems rather scarce right now."

"Excuse me, Mr. Nicholas, but who is that—" Aleksandra turned and pointed to the man, or where he'd been a moment before, but he'd disappeared. "Oh, he's gone."

"What is it, Aleks?" James came to her side and looked where she'd indicated.

"Nothing, just, there was a man, a *Māori*, staring at us, then at me. He's gone now."

"Could be anyone," Nicholas said. "They don't see many fair-haired women out this way, especially without a bonnet." He grinned. "Rather like it, myself, Madam," he nodded to her and slid down the rope into his boat.

Aleksandra's cheeks heated.

Mr. Nicolas returned with a big load of flax and then they were on their way, with well-wishings for the *Pākehā* trader.

"We should be back in a few hours," the captain called over the side.

"I'll hopefully have your *kumara* waiting," Albert said. He pushed off the side of the barque with an oar and stroked rhythmically back toward shore. Aleksandra waved as James' men began to weigh the anchor.

"Next stop is Ōpita Village, where the Ōhinemuri joins the Waihou, then we'll turn about and head for Pūkorokoro."

Aleksandra smiled and returned to coiling up the rope she'd just pulled back on board.

The mangroves abruptly disappeared and the ancient canopy trees and underlying brush of the dense forest were slowly replaced by rank swamp as they progressed inland. An hour on, a raised area with many *whares* appeared on the riverbanks.

"There used to be a *pā* here at Ōpita, but it was abandoned twenty years ago, for some reason," the captain said, as he steered the ship carefully toward the mooring site. "Now it's just a village." He waved at the men on shore and they pushed a canoe, piled high with *raupo* and flax from the swamp, into the stream and headed for the ship as the barque dropped its anchor.

"Most *Māori* dwellings I've seen have *raupo* walls and roofs," Aleksandra said. "Frontier settlers in America call it bullrush and use the seed heads to stuff pillows and burn for torches, but I've never seen it used for building."

"Most make their dwellings from it, even where it doesn't grow well, which is why we trade for it. Tight bundles of it, tied to a frame, make a home that's warm in the winter and cool in the summer."

Their exchanges at Ōpita took longer than anticipated, with several boatloads of *raupo* to collect from the shore. James glanced at the sun more and more often as it lowered in the sky. By the time he turned the ship around, he was looking decidedly nervous.

"Are we late for the tide turn?" Aleksandra frowned.

"Yes, but we should make it, all else going well." He took a deep breath and waved at the chattering children clustered on the bank.

Aleksandra busied herself reorganizing her knapsack as the barque floated down the river.

"Thank God for that," James muttered beneath his breath some time later.

Aleksandra turned to see Ōruarangi just coming into sight, its shore filled with people, and then a boat was pushed from the shore. She jumped to her feet and threw the line over the side, but her heart stopped at the upturned visages of the men in the boat. Their faces were closed, Nicholas wasn't there, and there were no baskets of *kumara* in sight.

ALEKSANDRA SPUN TOWARD JAMES. In a whisper, she told him what she'd seen.

"Not much we can do right now. We'll just have to see what's up." He gritted his teeth and tried to smile, with another glance at the sun.

Aleksandra froze as the man she'd seen staring at her earlier from the shore scurried, like a rat, up the side of the ship and over the rail.

He stood straight and addressed James. "Captain, our *rangatira* wants your lady to come and see the *kumara* pits."

"The *kumara* pits?" James blinked.

"They are the finest *kumara* pits," he said, as if that explained everything, then turned to go. "She will come in the boat with me. You, trader, will stay here." He pointed to the deck of the ship at his feet.

Aleksandra stared at James. "What does he want with me?" she hissed.

"The chief knows you're here and he's interested. In what, I'm not sure. To keep the peace, I recommend you go. I daren't leave the ship." He walked her to the rail, out of earshot of the others. "You need to go before any of my men mention you are Tama's woman, because then the *rangatira* will keep you for sure. Their *hapū* weren't on the best of terms, last I heard."

"Do we have time to make the tide?"

"We don't have a choice. They've been stirred up by the warrior," he whispered. "I won't leave without you, whatever happens." He bowed over her hand, his brow furrowed, and led her toward the balustrade.

The man popped his head back up over the rail. "Come now," he growled, "our *rangatira* awaits."

"I've got my *shashka* and three knives," Aleksandra said, beneath her breath. "I can swim out, if I must. Be ready to sail." She turned and glanced at Dzień, biting her lip as she climbed over the rail.

The shore rapidly approached as the men rowed. No one spoke to her.

On the shore, surrounded by an entourage, the old chief waited.

"Come," he said. "We will walk to the *kumara* pits, so you may see the wealth of our *hapū*."

Aleksandra put her head down and glanced around as they walked toward the nearby hills. The chief was silent, his breathing the only sound over the cheep-cheeping of the fantails. Then he stopped, reached out, and touched her braid.

It took all of Aleksandra's resolve to not cringe away from his touch. No one had ever touched her without her invitation, well, except for Vladimir and Symes, but those were entirely different situations.

"Beautiful hair," he said, and resumed walking. "I hope you like our *kumara* pits and stay with us. You may call me Wiremu. The rest of my name is too long for you to remember today."

She stared after him, frozen to the spot. He turned to face her and waved her on forward as he turned back toward his *kumara* pits of myth. She took a deep breath and followed. She was beginning to understand what he wanted.

"We had a visitor from Taranaki this morning," the *rangatira* said.

"Oh?" Aleksandra tried to keep her face a quiet mask as she turned toward him.

"He wanted us to join with him to fight the *Pākehā* in the Waikato."

"In the Waikato?"

"The *Pākehā* have invaded the Waikato to take land from the *Māori* who have lived there for many, many years. This cannot be allowed." The chief frowned. "The settlers need the food we grow and trade with them. We need to work together, not fight. These men from the Waikato tribes want our men to fight alongside them."

"It is sad it has come to this," she whispered. "There is so much land here, it is unfortunate the *Pākehā* settlers and their government think they should have all the best land, which has already been broken in by the *Māori*."

He turned to her and raised his eyebrows. "You understand this. I wish others of your race did as well."

"I grew up among the Shoshone Indians in America and understand very well what settlers want and what their governments will do to support them, at the expense of those who already live there." She hugged her arms to her chest and examined the toes of her moccasins as they moved along the soft dirt path in silence.

Finally, they stood before the pits. They truly *were* amazing. The individual plots were huge, perhaps six by twenty yards each, and they extended nearly as far up the valley as the eye could see. The plants were beautiful, their heart shaped leaves twining and trailing from the pits. A few white and purple flower heads showed above the greenery, pretty against the women digging among the plants.

"These are our *kumara* beds." The chief's chest puffed up and he grinned from ear to ear.

"They are truly great *kumara* beds, *rangatira*—Wiremu." Aleksandra enunciated her words and spoke slowly so there could be no miscommunication. "We will be proud to trade for whatever you wish to trade with us."

"I would like for you to stay here with me. We will trade many, many *kumara* together," he said, and again reached for her hair.

---

## 28

Aleksandra's chest was so tight she couldn't take a breath. She could barely swallow, and her hand strayed again toward her *shashka*. She tried again. "Your *kumara* beds are truly the best I have seen, but I have a husband and I must return to him. I will spread the story of your magnificent *kumara* beds wherever I go." She forced a smile.

"I will speak with your man about this." He frowned at her.

"The captain is not my man." She took a deep breath. Honesty had to be politic here. "My man is being held captive far away and I am trying to get help from his friend near Auckland."

He drew himself up to his full height and the warrior he would have been showed clear.

"You are traveling alone to seek help for your husband?" he thundered, the pulse pounding at his throat, then he gave a great sigh and was silent for a moment. "You are brave, *wahine*," he said. "If you care so much for your husband, I must let you go." He turned abruptly and walked back toward the ship.

Aleksandra offered up every prayer she could think of as she hurried after him.

The chief stopped to wait for her, then asked where she'd come from. She described her life in the Utah Rockies as the daughter and only remaining family of a trapper then told him of her time with the Pony

Express. She briefly touched on their time in California, and then they were standing beside the boat.

"Thank you for showing me your *kumara* pits. I'm sorry I cannot stay with you," Aleksandra said soberly, and climbed into the boat.

"I am glad you liked them. Go now and help your man," he said, and waved goodbye as the boat was pushed into the stream.

James threw a rope down to the man in the bow, then helped her climb back on board.

She heaved a sigh of relief when her feet were safely back on the deck.

"We're not going anywhere," he said, as he pinched the bridge of his nose.

"What's happened?" Aleksandra said,

"The *rangatira's* sent *kumara*," one of the men called up, and James went to the rail. He and Aleksandra waved their thanks to the chief, still standing on the shore, and helped the men from the boat transfer the tubers.

"I began to turn her 'round when I saw you returning," James said, tugging on the gaff attached to one of the sacks, "but the tide was too far gone and there wasn't enough depth where I tried to turn her." He stopped, and ran an arm across his forehead, then he continued, just above a whisper. "I've broken the rudder and jammed her on a sand bar. She's going nowhere tonight."

Aleksandra's knees wobbled as she gripped the rail. "I'm so sorry. How long will it take to fix? Can I help?" She sat down hard on the deck.

"We have to wait for a high tide to lift her out of the mud, then assess the rudder and see if we can make or find a new one. At the very least, it'll be several days." He looked as pale as Aleksandra felt.

She closed her eyes. The *Māori* from the shore, still standing on the barque, looked askance at her and the captain. "I'll need a guide," Aleksandra said.

"A guide? That's a swamp out there between you and Miranda. You need a boat."

"A boat big enough to carry a horse? Not likely." She turned and looked back to shore. "I'm going to ask the chief for a guide through the swamps. There must be a way. I'll not leave Dzień behind."

James stared at her, jaw dropped.

"Please row me back to the shore, gentlemen," she informed the rowers. They looked at her with lowered brows, then up at James, but they acceded to her request.

"PLEASE SIR...*RANGATIRA*...WIREMU," she dropped to her knees before the chief when she'd been delivered to the shore. "Our ship has been damaged and it's stuck on a bar. I must get help for my husband as soon as possible. Can one of your people guide me across the swamps to Pūkorokoro?"

"I can do better. I can send you in a canoe," he said, smiling.

"I thank you, but I must take my horse with me."

"A *hōiho*? A horse? Why?"

"I cannot leave him behind and I need him when I get where I'm going. He is a part of me."

He took a deep breath and stared off into space, then finally let it out. "Yes, it can be done, but there are few who know the way you need to go with a *hōiho*," he finally said.

"I can pay," she said.

He waved that away and shook his head. "I will send for him. Meet me here when you are ready to go."

"Thank you, *rangatira*. I will remember this forever." A tear ran down her face.

He wiped it away and pulled her to her feet. "Now go, *wahine*."

James was somewhat mollified when he heard she had a solution, but looked apprehensive that she was planning to cross the swamps, with Dzień, no less.

"You do realize you'll be walking, or possibly swimming, the whole way?" His brows lowered and his mouth pursed.

"There's nothing for it." Aleksandra shook her head. "I've little choice, especially if von Tempsky's gearing up for war. He could already be gone. Would you have me seek him on an active battlefield?"

"Of course not, Aleksandra," he said with a sigh, and reached out to jerk her braid. "You remind me of my little sister and I worry. I don't know of any *Pākehā* who's crossed that swamp. There are at least two rivers to cross as well, with sharks near the frith end." He scowled.

"I'll have to figure that one out when I get there, I suppose. The chief is seeking a guide for me right now."

"Then let's get you ready, and your pony off. He'll be annoyed to discover the ship was a better place than the swamp." He tried to grin, but his concern made it more of a grimace.

"Thank you for everything you've done for us. I'm sorry for my part in damaging your barque," she said, looking toward the wheel.

"You're not to blame."

"And I hope to see you again. I plan on it," she said as she turned to gather her gear and harness Dzień.

THE MAN WAITING on the shore looked positively feral. Standing a bit apart from the others, he was muscled and tattooed to within an inch of his life. The warrior appeared, to all intents and purposes, fierce enough to eat enemies with his gaze alone. Then he smiled and the facade dissolved.

Aleksandra breathed again.

"Ranui, this is Mrs. Argüello." The chief smiled at her and the warrior viewed her from the corners of his eyes, then turned back to the *rangatira*.

"A *wahine*? I am to take a *wahine* across the swamps? On a *hōiho*?" he sneered. Shaking his head, he looked away.

Aleksandra's blood began to boil. "I will walk Dzień. I can keep up, if that's what you're worried about," she said coldly, staring at him for long moments until he turned to face her.

He smiled and offered his hand. "Perhaps you will, perhaps you just will." He looked at the *rangatira* again. "I will do it, *pāpara*."

The old man nodded. "That is as it should be, Son."

Aleksandra bit back the words she'd been about to say. To insult someone who could get her where she wanted to go was foolhardy, but to verbally slap the son of a chief was suicidal.

"We leave at first light," he said and turned on his heel.

"Excuse me, sir, but if possible, I would prefer to leave now. I have traveling food ready, enough for both of us, and the horse needs only to be lifted from the deck. Since the tide is just turning, we should be able to swim across easily."

"That won't be necessary, *wahine*." The rangatira smiled. "You can lead the precious horse from the skiff. We will row you and my son across."

"What is so important that it cannot wait until morning?" Ranui's eyes narrowed.

"My husband is being held hostage on a ship at Tokomaru Bay by a man who could kill him in a mad fit at any moment."

He stared at her in silence, one eyebrow raised. "Tokomaru Bay." He blinked and said nothing for a moment, then continued. "An honorable enough reason." Ranui turned away. "We will leave as soon as I gather my traveling kit," he said over his shoulder and walked toward the *pā*.

Dzień was still glaring and swishing his tail by the time Aleksandra finished removing the ship's harness, water dripping from his now-clean coat. He'd swum across the river, led by Aleksandra from the *rangatira's* promised boat. He shook his body, soaking her.

"Are you happy now? I'm truly as wet as you are." She patted his neck and he rubbed his forehead vigorously on her shoulder.

Ranui stood by and watched for a moment before he shouldered Aleksandra's pack and headed off, carrying his carved *taiaha*. Aleksandra turned to wave to James, standing with the others at the rail of his damaged barque.

"Farewell, Aleks!" he shouted across the water and waved.

She waved back and turned to follow the son of the *rangatira* of the great Ōruarangi along a faint trail in the soft, damp earth of the *kahikatea* forest.

"It seems quite dry." Aleksandra looked up at Ranui. "Everyone said it's all a swamp, but if most of it is like this, it should be a simple enough crossing," Aleksandra said, as she caught up with him.

"It's a swamp, do not be fooled." He turned briefly and raised an eyebrow at her, his mouth quirked to the side. "This is the least waterlogged ground we'll see for the next few days."

"Oh." She took a deep breath. "I can tie my knapsack onto Dzień."

"Why?"

"Then we needn't carry it. It's light for Dzień."

"Any extra goods on the horse will not be to his, nor our, advantage. He'll have the most difficulty of all of us, even without the extra weight."

"Then I can carry my own pack." Aleksandra lifted her chin.

"I'm sure you can, but we'll make better time if I do. Besides," he grinned, "it's more likely to stay dry if I have it, because it will be further out of the water. In case you hadn't noticed, I'm a good two feet taller than you are."

"You do have a point." She flashed him a smile. "Perhaps it's better that you carry it. If nothing else, it will provide a handicap for me."

"Handicap? I don't know that word."

"Handicap…it means it might slow you down and make it easier for me to keep up." She chuckled and started to walk again, following as he turned to lead her deeper into the bush, his laugh trailing behind him.

THE SOLID GROUND beneath Aleksandra's feet soon disappeared beneath a foot of water and the going became difficult. As far as possible, Ranui held to what seemed a faint trail linking the clumps of closely-growing *kahikateas*. Their buttressed roots, hard up against those of their neighbors, may have provided stability for the trees in the soft peat, but they also made underwater obstacles over which she and Dzień were wont to trip. Frequently.

From time to time, the path diverged and a trail disappeared into the swamp in another direction. She grew to appreciate the short bits of higher ground. In between them, the water was often up to her belly and the leather of her moccasins became soggy and slippery within the first half hour. Dzień slogged along, muzzle tensed and held high over the water, his ears laid back. As Ranui had predicted, the pony had hardest time of all. His great weight and small hooves sank deep with every step.

"These mosquitoes really are hungry," Aleksandra slapped at what must have been the hundredth insect, "and they're getting hungrier as the day goes by."

"Yes, and the sandflies." He glanced over his shoulder at her. "Luckily for me, they love imported blood, so they're eating you, and not me."

"Would you like some *pemmican*?" Aleksandra held her hand out toward him.

"What is this?" His brows lowered as he sniffed it.

"Dried meat and berries mixed with fat, used for traveling food. I learned to make it from the Shoshone Indians in America. We brought a big bag of it on the ship with us."

"Oh." He tasted it, then finally a smile cracked his stern face. "It is good. And now you will have to taste my own sort of '*pemmican*.' It is called *kao kumara*."

"I haven't heard of that kind."

"It's not a kind, but the way it is prepared." He pulled a pouch from his haversack. "Try this," he said, handing the sack to her.

Aleksandra opened the drawstring and peered at the dark, crumbly, sweetly aromatic material within. "How do you make it?"

"The women wash and scrape many small *kumara* with fern and dry them in the sun for a few days, then they go into a *hangi* for a full day—"

"This is good." She grinned as she nibbled at a blackened morsel, then stopped, brows drawn together. "Sorry for interrupting, but what's a *hangi*?"

"It's a way of cooking. A fire is built in a trench and rocks are added, then the fire is raked out and flax baskets of food are placed onto the rocks. Ferns, then flax mats, then finally, dirt are piled on top, then it's left until the food is cooked."

"We did something like that, what we called a pit barbecue, in California at our *rancho*. We didn't use flax or ferns, but we did use fire and hot rocks." Her heart gripped at the thought of Xavier and she bit her lip.

"Sounds pretty close. Back to my story," he said. "The *kumara* are dried again in the sun after being pulled from the *hangi* and stored in flax baskets inside *patakas*. These are storehouses far above the ground, to keep them dry and to keep out the *kiore*, the rats."

Aleksandra pulled her attention back to him as he spoke. She couldn't help thinking how much more pleasant he was when he smiled. "How long can you store them?" she managed.

"This *kao kumara* is two years old, so at least that long, if you can keep it dry."

"It sounds like a lot of work, like making pemmican," she said, "but it's worth it to have good food on a journey."

"We usually crumble it, as you see it now," he nodded at her hand, "and mix it with water, but I think it's good any way."

They shared more *pemmican* and *kao kumara* as they carried on, while Dzień browsed on flax and *raupo* along the way.

Aleksandra slapped at another mosquito and scowled. Darkness was beginning to fall. It was getting harder to drag herself through yet another deep channel between the muddy, but relatively dry, hummocks around the *kahikateas*. Aleksandra struggled to move forward as her soaked buckskins weighed her down. Used to a lifetime of fitness, she wished for the hundredth time that she'd devoted even more time to walking around the deck during their sail from America.

*You're about to have to eat your own words about keeping up.*

"Now you know what the swamps are like," Ranui's voice seemed to come from far away, "you need to tell me which way you would prefer to go. The way straight ahead will shorten the distance you must travel if you are heading straight for Pokino, but it will require a third again as much swamp as going the other way, to the right."

She shook her head and examined her feet. She was more tired than she could remember ever being, even after riding over three hundred miles on a particularly bad Pony Express run. Perhaps she didn't remember being that tired because she'd eventually fallen asleep in the saddle. The station keeper had to rip the reins from her death grip when she'd finally arrived into the station. Not a chance of that here.

Dzień sweated from the exertion, despite his frequent dips, and his tight muzzle hadn't relaxed in hours. He was not a happy Mustang.

Ranui looked at her, his brows drawn together. "Are you all right, Mrs. Argüello?"

She shook her head to clear her brain. "Yes, just remembering something." She took a deep breath, then stepped into a hole and went underwater, her foot tangled in an unseen branch.

# 29

Strong arms grabbed her and pulled her head above the surface. Ranui held her firmly against him as she choked out water.

"And again, I ask, are you all right, Mrs. Argüello?"

She coughed again and shook the water from her eyes. "I'm OK, thank you," she somehow got out. He led her to the next hummock and sat her down on a log.

"Better?"

"Yes. I mustn't have been paying attention."

He sat down next to her. Dzień forgot to be annoyed and took advantage of their stop to eat some young rushes beside Ranui.

"You were talking about options, I believe, before I so rudely went swimming," she said, faintly. "What is our other option, Ranui? And, please, call me Aleks. I think we've gone past formal language and it looks as if we might be out here awhile." She looked down at her sodden attire.

"Fine, Aleks. If we head north now, we'll be out of the swamp sooner and you can ride along the shore of the Frith of Thames, but the trip will be much longer. Either way you go, we must cross the Piako River, but if you go to the coast, we will need to cross its wide mouth...and there are many sharks there."

"Sharks." She shuddered, as her stomach turned over.

"Also, I am less familiar with the swamps further to the west, but I believe they are boggier than those we've passed through and could hold more danger to your horse." He smiled as he scratched the fluffy bits around Dzień's forelock.

She rubbed her hand over her brow and her fingers through her hair, then looked up at him. "If it will be more dangerous for Dzień, let's go the longer way."

He nodded. "We'll just have to go upriver a little way to avoid most of the sharks."

She raised an eyebrow at him.

"Except that it's all mangroves at the edges, so it's a bit rough walking at high tide."

"What's the shoreline like?"

"There are also mangroves along the frith, but with wide mudflats, then a short bit of shell beach."

"And which tribe's *rohe* is it?" The new word he'd taught her earlier rolled nicely off her tongue.

"It is no one's, and everyone's. Our *rohe* encompasses the whole swamp, but along the frith is a wide band of free passage running from Opani pā, at the mouth of the Waihou, to Pūkorokoro. All may use it to reach the shared hunting grounds between there and Pokino."

"Is Pūkorokoro easy to find, once we get to the free passage beach?"

"Yes. It's just along the shore, after the coast changes to a white shell beach. We will see the *Pākehā* ships and the new redoubt up on the cliffs near the water."

"So could I find my own way once we reach the frith?"

"You could, as long as you don't get stuck in the mud." He grinned.

"You don't need to go any further than the Piako River, then, do you?"

"It might be a good idea for me to avoid the redoubt itself." He looked down at the tattoos covering his body, then raised an eyebrow at Aleksandra.

"I agree, under the circumstances," she said, with a frown. "I could surely go on by myself from the coast, then you could get back to whatever you were supposed to be doing today."

"Are you sure?"

"I should be fine." She sat for a moment, then gulped and looked up at him. "It's a free passage beach to the *Māori*, but will I be welcome there?"

"That remains to be seen," he said, and looked into her eyes without blinking.

As DARKNESS DESCENDED, Ranui found a relatively dry hummock above the level of the swamp. *Pukekos* squawked and the heavy whoosh of *kererū* echoed above as they swooped into the trees to settle for the night.

"Have you any dry clothing?" he asked her. "I'll get some wood for a fire to cook the pigeon you shot today."

"Thank you." Aleksandra sat down with her pack on a mossy log and stifled a yawn as Ranui walked away. She shook her head. He appeared as fresh as the moment she'd first set eyes upon him. She smiled, grateful he hadn't ridiculed her as her steps slowed near the end of the day, especially after she'd made such a fuss about being able to keep up.

Her hair still dripped from her last dunking, but it was pure luxury to pull off her soggy clothes and replace them with a dry linen shirt and a pair of Xavier's pants. She hung the buckskins from a branch in hope that they'd be drier by morning. She shuddered. The thought of donning the cold and soggy leather in the morning didn't hold much appeal.

"Thank you, Ranui, for your patience with me today," she said, when he returned. "It was harder going than I'm used to and I'm rather unfit." She peered up at him from beneath her lashes.

"It's all right." He smiled at her. "Besides, you caught supper. Where did you learn to shoot a bow like that?"

"I was raised in the Rocky Mountains, in America." She told him about her Shoshone family. "Dzień was their gift to me," she nodded at the pony, who was browsing nearby, "as was my bow." She reached out and rubbed a hand lightly along the smooth wood of the weapon.

"The *Māori* have never had bows and I've never seen one used before." He walked closer to her. "May I?" he asked.

"Of course," she said, handing it to him.

"Fine workmanship." He perused it for some minutes before returning it to her.

"I can teach you to shoot it, if you'd like," she said.

"I'd like that."

"They are a fine people, the Shoshone. It's sad they're being pushed from their lands, if they haven't already been," she said, looking at the ground.

"It's happening here, but I believe the English government will find we do not easily roll over and die," Ranui said, his voice edged with steel.

Aleksandra was silent. From what she had seen of the *Māori*, she'd have to agree. She sat for a moment longer on her *serape* as he struck a flint and started the fire with some fluffy material from a pouch, then she rose to gut and pluck the pigeon for their supper. He soon had a fire kindled and she shoved sticks into the ground beside the fire for a spit.

"The ground's soft, anyway."

"Soft isn't the problem," he said, his mouth twisting.

"*Kererū*, *kumara* and *taewa*. The best supper," he said, as he held out the root vegetables.

"I think I had these on the East Coast, cooked in a hot pool." Aleksandra took one of the small, knurled, dark purple *taewa* and studied it.

"When Captain Cook came, we already grew many kinds of *kumara*, but no potatoes. He gave these ones to my ancestors."

She handed them back to him and sat down on Xavier's serape with a twinge in her heart, thinking of her husband. She sighed and returned her attention to Ranui as he dipped a flax mat into the water channel beside them, then cut up the tubers. Wrapping them in the mat, he placed them by his side.

"When the fire's going well, we put these in the coals," he said. "I prefer them sweeter, as they get from slow cooking in a *hangi*, but it's not practical today." He gave her a rueful grin and sat down on a woolen blanket beside her.

"What's that bird, calling, there?" She looked up into the trees, but saw nothing.

He smiled. "That's a *koukou*, a morepork. A little owl."

She glanced at the fire, then skewered the pigeon carcass with a green stick and placed it on the forked branches to make a spit over the flames.

"You make shooting your bow look easy, but I'm sure it's only your experience showing."

She smiled at him "I appreciate your guiding me across the swamps, Ranui, and I don't expect you to do this for nothing. I'm happy to pay you."

"Consider it a favor to your friend, the captain James, but if you ever should find another bow and some arrows, they would be a good *utu*."

"*Utu?*" Aleksandra's brows drew together.

"It means...many things. Balance. To retain *mana*, one must reciprocate kind deeds, as well as seek revenge, if insult is offered."

"Done. I'll work on that as soon as we get to Auckland," she said, then sat very still. "Ummm... I'm not sure how long it will take to find a bow, though. I may have to get it from America. I can make one, but it will take time to find the right wood here."

"That's fine. I'm not going anywhere," he said, "except, maybe, the Waikato."

Aleksandra winced. "To fight?"

"The *Pākehā* and their government have turned upon the *Māori* who helped them survive here and sold them land. Now they want the best of the land, especially that already cultivated by the *Māori*. They are attempting to take it by force and trickery, but it will not go easily for them."

"That's what your father said to me today." She swallowed hard.

"Did he?" The tall man's brows lowered, his lips in a firm line. "He will not be pleased, but the young men are keen to go."

After they had eaten, Aleksandra sat staring into the fire, finally warm again. She looked up at Ranui as he rose and left the fireside with his Bowie knife.

He turned back to her for a moment. "Just getting some bedding. I'll return shortly," he said, and left the clearing.

She got up to check on Dzień. He was drowsing on the other side of the hummock, his coat finally dry, with one hindlimb cocked. The fading light showed most of the scrub in the clearing had been denuded of its greenery. She gave him a hug and a pat, then left him untethered. He wouldn't stray far. If someone planned to relieve her of her pony, it would make it that much harder without a halter on his head.

"Thank you for an excellent meal," she said, upon Ranui's return with armloads of bracken and tree branches.

"You provided half of it," he said, as he spread the branches down in two piles near the fire and covered them with bracken. He nodded to one of the newly made beds and lay down on the other one, wrapping himself in his blanket.

"I didn't know roast pigeon and *kumara*, much less potato, could taste so good," Aleksandra murmured as she curled up in Xavier's *serape*. Exhausted as she was, she barely finished speaking before she drifted off to sleep. From somewhere far away she thought she heard someone speaking, but she was too far into sleep-land to respond.

"Get some sleep," came the voice, "we've got to cross the Piako tomorrow and you'll need the strength."

ALEKSANDRA'S NOSE was tickled by the smell of fish cooking and she sat up abruptly, staring around her in the early morning light filtering through the *kahikateas*. Ranui had his back to her, crouched over the fire.

"What have you made now?" She inhaled deeply and he turned to face her, a smile on his face.

"I've tickled a *tuna*, an eel, and it's volunteered to be our breakfast." He handed her a piece, steaming in the early morning chill, on a flat bit of wood.

"It's a different sort of eel from what I've seen before." She frowned. These are huge," she said, at the thickness and size of the piece. It wasn't even the full width of the fish. "In California, the eels are thin, a third the thickness of my wrist, and have suckers in their mouths."

"These are different." He opened its mouth and showed her the row of sharp teeth and she shuddered.

"Do they bite?"

"Only if you let them get a hold of you," he said. "They're usually friendly and will let you touch them and feed them. I'm always a little sorry to eat them, when they're so quiet," the smile left his face, "but I always give thanks for their sacrifice, that we may eat."

"I understand. It's like killing deer which have no fear of humans where I come from. I, too, give thanks," she murmured.

"We need to leave as soon as we've eaten to catch the low tide across the Piako." He turned back to his fish.

"How far away is it?"

"An hour and a half, maybe less. We'll cut south to miss most of the tidal part," he said, and ducked his head.

"The sharks, you mean."

"Mmmm…"

"Thank you." She grinned at him when he turned to face her.

"Let's go up and take a look, make sure we're where I think we are," Ranui said.

Aleksandra frowned. "Up?"

He nodded at a cluster of *Kahikateas* and started to climb, wedging himself between the trees until he reached the lower branches. She tied Dzień's reins over his neck and followed. Trees big enough to climb were few in Utah, but she could sure climb rocks.

She soon stood beside him at the top of the two closest tall trees. She looked down once, but it made her so sick she didn't do it again.

"See those?"

"Those what?" she said, gazing around her at the seemingly endless expanse of gray-green *kahikatea*-forested swamp, a solid block of color that ending only at the edges, where darker green mountains reared above the tops of the swamp trees.

"Those are the Three Kings." He pointed back the way they'd come, east toward the Coromandel Ranges. "The triple peaks, just beside each other. They're up the valley beyond our *pā*."

Aleksandra turned around, carefully. The branches were thin, this high up. "Ah, I see them." She smiled. "And there's the river," she turned back the way they were heading, "just ahead of us. And the frith."

He nodded and they climbed down.

The occasional mangrove began to appear, but as they approached the river, the tough tidal plants became more numerous until they were struggling through a dense mangrove swamp.

"The band of mangroves is even wider nearer to the river mouth." He winced over his shoulder. "We're lucky we met it this far upriver."

"I'm glad for that," she said, tugging her buckskin shirt once again free of a mangrove snag.

"And there she is."

Aleksandra nearly ran into his back as he stopped and stood still, staring across the muddy waters of the Piako River.

"The tide's turning, isn't it?" The eddies swirled as the downstream current was checked by the incoming tide.

"It's low tide now and it's not going to get any shallower, so we'd better start swimming." His mouth set into a firm line. As he strode out of the mangroves and across the deep, thick mud of the tidal flats, he pulled the remains of the eel from a pouch at his belt.

"I thought you just had breakfast." She tried to smile, but didn't quite make it, as she willed her queasy stomach to stay put.

"Although it is something we wouldn't usually do, throwing parts of dead creatures back into the *moana*, the sacred sea, it might keep us alive," he said, and threw the chunk of meat and bone as far as he could downstream.

"Oh." Aleksandra gulped, and turned to Dzień. She kissed his nose and tied the reins over his neck. "Come on, boy, it's swim-for-your-life time again," she murmured, and tugged on his rein as she turned toward the water.

She was immersed nearly to her waist in the swiftly-flowing river when the water exploded just downriver, where Ranui had thrown the meat. The brown-green water churned to white.

"Swim," Ranui hissed, as he dove into the water and struck out for the other side.

Aleksandra chanced one more look at the swirling melee before she took a deep breath, let go of Dzień's rein and whispered to him as she dove in. Halfway across, she looked back. The buckskin was close behind her, his nose just above the water, water splashing around his pistoning forelegs. She turned back toward Ranui, put her head back down and ploughed through the water as fast as she could.

When she reached the far side, she ran from the water and tripped over a submerged log stuck fast in the thick mud. Ranui's arms once again caught her before she could hit the slime of the riverbed and held her tightly until her shaking limbs would hold her up again.

"Dzień?" She closed her eyes and froze, afraid to look behind her.

When the whaler arrived at Coromandel, it was full dark. Xavier and three other men rowed the longboat to shore, but the only people they saw were in the saloons, well into their cups. None of the rough miners remembered seeing a blonde woman without a bonnet, a blond young man, or a trading ship from the East Coast, although their ears pricked up at the mention of the woman.

"I think this is the last saloon," Xavier said, his heart sinking.

"It's a tavern, not a saloon," said one of the men accompanying him.

"Tavern, then," Xavier agreed.

"Your Aleks and that von Tempsky aren't around, else someone would've heard of them, especially if she doesn't wear a bonnet," he continued, "not many women like that around here."

"Guess we're done. Back to the ship we go."

"We must smell pretty bad, those men gave us a pretty wide berth," another of the men said.

Xavier had to chuckle. "The longer I live on the ship, the less I'm noticing the scent."

Lord knew when he'd be able to get it off of his skin and clothing. Probably never.

If he found Aleksandra, it would all be worth it.

## 30

A soft nose shoved roughly between Aleksandra's shoulder blades. She spun from Ranui's arms to wrap hers around the pony's neck and buried her face in his mane, shaking.

Ranui's deep laugh echoed behind her and she turned to look at him.

"You're a worry." He shook his head, his smile wide. "That pony will be fine. It's you that concerns me."

"Why?" Her brow furrowed.

"I've got to leave you soon," he said, his eyes scrutinizing the banks above them. "You'll be on your own after this, but I'll see you to within reach of the bay."

"Are we still in your *rohe*?"

"Yes, it's Ngati Hako nearly to Pūkorokoro, other than the free passage beach, but one of my brothers has recently…created problems, shall we say, with a few members of our *hapū* living over here. It's better I'm not found here," he said, gritting his teeth as his brows narrowed, then he glanced at her long hair. "It might be best, however, if you travel as a boy, especially when you get to the redoubts."

"So I've heard." She sighed. "Not a lot of women about, eh?"

"You look grubby enough to be a boy, anyway." He grinned. "I've never seen a woman get as filthy as you are right now." He ducked as she swung at him.

"Like I've had the chance to get clean," she growled.

"Look here, Aleks," Ranui laughed, "you've done better than any *Pākehā* woman I've ever seen in the swamps and I don't begrudge your getting messy, but I hope you'll accept a little gift from me before I go."

She eyed him sideways.

"Soon. We have a little way to walk yet. I don't want you stuck in the mangroves as the tide rises, so let's go."

As the river level rose, they had to walk closer and closer to the banks, tightly covered with the clothes-grabbing estuary plants. The thick mud, deepest at the higher side of the banks, sucked at her moccasins and left deep tracks, while Dzień struggled along, sinking to his cannons with every step.

"I think there's a track at the top of the bank. When I was here before, we crossed on a boat, further downriver towards the bay," Ranui said. He forced his way through the mangroves and clambered up the bank. Reaching a hand down to Aleksandra, she grabbed it and climbed up beside him.

"Oh," Aleksandra said, out of breath. "A trail, and on dry ground yet. Is there somewhere Dzień can climb up?"

They called the pony as they walked along the top and finally found a sloped gully where he could scramble up the embankment.

The track beside the river headed north toward the frith. If she looked eastward, she could just make out the top of a mountain peak over the mangroves and swamp trees.

Ranui pointed at it. "That's Te Aroha, that tall peak there." He turned back to face downriver. "You'll follow this trail to the frith, then keep left at the coast. There's a *Māori* village at Pūkorokoro, and up on the hill behind it is the first redoubt. From there, you just follow the *Pākehā's* road west past two more redoubts, to Queen's at Pokino, then straight north to Auckland. I'm sure you'll be welcomed there, though they won't want to let a woman go on alone."

"A woman won't be going on alone." She tucked her hair under her hat and stuck out one side of her lip, then slouched like a boy. A shortened bit of hair at the back of her neck hung down over the collar of her buckskins.

His raised eyebrows told her she'd succeeded.

"You don't look much like a *wahine* now. I guess they'll let you travel." He shook his head.

"James warned me about this too." She sobered and nodded. "I'll have to take my chances. Dzień is fast, though he's probably as out of shape as I am." She gave him a crooked grin.

"Be sure to save some of his energy for running from anyone who might want to capture you, be they *Māori* or *Pākehā*." He frowned. "The fact that you have a husband makes little difference to some of the men here. There are few white women for them to choose from and they might just take what they want."

"Hopefully they won't be prepared for weapons." She smiled at him as she drew her *shashka*. His eyes glittered at the sight.

"Wherever did you come by so fine a blade?"

"From Russia. My father was trained by a Cossack arms master, and he trained me."

His eyebrows shot up and he stared at her. "Even in *Aotearoa*, we have heard of the Cossacks. Someday, perhaps, you will show me your Cossack skills when the terrain is more suitable." He lifted a brow at the sodden landscape.

"Your English is excellent," she remarked. "How did you come to learn it?"

"At the mission school that used to be at Puriri, before the mission was moved to the Kauaeranga River Valley. My father thought we would have need to understand what the *Pākehā* knew, whether it be their language or their knowledge of the world, so he sent my brothers and me to their school from an early age. Later, we attended Wesley College in Auckland."

"You've done them proud, as we say in America," she said, nodding at him.

"How are you going to get back across the river?" Aleksandra's brow wrinkled at Ranui.

"Same way I got here, only a bit further upstream." He grinned at her.

"Now who's the worry?"

"I've done it all my life. I was just afraid for you. I didn't know if you could really swim and I didn't fancy ripping you from the teeth of a shark or two."

"That wouldn't be my idea of fun, either," she said, with a gulp.

"We're getting close now. Around the next bend, we should see the frith. It's tidal flats, with many shellfish beneath, until you reach

Pūkorokoro. It should be easy going for you both, but remember to watch for the soft spots."

"How long will it take me to get to there?"

"An hour or two from here, if you do a bit of trotting and a bit of walking, you'll come to the Waitakaruru. You'll have to cross it. The flats near it can be swampy, so have a care."

"Another river?" Aleksandra's throat began to constrict.

"Yes. It's smaller than this one and probably too shallow for sharks, but here," he handed her another piece of eel, "just to make you feel better. Are you sure you don't want me to come?" He frowned.

"I'll be fine," Aleksandra said, with more confidence than she felt. She took a deep breath and turned back to Dzień and scratched his withers. "You've kept more eel for yourself, haven't you?"

"Of course," he smiled, "but thank you for asking. You'll know you're nearly there when the mangroves give way to a shell beach. Soon after that, you'll see the village and redoubt." He gritted his teeth. "You likely won't see anyone in the village, though. I hear it was abandoned after the colonial troops bombarded it from their ships."

She closed her eyes and bit her lip. "I'm so sorry, Ranui. I wish there was something I could do."

"There's little you can do, but I appreciate it, nonetheless. Anyway, after you cross the Waitakaruru, a little stream runs off the bank in a waterfall. When you get there, you might want this." He handed her a flax-wrapped packet.

"What is it?"

"Unwrap it and find out."

Aleksandra bit her lip as she worked at the tiny knot in the flaxen string tying it together, then stared at it in awe. She sniffed at it and her mouth dropped open.

"Wherever did you get this? Soap?"

"I made it after my time on a whaler."

"You were on a whaler?" Her stomach flipped over and she stared at the white lump in her hand, wondering if she dared drop it in front of him.

"Yes, for a short time. It wasn't the life for me."

Aleksandra's hands shook. The urge to throw it at him nearly overpowered her sense of self preservation. She swallowed hard, then glared at him. "The thought of those magnificent—"

"—yes, I know," he cut in. "You don't have to say it. I understand completely."

"Then how could you—"

He grabbed her hand and wrapped her fingers tightly around the package. "That's why," he said, in a quiet voice, "this soap is made from coconut oil. It's not made from blubber. I obtained the oil in the islands. It is a gift, for you."

"Thank you," she whispered, as tears flooded her eyes, "and thank you for not killing whales to make it. I know it's silly, because they're like anything else I'd hunt, but...I still feel that way. They remind me of horses," she said, with a shrug.

"I'm glad you appreciate it." Ranui smiled at her and shook his head.

"When I jumped Dzień over the gunwale to escape the ship, the last thing on my mind was soap." She grinned through her tears. "I appreciate this more than you know."

"So when you reach that stream, enjoy your treat. I know you will."

"Oh, will I." She shook her head. "I don't know how to thank you enough for guiding me through the swamp, but I'll find you a bow and arrows. I'll teach you to make arrows next time we meet, as well. Start saving thin hardwood, about this size," she indicated with her fingers. "And, feathers, too. Long, straight ones.

"I'll do that. You please take care, won't you? I don't envy you the ride to come. The districts are in an uproar."

"I know," Aleksandra said, and chewed on her lip.

"You won't be safe anywhere, redoubt or *pā*, so keep to yourself until you find von Tempsky. His reputation alone will keep you safe, at least among the Government troops. I don't have to tell you not to say his name to a *Māori*, do I? So just don't, eh? I'd like to see you alive again."

"I'll keep that in mind." She laughed and stood on her tiptoes to give him a quick hug.

"Here, take this." He handed her his pouch of *koi kumara*.

"But you might need it," she protested. "No, better," she slid out of her pack and riffled through it for a moment, "you take my *pemmican*." She grinned. "Enjoy it. It'll have to last until your bow and arrows arrive."

"Thank you, my lady. The pleasure has been all mine," he said, and bowed.

"Oh, they *did* teach you things in that school!"

"Yes. Mostly how to be as *un-Māori* as possible. They didn't even allow us to speak our own language, but my heritage will not be denied," he said, his brows narrowing as his lips set into a firm, hard line.

"That is as it should be. Farewell, Ranui. Thank you again, and please, stay out of trouble?"

He leaned toward her and shared with her a long, lingering *hongi*. They stepped back and smiled at each other, then Aleksandra gave him another quick hug. She waved goodbye as she turned and slipped away, Dzień following closely behind.

ALEKSANDRA LOOKED CAREFULLY about her before she led Dzień out into full view of the Frith of Thames. She couldn't help but stare at the lovely bay opening up before her. It was huge, bordered on both ends by high, bush-covered mountains, dotted with distant mist-shrouded islands. Nothing moved except for the little waves at its edges and the inevitable mangroves, which barely waved in the breeze.

"Getting hungry, eh boy? Not a lot for you to eat out here," she said, as she fed him a few handfuls of grain. She took a good drink from her canteen, then poured the last of the water into her hat and held it out to him. The thirsty pony drank until it was gone, then they went on.

As Ranui warned, the sand was soft in places, but plenty of it was hard-packed. They paid attention and picked their way along, Aleksandra swinging her arms as they walked side-by-side. Dzień picked his head up and sniffed, then quickened his stride.

"Food or fresh water, Dzień?" He was good at finding both. In the distance, figures on the water along the coast to the west might have been boats, but she couldn't be sure.

They'd been walking for well over an hour when a river mouth opened up before them.

"The Waitakaruru, Dzień. One more swim, sorry, lad," she said, "but hopefully, it's the last."

The buckskin walked on ahead, then turned his head back to her, as if to hurry her up.

"Oh." Aleksandra wrinkled her brow and scowled at the river. "We needn't have hurried to get here. The tide is just beginning to go out. We'll have to find somewhere dry to take a rest for a few hours, pony."

He shook his head and followed her back along the edge of the mangroves until they found a dryish clear patch. Aleksandra ate some *koi kumara* while Dzień munched more of his dwindling grain supply and dozed. She stood up to take a good look around. Satisfied no one was anywhere near, she went to sleep.

Aleksandra awoke refreshed. They returned to the river to find the tide had dropped, so she tied the Mustang's reins up around his neck and packed her gear, wrapping it tightly against water. She shouldered her knapsack and fished the eel from her pocket.

Dzień turned his lip up when he reached toward her hand to see what she held.

"Starting to smell, isn't it?" She grinned at him. The water looked much shallower than the Piako, but she wasn't taking unnecessary chances. "Let's go, boy. Same as last time," she said, and threw the piece of fish as far downstream as she could. She watched, but no flurry of activity altered the light ripples of the water's surface. "Swim time, come on!" she said, and gave his rein a tug. She took three steps into the water, then dove and swam. She looked back once, but Dzień didn't need to be told twice. He was swimming after her. She turned and swam for the far bank.

They emerged dripping, but the anticipation of a freshwater bath made Aleksandra smile as she hugged the Mustang once they were clear of the river.

Sure enough, a little waterfall made its way off the riverbank. It tasted fresh when she cupped her hands and dipped her tongue into it.

"How can water be fresh in such a place, surrounded by a swamp?" she asked the pony. "It must be from an underground spring."

Dzień just shook his head again.

Wherever it came from, it was clean and drinkable. She filled her canteen and her hat for Dzień. He drank his fill and ate more feed.

Aleksandra drew out the precious soap from her pack. Sniffing it once again, she closed her eyes in ecstasy before stripping off and having her first real wash in nearly three months.

The light was beginning to fade by the time she was done, but she was clean, truly clean. She could hardly stop the idiotic smile that stretched her face.

Aleksandra dressed and swung on her knapsack, then started walking, her wet hair drying in the light breeze. Dzień snorted at a seabird which froze as he walked up to it. It finally flapped its wings at him and flew away. Birds were everywhere on this stretch of beach. Gulls, sandpipers and oystercatchers pecked the muddy sand as the water rose higher by the minute to cover the little crabs that scurried out of Aleksandra's way.

Ahead showed the white sand beach that signified she was nearing the redoubt. She stopped and twined her fingers in Dzień's mane, considering. It was only an hour or so away, but it would be full dark by then. Being shot by a sentry in the gloom wasn't in the plans, so she kept an eye out for a dry clearing in the last of the mangroves and found one, just as dark fell. She clambered into it for a good look, leaving the pony standing just outside.

When she stepped back out to get Dzień, a fire showed in the distance on the coastline to her right, toward Coromandel.

As she stood watching, her heart began to race as more and more fires lit up the sky. They soon dotted the far coastline around the whole eastern side of the frith. They weren't little campfires. These were big signal fires.

It couldn't mean anything good for the *Pākehā*. As far as she knew, there weren't any *Pākehā* settlements along that coastline other than Coromandel, and she counted at least seven fires by the end of a half hour. When she looked toward where the redoubt should be, a few spots glowed, but nothing like the pyres burning on the far shores.

After praying for the safe release of Xavier, Aleksandra somehow slept soundly. She was awake to watch the sun rise over the Coromandel Ranges as she broke her fast with *koi kumara*. Dzień finished the last of the oats, then nibbled the younger mangrove shoots.

By the light of day, the new redoubt showed in the distance. Men swarmed over the hillside like so many busy ants behind the tall masts of the three tall ships standing at anchor in the bay. With a look about her, she swung up and pointed Dzień northwest along the coast. He moved off quietly, then threw his head up and sniffed deeply as the wind changed direction. He whinnied, then quickened his pace toward the activity.

"Horses there, eh pony?" Aleksandra smiled. "Can't say but I'd appreciate a cooked meal. There's bound to be some grass up there, too. You must be getting tired of eating mangroves." She patted his neck as he broke into a trot, nose to the ground, carefully negotiating the softer patches in the packed mud.

Soon the beautiful white shell beach crunched and slithered beneath her mount's hooves. Aleksandra dismounted and picked up a double handful of the glossy, iridescent chips of shell, the fragments ranging in color from purple to white to russet. She let the chips run between her fingers while Dzień tugged on the rein, pulling her onward.

Up on the bank to her left stood the *Māori* village's *whares,* behind a fence of tree branches whipped together with flax. Several of the dwellings had been torn apart. Most were blackened and a few were merely piles of charcoal on the ground. There was no movement within the settlement.

Aleksandra bit her lip. Yet another indigenous group moved on.

*When it would stop?*

A way off to the right stood the ships she'd seen from afar. One revealed itself as the gunship "Sandfly." She shook her head. "Appropriate. They bite, as I'm sure the balls from those big guns do."

As she neared the cliffs below the redoubt, a sentry shouted something at her and she waved. She halted Dzień as the young man in a blue uniform ran toward her, rifle at the ready.

She raised her eyebrows at him from beneath the brim of her hat.

"Oh, it's only a boy!" he said, lowering the muzzle. "What's your name, lad? What are you doing out here on your own?" He looked behind her, then frowned.

"I'm seeking Mr. von Tempsky at Queen's Redoubt. I was told I could get there this way," Aleksandra said, remembering just in time to lower her voice, as she'd done when riding as a boy for the Pony Express.

"I don't know about any von Tempsky, but you can get to Queen's this way. Follow me," he said, spinning on his heel and marching up the beach. Ahead of them, a wide, tidal river mouth opened up to the frith from the west. "That there's the redoubt, up on the top of the hill," he said, pointing to the hive of activity at the top of the steep bluff.

"Are they building two? What's that, to the south of it, by that big tree?"

"Oh, that's just a little picquet post. We post a piquet there at night. The signaling is done from there, to the ships and the next redoubt at Maipu."

The rattle of an anchor chain came from a ship, smaller and closer in than the others, and Aleksandra glanced its way to see a boat being lowered over the side. She returned her attention to the sentry. "How far away is Maipu?"

"It's about four and a half miles."

"They signal over that distance?"

"Yes. Semaphore, you know, big flags. The signalmen have telescopes and flags so they can read messages from far away."

"Oh, with a telescope."

"Yes. They'll be calling that redoubt at Maipu 'Esk', after that ship, there." He turned and pointed at the 21-gun corvette at anchor to Aleksandra's right. "This is Pūkorokoro, like the river at the base of the bluff. We're calling the redoubt 'Miranda', after *that* ship," he pointed at the closest warship. "We need good communication to block the rebels. The Kingites at Paparata pā were threatening the rear of Cameron's army and raiding rebels were crossing the frontier whenever they wanted." He rubbed a hand over his face. "They could get across the Grey's line and rove the Wairoa ranges."

"Grey's line?"

"Governor Grey's line." He frowned. "Don't you know? In July, he issued a proclamation that Waikato *Māori* living north of that line, along the Mangatawhiri Stream, would be banished south of there if they didn't declare for the government. The governor sent out another proclamation to the chiefs that any *Māori* who didn't lay down their arms would forfeit all their lands."

Aleksandra gripped her buckskins with her free hand as her heart hit her boots.

## 31

Crowned by a spired white church, a high, rocky headland jutted out of the coastline to their port side. The captain of the whaler steered wide of the breakwater extending from the point and headed his ship into the next big bay.

"Auckland," the captain said, nodding his head at the sprawling city behind the ships filling the inlet and docked at the wharves.

Upon the headland ranged several cannon and many one- and two-storied stone buildings. A Union Jack, flying from a flagpole, presided over the site.

"Complete with fort?" Xavier said.

"Fort Britomart, on the point of the same name." Thompson nodded at the cluster of buildings. "Built on an old *pā* site."

"Big ditches around the outsides and all," Xavier said, staring up at them as they passed.

"They'd be the original *Māori* trenches," the captain said, never taking his eyes from the rocks to their port side. "We'll dock at Queen's Wharf," he added.

The city of Auckland spread out before them, rising up the gradual slope beyond the bay. The fort was sizable, but the church dominated the skyline behind Point Britomart. Warehouses and stores lined the road running along the water's edge and houses covered the hills in the background.

"That's a bit grand for this little place," Xavier said, pointing to the church.

"Eh? Oh, that's St. Paul's Anglican. It was the first one here. It's been there for twenty years, already. And up there," he jutted his chin up the hill a little further, "is St. Patrick's. Take your pick. They're both grand."

"I think I'll find Aleksandra before I start looking around at churches," Xavier said, with a grin.

The sounds and smells of port hit him when they edged up to the wharf and threw out their hawsers to the waiting men. As soon as the boat was moored, Xavier grasped the hand of the captain and thanked him profusely, then climbed down the rope ladder to the dock.

"Von Tempsky shouldn't be too hard to find," the captain called down after him. "Just ask at Fort Britomart. They'll know where to find him."

"Thanks again," Xavier said, waving, as he headed for the point.

The rough scoria of the road surface grated on the soles of his boots as he passed the church. With its tall spire and elegant lines, it was truly beautiful. Certainly a finer building than he'd expected to find here. Perhaps it wouldn't be such a backwater, after all.

His legs were proving a bit unsteady from his time at sea, so he stretched them out as he walked, nodding to passers-by, many of whom turned their faces away as he neared them. He grinned, despite himself. He must smell like a fiend after being on ship for three months, and the last of that on a whaler. Once he set the wheels in motion to find von Tempsky and Aleksandra, he'd get a room and a bath. He could almost feel the warm water of a scented bath enveloping him.

"Hold there," the guard at the entrance to the fort challenged.

He held up his hands and stood still, coming out of his daydream.

"Hello," Xavier said. "*De veras*, of course."

"State your name and business," he barked.

"Xavier Argüello, looking for Captain Gustavus von Tempsky. I understand he may be near Drury?"

Several men looked up at his comment, brows narrowed.

"Right this way," the guard said, giving him a sideways glance, his hand on his sword hilt.

The other men melted away, then the guard stood aside for him to precede him into a stone building.

The door slammed behind him and metal scraped upon metal.

Xavier turned, but the guard was nowhere to be seen.

He surveyed the waiting room. A five by five room, with only a wooden bench against one wall and a high, barred window.

*Some welcome.*

If they were trying to discourage visitors, they were doing a good job. He knocked on the door. A shiver ran up his spine when no one replied. He tried to lift the latch, but it wouldn't budge. Even when he shook it. "Hey, you've locked me in! Guard!"

Only silence, then retreating footsteps on the boardwalk outside the door.

It finally clicked.

This was a gaol cell. But why? Had von Tempsky disgraced himself?

Xavier sat down to wait patiently, but eventually he rose to prowl from one wall to another. He pulled the bench before the grilled window, but it didn't give him enough height to see out, so he put it back and continued to walk the walls.

There must be some mistake.

"SOON AFTER THAT, we invaded the Waikato," said the young sentry. With a grin and a wink at Aleksandra, he rattled on, clearly misunderstanding the look of horror that must surely show on her face. "Had to, you know, the government had already promised the *Māori's* land to the men from other countries who've come to help us win this war." He strutted as he spoke, with a wide grin.

Aleksandra turned away and clamped her mouth shut, fists clenched at her sides. Voicing her opinions in wartime would land her in serious trouble, but stabbing a soldier would get her shot. He was still talking by the time her head cleared and she attempted to feign interest.

"—from Esk, they'll signal to the new Surrey Redoubt that's just being built—"

"—and from Surrey, they can signal all the way to Queen's," Aleksandra said, her voice flat.

He grinned. "You got it, boy! You're a fast learner." His smile melted and a shadow crossed his face. "So how come you're not in a regiment?"

"I've just come from America. We were shipwrecked. I have to find Mr. von Tempsky to help get my family to safety."

"Oh." His brows still narrowed, he mumbled beneath his breath. "I'll take you to the commander at the redoubt." He scowled and marched faster.

They'd come level with a dock, if it could be called that, a short structure on long poles isolated far out in the low tide mud flats.

"We've just built that," he nodded at it, "so we can get supplies from the bigger ships, at least at high tide. It took forever to make a passable causeway from the dock." He indicated the long pathway of tea tree fascines tied together with flax and rope. "We wonder if it'll still be there every time the tide goes out."

"Shall we avoid it? It looks a bit rough." Aleksandra glanced at the construction. Dzień's legs probably wouldn't survive walking across it.

"If you wish," he said, looking at her sideways, his lips in a firm line.

Aleksandra sighed. She gave it wide berth and returned her attention to the ground, avoiding the deeper mud as they approached the river. Aleksandra changed her mind about the rough causeway when they approached the junction of the swampy delta and the bluff of the redoubt, where the compacted tidal mud had been churned to a deep morass. She slid to the ground and led the pony onto the rough walkway.

"I'm part of the coast guard," the soldier said. "Most of us are navy men, not landlubbers," he said, pursing his mouth. "We had to stand off shore in the Waiheke passage on account of the weather for eight days. Ships full of newly recruited colonial militiamen from Auckland, half of them only boys. Never been on ship before." He rolled his eyes. "At least the Australians in the lot knew what a ship was about." He shook his head.

"Looks pretty busy up there," Aleksandra's brows narrowed as she looked at the redoubt. "Is the redoubt that big?"

"The flotilla from Auckland had over nine hundred troops and nearly fifty officers."

"For this redoubt?" Her jaw dropped as her chest tightened.

"This one's only being built for a hundred and twenty men. Took awhile to get 'em all in, though" he said, one eyebrow raised. "We had to land way up the coast on account of the shallow mud flats. We slung the horses off, then had to get all those men and the horses through two swamps and over that ferny ridge." He nodded his head at the steep hills running from the coastal swamps toward them. "Took us a whole day to get to Pūkorokoro River."

"Some effort," Aleksandra said, eyeing the hills and the swamps between.

"We got to pursue some unfriendly natives from the Pūkorokoro village, though, just south of the river," he said with a grin. "They'd dug rifle pits and were going to use them, but we scared 'em off, then bivvied for the night. In the morning, the Colonel decided where we'd build the redoubt. We've been working at it ever since."

"Unfriendly natives?" Aleksandra lifted a brow at him.

"Well," he glanced down, his lips twisted, "I guess they'd some right to be unfriendly. The *Miranda* and the *Sandfly* visited a fortnight ago and shelled three of the rebels' villages hereabouts." He turned away and kept walking.

Aleksandra gritted her teeth and buried the fingers of one hand deep into Dzień's mane. She tried to breathe slowly and focus on the cliffs and the river just ahead. "Can you get boats up the river?" she asked.

"Small ones, at high tide. We only have four feet to play with, but it's better than nothing. Took some work to clear the river, though. The *Māoris* blocked it with big *pohutakawa* branches after the *Miranda* and *Sandfly* were here last."

Aleksandra nodded and turned her head turned away to hide her tight jaw, as he continued.

"It was tricky to get supplies up to the redoubt site in the beginning, though." He frowned back over his shoulder. "We dragged everything up the face of the bluff and lost quite a bit of gear. Eventually, we built this road up to the top, but it took forever, going through swamp and mudflats." He shook his head.

The sentries they passed glanced at them, eyebrows raised.

"They don't see too many *Pākehā* traveling alone out here," he said, and turned left toward a steep road cut into the hillside that led to the top.

When they finally reached the redoubt, the ants became soldiers, more than she could count, digging, carrying logs and planks or stomping down dirt. The trench-diggers, working in ditches deeper than their own height, threw shovelfuls of dirt from the perimeter of the huge redoubt upwards onto the growing mounds beside them.

"After it's tamped down, that dirt they're tossing will become the palisades surrounding the redoubt." Her escort pointed out the rectangular bastions rising on its corners, then directed her gaze to a rise a few hundred yards to the south. "That's the piquet post you asked about. It's nearly done." He nodded at the structure. "Wait here," he said.

Aleksandra's jaw dropped at the view. She stared east at the

Coromandel Ranges rising high over the *kahikatea* swamp she'd just traversed, somewhere beyond which lay Xavier, hopefully still alive. She gulped and turned to look south at 'The Waikato', as the sentry had called it. He'd jutted his chin north to show where Auckland lay.

"My man tells me you appeared out of nowhere," said a powerfully built, black haired man, as he walked up behind her and stood to attention. "Lieutenant-Colonel Carey. May I be of assistance?"

Aleksandra spun about. "Yes, sir," she said, then nearly kicked herself as she remembered to lower her voice again. She gulped. "I was hoping you could point me in the direction of Queen's Redoubt."

"You do realize, son, that it's wartime? What could you be thinking, out on your own?"

"The rest of my family's on a shipwrecked vessel awaiting help from Mr. von Tempsky, a journalist an—."

"—von Tempsky? He's with Jackson now, near Drury, but his journalist days are over. He's in the Forest Rangers. I hear he's been quite effective in the bush."

"That would be the man." She put her head down and made a figure in the dust with the toe of her moccasin.

"You can go on to Esk with a detail leaving tomorrow, and on from there. You say your family is shipwrecked. Just where are they?"

"A long way from here. East Coast."

"You've come from the East Coast." One brow raised, he stood, hand on hip and stared at her. "You and this pony... and I'm meant to believe that?"

"Yes, Colonel, sir." She dared to look up at him and told him her story."

He listened in silence, his mouth quirked to the side. "By yourself," he said, and stood in silence for a minute. "How would a youngster like you defend yourself against hostile natives?"

"I've not yet found any to be hostile, sir," she said, with a raised brow, "and I know about hostile...I rode for the Pony Express in Utah and Nevada," she said softly, "a few years ago."

"Is that right?" he said. His hand fell from his hip and he stared at Aleksandra. "Your name, young man?"

"Aleks—Aleks Argüello."

"All right, Aleks, I'm not sure I believe your story, but just so you know, everybody in the country will be called upon to fight, so make sure you do your part, eh? I'll be asking after you when I get to Queen's next."

He looked at her out of the corners of his eyes, then took a deep breath. "You can get a feed for yourself and your horse over at that tent there. The troop leaves at first light for Esk. Be sure you're ready."

"Thank you, sir." Aleksandra swallowed hard. "If there's anything I can help with while I'm here, please let me know."

"I might just do that," he said, then added in an undertone, "though you look like you could use some feeding up, not hard work." He turned and disappeared into the mass of men, already sweating as they labored in the early morning summer sunshine.

She led Dzień beyond the other horses' picket lines to where he could find some grass and slipped his reins beneath a rock, then headed for the mess tent. She was in luck; there was some breakfast left. With a bucket of feed for Dzień and a plate of stew for herself, she made her way back to the Mustang. She stored some grain in her feed bag and put the rest in her hat for the hungry pony while her stomach grumbled from the smell of her own breakfast. She finally sat on a log and ate her ration. Hot stewed beef and biscuits had never tasted so good.

All went well until Dzień finished his grain and smelled her biscuits. She shared a bit and dunked the rest into the stew. Turning up his nose at the combination, Dzień returned to the wispy grass. Aleksandra turned him loose to scavenge what grass he could find, and he made a beeline for the edge of the bush to browse while Aleksandra finished her meal in peace.

"Argüello," a voice boomed out behind her.

Aleksandra swung toward the sound to see the Lieutenant-Colonel looking her way. She jumped to her feet, bowl in hand.

"Job for you," he shouted, walking toward her. "Where's that pony of yours?"

"Eating, sir," Aleksandra nodded her head down the hill at the buckskin, barely visible just inside the bush.

"I've a dispatch for Surrey that can't wait till tomorrow. Since you've ridden for the famous Pony Express, I thought you might be willing."

"Glad to be of service, sir, but you'll have to tell me the way."

"There's a clear wagon road all the way through," he raised an eyebrow and grinned, "or something of the sort. It's the *only* way through, unless you're a native."

"Truth be told, I'd rather be getting on, anyway."

"Get some rations for you and your pony while I ready the dispatch. Sure you're happy to go alone? None of the others are keen."

"I'm used to it," she said.

"That track isn't actually the safest place to be right now," he looked at her beneath his brows, "lying as it does near Governor Grey's line."

"I've been through worse." She winced.

"I wouldn't ask anyone to do this, but it's important." He sighed. "The working detachments sent to build the Esk and Surrey Redoubts along the Miranda-Mangatawhiri line are about to make a reconnaissance of the Kingite's Paparata pā. I've just received vital information the men need before they march," Carey said, turning to leave. "Their commander must get this immediately."

## 32

Eventually, someone came to the door of Xavier's cell, or rather, several people did.

"Stand back, Argüello," came a harsh voice. "Don't try anything, or we'll shoot."

He blinked. "Shoot?" Xavier stumbled backwards, away from the door as a key grated in the lock.

Five men, bare bayonets glinting in the light shining through the high window, moved slowly into the room, all facing him.

"There must be some mistake," Xavier said, to the man with the most impressive uniform, while eyeing each of the bayonets in turn. "What seems to be the problem, sir?"

"You are under arrest for murder."

His mouth dropped open and he never moved as more men entered and moved past those holding the rifles at his chest. They grabbed him by the arms.

Xavier's breath caught in his chest. "You must have the wrong—"

"—save your words for the magistrate, if you even get a trial," he growled.

Xavier's vision blurred as the men locked manacles on his wrists behind his back and shackled his ankles together with a short chain.

There was no point in fighting and his skin was just beginning to heal from their last period in chains on the ship, so he made no fuss as they led him from the room and out of the fort. This was bad enough, but he needed to find Aleksandra. It didn't bear thinking about—her alone in this godforsaken place?

People turned to stare as they led him back past the church along the scoria road and up the hill toward the built-up part of the city. The men surrounding him strode out, but his legs were shackled close. He had to take two step to their one, but he kept up.

A hundred yards or so later, his gaolers slackened the pace. One man ran ahead and pounded on the door of a small shack. No one answered. To the left of the shack stood the Auckland Courthouse, if its sign were to be believed, its pillars reaching toward the sky.

"Be with you in a moment. Just let me get this last debtor…" a man in a blue uniform said, as he finished locking a man into a set of stocks attached to the right hand wall of the shack, "…into place." He turned to the man in the stocks. "There. Enjoy that, sir, and remember to pay your—"

"Gaoler!" shouted the army man leading Xavier's contingent. "We have a dangerous criminal on our hands. Open the gaol so we can get him off the streets. He's wanted for a grisly murder on board a ship."

Faces turned in the street around them as they waited. The gawkers' numbers grew by the minute, all staring at him with grim fascination.

"Will you please find Gustavus von Temp—Captain von Tempsky? He's with the Forest Rang—"

"—I told you to shut up," his captor growled, and swung a heavy fist. He ducked and the man missed.

"Come along, then," the gaoler said, and led the way to his gaol.

Once inside the tiny, windowless cell, the gaoler searched him. "Here's the murder weapon we've been told about," he said, swinging Aleksandra's father's *shashka* through the air. "And a knife. No, two knives."

Xavier closed his eyes, shook his head, and held his peace. He'd try again after the military men left.

"You'll be heading to Esk Redoubt first," Colonel Carey said, as he led her to the top of the picquet post. "It's at Maiapu, on that high ridge between here and Surrey. Here," he said, handing his telescope to her, "you can see the flags signaling from Esk."

"On that highest mountain peak?"

"Yes. And to your right are the Waikato Heads," he said, pointing out the shimmering blue waters of the western bays, far across the island. "Queen's Redoubt lies before them, near the Waikato River."

"I can't make out the men clearly, but I can see the flags." The signalman's regular movements were uncanny in the telescope glass.

"The horses and wagons have carted goods and timber from here to Esk, so it really is a road, of sorts."

"I've seen those before, sir," she said, jamming her hat down more firmly on her head. "We'll get it there."

He chuckled.

"If you have your signal system set up and it's working, why do you need the message delivered?" Aleksandra frowned.

"The taking of the Paparata pā is of utmost importance to the success of the colonial forces." He stopped for a moment and looked about him, then turned back to her and lowered his voice. "This string of redoubts from here to Queen's was built to cover the flank of Cameron's army and take a firm hold on the Wairoa Ranges. Paparata pā currently provides a clear pathway and support for the *Māori* to route troops from the Wairoas or from east coast, via the Piako swamps and the Frith of Thames, to reinforce their army in the Waikato."

"Oh." Aleksandra let out her breath with the word.

He went on, his words spoken between gritted teeth. "The stronghold must not be allowed to remain in the hands of the natives."

"But why don't you just signal the message?"

"We suspect messages are being intercepted by the enemy or that there's an intelligence leak at Queen's."

Aleksandra nodded slowly.

"The upcoming Forest Ranger raid is so vital that Governor Grey has ordered this transmission to be carried by boat from Auckland this morning and hand-delivered to the redoubt commanders along the way."

"The boat I just saw coming in?"

He nodded.

Aleksandra jumped up and reached for Dzień's bridle. "I'll be going now, then, sir?"

"Where's your saddle, Son?" he said, his brows lowering.

"Don't have one."

"Are you prepared to defend yourself?"

"Let's just say I have at least three good blades on my person," she said. She slipped the bit between the Mustang's teeth and turned back to face him.

Both of his eyebrows were raised. "Sure you don't want to stay on in my regiment?"

"With all due respect, sir, I need to get help for my family but I appreciate the compliment." Aleksandra smiled and tipped her hat, then clucked to Dzień. He broke into a lope as she vaulted on and they slid down the steep, muddy track, headed for Esk, Surrey and von Tempsky.

Aleksandra sighed with pleasure as they rode away from the teeming mass of sweating men, the Lieutenant-Colonel's packet of papers tucked into her shirt. Dreading the thought of a night among the rough soldiers and navy men, she was only too happy to ride away alone on a track she "couldn't miss".

Rounding a corner on a steep uphill, Dzień's head shot up and he stopped short. Before them, twenty-odd men dragged a native canoe behind them up the road through the bush. Even without uniforms, the men showed their origin by the sea shanty they sang, as they rhythmically heaved on the ropes yoking them to the hollowed-out tree trunk.

As she neared the sweating men, one of them glanced over his shoulder, fear in his eyes, then gave her a faint grin and sighed. The rest spun around, then shared relieved glances, mopping their brows on their sleeves.

"Well done, men," Aleksandra shook her head at them, "but I don't see any water to float it up here."

"The *waka's* to help rebuild a bridge across a stream. Make it easier for the horses," one man puffed, his reddened cheeks glowing in the dappled light. "There was one there before, but it collapsed when we tried to pull the big gun across it last week." He shook his head and sat down for a moment, then looked at her, his brow scrunching up. "Are ye alone, laddie?"

"Yes, but I'll be fine." Aleksandra smiled.

"You'll take care, won't ye?" The man's brows furrowed as he waved her on by.

"That I will, thank you," she said, riding past the beautifully carved *waka*, lying incongruous, deep in the forest.

She rode down the other side of the mountain, cautiously surveying the open area before her as the track emerged from the dense bush and skirted the edge of a swamp. On the other side of the valley it entered the forest again and headed uphill. Finally, before her stood the steep incline

Carey had mentioned. Esk was as yet invisible, but no one could've missed the noise from the men.

A whinny sounded in the distance. Dzień trumpeted in reply, then put his head down and hit a long trot up the track, his ears pointed hard forward.

"Will your ears make you fly there faster, pony?" she said, and he flicked them back at her.

A boy, looking too young to be wearing a colonial troop uniform, stepped out of the shade of a *Puriri* tree. Waving his rifle in her direction, he called out for her to stop.

"Message for your commander," she shouted and pulled the envelope from her shirt. She waved it in his direction as they slowed to a halt.

He looked at it and looked again, mouth twitching. "Seems in order," he murmured.

She wondered if he could read. "Thank you, sir." She nodded, then trotted for the redoubt.

The view in every direction, as she approached the top, was staggering. To the east, south and west the terrain was *kahikatea* swamp, with hills and small ranges rising from it at intervals. Seas shimmered to the east and west.

Esk Redoubt was well progressed, its trenches already deep. The scarfs up to the resulting parapets were steep, nearly vertical, and already higher than the men's heads. Two north-facing rectangular bastions and a southwest circular one extended out from the corners and several of the soldiers' dwellings were well-started. Her guts clenched as she looked around the site. There should be many more men here than the twenty working on the fortress.

"Hello, message from Colonel Carey," she called out loudly.

The men stopped their labor and as one, turned to face her. A blonde man approached her, dirt falling off his uniform as he walked toward her.

"Good morning, sir. Urgent orders for the march on Paparata from Colonel Carey."

"Let me get the commander, one moment," he said, and ran for a tent on the other side of the encampment.

A tall officer in a tidier uniform approached her.

"Good morning, sir. Orders from Colonel Carey," Aleksandra repeated.

"Thank you. Who might you be, and," he looked down the way she'd come, "why are you alone?" He raised an eyebrow. "A drink for your pony?" he asked, indicating the trough Dzień was already pulling toward. The commander motioned to one of the men, who scurried away quickly.

"Name's Aleks, and Colonel Carey asked me to carry this message for him. I'm heading for Queen's to find Mr. von Tempsky."

"Ah, the intrepid Mr. von Tempsky. That's Captain von Tempsky, now." A tic showed in his jaw, before he shook his head and continued. "The men left hours ago."

It was late the following day before Xavier was able to speak with the gaoler, and then, only through the door. His only other human contact had been early that morning—a woman who wouldn't speak to him, as she passed a dish of some crude gruel through the narrow slit under the metal door.

"Please, sir, can you get a message to Captain von Tempsky? He's with the Forest Rangers, in Drury. I need to find him. My wife was trying to get help, to save me from the first mate who killed Capt—"

"—save your breath," he said. "The magistrate will hear you, maybe. He's pretty busy with all the prisoners we've captured from the war in the Waikato. Just be happy you're considered too dangerous a criminal to be tossed out onto the *Marion*."

"The *Marion*?"

"The prison hulk out in the bay. That's where they're storing the *Māori* prisoners they've taken until they can ship them off to an island somewhere. You wouldn't last a day out there, anyway." He chuckled. "And that would cheat the crowd out of the spectacle of your hangin'. No fun in that," he said. His laughter faded as he walked away.

Xavier's stomach grumbled at the lack of food but it was his heart, breaking into shards for Aleksandra, that did him in.

Somehow he slept, with no idea of what his future, their future, would hold.

# 33

Aleksandra's heart sank.

The officer's brows narrowed as he perused the letter briefly. "You should be able to catch them before they leave Surrey for Paparata," he said, his hands turning white as he gripped the paper.

"I hope so." She took a deep breath. "The Colonel said they need this information before they get there."

"Thanks for your message, Aleks," the officer said, turning to take a canteen and paper-wrapped packet from the approaching soldier.

"No problem, sir."

"Take these," he said, handing her the vessel and the package, "and ride safely. The last hill up to Surrey's a killer."

"Thank you, sir." Dzień finished drinking and she backed him away from the trough, then turned him on his haunches and waved. Dzień broke into a canter as they traversed the first switchback on the steep track down the mountain.

Once they reached the flats, she opened the packet to find bread and cheese. She ate them as she rode down a ridge back toward a swamp. They swept around the marshy edge in an arc, the vast *kahikateas* towering above them. A pair of *kererū* whooshed past them into the trees. She cringed at the thought of the meal she and Ranui had made of one. Though delicious, she rather preferred watching the seemingly ungainly, massive pigeons easily negotiate their way at speed among the closely-packed branches of the treetops. Dzień shook his head when one swooped near them.

Aleksandra rubbed his neck as they trotted down into a rocky, shallow stream running from the hills to the north. Dzień stopped for a drink while she perused the wagon road ahead. It rose gradually upward from the river, then turned straight up a hill. At a decidedly lofty elevation, she could just make out the hard horizontal line of brown against the dark olive-green of the native bush which could only be the rising parapets and bastions of the Surrey Redoubt. The tiny figures crawling over its surface must be soldiers with their mattocks.

She took a deep breath. The officer at Esk had that right. It would be some trek to the top. After a good look into the bush around her, she slid from Dzień's back.

Dzień snorted down her front as she rubbed the sweaty hair beneath his forelock.

"Well, boy, let's get up that hill. The sooner we get it over with, the sooner I can pass on this message." She slid a hand down his body and took hold of his tail. At her click, he headed off at a slow trot and Aleksandra ran along behind him, up the precipitous ridge to the northwest. The pony still hadn't recovered his fitness after his long sojourn in the ship's hold and she wanted to keep a little in reserve.

She looked back down the hill from time to time as they climbed the track. The bush-covered hillside was deeply cut with wheel tracks and random hoofprints. The downhill side of the track before them had given way. Vertical skid marks off the side and down the bank showed where a team and a heavy wagon or gun must have slipped off the road, only stopping before an ancient, towering *Puriri* tree. Its bark was newly torn and the thick trunk gouged. She pitied the horses who'd pulled the wagon up to the redoubt site, likely more than once.

"Lucky for them that tree was there," she said to the pony. "Nearly to the top, lad."

"Stop right there!" someone shouted.

Aleksandra couldn't see him. He was on the other side of Dzień. She scrambled up to his head and stood, gasping for breath, looking at the soldier pointing his Enfield at her.

"What's your business? Who are you?"

"I've a message for your commander," she said shortly. "Urgent, needs to get to him before the men," she panted, "leave for Paparata."

He lowered the muzzle and walked toward her, hand outstretched. "I'll take it," he said.

"I'm to give it to no one but your commander."

"Well, then," he said gruffly, "better get a move on, they've already left."

Aleksandra took a deep breath, swung up on Dzień and galloped past the man while he shouted behind her. She lay low on the pony's neck in case he planned to make an issue of being left behind.

A square bastion rose before her as they crested the hill. Men with tools, nearly invisible in the deep trenches, hacked at the earth and threw it high up onto the rising parapets. She was challenged again as she neared the fort and waved the papers at them, not slowing down.

"I need to see your commander immediately," she shouted. "Urgent message from Colonel Carey!"

They swung around and pointed towards a tent, from where a red-haired man emerged, rifle in hand.

Aleksandra slid Dzień to a halt before him, ignoring the officer's lowered brows and the muzzle of his rifle. "Sir, message from Colonel Carey. The men are not to proceed to Paparata pā without this information," she said, handing him the missive.

"Where have you come from?" he growled at her.

"Miranda," she cocked her head at him, "sir," she added.

He took a deep breath and gave her the hint of a smile. "And where is your uniform, young man?"

"I'm a civilian, sir, just doing my part to help."

"Alone? I'm meant to believe that?"

"My family is being held prisoner and I seek Mr., ah, Captain, von Tempsky." She looked him in the eye. "I'm told he's at Queen's."

He frowned at her over the open missive, then turned to his aide. "Send Hughes on his fastest horse to intercept the men heading for Paparata pā," he said. "Tell them to return immediately."

Aleksandra stood quietly, slowly getting her breath back, until he was finished. "Excuse me, sir, may I water my horse?"

"Oh, of course." He snapped to attention and led her toward a trough and picket line. "I'm Sergeant Cole. What's your name and how did you become involved?"

As she answered, a glance across the camp showed the sergeant's aide dealing with the regular who'd challenged Aleksandra on the hillside. The soldier's face was dark as he turned and stomped back down the hill toward his post.

"Do you have a letter of introduction, in case you're stopped?" the officer asked.

Aleksandra turned back to him and shook her head. "There wasn't time and we were more worried about catching those men." She raised her brows at him.

"Come to my tent and I'll write one," he said, lifting his tent flap. "I appreciate your assistance in this situation. Many lives may have been lost."

"I'm glad I was able to get here in time," she said.

"We'll be better off with the help of the new Forest Rangers division. The move on the Paparata pā will be made by their unit."

She choked on the water she'd just sipped from her canteen and he looked at her sideways.

"The Forest Rangers will carry out this foray. The rebels surely expect our attack and our regular troops would be slaughtered. The Rangers will be a surprise, arriving from a different direction, with a level of stealth the natives would never expect."

Her heart stopped at the thought of von Tempsky, her new *Māori* friends, and her part in it. She closed her eyes, her heart leaden. "Was that the news I just carried?" she whispered, all air gone from her lungs.

"Yes, so thank you very much." He dipped his quill into a tan ceramic inkwell and quickly scrawled out a note. "Have you eaten?" he asked, as he blotted the ink on the parchment.

"A little," she murmured. She shivered as sweat dripped down her back.

"We'll get you fed and when your horse is ready to go on, you can head out."

"Thank you, sir. If I may take care of my horse first, please?"

"Don't worry about him, one of the men—"

"—if you don't mind, I'll care for him myself, please," she interrupted.

At a nod from the now-smiling sergeant, she walked the pony cool, gave him another drink and tethered him away from the other horses. Back at the sergeant's tent, he waved her in. Her mouth watered at the sight of the table, set with of fresh meat, cheese and the inevitable hardtack. The shade and breeze through the open tent flaps were welcome and she cooled as the sweat covering her body dried.

"So you're seeking von Tempsky. Would you care to tell me—"

The captain was cut off once again as Aleksandra leapt from her seat with a shriek, heading for Dzień. A young soldier was about to hit the still-thirsty pony as he nosed a bucket of water the boy carried past him. The soldier stayed his hand, but she kept coming, only to fall headlong when she tripped over a tent peg. Winded, she leapt to her feet, gasping for breath, and shoved her hat on tighter as she continued toward Dzień.

"Don't you touch that pony. He's just thirsty. Don't you have an ounce of kindness in you?" Aleksandra growled. She jerked the bucket from the boy, who stood stock still, stunned. When the pony had drunk the lot, she thrust the bucket at the soldier and shoved him away with all her strength, turned on her heel and stalked back to Sergeant Cole's tent.

His brows were narrowed and his lips pursed when she arrived back at the tent.

"I'm sorry, sir, but that pony's saved my life more times than I care to remember. I cannot abide to see him abused," she said in a soft voice.

"Why don't you take off that silly American hat? You might be a little cooler," he said in his clipped British accent, reaching for her battered ten-gallon hat.

She spun, one hand on her hat and the other reaching for her *shashka*. Her feet found a tent peg again and she fell headlong into the side of the adjacent tent and went down in a heap. She extricated herself from the canvas and ropes and stood looking at him. His narrowed eyes were now on her chest and she glanced downward.

Her breasts, thankfully still inside her buckskins, hung partly free from what was left of their restraining leather wrap. She broke out in a sweat again as she glanced behind her and stepped backwards, away from the sergeant. The old cracked doeskin she'd worn to bind and hide her woman's chest so many years before, riding the Pony Express, had finally given up the ghost. She managed to stifle the insane desire to giggle at her uneven bust. She had one large breast and one mostly flat, off to the side. She sobered quickly enough when the officer caught her by the arm and dragged her into his tent.

"You're obviously not who you say you are, 'missy'. How about you come clean and start by telling me who you really are and what your mission is here."

Aleksandra could only look miserably at the ground while her mind raced for a reply.

"How about starting with your name, your real one?" The officer's good temper had evaporated.

"Aleks," she said in a small voice.

"Try again," he growled. "The rest of it."

"Aleksandra Argüello."

"You don't look like any Spaniard I've ever met."

"My husband is Argüello, if he yet lives," she whispered in a faint voice.

"So you've run away? There are rules against that here."

Aleksandra gritted her teeth and drew herself to her full height as she glared at him. "I run from nothing," she snapped. "If you truly want to know, we were shipwrecked on the East Coast near Tokomaru Bay, I jumped that Mustang over the bulwark and into the sea, climbed over hill and dale with the son of a *Māori* chief, caught a trader's boat around the Coromandel, up the Waihou River, and when *that* ship broke a rudder and became stuck on a bar, traveled across the Piako swamp with a son of the chief at Ōruarangi. He left me at the Piako River and I've come by shore to Pūkorokoro, that's Miranda to you, and I've carried messages for Colonel Carey since then. What else do you want to know? I told the truth about my husband and seeking von Tempsky."

"Implausible enough story. Why do you ride as a man?"

"How far do you think I'd have gotten if people knew a lone woman rode across the island?"

He took a deep breath and slowly breathed it out, one eyebrow cocked, then relaxed back into his seat. "So why do you want von Tempsky?"

"He's an old acquaintance of my husband and I hoped Gustavus might be able to save him from the madman who holds him on the ship. From the stories he tells, von Tempsky fears nothing and if anyone can save my man, it's him."

"Having met the Pole, I'd have to agree with you," he said with a twist to his lips. "I'll give you an escort to ensure you get to Queen's, Aleksandra. That should keep you out of trouble for a few hours."

"I don't need an escort. I rode for the Pony Express in Utah. This country holds no fears for me," Aleksandra said, through tight lips.

"Let us just say it's for both of our protection. You fooled me once. I don't want the army to suffer because I believed you when I shouldn't have," he said, with a steely glint in his eye. "Stay in the tent."

She gritted her teeth against the retort she daren't utter. He stalked away and called out a name, in a voice that boded no good for someone. Probably herself.

Whipping off the doeskin band, she tied it back together and succeeded in trapping her errant breasts again, just before the sergeant entered the tent with a middle-aged man.

"Ma'am," the burly, grizzled man said, with a nod to her.

"Corporal Blakely has volunteered his services to escort you," the officer said.

Aleksandra raised a brow at him and turned to Blakely, while the sergeant continued.

"He knows you're a woman and will take care to deliver you safely to the commander at Queen's and to von Tempsky, if he is in residence there," he paused, "if von Tempsky will claim you."

Aleksandra tightened her jaw but held her peace.

The sergeant turned to her and lifted a brow, almost daring her to comment.

"Thank you for your offer, sir." She attempted a smile at the unlucky Blakely. "I don't need the escort, but if that's the only way I'll be leaving, I welcome your company."

"So that's Paparata pā, over there?" Aleksandra pointed out over the edge of the developing rectangular bastion at the northwestern corner of the Surrey walls.

"Yes. That ridge, and the valley past it, through to the next ridge," said Corporal Blakely. "It's a huge village, but we've not seen much activity there lately. We think they've drawn down into the part of the valley we can't see from here. They've set scouts to watch our movements toward them."

The panorama from Surrey was more astounding than the views from Miranda or Esk. Even without a telescope, the Waikato Heads stood out against the glistening sea when the Corporal pointed them out.

"Why have the men been recalled from their reconnaissance of Paparata?" he asked, brows drawn together.

"I'm afraid you'll have to ask Sergeant Cole, sir."

"Well let's get on," he said, waving an arm at the sergeant's tent, where the man himself stood outside holding a scrap of paper. He waved at them and disappeared into the tent.

"Thank you for the escort." Aleksandra gave Cole a wry grin as she turned her pony around and headed down the ridge toward the shimmer of water in the Mangatawhiri Stream. Corporal Blakely urged his less-surefooted horse on, to make some attempt at keeping up.

Dzień slid down the steep grade from the redoubt, then the trail leveled a little, switchbacking down the southern side of the hill. They rode west along the edge of the bush, keeping out of the swamp to their left until the trail tracked upward, away from the wetland. They turned toward the south, leaving the edge of the bush and followed a rutted wagon road along the ridges toward Queen's Redoubt.

They were out of the swamp, but still had to traverse several streams crossed by log roads. Aleksandra let Dzień seek out more stable and safer fords, instead of crossing on these.

"You'll add miles to this trip," grumbled Blakely.

"And I'll have a sound horse at the end of it," she said, raising a brow at him. She glanced at the spindly horse he rode, struggling along beside Dzień.

He gritted his teeth and said nothing for miles.

Dzień grazed as he walked, swinging along at a steady pace. Aleksandra scratched his withers and stretched. It'd been a long few days.

A few hours later, the Mustang's head shot up, ears pricked, as row upon row of white tents appeared over the crest of a hill.

"That'll be Queen's, headquarters for the colonial troops invading the Waikato," the Corporal said.

It looked like the tent settlement at Fort Churchill, but Utah had never been so green, nor was the approach to that fort so muddy. As they approached, the immense parapets rose to block out the remainder of the sun, sinking further to the west.

"That's the southeast bastion, there," he said, pointing.

She nodded. Surely he thought she should be impressed, but sadness was all she could muster. Sadness for the Indians, sadness for the *Māori*, sadness for invaded and displaced peoples everywhere. She turned her head to the fore, away from her escort's narrowed brows.

"We'll soon find von Tempsky, and then we'll…see what's what," he said.

She glanced back to see him eyeing her with suspicion.

"Don't try anything funny, eh, girl?"

She blinked and shook her head at him, allowing her own forehead to furrow. "Let's just find him, eh?" she said, "and then you can be rid of me."

He said nothing, just continued to stare her way.

# 34

"Aleksandra? Aleksandra Argüello?" The voice of the wiry man speaking with Corporal Blakely boomed across the tent camp. "Where is she? *Alone?*"

The corporal nodded in her direction, then hurried to keep up with the man, presumably von Tempsky, as he spun and strode toward her at an astonishing pace. He didn't muck around. From the stories Xavier had told her, she wasn't surprised.

Blakely was still spluttering at him as he took Aleksandra's hand and bowed over it as if she were a princess.

"I am Gustavus von Tempsky. Are you Aleksandra?" he said.

She nodded and bowed slightly. "*Dzień dobry.* Yes, I'm Xavier's wife."

"Ah, you make my heart glad," he said with a sigh, and beamed. "I have not heard my native language spoken in many years. *Dzień dobry* to you as well. But where is Xavier?" he said, in his thick Polish accent. The Prussian glanced behind her, then back, his brows nearly touching.

"It's a long story, sir."

"Then you may tell me over a meal." He motioned to the corporal. "What is it you're trying to say?"

"Ummm...sir..." he hesitated, then set his jaw with a gulp. "My commanding officer was concerned she might be a spy."

"Does she look like one?" he growled. "She looks like an exhausted and lonely woman. One who is married to someone I consider a special friend." His voice raised as he continued. "Tell your 'commanding officer' to mind his men. I will care for her and find whatever it is she seeks. Do I make myself clear?" He finished at top volume.

"Crystal, Captain von Tempsky," the corporal squeaked, standing stiffly at attention.

"See that you return with your news at first light," von Tempsky barked.

Blakely turned on his heel and retreated as fast as he could march.

"Thank you for the escort," Aleksandra couldn't help calling out.

"Now, where were we?" Von Tempsky's voice was light again. "And where is that husband of yours?" he said, offering his elbow to escort her to his tent.

She told him her tale over a light repast.

When she was finished, the Pole took a deep breath and let it out slowly. "I'd just received word I was to be passed over for a foray into the Wairoa Ranges which I'd helped plan," he gritted his teeth, "but now I see it was for the best. I've been ordered to go to Auckland to report on our position. Now it seems it will be beneficial to assist in finding Xavier."

"So when do we leave?"

"We?" He blinked.

"We."

"You, madame, will go with an escort to the home of my wife and children. I must leave at first light and your Mustang, he needs rest."

"But—"

"—no buts about it. *Przepraszam*, I'm sorry, but your escort will be arranged," he said firmly, then his voice softened. "I may not be able to go to Xavier myself, but will send my second-in-command with a troop on a ship to see he is rescued. That is the best I can do right now, under the circumstances."

She opened her mouth to protest again, then slapped it shut. She wouldn't get a better offer and Xavier's life was at stake. Time to swallow some pride.

"With you, I will send this token," Gustavus said, as he removed his hat. He unlatched the silver pin from its front with care. "There are few enough of these around and if you tell anyone of importance whose it is, you will have free passage wherever you wish to go."

She stared at the pin, glittering in the sunlight. The badge was created of silver letters F and R entwined in swirling script, and its surface was inscribed with flowing designs.

"I will guard it with my life," she whispered, and slipped the cord of her beaded buckskin pouch over her head. She placed von Tempsky's pin inside and gripped the old bag like the talisman it was.

"*Dziękuję Ci*, thank you, Gustavus," she managed.

"I'll find a tent for you now. You and that pony get some rest and we'll see you all soon in Auckland," he said, as he led her from the camp to where her pony was being led around to graze.

ALEKSANDRA WAS FEEDING Dzień at first light when Gustavus von Tempsky found her.

"You're up already? I'm arranging for your escort."

"Yes, sir." She managed a smile.

"I know it is hard to wait when one is concerned, but you can take your time traveling to Auckland. I'm sure your horse will be appreciative. It is really a beautiful trip," he winced, "other than the mud, but be sure I'll make the utmost haste to find Xavier."

Now her smile was genuine. "Thank you, with all my heart. I'll go to your wife. Do you have a letter for her?"

"Here it is." He fossicked in his belt pouch and handed her a wrinkled missive. "Please give it to her, with all my love."

"I promise. And please…hurry."

"Your husband is important to both of us," he said, with a laugh. "Rest assured I will do everything in my power to ensure his rapid release." He kissed her hand, then looked around at two men who approached. "And here are your escorts, as we speak." He introduced them.

"Mrs. Argüello." One nodded and his eyes barely met hers.

"Are you men ready to leave?" Gustavus said.

"Yes, sir," the other man barked, as they both stood to attention.

"Well then, get your packs."

They spun on their heels and bolted toward their tents.

"Whatever did you tell them?" Aleksandra eyed von Tempsky. "They scarcely looked at me."

"That I'd have their guts for garters if anything happened to you. They're not from my regular troop and they've heard stories." His eyes glittered.

She took a deep breath. "I am armed, well-armed. I'm used to looking after myself, but thank you for your attention."

"I'm off, then. I desired to see you sorted prior to my departure."

"Couldn't I just go with you, since you're going to Auckland?"

"I must make a small detour into risky country and I do not wish you to be endangered needlessly. Lord knows there is enough danger on even the Great South Road. We've had to detail troops to cut the bush back on both sides by twenty yards, and more, in an attempt to prevent ambuscade by the *Māori*. They have been attacking the supply trains and it has seriously impeded our push into the Waikato."

Aleksandra winced. She didn't blame them for trying to protect what was theirs. Surely von Tempsky wouldn't share her views.

He took her hand again and bowed low over it. He wouldn't be out of place in the Prussian or Austro-Hungarian court, one of which was probably where he'd learned his manners.

She smiled as he turned to go. "Thank you again. We'll meet soon, I trust."

"Soon, at our home in Auckland, with your husband in tow. Care well for yourself, *mój przyjaciel.*"

"You take care, too, my friend," she replied, as he turned and walked to his horse.

Her escorts approached, their steps tentative. "We're ready when you are, madame," one said.

"Give me ten minutes and I'll be ready to ride," she said. "And don't worry, I don't bite."

They looked relieved.

XAVIER WINCED as the gaoler shoved him the last few feet to the bench before the magistrate. The shackles dug into his shin as one of his feet caught on the step.

"Who's this?" the bewigged judge asked, never looking up from his papers.

"The murderer from the ship, the Spaniard Xavier Argüello."

"Oh, him." The man looked up and peered at him over his spectacles, then shuffled through his papers. He stopped halfway through the pile and read for a few moments.

"We really don't have time for this," the magistrate's clerk said, turning up his nose at Xavier, "why don't we just string—"

"Magistrate," Xavier interrupted, "please sir, I am Xavier Argüello, of Rancho de las Pulgas, in San Francisco, but I'm no murderer."

The judge raised his brows. "And I am the Queen of England. Silence!" he barked.

Xavier barely stopped himself from shaking his head.

"You've been accused of the murder of one James—"

Xavier blinked. "Who, sir?"

"No talking. James Morrison Fitzwilliam III, going by the alias of Seaman Walter Symes."

Xavier mouth dropped open.

When he was finally permitted to tell his story, it became clear nothing he could say would make a scrap of difference. The accuser was not even present, but that didn't seem to matter.

"You will be hung from the neck until you die, three days from now," he said, with a crack of his gavel on the bench. The magistrate stood, his wig askew, turned, and walked out through the door behind his chair.

Xavier was past sinking now. Only finding Aleksandra mattered now. And it might be too late. They wanted a scapegoat for the death of a peer of the realm and he was a sitting duck.

*Von Tempsky, where are you?*

Xavier's head spun as he was dragged back, uncaring, to his cell and dumped without ceremony onto the floor.

As GUSTAVUS SAID, vast numbers of soldiers were working to widen the roadsides, sweating in the early morning sun as they cut and dragged trees from the forest's edge. There were more men on this detail than Aleksandra had seen in the whole camp at supper time.

"So why aren't you men out here cutting timber?" Aleksandra couldn't help asking.

"I've got an injured hand," one said, "and he's," he nodded at his mate, "got an injured foot."

"Really? You're riding well. How fortunate," she said, as the first man rapidly switched both of his reins to one hand and dropped the other from view. Aleksandra shook her head.

By the time she and her escorts were half way up the hill from Queen's along the ridge they called "The Razorback", the two men were already dragging their figurative feet.

"We live just ahead, there." One pointed ahead, slightly to the west, and gritted his teeth.

"Yes, I've left my wife alone in our cabin. I'd sure like to go see her, but I've no leave for two more weeks," the other said, with a deep sigh.

"You've left her alone?" Aleksandra frowned.

"Well, we have stock to feed and she's very pregnant."

She closed her eyes and counted to ten. If she couldn't get away from them soon, she could save the *Māori* some trouble and kill these two herself.

The road dipped, rose and dipped again.

"Keep a close lookout for ambuscade, especially over these bridged gullies," the younger man said.

"With so many men working on the road, it seems a bit of an unlikely place for an attack, wouldn't you say?" Aleksandra said dryly.

"You never can tell," the older one said.

The two men's fidgeting increased as they progressed onto the flats. They kept shooting dark looks at Aleksandra and making inane comments about the army and the *Māori*.

She found her hand once again on the hilt of her *shashka* and her teeth clamped together. "Gentlemen, truly, if you'd like to go home, I really don't need an escort. I only accepted it because Captain von Tempsky wouldn't let me go on without it."

They looked at each other doubtfully, then one quirked his lips. The other glanced ahead to a road heading off to the left before them.

"Are you sure?" They spoke at once, then laughed—short, tension-filled barks.

"Of course. I can go faster without you two," Aleksandra glanced at their gaunt horses, "and get to Auckland sooner."

They eyed at each other again, then saluted her. "Thank you, Mrs. Argüello," said one.

"Yes, thank you," the other echoed. "The road's clear from here, easy all the way to town." With that, they bolted away as if she might change her mind.

*As if...*

She laughed and let Dzień trot on across the level trail. He shook his mane and gave a little buck. She nearly took her hair out of her hat, but thought better of it.

Finally, things were happening. She was going to win this one. She took a deep breath and smiled, again fingering her *shashka*, but this time with pleasure. She'd done all she could. Gustavus was on his way to save Xavier and she'd be in a real bed tonight, or at least indoors, at the von Tempsky residence in Auckland.

It was all coming together again for her and Xavier's little family. They *would* be a family. She was sure of it now. They rode up a rise and Dzień dropped back into a walk. Thankfully, she hadn't been sick anymore. She's tried not to think of it during her dash across the island, but now she smiled at her secret. She reached down to cuddle Dzień, then launched into a lullaby as they walked on, his head swinging along with her song.

"I appreciate the *Pākehā* working so hard to help us." Tangawai watched the uniformed men in the distance to the southwest of his outpost, high atop the Maketu pā.

"They clear the bush beside the Great South Road to keep their supply trains safe from us, not to help us," Mahi replied in *Māori*, his brows drawing together as he looked at the young *rangatira* from the corners of his eyes.

"Their stripping back of the bush from the road also lets us see who comes and goes on their road." Tangawai grinned and raised the telescope back to his eye. The colonial army soldiers continued to toil and wear themselves out in the morning sun. He wiped sweat from his brow with the back of his forearm. The weather was already hot and humid for this hour, and he wasn't swinging an axe.

As he scanned the Great South Road northward from the loggers, three mounted men came into view, trotting toward Auckland. Two wore military uniform and one was clad in a ragged-edged leather tunic.

"Tangawai," a female voice called up to him from below.

He handed the scope to his cousin and leaned over the wall. The woman was climbing the steep side of the *pā* before him, a flax *kete* on her back. He threw a coil of rope to her and she climbed the last bit with its help.

Tangawai smiled as he took her hand and helped the slim, but heavily pregnant, young woman over the last parapet. "It must be getting difficult to climb, my Tūī." He pulled her to him and kissed the top of her head on her glossy black hair.

"It won't be long now, and your son will be on my back instead." She smiled up at him and pulled his *kai* from the satchel.

He sat and ate with her while his cousin kept watch.

"Tangawai," Mahi called over his shoulder, "weren't there three riders heading north before, from Williamson's Clearing?"

"Yes, two in uniform and one other."

"There's only the one *Pākehā* now."

"Can you see the uniformed men?"

"No," he said, and watched for awhile more. "Ah, there they are… they're going away from us, toward the homesteads on the west side of the road. It might be a trap."

"We'd better go spring it, then." Tangawai frowned and pulled Tūī to her feet. "I'll signal the village to ready the riders, but you'll need to get down there and explain. The rest need to be ready to disappear into the bush. The *Pākehā* won't follow them there." He gave her a quick hug and a kiss, then she slid over the edge and lowered herself on the rope. Tūī waved from the bottom, then turned and ran down toward the village.

Yes, the *Pākehā* made it easy to see their road…and easy to see the figure on a small buckskin horse. Alone, when he'd just had a military escort. Why *had* they left him alone? This was a new trick.

He signaled via mirror to the village below and four men made ready. They approached Tūī when she reached the encampment and stood beside her for a few minutes, gesturing, before they mounted up and raced from the encampment. Their horses were gaunt and hard from their time in the bush on rough feed, now that the *Māori* were beginning to be pushed from the lands of their ancestors.

Tangawai returned to his telescope and scanned the horizon as his men galloped down the hill toward the newly-cleared road. The dust cloud raised by their passing diminished as the warriors settled themselves just inside the bush on both sides of the track to await the lone rider.

He was soon in their own trap. Tangawai gripped the parapet before him as his men surrounded the *Pākehā*. The rider looked small and puny, now that his *whanau* surrounded him. His men seemed to be speaking to the rider, then the little horse made a dash to escape, but its way was blocked. The *Pākehā's* horse reared and sunlight glinted off metal near the hand of the rider as his men rushed toward him.

The rump of the gray horse was stained scarlet by the time the diminutive rider was dragged off the buckskin by two of his remaining, seasoned warriors. The man who'd been riding the gray crouched next to his horse, holding his bleeding forearm, and the other lay face-down on the ground. Tangawai shook his head and swore, while the men beside him on the walls stepped further away from him. He watched as his men picked the rider up off the ground and shook him.

And knocked his hat off.

Tangawai took the telescope away from his eye and blinked, glanced at the telescope, then peered through it again.

It was still there.

The blonde hair, down past his knees.

*Pākehā* men didn't wear their hair that way.

The man who'd just bested two of his finest warriors had blonde hair cascading down past *her* knees...for it had to be a *wahine*.

This wasn't normal, by anyone's reckoning.

By the time Tangawai set enough guards to observe all directions from the top of the *pā* and sent his entire *hapū* into the bush to safety, the group racing toward him had already begun the steep climb past the cemetery and St. Brigid's Catholic Mission Church.

He peered toward the priest's home and let out a breath. Father McDonald was otherwise occupied in the kitchen shed, probably making medicines for his parishioners. He twisted his lips into the parody of a grin. The old man would not have been pleased at the entourage about to pass his front step.

The *rangatira* met the group just before the churchyard and hurried his warriors and their captive past, motioning them off the trail toward the church to ensure the Father didn't see them. As the bay colt bearing his downed warrior passed, he heaved a sigh of relief. He still breathed. He didn't look at the face of the bound and gagged girl on the buckskin pony as she passed, though her fair tresses seemed to catch fire and glow in the sunlight. Enough time to interrogate her when she was safely in the *pā*.

## 35

"Who sent you and what is your mission?" said the biggest of the men. By the attitude of the others toward him, he must to be their leader.

Aleksandra shook her head once again, her cheeks burning. Hair fell across her face as she drooped from the tree to which she was tied.

"I'm trying to get help for my husband, as I told you," she repeated. "He's on a damaged boat on the East Coast, captive. I just want him out. I want nothing to do with your God-forsaken war. I had enough of it in Utah with the Indian wars."

"What is this of von Tempsky?"

"What of him?"

"My men said you called out his name after they knocked you off your horse, after you tried to kill them," the leader said, his voice terse. "Just how *did* you injure my men, incidentally?"

"With this, Tangawai," one of the men called, brandishing Aleksandra's *shashka* in the air.

"Bring it to me," the leader said, his brows narrowing still further, if that were possible.

Aleksandra growled, deep in her throat.

"This is a fine blade, too fine for a woman's hand. From whom did you steal it?"

Aleksandra struggled against her bonds, but they held firm.

"My papa gave it to me and taught me to use it," she spat, from between gritted teeth. Her cheek and forehead hurt where they'd hit her, but she'd gotten off lightly. The Indians she'd grown up with would have killed her long before this for her trespasses unless they wanted to learn what she knew.

"That is clear." He glanced at the still-unconscious man lying in the shade and the other warrior, his forearm sliced to the bone, who was having his arm bound. He was moaning, despite the laudanum he'd been given.

"Von Tempsky." He enunciated every syllable. "What is he to you? This is the last time I will ask. After this, you will be happy to provide me with any answers I want and you'll not like it."

"My husband knew him from the San Francisco. We were to join him in Coromandel, but when our ship was wrecked on the East Coast, my husband was taken captive by the man who took over the ship and I've come to find his friend von Tempsky to help free him."

His brow lowered and he tilted his head toward her. "If I believed you could've made it here from the East Coast, maybe I could believe the rest of your story, but it is impossible."

Aleksandra stared at him. "If it were impossible, I couldn't have done it, but I have."

"How?"

She told him, adding: "I was given an escort by von Tempsky, but I sent them home..."

The man looked at her as if she were mad. She was starting to wonder herself. "You sent your escort *home*?" His eyes bulged as his jaw dropped.

"Yes. I rode for the Pony Express, I can certainly take care of myself here." She raised an eyebrow at him, then realized what she'd just said and bit her lips together and closed her eyes.

"Like you've just taken care of yourself." He shook his head. "Now you're my captive."

"Seems so, doesn't it." Aleksandra took a deep breath. "What do want with me?"

"I want what information you hold. Are you a spy? Why would anyone in their right mind, with the climate such as it is right now, send a woman alone on their 'Great South Road' unless she were a spy?"

Aleksandra shut her eyes and shook her head.

*How could he be so dense?*

"I would imagine those men have by now realized their error and begun seeking me. Von Tempsky's temper is legendary and I cannot imagine he'll be pleased to know I'm traveling unguarded." She couldn't help a little grin.

The leader shook his head and looked around at his men and the women who'd come from the bush to care for the injured man. He fired a stream of *Māori* at the women not immediately attending the man. They ran into the bush and returned with flax bags, which they tied to the horses. One of the men who had captured Aleksandra untied her and wrapped a rope roughly around her wrists. He half-dragged her to Dzień and muttered beneath his breath as he looked where her saddle should be, presumably for somewhere to tie the rope. He had to content himself with holding to the end of it and mounting his own horse.

"Be happy you're allowed to ride. I'd prefer to drag you, but the *rangatira*," he nodded at the big man, "wants you in one piece, for some reason. If you try to escape, I'll pull you off your horse and you can keep up as best you can for the rest of the journey," he said, his eyes narrowed and his mouth hard, "so stay with us."

"Where are we going?" Aleksandra asked.

"Far from help for you," said the *rangatira*.

"I have to get help for my husband," she whispered, and fell silent. She hadn't a choice in the matter. She put her head down and sat quietly as they mounted their horses. Aleksandra took a good hold on Dzień's mane when they set off at a ground-eating lope, straight up a steep hill. Dzień stayed close to the flank of the bay at his side. At the top, they passed a *pā*. On its rocky outcrop, silent men stared at her as their group rode past, their horses puffing from the climb. The trail leveled off and the bush ran as far as she could see ahead of them, broken only by the massive swamps in the distance to the south. Behind her, in a sea of green, the jagged brown slash that must be the Great South Road showed harshly against the silvery blue shimmer of the ocean behind it. Could she have possibly crossed the full width of this island nation? She turned her head forward and took a deep breath, even as a band tightened about her heart. She had to get free and survive. At least she'd found von Tempsky, who was hopefully even now sending help to Xavier.

The wide trail ran for miles along the ridge, most of it under the cover of trees. *Kererū,* startled by the passage of the horses and men, whooshed by from one perch to another in the ancient forest or sat in the branches watching them, while fantails flitted about their heads when they walked to spare the horses on the downhills.

Her captor turned to her and grinned. "Getting tired, *Pākehā*?"

"I'm used to this." Aleksandra shot daggers with her eyes. She wasn't about to tell him she hadn't been on a horse for three months up until a short week ago.

His face fell and he gave the rope a vicious jerk. "You should be walking as a true captive. I don't know why he lets you ride," he snarled, and turned to face forward.

"Manu, leave her," the *rangatira* said, not even looking around.

"Tangawai, why does she ride when she deserves to walk?"

"The *wahine* is my business. Yours is to hold to the end of her rope and see she stays with us." The chief glanced around briefly, his face impassive.

Aleksandra let herself drift off, as she'd done many times riding the Express. It seemed forever ago, when it was actually only a few short years. So much water under the bridge since then. When she roused herself enough to notice her surroundings, it was gathering dark. She checked the rope tying her wrists. It was fast and not likely to give without a knife. She wriggled her foot, deep in her high moccasin and broke out into a cold sweat.

Her throwing knife was still there. Somehow they'd missed it. She'd have to choose her moment carefully. This was their territory and she didn't know the way out…but she'd find it.

The little band stopped at a clearing and the men dismounted. The young *rangatira* walked toward her. She daren't move. "We'll stay the night here and move on in the morning."

"Why do you keep me? I'm no good to you." Aleksandra shook her head. "Surely you have better things to do than to escort new immigrants through the mountains."

"On the contrary, miss, this takes precedence."

Aleksandra's mouth dropped open, then she closed her eyes and shook her head. When she opened them, he still stood before her. "I don't know who you think I am, but I'm of no use to you nor anyone else," Aleksandra said.

"That is up to our leader to decide. Your friend, von Tempsky, is not unknown to us. You might prove valuable in the coming months."

Aleksandra's world swam about her.

*Months?*

Xavier would have rotted on that hulk by then, if von Tempsky's men didn't find him. "But I know nothing that can help you," she repeated, "though I suppose I should be happy you're not going to kill me." She couldn't repress the ghost of a grin.

The *rangatira* chuckled and shook his head. "Don't stray too far from me and give Manu any excuse. You injured his brother and he'd like to return the favor, with interest."

"Other than this trail, I'm not too sure where I'd go, exactly." She raised an eyebrow at him and shrugged.

"You're clearly used to spending hours on that horse and ride as if you were part of him. I'm sure you'd figure it out. Don't try it."

Aleksandra looked up at him, silhouetted against the rays of the setting sun. He was striking, his features not unlike Xavier's.

He began to speak, then fell silent. Finally, it seemed he had to ask. "What is your training, that you could beat two of my warriors?"

"My father taught me." Aleksandra wasn't giving anything away.

"And where is this father of yours?" The chief's voice was soft now, but somehow menacing.

"In heaven."

He took a deep breath and his features softened. "I'm sorry to hear that. My name is Tangawai. What is yours?"

She said nothing, and he reached across and gave her a little shake. "That is not a trick I would try when we get to our destination. The *rangatira* will not hesitate to use whatever force necessary to extract information from you. He is not above handing you to his troops to use as they see fit. We regard prisoners as slaves and use them as such. We are, in case you don't know, at war with the *Pākehā*," he growled, "whether we like it or not."

"I thought you", Aleksandra said, with a lift of her brow, "*were* the *rangatira.*" She bit her lip and played with the fringe of her buckskins as the imposing man looked her over slowly, his brows lowering.

"I am *rangatira* over the Maketu village and *pā*," he finally replied, "but we journey to the chief of all the local *hapū*. He will lead us into battle against the *Pākehā* who have made such outrageous demands upon us in our own country."

I MUST PAY ATTENTION.

Aleksandra's head began to swim as they rode out the next morning, perhaps from the pounding she'd taken, or perhaps it was the lack of food.

Either way, it worsened as the day progressed. At least, she no longer carried her pack. She hadn't seen it since they'd picked her up on the Great South Road. Nothing she could do about it now.

She rode with her head bowed, but took care to note the directions they turned. Their climb eventually led them to a ridge trail. There wasn't much moss on these trees, but what moss there was allowed her to tell north and s—

She closed her eyes and took a deep breath.

She was in New Zealand. Southern hemisphere. All of her directions would be off. How could she have missed that?

At least she knew where east and west lay from the sun, still warm on her face before her. Far below the ridge trail on both sides were swamps, smaller on the left. The ones on the right grew in size until she realized it was the swamp along which she'd already ridden.

Then it clicked. They must be headed for the Paparata pā. She opened her mouth to say it was useless, but she clamped it shut. Who knew, the army might still be there? She had no idea when the Forest Rangers were due to make their assault. She kicked herself for not asking.

A few hours later, the scout they'd sent ahead returned and spoke to Tangawai. His face was flushed and he spoke clearly, coldly, and with deadly anger.

Aleksandra's captor left her horse's rein in the hands of one of the women and the men crouched in a circle, speaking in terse, sharp tones, sending black glances her way.

Tangawai came to her and took Dzień's reins himself, saying nothing. He mounted and led off, and the rest followed.

The trail became rougher as they rode north down the steep hill to the edge of the swamp below. They skirted more swamps until another huge mountain stood before them. A short, intense climb later, and they were on another ridge trail, which they followed until the sun was low in the sky. As the sun began to set, they met a river and turned to ride along its shore.

Aleksandra's head drooped. She could keep her eyes open no longer. She wove her fingers into Dzień's mane and slept.

# 36

Aleksandra's ears roared. She shook her head to clear it, but the sound still reverberated as the tough men on their even tougher mounts before her pushed through the trees into a clearing.

The sound diminished as the horses slid down a steep bank of dense bush and came out into another clearing. Now the roaring was louder than ever. It must be from outside her, but in the darkness she couldn't make it out. She and Dzień were led through a narrow channel of deep, fast-running water. The very air about her was damp and smelled musty.

The moon rose as Dzień exited the water and the origin of the sound became clear. Her jaw dropped at the sight of the most magnificent waterfall she'd ever seen. It looked like the tail of a giant, white horse towering above her, a hundred feet high. Then she lowered her eyes.

She goggled and snapped her mouth shut when she saw the encampment in the clearing between her and the falling water. Not only warriors, but women and children, too, all staring their way. Her guts chilled to a solid mass of ice as they rode into the camp.

She flicked a glance at her captor and he raised a brow at her.

"What did you expect?"

She shook her head. Whatever she'd expected, she couldn't have imagined this. This was as bad as coming over the ridge into the secessionist's camp in Nevada, only this time she was the captive instead of Xavier.

A tall old man with tattoos covering his face strode toward them and spoke in *Māori*, his words clipped and hard.

Her captor sat up straighter and lowered his eyes as he answered firmly, but with respect. They both turned to glare at her, and the older man barked something more at her, still in *Māori*.

"I don't understand you," she answered, in Shoshoni, "but this is the language of my native friends in America."

If the situation weren't so dire, she would have laughed at the confusion on their faces. As it was, she satisfied herself with a brief tightening of her lips before turning her head away.

"What, in God's name, language is *that?*" Tangawai said.

She couldn't help a grin now, and told them. The two men shook their heads.

"Shall we speak in a language we may all understand?" said the older of the two. By the deference shown him, he must be the *rangatira* of which her captor had spoken.

She tightened her lips and nodded.

"My son tells me," he continued, and Aleksandra eyed Tangawai briefly, "that you are a friend of von Tempsky, that scourge upon the face of *Aotearoa.*"

Von Tempsky's silver Forest Rangers badge shone in the torchlight as the *rangatira* held it up. She blinked and remained silent while she reached for her buckskin pouch. It was still there.

"He also said you fought like a warrior, better than most *Pākehā* men."

She raised a brow but bit back the retort she wanted to make.

"What were you doing, traveling alone through hostile territory?"

"Heading for Auckland to find a ship to rescue my husband."

Now it was his turn to blink. "Where is he?"

"Last I saw," she frowned at him, "Tokomaru Bay."

"That is impossible."

"You know nothing of—" cut off as his son jerked the rope binding her wrists.

"Your life is in his hands, *wahine,*" he hissed. "Have a care for your words."

She bit her lip.

"Hop down," the leader said, "and I will hear your story."

She slid from Dzień's back, then followed the pair to a seat on a log apart from the others.

When she was done, he sighed.

"You understand this war of ours?" The *rangatira* raised a brow at her.

"Better than most, I suspect," she whispered. "I was raised among the Shoshone. I have watched, with tears, to see the annihilation of their tribes, the desecration of their lands... and the loss of their lives. I do not wish to have any part of the destruction of your ways. Von Tempsky, a friend of my husband's from his mining days in California, wrote to us there."

"Von Tempsky," her captor growled, but quieted at a glance from his father.

"He told us," Aleksandra glanced at him, then went on, "that the settlers and the *Māori* worked together as one. It was the answer to my prayers. I was unable to help the plight of my Indian friends there. At least we could go somewhere we could be at peace." She was silent for a moment, her heart squeezed in a vise. She struggled to draw a deep breath and went on. "And then, this?" she hissed, and waved one arm at the natives, clustered together in refuge. "Hiding out? Preparing to defend yourselves? Back to the same, again?" She shook her head and dropped her eyes to the ground as her heart fragmented into jagged shards.

The men were silent.

She lifted her face to theirs again, but they blurred before her eyes as tears ran cool down her cheeks.

"*Rangatira*," the leader's son continued in *Māori*, his voice rising toward the end. He flashed a heated look at Aleksandra, then stomped away, muttering.

The older man watched him go, then turned back to Aleksandra. "What were you doing out there alone? My son believes you were a trap, set to lead the colonial troops to follow us and find our stronghold."

"The two men von Tempsky assigned to escort me were...slow."

"Useless?"

Her grin answered him.

"You'll have to know that von Tempsky is the arch-enemy of *Māoridom*, don't you?"

"He was a mercenary in South America and learned to fight in the bush there, so I guess he would be."

"Until he left his employ as a newspaperman and became a soldier," the *rangatira* continued, his face tight, "the colonial troops feared to enter the bush. Then he and Campbell, a *Pākehā* who also has no fear of the bush, were given free rein in the army as 'Forest Rangers' and they began to fight us on our own, previously impenetrable, territory. The army hasn't found us here yet, at the falls."

Her pulse pounded in her ears as her hands grew colder and colder. "So you won't let me go, will you?" she whispered.

He tightened his jaw, but said nothing, then his granite features seemed to soften a bit.

"My husband will be killed by that lunatic on the ship and I cannot go to help him?"

"You know I cannot, *wahine*. Our lives would be forfeit. Our entire village, our race."

"But I won't tell anyone," she pleaded. "Truly."

He looked her squarely in the eyes. "I believe you, but they," he glanced at a group of young warriors, their faces frozen, staring in their direction, "would not. They have young children and women to consider."

"But…"

"Both you and they know how the natives in America have been treated, and those in the other British colonies. Do you think they want that for their own?"

She hung her head, her guts tightening by the second. "So, you'll let an innocent man die."

"Thousands of our innocents are dying now at the hands of the colonial troops. Would you see one of our last strongholds in these Wairoas breached?"

"I don't know how to find it."

He quirked his lips. "With as much fear as you've shown, or not shown, rather, I'm beginning to believe you would be capable of nearly anything."

She frowned, then looked at her boots again.

He nodded again at the men grouped behind her.

"And they will only see your husband as one man they do not need to kill. Do you think his life matters to them? We were given an ultimatum by the colonial government."

She glanced up. "I heard," she whispered, but he went on.

"Those *Māori* north of the Mangatawhiri Stream, just south of here, you would've crossed it, could declare for the Queen and surrender our arms, or else everything we own would be forfeit. You know how long we were given to decide?"

She shook her head slowly, staring at her fingers, twisting the fringe of her buckskin shirt.

"Three days."

Her head shot up. "No," she whispered.

"Yes. Three bloody days. Most of the *rangatiras* had not even received the second proclamation, issued two days after the first.

"And then?" she whispered.

"They invaded the Waikato the day after the second was issued. Through our fields and orchards, our crops. And they call us savages..."

Aleksandra closed her eyes and shivered at the darkness pushing at her soul.

Neither spoke for some time.

"Your English is better than most of the settlers I've met," Aleksandra finally said, for want of something better to say.

"The missionaries ensured we were well-taught in Auckland. We have 'become civilized' and now they want the land we have tamed and cultivated. We are vilified and pushed from the heritage of our ancestors."

Aleksandra steeled her heart against his tirade, but tears still flowed from her squeezed-shut eyes.

*They will never let me leave.*

"Please?" she whispered.

"I'll probably have difficulty even keeping you alive. It is lucky for you that you are worth more alive than dead. It is impossible, *wahine*. These men, they have seen too much death at your peoples' hands."

"They're not my people."

"They are, whether or not you agree." He was silent for a moment, then continued. "You will remain here, for now."

She let out her breath and slumped, shaking her head, tears falling freely.

"There is a cave at the base of the waterfall. I can keep you safe there. Too many of our men wish you harm to house you elsewhere. There is only one entrance to it and I can keep that guarded. Now, tell me the rest of your story."

They sat together, her talking and him nodding and questioning, until late into the night. A woman offered them food. After a moment of hesitation, she took it and offered the hint of a smile of thanks.

"And so, here I am," she said, as she finished, then sat up with a start. "I must care for my Mustang. He—"

"—the little one has been cared for, although he has been tugging at his lead to come to you. I will have him brought to you in a few minutes,

then he will go to graze with our own. I will see a bed prepared for you."
He rose, with a hint of a grimace, and left her.

Another woman approached and motioned for her to follow, then
Dzień was there, his warm bulk solid beneath her shaking hands. She
turned her face into his mane.

He nosed her derriere as she sobbed silently into the dried sweat on
his coat. Her chance of escaping this veritable fortress, closed in on three
sides by the sheer walls of the waterfall and on the fourth, by hundreds of
seasoned warriors, was slim to none. She would never have the family of
which she'd so dreamed. Xavier would never get to know he would have
been a father again.

Her insides clenched as she gripped the pony's mane. Fatigue and
despair pulled her so low that when the woman came to collect her and
take her to her prison, she merely kissed the pony on the nose and
followed without a fight.

She wakened to the roaring of the waterfall. Light shone in from a
small window in the rock at the back of the cave. She crawled toward it
and peeked out. The water fell from above into a huge pool, where ducks
of many colors played in the swirling eddies. Toddlers along the shore
were watched over by older girls and hauled back when they approached
the water's edge too closely.

Her Shoshone family would have retreated to a hideaway like this,
only to be slaughtered or moved on, again and again. With each thought,
her heart sank to greater and greater depths.

GUSTAVUS VON TEMPSKY, with a troop of regulars behind him, rode
down Auckland's Queen Street to the waterfront on Shortland Street.

"Men, gather round. You're to report to the barracks tonight at Fort
Britomart, right there." He nodded at its guarded front entrance, just
down the road. "I'll be with you in the morning, but I have business to
take care of right now. Are any of you seamen?"

Two of them put up their hands.

"Right. You two will take ship tomorrow for a rescue mission of the
husband of the woman who came to Queen's yesterday from Miranda.
Meet me and Jacobsen, my second in command, at Queen's Wharf at
half-five." He looked at the remaining men. "The rest of you, I'll see you
outside the fort at six. Be ready to ride."

Several groans met him, halted abruptly by his look, and the men turned their weary mounts toward the fort.

Two more duties before he rode to their little home on Grafton Street to see Emelia and Aleksandra. He smiled. Aleksandra would get along well with his wife and their three children. His wife was left alone far too much for both of their liking, but war was war.

He went to the wharf and started asking around for a ship with a hoist, big enough to take the Argüello's stock and belongings. He passed up five potentials, but finally found one which could be ready to leave in the morning. He was stepping down onto the pier when a gang of seamen, clearly on the grog, pushed past him.

"That uppish Spaniard, 'e'll get 'is comeuppance," said a tattooed seaman with pale blond hair. "Magistrate's found 'im guilty yesterday, an' 'eel 'ang in a couple days." He laughed. "Bloody 'ol Symes…'ee 'ad it comin'. I say good one, but Broadhurst, 'ee said Symes were royalty-like, and Argüello'll 'ang fer sure."

Gustavus stopped in his tracks and spun around.

The man was still nattering on when von Tempsky gripped him by his shirt-front, lifted him off his feet, and slammed him against a wharf pile. His Bowie knife glinted in the light of a ship's lantern as he held it firmly against the man's throat, while the blond's mates backed off and slunk away into the darkness.

He wasn't as drunk as he sounded and he started to whine. "It were all Broadhurst's doin', 'ee—"

"Where is Broadhurst now?"

The seaman tightened his lips and Von Tempsky let the razor edge of the blade slide just a little. A drop of blood ran down the shiny steel.

"Where?" he repeated.

" 'ee-'ee were nearly dead when I left 'em at the beach near the whalin' station, what with the cut to his arm what the blonde gave 'im. It weren't my fault," he sniveled. "It were a dyin' man's last wish, 'at the devil Argüello die fer killin' 'is mate Symes. 'Ee said 'e wanted a chance with the blonde angel, an' didn't want Argüello to get 'er back."

"So you left him on a beach, half dead, and came here to blame someone who may be an innocent man?"

"Broadhurst said it were 'im what did it, an' I b'lieve 'im."

"You're coming with me to visit the magistrate. He'll probably keep you for the murder of Broadhurst."

That finally got through. The sailor said not another word as von

Tempsky dragged him off the wharf and up the road to the gaol.

ALEKSANDRA SLEPT most of the next day. She'd had precious little sleep for the past week, and although she was confined, she was also warm and fed. She hoped Dzień was, too. Her prison was set into the cliffs, just to the right of the waterfall. The mist from the water thankfully drifted away from the cavern, so at least she was dry. She'd been provided with a thick bed of *raupo* and the roof was high enough for her to just stand erect in the center of the cave.

The woman who'd brought them food the previous night took her out again to see Dzień and walk a little. The Mustang seemed happy enough. The horses comprising the small herd of hard-done horses grazed a cleared, grassy area or browsed the trees along its edges. Most of them were hobbled, but Dzień was free. He whickered to her and trotted to her side, rubbing his forehead on her. She wrapped her arms around his neck and sobbed until she was cried out.

She took careful note of the terrain when the woman escorted her back to the cave, but her spirits drooped at the sight of the bush near the entrance. The near-vertical bank was too steep to climb and the pile of loose rocks at its base, combined with the denuded patches farther up, indicated it was none too stable.

She worried about Xavier. Would von Tempsky's men find him in time? Broadhurst had been seriously cut—she'd felt the tendons ping and her *shashka* had grated on bone. If he survived, his retaliation would surely mean death for Xavier. The ship's surgeon would hopefully keep him drugged to the gills, given the choice, but there probably wasn't enough laudanum left on the ship to keep him sedated for long.

She turned over and curled into a ball. With a deep breath, she forced the thoughts away.

*I am alive. Where there's life, there's hope.*

She would survive. She would somehow get away and find her husband. She wasn't yet sure how, but it sounded like she might have plenty of time to consider it. She winced and laid her head down for some more sleep. If she managed to escape, she might not have a chance to rest for days.

GUSTAVUS COULDN'T REMEMBER HAVING BEEN BEING so very angry in his entire life. The magistrate must have rocks in his head.

Von Tempsky had spoken with Xavier, very quietly, through the wall of his cell last night under the cover of darkness. He now had the whole story. If the dead 'Seaman Symes' hadn't been a peer of the realm, this case would have merely disappeared somewhere beneath the scuffle of the war, but as it was, he'd have to do some fast talking. Past exhausted, he headed for the fort to report, then towards home.

Unfortunately, when he arrived at their two-room Grafton Street house in the wee hours of the morning, Aleksandra wasn't there, nor had any message come of her whereabouts. It took all of his self control not to jump back on his horse and head south, but neither could he leave Xavier to be hung.

At least his wife was pleased for the opportunity to spend some time with him.

After postponing the ship and putting his men to work on other projects, he spent much of the next day waiting to be seen by the magistrate.

They discussed, he cajoled, and they argued. And got nowhere. The man needed a name to attach to the missive to the Queen, proving he'd done his duty by a nobleman.

Gustavus spent the next day in like manner and rode home dejected. In the evening, however, two messengers arrived at once.

The good news was that the magistrate would release Xavier the following morning into his custody. It seems the captain of the ship upon which Xavier had travelled from Tokomaru Bay had gotten wind of the *Californio's* plight and had words with the magistrate. The bad news came from one of the men of his regiment, about the two slackers set to escort Aleksandra. They had somehow "lost" her...left her and gone to see their families...and they suspected she'd been picked up by the *Māori* near Te Makatu pā.

He would hang those boys from the highest tree he could find when he caught up with them. By their fingers.

Von Tempsky sent word with his man to gather his troop of Rangers and meet him the following evening on the Great South Road near where the escort had deserted her.

The man saluted sharply and disappeared into the shadows. He smiled, for the first time in days.

He loved his Rangers.

## 37

The following midday, the chief dismissed the guards at the cave entrance and entered. "Aleks, would you like to walk with me?"

She took a deep breath, then nodded. She followed him out to where the horses grazed and they spoke at length of horses and what she knew of the US Army.

"And what of this, this Pony Express? My son said you rode for them, as a man?"

Aleksandra laughed at the look on his face. "Yes, I did."

"Why would a woman have reason to do this? I understand it is dangerous, with Indians on the warpath, snow, salt deserts, not to mention wild animals and men." He frowned at her. "Didn't your family object?"

She stared at the piece of grass she was shredding between her fingers. "They're all dead."

His face was motionless.

"So, you see why my husband is so precious to me? Especially after I have lost two children and it seems I may never have a family again?"

Neither spoke, though the men guarding from a discreet distance shuffled their feet and scowled.

He finally looked at her. "You may not understand this, but I have no choice if I want you to survive. I may be chief, but I am an old man.

These young men would hunt you down. You would not make it from the forest."

She glanced over her shoulder at their dark faces and couldn't think of anything to counter his argument. "So I'm here for awhile, am I?"

"It appears so."

"Well, I cannot just sit in my cave. I will go mad. Do you have anything other than grass wisps to groom these horses?" she said, looking around at the scruffy bunch of horses.

"They will do." The old man smiled. Grabbing a handful of long grass, he twisted it into a wisp and handed it to her. She smiled and began on Dzień, while he made one for himself.

"My men tell me you look like a mythical centaur when you ride," he said, after they'd groomed the horses in silence for awhile.

She raised her brows at him.

"Some of them thought it might be magic, after you bested the warriors at your capture."

"Nope." She grinned, then shook her head. "Just hours and hours on a lunge line with no saddle, no reins."

"You didn't learn to fight like that on a lunge line."

"No, my papa was trained by a fine arms master in the *schlacta,* or noble, house where he was raised in Poland."

Now his brows shot up. "Some history," he said.

"Papa was also trained in *džigitovka,* which he has taught me."

He frowned. "What, in heaven's name, is that?"

"Cossack military show riding. Originally, they were war movements, and they have stood me in good stead. For example, against young Manu's unfortunate brother and the others."

"This I should like to see. Will you show me?"

She considered, her heart thumping like a jackhammer. She could possibly get away, once on Dzień, but she must plan carefully. "Can I show you tomorrow?" she said. "I'm still pretty sore from the beating at your men's hands."

His brows lowered. "Of course. I'm sure the others would like to see, as well."

*Mistake.*

She should've done it now, and there would have been fewer people to impede her escape. She went back to grooming. Her hands were busy, but her eyes, surreptitiously surveying the surroundings for anything that could resemble a trail, were busier. Her heart twinged at the thought of taking advantage of the kind chief, but she had to get back to Xavier in one piece.

THE NEXT DAY, the *rangatira* accompanied Aleksandra to the clearing, followed by most of the camp.

This hadn't been her intent, but it was still a chance. Slim, but a chance.

Dzień's coat shone. She raised a brow at the leader over the pony's back and he grinned.

"I like him. What sort of horse is he?"

"He's a Mustang. Given to me by my Shoshone family." She gulped. "Thank you for grooming him." Dzień nuzzled her hand and she scratched his forehead. "He looks well," she said softly.

"The feed," he hesitated, "it is not ideal, but it is what we have."

She winced. The *Māori*, from the children through to the horses, had been stripped of nearly everything. Well, she'd give them a show before she left. "Even the worst feed in this blessed country is better than what passes for grass in the high desert where Dzień was raised."

The *rangatira's* eyes glowed at that.

She braided a loop into Dzień's mane, then pulled the bridle on over his ears.

"May I use this?" she asked the chief, indicating the blanket she'd brought with her from the cave.

He looked perplexed, but nodded.

Aleksandra folded it several times lengthwise and pulled it around the pony's barrel like a surcingle. She knotted it firmly, then looked the *rangatira* squarely in the eye, bowed, clicked her heels together and spoke a brief command to Dzień in Polish. He struck off into a canter as she lightly vaulted to his back. She slowed to a walk to check the field, then warmed Dzień up slowly at a walk and a trot around the perimeter of the clearing. She kept her face forward, but her eyes scanned the hills for any trails.

"There don't seem to be any holes," she said, upon her return. "I cannot do many of the moves without my saddle, nor my *shashka*," she grinned ruefully, "but I will show you the ones I can."

He nodded and stepped back.

She set the pony to a canter again and circled the makeshift arena. It was many months since they'd practiced, but Dzień knew his job, speeding up on the straights and slowing for the bends.

"This is when, normally, I would ride fast beneath a pine tree, lop off a pinecone, catch it on the tip of my *shashka*, and deliver it to you," she called to him. "But, as you see," she shrugged, "no sword."

He raised a brow at her and shook his head.

She called to Dzień and he increased his speed. She kicked her right leg over the Mustang's head and sat with her toes pointed together, perpendicular to the horse as he speeded to a gallop down the long side of the arena for four strides, then returned her leg to the correct side and settled in for the turn. On the next straight, she again flicked her right leg up and over Dzień's head, then gripping his mane tightly, slid off and ran four steps beside him, then vaulted back on.

"I can't go from side to side without a saddle," she shouted.

The watchers, previously muttering among themselves, stood quiet, transfixed.

She'd always had her surcingle snugly fitted over a saddle. Would the makeshift bellyband hold? She tried not to think of the consequences if it didn't. The consequences of not trying, however, could be infinitely worse.

"I haven't tried this without a saddle, but for you, I will," Aleksandra yelled back over her shoulder as she started down a long side of the area. She took a deep breath, slipped her right arm through the mane loop and grabbed a huge hunk of mane, slipped her right foot inside the blanket band and twisted it around, then slipped her knee beneath it too, cringing as she did so. Her papa would have hung her for this, because of the danger. She tried not to think of it, as in one fluid movement, she swung her left leg over the bouncing rump of her pony, and extended it toward his tail on the far side from the *rangatira*. After she raced past the chief and the group, she bounced up onto Dzień's back, back into full view of the crowd again.

A few tentative claps turned into a thunder of applause. She smiled at them as she passed again and slowed to a halt before the chief.

"Can you put something on the ground for me to pick up?"

His brow wrinkled.

"Something small and shiny, so I can see it? Maybe von Tempsky's badge?"

He gave her a look, calculating, but pulled it from a pouch on his belt and placed it on the ground, a few yards in front of his feet.

Aleksandra circled, then picking up speed, hooked her left foot into the surcingle, praying it would hold, and started to lean back to the right.

She gritted her teeth as the blanket slipped. She grabbed for a bigger hank of mane, but it eluded her fingers and she begged for the loose knot to hold. It failed. She crashed to the ground in the path of the Mustang's flying hooves but somehow managed to roll free.

Aleksandra lay still on the ground in the silence, blinking, her head awhirl, before hands reached for her.

"Just let me lie for a second, please," she said, and closed her eyes.

Everyone backed up and soon warm breath and whiskers nuzzled her face. She couldn't hold in the giggle as he lipped at her belly and she sat up. Aleksandra looked around at the circle of concerned faces and climbed up Dzień's leg to stand beside him. The ground slowly stopped spinning.

"Let's try that again, but I'll tie it properly," she said.

"That won't be necessary," the *rangatira* said. "You don't need to kill yourself."

"Oh, but it's the best move. I can do it, as long as I tie the band right, though it's easier with a saddle," Aleksandra said.

She knotted it properly this time, and more tightly. It needed to be. This was her only chance.

At a full gallop, she hooked her left foot into the surcingle and fell backward to the right, next to Dzień's bouncing barrel. Her hands reached for the ground, head and arms only inches from the pony's flying feet. She dragged her fingers through the grass for several strides and flicked herself back up to sit astride, waving the shining silver brooch.

"Bravo, well done," called the *rangatira*.

She bit her lip, sorry for her next move. He had been kind.

The crowd cheered as she shot past their leader and bolted for the trail she'd seen, heading into the bush and out of the valley.

The cheering behind her turned to shouts, then to gunshots. She pulled her knife from her moccasin and dropped into a hang again on the far side of the pony from the crowd as they entered the forest.

Dzień shied hard against her and skidded to a halt. Aleksandra glanced beneath the racing pony's neck and saw Manu, his hand reaching for the mustang's reins. She tried desperately to flick herself back on, but the surcingle slipped again. She managed one swipe with her knife before he swung his *taiaha* with an unearthly shriek.

Her head exploded and the world went black.

ALEKSANDRA STRUGGLED TO A SITTING POSITION, her head throbbing. She blinked in the darkness and then remembered the scene she'd left, just before the blessed darkness had overtaken her.

They would roast her alive for this. Her life would surely be forfeit now. She closed her eyes against the aching in her head. She must have fallen hard—her neck was rigid and sore. She twisted it around until it clicked back into place and sighed, but her relief was short-lived.

Her soul was a shell. There would be no escape now. She would truly never have a family again. She cradled her barely-swelling abdomen. Her baby, unborn, would never see the light of day, if indeed, it survived today's two falls from Dzień.

The sound of a small splash came from the waterfall pool outside the hole at the back of her cave.

She frowned and stared into the utter darkness, but nothing, or no one, appeared.

"Plink." Metal sounded on stone in the gloom. A whisper came, just over the sound of the falling water.

"The warriors may no longer respect my wishes tonight. Manu is even now riling them up. If they come for you, and your *tamaiti*, your baby, inside, at least you will have a chance of escape." It was the *rangatira*. A rush of relief washed over her, then uncertainty.

He knew she was pregnant? When she barely knew herself?

Aleksandra's heart sank at her deceit of him yesterday, and sadness overcame her for this old chief, whose word might no longer be the law.

"Thank you, I'm sorry," she breathed, but had no way of knowing if he heard.

Another splash, then only the constant rushing of air and water could be heard.

She crawled toward the gap from which the voice had come, crouching and ducking her head at the lowering ceiling.

Cold steel met her fingers. A blade. She scarcely dared breathe as she ran her fingertips along the blade, then onto a leather grip that fit like a glove as her hand closed over it. Her heart warmed at the familiarity. She cried for the aging *rangatira* as the rush of gratitude for the old man overwhelmed her. Her tears ran cold in the breeze from the hole in the rock before her.

If only she could squeeze through it...but it was impossible. She'd checked the day before. Impossible.

What could she leave for him, after she was finally dragged out and punished?

Hands trembling, she wrapped a fossil from her beaded pouch in a scrap of fabric torn from her blanket. Her papa had fossicked it for her from the rocky ledges of the Onaqui Mountains of Utah. Her most prized possession.

She placed it with care on her bed in hope that whatever happened, he would find it. She lay down and said her prayers in exquisite detail. More than likely, they would be her last.

SHE MUST BE DREAMING. She pulled the blanket over her head. Only wishful thinking.

"Aleks," the voice hissed again and water splashed outside her cave.

She sat bolt upright and bumped her head on the ceiling of the cave. "Ow, Xavier?" she breathed.

"*Sí.* Climb out this way," he whispered.

"There's not room. I tried," she said, her voice nearly cracking in despair. There was a whole camp full of men out there. Now he would die, too.

The sound of rifle fire erupted but it sounded far away. Men and women shouted, close at hand, then nothing more was heard over the rushing water.

Xavier whispered again in the darkness. "Von Tempsky's diversion. Come on, it's only roots at the top, with rocks stuck in between them. I think I can pull enough away so you can squeeze out." A sharp intake of breath as something splashed. "Dropped one. Here, take the rest and put them behind you."

Aleksandra scrabbled for the rocks, breaking out in a sweat at the thought of the sound they would have made falling into the water all at once.

"I think there's enough room for you now—try," he said.

Aleksandra didn't need to be told twice. Stuffing her *shashka* into her waistband, she scrambled for the gap and grabbed Xavier's warm hand.

A flicker of light showed behind her. She turned her head to see Manu, torch in hand, duck into the cave.

She let go of Xavier's hand at the same time a bloodcurdling screech erupted from the warrior. She prayed he hadn't seen Xavier's hand disappear back out the hole.

"This time, *wahine*, you die," he said, as he leaned the flaming branch against the rock wall. "Someone is attacking our village and it is because of you. For the lives of ours who will die, so will you."

He rushed toward her, *taiaha* in hand.

She crouched as she flicked out her *shashka* and held it before her.

He jerked at the sight of it, nearly hitting his head on the low ceiling. His eyes narrowed. "Where did you get that?"

"It's mine," she said, staring into his eyes of flint, daring him.

"The *rangatira* gave it to you," he said slowly, "didn't he?"

She said nothing.

"He will die this night, too. That will not be countenanced," he said, as he dashed the few steps toward her.

She'd meant only to defend herself, but if he was going to attack the chief...well, that changed things. She wouldn't let that happen, not while she was alive.

He swung his *taiaha*, but it struck the wall of the narrow end of the cave wherein she crouched and the blow never caught her. While he snatched it back, she sprang with her *shashka*, thankful for its short blade. He dropped the long weapon and lunged for her as he drew the *patu* from his belt, its length flashing green in the torchlight.

He never got to raise the weapon. Whether he'd seen her *shashka* before him or not, she wasn't certain. It plunged straight into his chest and he fell off the end of her blade, gasping.

She didn't wait to see if he'd move again, but drew her blade from his body and dashed for the gap to Xavier.

"He's dead," Aleksandra whispered, "or on his way there."

Strong hands gripped hers and Xavier drew her from the cave. It was a tight fit, but she made it.

She found a ledge to brace her feet upon while he undid the knot tied around his waist. She glanced up the sheer rock wall above. The rope that supported them both disappeared somewhere high up the cliff.

"Easiest way is down. I'm not sure this rope will hold both of us for long," he breathed in her ear, "but hold on and we'll go down the rest of the way to the water."

"But there are 400 tribesmen out there," she whispered. Xavier chuckled beneath his breath.

"They're at the other end of the valley or gone bush."

"Manu wasn't."

"Manu? Oh," he jerked his head back toward the cave, "him. True, but we can't go back up. We can pull ourselves on our bellies down the stream and hope no one notices. No more talking now."

"Dzień?" she whispered.

"I saw him earlier. He'll come to your whistle when we get out of this," Xavier said, as he lowered them toward the inky darkness of the water.

She gasped, then bit off the sound as the water slipped beneath her buckskin shirt, but she couldn't repress a shudder.

"*Sí*, a bit like that, isn't it?" His voice was like the touch of a breeze beside her ear.

He let her go and breaststroked silently toward the outlet of the waterfall's pool. She followed, clenching her teeth to keep from chattering, while she glanced around. Nothing moved in the campsite.

A tug on her shirt and Xavier was pulling her from the water.

"A trail, up here to the left," he hissed, and she climbed from the water and up over some rocks, her buckskins heavy with water.

He gripped her hand and pulled her into the shelter of the bush.

"*Te quiero, Querida*," he said, his voice shaking. He held her close for a moment, then they were climbing. It wasn't much of a trail, but it was a way out.

"I cursed this moonlight earlier, but I'm giving thanks for it now," he said, as they stumbled as quietly as possible up the steep bank to the ridge. Rifle fire still sounded in the distance, but the woods around them were still.

"Let's climb up these trees and we can see where they all are, or those who are shooting, anyway," Aleksandra said.

From the top, gunfire flashes showed, but they seemed to be coming from only one direction.

She gripped his hand. "The distraction? Looks like the rest have gone."

"Why would the *Māori* go?" he asked.

"This is their last stronghold in the Wairoas. All their woman and children were here," she said, and stopped, unable to continue.

"Let's go on, then. We're to meet the rest up the valley." Xavier squeezed her hand and kissed her, then he put fingers to his mouth and the eerie call of a barn owl came out. He repeated it three times, then waited through another barrage of gunfire. He repeated it again.

The call returned, faintly, from the direction of the shooting.

Xavier called again and the rifle fire stopped altogether. The sound of owls, from far away, came on the breeze.

Sporadic rifle fire resumed, but it only came from one spot.

"Let's go, that man's the final diversion."

Climbing down was harder than going up, but they hit the ground running and soon burst into an open field. They melted back into the shadows at its edge and ran until they met the next ridge. A big shadow moved, then many men, rushing toward them.

Her heart slammed against her chest wall as she stood frozen, *shashka* in hand.

# 38

-------

Dzień's whicker came from the darkness and he ran toward her. She threw her arms around him and Xavier joined them.

"Up you get, *moje drogie*. We're off," said Gustavus von Tempsky, from behind them, and he gave her a leg up. "Well done, Xavier. Let's go, before they come after us." His words trailed off as she and Dzień raced for the ridge, headed out of the Wairoas. Dzień cantered eagerly up the slope, then they waited at the top for the men, who raced behind them on foot. She surveyed the terrain between her and the men, but saw no other movement.

"Our horses are a long way away, but we'll get you to safety, then go get them," Gustavus said, when the group reached her.

She nodded and looked to the east. The faintest edge of light was beginning to creep over the horizon.

They soon reached a scoria road and turned west. A short time later, they passed a house, then another, and finally, a big shingled farmhouse, well fortified.

"This is Travelers' Rest. You won't find a better welcome anywhere than with the Smiths," von Tempsky said, with a flourish.

Old Smith met them in the yard. "Come in, come in!" he called. "My boys'll take your horse. The rest of the Forest Rangers aren't in right now, so we have plenty of room." He grinned and clasped hands with Gustavus.

Aleksandra gazed around the walls inside with awe. They were lined with thick planks taller than Xavier's head and rifle loops showed everywhere around the interior. The man was serious.

Smith caught her eye. "When they told me to evacuate, I wasn't havin' a bar of it. My family can hold this castle just fine."

"Xavier, you two stay here and we'll return with a horse for you, then we can finish the trip Aleksandra started so many miles ago," von Tempsky said, patting Aleksandra's cheek. "The Smiths will take good care of you and I'm sure you two have plenty to talk about." He winked at Xavier, turned on his heel and disappeared out the door.

MRS. SMITH SEATED them at a long, scarred table. Xavier tried not to look at the bullet holes penetrating the walls and the parchment windows. Glittering fragments at the corners suggested the windows had once been glass. He caught Aleksandra staring at them and she shuddered. She must've seen them too.

Xavier pulled her snugly against his side as they waited for their breakfast.

They ate until they could eat no more.

"Eggs and salt pork have never tasted so good." Aleksandra said. "Thank you so much, Mrs. Smith, and you too, girls."

The Smith daughters flushed and returned to the kitchen.

"I'll show you two to your room," Mrs. Smith said, and hustled them down the hallway.

Despite the hour, they stripped off and had a wash from the basin on the sideboard, then went to bed.

"Xavier...however did you find me?" Aleksandra lay propped up in the curve of his body. She shook her head and reached up to kiss him. "That's one big forest."

"The evening I was released from gaol in Auckland—" he gripped her hand, when she spun to stare at him, mouth open.

"—gaol?" she interrupted.

"—it's a long story. Let's finish this one first. That night, von Tempsky received a report about the escorts who'd left you on your own."

She winced.

"So you *did* make them leave you alone, didn't you?" He enunciated each word.

The barest nod from her. "I'm sorry, Xavier," she breathed.

"I wondered." He closed his eyes for a moment. "I could almost feel sorry for the idiots…almost. Anyway, the day after your escorts deserted you to visit with their families," he gritted his teeth, "they met up for their return to Queen's, and…realized their mistake. I suspect when von Tempsky gets his hands on them, they'll realize just how big a mistake it was." He flicked his hair back with one hand and continued. "I'd rather be in combat than face that man in the temper he was in this morning."

Aleksandra paled.

"So what did they do then?" she asked, looking up at them from beneath her lashes, her hands gripping the sheets.

"They at least thought to check the next redoubts to make sure you'd shown up there on your way to Auckland. When no one had seen you at Drury, nor at the next one, they raised the alarm. Gustavus and his troop and I left the moment I was released. When we reached the place on the Great South Road below Te Makatu pā, the blood and signs of a scuffle showed us where to go, along with a knapsack—containing a bow and a pair of my trousers. Thank God there hadn't been any rain. Gustavus and his men tracked you to the falls."

They were silent for long moments.

"I never thanked you for saving me," she whispered. "It's a good thing you did, because there's more of me than you know."

"How's that?" he asked, frowning at her.

She glanced down at her belly and rested her hands on her gently curving abdomen.

His heart jerked, then began to fill, slowly, to bursting.

"We've been given another chance, Xavier. This new country, for all its trials, might be the place for us to start again."

He drew her against him, stroking her hair, her face, her body. So many challenges and she was still here beside him. She wouldn't leave him. Together they would build a family, a life, despite whatever came before.

She lifted her lips to his for a long kiss and he spread his hand over hers.

"Forever. I finally believe it now, *Querida*."

"Me too," she breathed, and held her face up for another kiss, and another, until the sun's rays streaming in though the window disappeared into oblivion. There was nothing but the light shining from Xavier's eyes as he rolled her over and lay his length along hers, molding them together for all eternity.

## The End

*Thank you for joining Aleksandra and Xavier in*
*A Sea of Green Unfolding.*
*They will be returning in the Tatiana series.*

*Enjoyed the story? If so, would you please...*

**Leave a short review** *on Bookbub, Goodreads and your favorite eBook retailer. I'd be grateful for your help in spreading the word! Thanks for helping an Indie become known!*

**Sign up** *for Lizzi's VIP Reader Club to hear about new releases and specials, plus get your free sampler gift at www.lizzitremayne.com/vipsea/*

**Ready for the next book?** *Find Lizzi's books at www.lizzitremayne.com/books/*

# FIND EBOOKS & PAPERBACKS

## Find eBooks

at your favorite online retailer via buy links at www.lizzitremayne.com/books/

## Find Paperbacks

Signed print books are available in standard (and some in large format) print from the author and and unsigned print books are available from most online retailers.

Contact the author via her website at:

https://lizzitremayne.com/contact-lizzi/

### *New Zealand Schools*

Available from Wheelers and AllBooks (print and digital)

# LIZZI TREMAYNE
## BOOKS

## COMING SOON!

WITH LOVE FROM
NEW ZEALAND, RUSSIA, SCOTLAND, AND U.S.A.

# BOOKS DETAIL AND UPCOMING RELEASES

*The Long Trails Series*

Book One: *A Long Trail Rolling*

*A dangerous job. Is it a convenient escape route... or a death trap?*

**Winner of True West 2016 Best Western Romance, Romance Writers of New Zealand: 2014 Pacific Hearts Award and 2015 Koru Award**

UTAH TERRITORY, 1860. *Alone.* Aleksandra has spent her whole life training for the inevitable. So when a brutal Cossack tracks down and kills her father, she knows what she must do. She flees, disguised as a Pony Express rider, in an attempt to keep her pa's killer from discovering their family's secret.

Xavier has kept the world, especially women, at arms-length since he ran from his troubles as heir to his *Californio* rancho family. As a Pony Express Station Keeper, having a girl riding the Pony out of his station wasn't ever part of his plans... but somehow it happened, blackmail being what it is. Curiously, he didn't want to let this one out of his sight.

They begin to let each other into their hearts, but the cards are stacking against them as the minutes tick by and Aleks rides full speed into the Indian Paiute War. Can they learn to trust in time to escape the Indians, evade the killer, and save both their love and Aleksandra's family legacy?

Book Two: *The Hills of Gold Unchanging*

*As the Civil War rages, secessionists menace California. The Confederates want the state and they'll stop at nothing to they'll stop at nothing to take it.*

UTAH TERRITORY, 1860. On a wagon train headed for the Golden State, Aleksandra makes a dangerous enemy of a gun-running Confederate when she fights her way out of his unwelcome embrace.

After a late-night poker game, Xavier's new friends realize he's heard too much to be allowed to live.

Embroiled in the Confederates' fight to drag the new state from the Union and make it their own, can Aleks and Xavier survive? The secessionists mean business.

Book Three: *A Sea of Green Unfolding*

*They set sail for the peace and calm of New Zealand, but they hadn't counted on murderers, mutineers, and a land war in paradise.*

SAN FRANCISCO BAY AND NEW ZEALAND, 1863. Aleksandra and Xavier have finally found happiness on their Rancho de las Pulgas, but tragedy and death strike far too soon. Sickened further by the U.S. government's treatment of their Native American friends, they only want out. Of everything.

They are thrown a lifeline by an old friend of Xavier's from the California goldfields. This Gustavus von Tempsky, with his shadowed past, is now a newspaperman in Coromandel, New Zealand. His invitation draws them to a new start, with a part to play in the development of the peaceful young country —but by the time they arrive in Aotearoa, everything has changed.

Aleks thought mutineers and scoundrels aboard ship were the worst of their worries, but she hadn't planned on disembarking into a turbulent wilderness and befriending the helpful local Māori, only to find von Tempsky leading the colonial troops into the bush against the natives who'd saved her life.

Box Set: *The Long Trails Box Set*

*Can an orphan, with only her Mustang and a Cossack sword, survive alone on the frontier?*

From the deserts of Utah, through the gold mines of California, to the turbulent wilderness of Colonial New Zealand, Aleksandra rides, loves, and fights—with only her Cossack skills to keep her alive.

**\*\* From multiple award winning author Lizzi Tremayne \*\***

**UPCOMING: *The Tatiana Series*** (with links to *The Long Trails* series)

Book One: *Tatiana I*

*Stableman's daughter Tatiana rises to glamorous heights by her equestrienne abilities —but the tsar's glittering attention is not always gold.*

MOSKVA, RUSSIA 1842. Tatiana and her husband Vladimir become pawns in the emperor's pursuit of a coveted secret weapon. While Tatiana and their infant son are placed under house arrest, Vladimir must recover the weapon or lose his wife and young son. With the odds mounting against them, can they find each other again—half a world away? *Coming soon!*

Book One: **Somewhere Called Home**

*Highlands to Waterloo—can love prevail over fate?*

SCOTTISH HIGHLANDS, 1813. Lachlann is disowned for refusing to become clan tacksman after his father and heads for the city, alone, to build a life for himself and his beloved Annis. Annis' waiting turns to despair when her mother buys safety during the clearance of their village—leaving Annis at the mercy of the laird's degenerate son. Lachlann emerges from the hell of Waterloo wanting only to see Annis again... and his father. *To be released soon.*

## The Once Upon a Vet School Series

**Drama and humor abound as Lena pursues her childhood dream of becoming an equine vet—and beyond—in this upcoming, unique series of six independent novella sequences:**

*~Junior Years~*

After Lena hears she needs good grades to become a veterinarian, things start to get tricky. Even her pony doesn't get out unscathed. (Middle Grade) *USA 1972-1976*

*~High School Days ~*

When your high school counsellor says vet school's too hard for you and your HS sweetheart offers you a dream life of farming, writing, and babies, what do you do? Is vet school really the be-all, end-all? (Young Adult) *USA 1976-1979*

*~College Nights*

How can you have a life when you need an A in every class for four years to get into vet school... on top of 800 hours vet practice work? Something's got to give. (Young Adult and up) *USA 1980-1984*

*~Vet School 24/7~*

Now they're in, the pressure for grades is off and vet school social life is upon them... there's only the tsunami of 200 years of veterinary knowledge to pack into their heads. Can Lena and her friends stay afloat? (Young Adult and up) *USA 1984-1988*

### ~Practice Time~

Finally graduated, prima ballerinas of the university, Lena and her vet school classmates disperse to far-flung practices... and real life. What could possibly go wrong? Late nights on-call, mud, blood, and finally, a light at the end of the tunnel... unfortunately, it's only the penlight of a dictatorial vet technician in Lena's eyes after she passed out on the floor. (Women's Rural Fiction with Romantic Elements) *USA & New Zealand 1988-2012*

### ~Long in the Tooth~

When Lena suffers another catastrophic back injury in New Zealand, what's she to do to feed her family and keep the farm? She can't breathe around cats or birds and what good's an equine vet who can't hold up a horse's leg? Time for Lena to go back to school. Again. (Women's Rural Fiction with Romantic Elements) *New Zealand 2012- ...*

### Currently Available Reads:
### ~Vet School 24/7~

### Fifty Miles at a Breath

*Horses bring them together and their future looks rosy—it's the present they can't handle.*

When equine veterinary student Lena and veteran pilot Blake fall in love, vet school and the past intrude. Add in a long-distance relationship, and things get just plain hard. A grueling endurance race forces them to draw on their strengths and face their fears—together.

### Lena Takes a Foal

*She needs help... he needs to stay away...*

Lena's got a problem—one that might prevent her from graduating. When her horse flips over and lands on her, it has to be the dashing resident, Kit, who finds her. Luckily, she's sworn off relationships after her last debacle and sea-green eyes and rugged good looks are the last things on her mind. Besides, to a veterinary school faculty, relationships between residents and students are like oil and water.

They just don't

mix.

*~Practice Time~*

### Greener Pastures Calling

*A new country, a great job, and a good Kiwi bloke. Life couldn't be better.*

*Until it gets worse.*

Newly emigrated to New Zealand, Lena wants a 'good Kiwi bloke', but they're elusive as their nocturnal namesake. Nigel's avoiding females, unless they're cows, horses, or his mother after his first marriage. Sparks fly when they meet—but not the first time, over the dirty instruments in a filthy cowshed. They seem to be made for each other, until Nigel remembers where he first saw her. And then the questions start.

### *Understanding Modern Vet Med for Owners*

The new series of veterinary books for horse owners to let you use what vets know to keep your horses healthier and happier. *First volume due out soon!*

Sign up for Lizzi's VIP Reader Club to hear about new releases and specials, plus get your free sampler gift at

www.lizzitremayne.com/VIPSea/

# AUTHOR'S NOTES

This, of all my tales, is the story of my heart. I began my first novel about a girl who rode the Pony Express. The series has evolved into so much more than a tale about an express mail service. It is a gift to those in my old Bay Area haunts and my adopted country of New Zealand. New Zealand's history, like most countries, is one of conquest and takeover... or not, as it turns out. Sometimes it's more like this one: settlement and agreement, then breaking of that agreement, invasion and takeover. In New Zealand, however, the original treaty, in some form, still holds some sway. Much of the history is... not hidden, but certainly not offered in schools, so it remains locked away, far from most people's psyche. This is my offering of a little of the history of both places, history some would rather forget, for their own reasons. I consider it important enough to put it out there. I hope you enjoy this story as much as I loved writing it.

Aleksandra's hero Xavier, is a Californio, an old Californian of Spanish descent, and as such his name is pronounced 'HAV-ee-air.'

Aleksandra, Xavier, and several others in the story are completely fictitious characters, but the incidents portrayed are not. Many of the historical figures included were real people, however, and I have used artistic license to describe their actions. I have utilized actual people and incidents to offer history to some who may never pick up a book of historical nonfiction, while offering history buffs historical figures in a different light. Some of the dates have been altered to make the story work, but otherwise I have presented the history of the events and the people as best I understand them from the historical record. Of particular note are some of the dates pertaining to my hero's family. This is historical fiction, after all. :) Luis Argüello, the husband of Maria and the father of fictitious Xavier never lived at Rancho de las Pulgas. He was the first governor of California under Mexican rule and governed from 1822-1825, usually living at the Presidio. After Luis' death in 1830, his wife Maria Soledad Ortega de Argüello was granted the four square leagues of Rancho de las Pulgas by the then-governor of California and moved there with her children. She ran the big rancho, recorded to have 4000 cattle and 2000 horses in 1838, from then on. When California was ceded to the USA, Maria had to claim to retain the family's land grant. In 1852-3 the claims were rejected. SR Mezes (lawyer for Maria) was successful in 1857 and they were able to retain the land, less the 3/20ths for Mr. Mezes. By 1859, before the time of this story, she had already sold the remains of Rancho de las Pulgas and moved to Santa Clara County. Thus, the rancho was not lost to a gambling fictitious son, and it was sold prior to the time of this story. In 1976, the City of Redwood City renamed a downtown plaza at the intersection of Broadway and Argüello Street as Argüello Plaza. A bust of Maria Argüello was erected in September of the same year in that plaza. The bust is on the edge of the train and bus depot, next to the Broadway train crossing.

I have not been able to discover whether de las Pulgas had its own proper chapel or not. In any case, it would not have been where Xavier was christened, nor where his mother and father were married, as they only obtained and lived there after the death of Maria's husband. The first local Catholic Church was not built in Redwood City until after this time.

If you have any doubt as to the damage that may be done with a shashka, check out this You Tube video on clay cutting with a shashka, from Russia, late 19th C.

https://www.youtube.com/watch?v=xL6zZ7McaO4

Throughout, I have used "Indian" to denote the peoples currently called Native Americans, due to the nomenclature of the period represented in this story. For the same reason I have used the term "native" for the Māori, as used by people such as the missionary wife. No disrespect is intended.

The names for the group of Native Americans originally occupying the San Francisco Peninsula prior to the arrival of the Spaniards are up for debate. Many call them tribes of the "Ohlone" language group. Others refer to them as Costanoans. "Costanoan" is derived from the original Spanish explorer's name for the natives of the region as Costeños (Coastal people), which was later Anglicised to Costanoans. "Ohlone" may have been derived from (or vise-versa) the name for a Spanish rancho called Oljon, and refer to a single band which inhabited the coast near Pescadero Creek, and as it refers to one band, some current members of the group object. Some members wish to use the name Muwekma. I had to pick one name. The tribes and villages of the Costanoan Native Americans of the Ohlone Language group who lived on what later became the Rancho de las Pulgas lands of the San Francisco Peninsula include the Lamchin (present-day San Mateo County, Bay shore from Belmont south to Redwood City and valleys to the west), Ssalson (along San Mateo Creek, in San Andreas Valley. Had 3 villages along San Mateo Creek), Puichon (near present-day Menlo Park, Palo Alto and Mountain View), and Suchihín (south end of crystal springs reservoir). Their lack of a written language and the scanty mission records leave much of the detail up to debate.

Grease monkeys and skid rows or skid roads: this terminology may or may not have been used in 1860, but it was certainly used by 1910, and the techniques described were in use at that time.

Please indulge me here, with reference to the detail in the discussions in Sausman's store. This is a gift to the communities in which I grew up: La Honda, Pescadero, San Gregorio and Half Moon Bay, about the origin of the road that links them (still the only road that links them).

Cole Younger and the James-Younger gang used to hang out in La Honda. That's the story I grew up on in that small town. In reality, Thomas Coleman "Cole" Younger was a guerrilla for the Confederacy during the American Civil War and later a leader with the James-Younger gang. Unfortunately, Cole didn't live in La Honda in 1863, but I wanted to include him in the story, so I've tweaked the time he lived there. And he did hang out at the Ray Ranch. :)

Captain Cook returned to Britain in 1771 after his exploration of New Zealand. He touted the swamps beside the Waihou River (he called it the Thames) as potentially rich farm land (once it was drained), filled with tall trees suitable for building and masts. Some seventy years later, settlers flocked there. Though the kahikatea may have been slightly less ideal for masts than the later-discovered kauri, the great kahikatea forests were decimated for masts and building, and in much later years, for butter boxes. The swamps were, indeed, drained for farmland. Today, this land, much of it peat, is now called the Hauraki Plains. It is prone to flooding and has a high water table. My son lives down there and if he digs more than two feet into the ground, he has a swimming pool. But I digress. In the story, Aleksandra travels up the Waihou on a trading vessel, and the trees crowd close on the river. I have yet to find exactly when the Waihou was stripped of its trees, so I have left the trees for her, and you, to discover that little part of New Zealand as it once was.

The body of water in the North Island of New Zealand now known as the Firth of Thames, was in 1863, on maps, anyway, called the Frith of Thames. Perhaps a hangover of Scottish mapmakers, who would have used Frith and Firth interchangeably.

Paparata pā had already been taken by the colonial forces as of the date Aleksandra delivered her message. I altered the date to make it work in the story.

The concept of "Iwi" is relatively new. In this era, I understand that hapū was predominantly used.

While I have used primarily American English spelling for most of the book, I've left the term "gaol" instead of "jail", as that was a current spelling, even in some places in the USA at the time. I've used the spelling harbor in general text, but retained the New Zealand spelling in place names as they exist in New Zealand.

For some interesting info on old time logging, check this out:

http://www.mendorailhistory.org/downloads/LoggingwithOxTeams.pdf

For some interesting info on džigitovka: NB, it was Caucasian, and later Cossack, before Russian.

https://www.youtube.com/watch?v=QjN96pu8TZE&list=PL7AF37547AEE9E870&index=5

I hope you enjoy your foray into my world of historical romantic suspense. If you liked it, help others find it by leaving reviews and comments where you purchased it, on Goodreads, and on my webpage. If you want to pass on a comment, please find me via my *Connect with Lizzi* page.

Warmest regards,

Lizzi Tremayne

www.LizziTremayne.com

# NEW ZEALAND PLACES:
## THEN & NOW

Mauao or Maunganui ~ Mount Maunganui
Ōpita ~ Paeroa
Ōruarangi ~ Hikutaia
Pokino ~ Pokeno
Poverty Bay ~ Large bay at Gisborne
Pūkorokoro ~ Miranda
River Thames ~ Waihou River
Wairoa Ranges ~ Hunua Ranges

# GLOSSARY OF FOREIGN WORDS
## OR TERMS

amor ~ S ~ love
año ~ S ~ year
arroz ~ S ~ rice
asada ~ S ~ roasted
bebé ~ S ~ baby
buenos días ~ S ~ good morning
californio ~ S ~ of Spanish Californian descent
calzones cortos ~ S ~ knee breeches
carta ~ S ~ letter
casa grande ~ S ~ big house or mansion
casamiento ~ S ~ marriage
cena ~ S ~ evening meal, supper
chaleco ~ S ~ waistcoat
chaqueta ~ S ~ Short, fitted men's jacket
cómo ~ S ~ what? how?
con ~ S ~ with
todo mi corazon ~ S ~ all my heart
cumpleaños ~ S ~ birthday
de seguro ~ S ~ of course, to be sure
de/ del ~ S ~ of
digame ~ S ~ tell me
Dios m'o ~ S ~ my God

dzińkuję ci ~ P ~ thank you

dzień ~ P ~ day, also name of Aleks' horse

džigitovka ~ R/P ~ Caucasian, then Cossack then Russian military show riding

El Camino Real ~ S ~ The Royal Road

el ~ S ~ he/him

ella ~ S ~ she/her

nuestra familia ~ S ~ our family

estan viniendo ~ S ~ they are coming

faldas ~ S ~ skirts

fiesta ~ S ~ party

gracias ~ S ~ thank you

hacienda ~ S ~ ranch house

hāngī ~ M ~ earth oven to cook food with steam and heated stones

hapū ~ M ~ group of multiple whanau with a common ancestor

hermano ~ S ~ brother

hijo ~ S ~ son

hōiho ~ M ~ horse

kai moana ~ M ~ food from the sea

kākā ~ M ~ large native colorful parrot

kerer_ ~ M ~ large native wood pigeon

kete ~ M ~ bags woven from flax in NZ

kia ora ~ M ~ hello, greetings, best wishes

kina ~ M ~ common sea urchin, sea egg

korimako ~ M ~ bell bird, an olive green songbird

koukou ~ M ~ Morepork, a small owl native to NZ and Tasmania

kumara ~ M ~ sweet potato

kwahaten ~ Sho ~ antelope, Alek's Shoshone name

lo siento ~ S ~ I'm sorry (for it)

mi ~ S ~ my

mierda ~ S ~ crap, feces

mío ~ S ~ my, mine

niños ~ S ~ children

modiste ~ F ~ a fashionable milliner/ dressmaker

mój przyjaciel ~ P ~ my friend

moje drogie ~ P ~ my dear

moko ~ M ~ traditional Māori tattoos

no se ~ S ~ I don't know

nuestro ~ S ~ our

pā ~ M ~ fortified Māori village/ hill fort
palillis ~ S ~ fried puffy, sugared festive bread
pāpara ~ M ~ father
parareka ~ M ~ king fern, horseshoe fern: edible starchy underground stems
patu ~ M ~ club of hardwood, whalebone or stone (including greenstone)
pemmican ~ C ~ fat/protein food used by American Indians
perfecta ~ S ~ perfect
piececitos ~ S ~ little feet
pipi ~ M ~ bivalve from under sand in sandy NZ harbors
pīwakawaka ~ M ~ fantail, native bird, gregarious and insectivorous
pobre niña ~ S ~ poor little girl
pollo ~ S ~ chicken
pononga ~ M ~ slave, also many other words for slave/ enslavement
poquita ~ S ~ little one (fem.)
por supuesto ~ S ~ of course
primogénito ~ S ~ firstborn
przepraszam ~ P ~ I'm sorry, apologies
punch ~ E ~ bull driver on logging team
que le vaya bien ~ S ~ (I hope that you) go well
qué será será ~ S ~ what will be, will be
querida/querido ~ S ~ my dear, darling, love, lover
rangatira ~ M ~ hereditary leaders of hapu, chief
raupo ~ M ~ a type of rush, cattail
recuerda ~ S ~ remember
rewena bread ~ M ~ bread made with a potato culture
rohe ~ M ~ tribal territory
schlachta ~ P ~ Polish noble
serape ~ S ~ Latino shawl/blanket worn as cloak
serpiente de cascabel ~ S ~ rattlesnake
señorito ~ S ~ little or young master
shashka ~ S ~ Sharp guardless, single edged Caucasian, Ukranian and Russian saber
sí ~ S ~ yes
sirvienta ~ S ~ female servant, often American Indian, in Californio households
sirvientes ~ S ~ servants likely indentured or apprenticed =slaves
siempre ~ S ~ always
sopapillas ~ S ~ small flat fried breads

suglar ~ E ~ one who rode the first log in logging behind oxen
taewa ~ M ~ potatoes, small, knobbly purplish Māori potatoes
taiaha ~ M ~ traditional staff weapon of carved hardwood
tamaiti ~ M ~ baby or child
tan ~ S ~ too much
tapaderos ~ S ~ long stirrup covers to protect boots from thorns
tauhou ~ M ~ waxeye, silvereye. Small NZ bird
te quiero ~ S ~ I love you, I want you
ten cuidado ~ S ~ be careful, have a care, watch out
tía abuela ~ S ~ great aunt
tūī ~ M ~ native bird, white feather tuft, nectar eater
utu ~ M ~ seek reciprocity, whether kind deeds or revenge, to retain
balance of mana
wahine ~ M ~ woman
waka ~ M ~ traditional canoe
whanau ~ M ~ extended family/group may include friends
whare ~ M ~ house or building, historically of raupo
y para ti ~ S ~ and for you
zakwas ~ P ~ rye sourdough starter
żurek ~ P ~ white borscht, traditional Polish stew

**Key:**
**Cr: Cree Indian / E: English / F: French / M: Māori / NZ: New Zealand / P: Polish / R: Russian / S: Spanish / Sho: Shoshone**

# RECIPE: REWENA (MĀORI) BREAD

**Starter bug (Hua Rēwana)**

Ingredients:

2 cup parāoa (flour)
4 tablespoons huka (sugar)
2 cooked rīwai (potato) or kumara (sweet potato)
wai (water) for cooking potatoes

Instructions:

Cut up and boil potatoes or kumara. Save water and mash by hand in cooled potato water.

Mix all ingredients together and put into a sterilized jar. Cover. Let it grow in a warm place. (Not a heating pad, too hot).

Feed the bug daily for five days with: 1/2 cup flour, 1 tsp sugar and enough water to mix it all in. Lumpy is fine. To improve bug for rising, at least once per week, mix into rēwana: 1cup flour, 1/2 cup sugar and boiled warm (not hot) potato water. Important: If your water is chlorinated, boil it first, so the chlorine doesn't kill the bug.

**Rewena Bread**

Ingredients:
4 cups high grade parāoa
2 tablespoons huka
2 cups wai
2 cups hua rēwana

Instructions:
Mix the flour and sugar, then make a well in the dry ingredients. Add the bug and the water, then stir to combine.

Do not beat it. Knead it gently, ONLY until mixture loses its stickiness, maybe two–five minutes, with minimal flour. It will be soft and satiny.

Place in greased Dutch oven. Cover with cloth and leave to rise in warm place until doubled in size.

Heat oven to 425 degrees F / 235 degrees C. Bake 10-12 minutes, then turn oven down to 360 F / 200 C for 10-12 minutes, then cook at 338 F / 187 C for about an hour.

Enjoy with butter, honey, jam, meat, whatever!

# ABOUT THE AUTHOR

Lizzi grew up riding wild in the Santa Cruz Mountain redwoods, became an equine veterinarian at UC Davis School of Veterinary Medicine and practiced in the Gold and Pony Express Country of California before emigrating to New Zealand. She has two wonderful boys, a grandson, and an awesome partner in that sea of green. When she's not writing, she's swinging a rapier or shooting a bow in medieval garb, riding or driving a carriage, playing in the garden on her hobby farm, singing, cooking, teaching, or looking into a horse's mouth in her equine veterinary dental practice. She is awarded and multiply published in fiction, nonfiction, special interest magazines and veterinary periodicals.

**With her debut novel, Lizzi was:**
Winner 2016 True West Magazine
Best Western Romance
Winner 2015 RWNZ Koru Award
Finalist 2015 Best Indie Book Award
Winner 2014 RWNZ Pacific Hearts Award
Finalist 2013 RWNZ Great Beginnings

# CONNECT WITH LIZZI

**I'm looking forward to hearing from you!**

**Join conversations and find story excerpts, buy links, and more here:**

www.lizzitremayne.com/VIPHills
www.lizzitremayne.com
www.horseandvetbooks.com
www.bookbub.com/profile/lizzi-tremayne/
www.facebook.com/lizzitremayneauthor/
www.instagram.com/lizzitremayne/
www.tiktok.com/@lizzitremayneauthor
www.twitter.com/LizziTremayne/
https://www.youtube.com/channel/UCylITovsoX1H1E17lJZTxTQ
www.goodreads.com/LizziTremayne/
https://nz.pinterest.com/lizzitremayne/

# ACKNOWLEDGMENTS

Thank you to:

Matt. For everything. With or without you, as you say, this book would have been written...but it would have taken many years longer sans your love, kindness and support. My readers (anticipating Sea of Green for the past four years) and I thank you. (The 'four years' is a long tale...see my blog for a giggle.)

Elliot, Stuart, and Tamiee, for giving me a reason to strive and for your encouragement, and to Kirsten, for your boundless energy, inspiration and continuing to love, like Maria. I love you guys heaps and buckets.

My most magnificent beta readers. Several of you have come back for more after beta reading Book One, Book Two, or both. Without you, this story would be much the poorer. Thank you for your thoughts and ideas —you'll see them in the story. I had a blast with you all, and I'd be honoured to welcome you back for my (our) next story! My most profound thanks go out to Kate Le Petit, Kirsten Davidson, Greta Gordon, Tanya Sherborne, Danielle L Hadfield, Mari Schabardina, Jude Knight, Shelagh Merlin, and Matthew Tremayne, Larn Wilkinson and Mara Rare.

John K. Smith, for introducing me to bushcraft, hunting, bows, and some special places up the Maratoto, which we won't talk about. More importantly, my forever appreciation for your kindness and care for my boys, and even after all these years, still including us in your family.

My fantastic, encouraging friends from RWNZ and Authors of Main Street. With groups like this at your back, how could one not succeed? Love you all.

Kajai Lang, for the lovely author photos.

Kathy (Zanone) Wolf and Bob Doughtery, for your awesome

knowledge and assistance with research on my old home town, La Honda, California—before it became yuppified.

Jacqueline Higuera McMahan, for your book: *California Rancho Cooking*. I have loved it since the day I found it nearly two decades ago!

Larn Wilkinson and Mara Rare, for your invaluable advice and help with concepts Māori.

Linton Stuart, for your enthusiasm, kindness and willingness to drag me up hill and down dale, from Miranda Hot Pools to the Miranda Redoubt (Thank you John Killick for showing us the Miranda Redoubt, and thank you to Michael and Brenda Karl, the current owners of the property!), then to the farm of Carolyn and Bryce Shuker (Thank you both so much!), who kindly showed us up the steep hill (as steep as it was in the story) to Surrey Redoubt and their exquisite antique inkwell from the site (featured in the story). Linton continued on with me to Bombay to meet with Murray Sutton, and together the three of us visited Te Makatu pā near Ramarama, the old church, and more on the Great South Road. What a day. Thank you all!

The Mangatangi Historical Group, for the fantastic detail I was able to use in my story from your information about "The Thames Expedition" and for the opportunity to speak with your group.

The wonderful curators and librarians of The Museum of San Carlos History, the Papakura Museum, the Auckland War Memorial Library (Thank you, Rose, for your lovely book on von Tempsky!), the Sir George Grey Special Collections at the Auckland Main Library, the Katherine Mansfield Room at the National Library in Wellington, and Stephanie at the Tauranga Library for patiently dealing with my endless queries.

Dave Smith, for your assistance and information about the Forest Rangers…and…your book is on its way home. Thank you! :)

The Speedys, third generation farmers of the Hauraki Plains near Ngatea, (which was once part of the Kahikatea swamp in the story) for allowing me to visit their old piece of native bush.

Eric Muir and the Franklin Historical Society, for welcoming me, and inviting me to speak with them.

the many others who have helped in so many other ways, including your everyday encouragement to finish this story and get it out! Thank you all. I couldn't have done it alone.

xx
Lizzi

# EXCERPT FROM TATIANA

M *id-1842 Moskva, Russia*

BY THE TIME I was fifteen, and Vladimir sixteen, we were inseparable. No longer did he clean stalls as punishment, but to help me before his Training School classes began. This gave us more time to fit ourselves and prepare our combined *džigitovka* performances. We had been selected as part of the team to perform for the Tsar on his next visit to Moskva from St. Petersburg.

The tsar's creepy messenger, who came to our door with increasing regularity for no seemingly good reason, had delivered the invitation for our group to give the performance. His terse smile showed through the lace curtains as he stood before the door. I managed to talk Papa into answering it, claiming I couldn't leave my cooking pot.

The messenger, whose name I never asked, but he told me anyway, was Sambor Andropov. Due to his frequent visits, I had taken to ignoring anyone knocking on the door when I was in the house alone. His mere eyes on me made my skin crawl, and I felt I was being undressed before his eyes. Although a servant of the tsar could not be ignored without serious repercussion, if he didn't know I was there, all would be well. If the message was important, he would return, or Mrs. Bagrov would get the door if she was in.

I had the grace to be embarrassed when I realized he had carried such a special invitation to our door after I had avoided him. It was just that men and boys in Papa stableyard never looked at me like that, so perhaps I was being overly sensitive. I vowed to be kinder to him when I saw him next. He was, after all, just doing the tsar's bidding.

After this missive, our training intensified. We only had a month to prepare our troop for our presentation before Tsar Nicholas and his Empress Alexsandra Feodorovna.

There were eleven men in our group, plus me. We were drawn from the wider area around Moskva, but bragging aside, Vladimir and I were the stars of the show.

We had a joint act, with a quadrangle, jumping and shashka work, but our own little act was the best one. It began with Vladimir and I standing in Sarda's saddle, with me just behind him, one hand in the air, waving at the audience. We would then do a lift, ending up with my standing upon Vladimir's shoulders—at a full gallop.

It was a truly tricky maneuver, and one that few ever attempted. We lived, ate and breathed *džigitovka*. In any spare time, we worked out together— running, press-ups, sit-ups— we needed all the strength we could muster, and on the day of the performance for the Tsar Nicholas and Tsarina Alexandra Feodorovna, we triumphed.

During our bows to their Excellencies, the Empress Alexandra Feodorovna beckoned us closer.

"Your skills," she said, "for such young people are to be rewarded. I should like to see you both again." She paused for a moment. "Perhaps," she glanced at the tsar, who lifted an eyebrow at her, and then turned back to us, "you would like to attend the ball at the Kremlin tomorrow night?"

I swallowed hard.

"We should be honored, your Excellencies," Vladimir said, his voice smooth.

"We will see you there." The tsarina nodded and turned back toward her husband, dismissing us.

I curtsied as gracefully as I could, holding a pair of reins and wearing jodhpurs and boots, lacking the essential skirts. Vladimir drew me to my feet and escorted me away.

"A ball at the Kremlin?" I blinked and took a deep breath. "However will I find a ball dress before tomorrow night?"

"You have none?" He looked at me, jaw dropped.

I peered from beneath my brows. "How many balls have I attended since we met?"

He stared at me. "Well…"

"Exactly. I attended the end of year cadets ball with you last year, but that dress will hardly be suitable for an audience," I indicated my breeches and boots, "other than this, of course, with the tsar and tsarina. It's easy for you. You simply need your Training School dress uniform."

"Sisters. Yes, that's it." He spun to face me. "Olga and Sonja will have a dress to fit you."

My jaw dropped. His sisters were elegant young ladies. I'd been introduced to them before, but they hadn't seemed impressed by the stable girl performing with their brother. "But they live a full day's ride away. I'd never be able to ride there and return and still take care of my stable duties."

"I'll go. I can get one of the other lads to do my work for me, if your father permits."

"I permit," he said, walking up in time to hear the end of the conversation.

"Thank you, sir. I have three sisters, most of them close in size to Tatiana. With your permission, I will leave as soon as I cool out my horse."

"We'll take care of that and inform the headmaster. Well done, both of you. Your performance was without equal," he said, taking the reins of Vladimir's horse and leading him back toward the barn.

"Papa," I said, and he turned. I reached out for Sarda's reins. "Thank you, for all you've done for me, for us." I glanced at Vladimir's retreating back.

He handed them to me and hugged me, his eyes glistening with unshed tears. "You have made me so proud, both you and Vladimir. What a team you make."

"We could've never done it without you."

"Soon he will be finished here and must enter the tsar's army." He took back Sarda's reins and together we began walking the sweating horses. "Have you considered what you will do then?" His eyes looked at me—through me—and I shuddered, then swallowed and looked at the floor.

"I honestly do not know, Papa."

"A life of horses is hard for a man, much less a woman, and I won't be around forever."

My eyes snapped up to his. "What?" For the first time, I saw his weathered visage, the grayness of his skin at the edges, and my stomach clenched. "Papa, are you ill?"

He took a deep breath. "I'm not sure, but my heart, it does funny things sometimes. Not badly, but it's enough to give me pause—to question and to ensure you are provided for."

The walls of the Kremlin swayed around me. Papa was my rock, although I'd been increasingly leaning on Vladimir as we had become close friends, and now, it seems, something more.

"Have you been to a doctor, Papa?" Knowing he hadn't.

"No, but there is little they could do."

"You don't know that..."

"Trust me, I know. Anyway, *princessa*, you will be going to the ball and dancing the night away on the arm of your prince.

"Will you becoming?"

"The invitation was only for the two of you, but I will be awaiting your return with bated breath." I offered the horse a few sips of water from a bucket then pulled Sarda away and we resumed our walk.

"This will be my first ball without you, Papa..." I searched his face, seeking to know the extent of his sickness, but nothing showed.

"My *solnishko* has grown up." New tears in his eyes threatened to fall. "You will be the loveliest woman there."

*Woman.*

I'd never thought of myself as that...it would take some time to sink in.

***Due out soon! Look for it!***

Sign up for Lizzi's VIP Club to hear about new releases and specials, plus get your free sampler gift at www.lizzitremayne/VIPSea

*Thank you for reading.*
*I hope you enjoyed A Sea of Green Unfolding!*
*To join Lizzi's VIP Club and hear about new release and specials, plus get your free book!*

*It's right here:*

*www.lizzitremayne/VIPSea/*